S I G N A L S

S I G N A L S

(((•)))

Tim Gautreaux

ALFRED A. KNOPF · NEW YORK

2017

THIS IS A BORZOI BOOK
PUBLISHED BY ALFRED A. KNOPF

All rights reserved. Published in the United States by Alfred A. Knopf, a division of Penguin Random House LLC, New York, and distributed in Canada by Random House of Canada, a division of Penguin Random House Canada Limited, Toronto.

www.aaknopf.com

Knopf, Borzoi Books, and the colophon are registered trademarks of Penguin Random House LLC.

Several stories were previously published in the following publications: *The Atlantic:* "Attitude Adjustment," "Died and Gone to Vegas," "The Safe," "Welding with Children"; *Fiction:* "Sorry Blood"; *The Guardian:* "Gone to Water"; *GQ:* "The Bug Man," "Easy Pickings"; *Harper's:* "Deputy Sid's Gift," "Something for Nothing"; *The New Yorker:* "Idols"; *Ploughshares:* "Resistance"; *Story:* "Good for the Soul"; and *Vintage Shorts:* "The Furnace Man's Lament"

Library of Congress Cataloging-in-Publication Data
Names: Gautreaux, Tim, author.
Title: Signals / Tim Gautreaux.
Description: First Edition. | New York: Alfred A. Knopf, 2017.
Identifiers: LCCN 2016019485 (print) | LCCN 2016026460 (ebook) |
ISBN 9780451493040 (hardcover) | ISBN 9780451493057 (ebook)
Subjects: | BISAC: FICTION / Short Stories (single author). | FICTION /
Literary. | FICTION / Family Life.
Classification: LCC PS3557.A954 A6 2016 (print) | LCC PS3557.A954
(ebook) | DDC 813/.54—dc23
LC record available at https://lccn.loc.gov/2016019485

Front-of-jacket images: (top two) Stacy Kranitz; (bottom two) Alec Soth / Magnum Photos
Spine-of-jacket images: (top) Eliot Dudik; (bottom) Maude Schuyler Clay
Back-of-jacket images: Eliot Dudik
Jacket design by Kelly Blair

Manufactured in the United States of America

First Edition

For Haley and Melissa,
who gave us grandchildren

Wake me up early, be good to my dogs
And teach my children to pray.

—JOHN ANDERSON

Contents

Contents

SIGNALS

Idols

Julian was living in a sooty apartment building next to an iron foundry in Memphis when he received a letter announcing that his great-grandfather's estate had finally been cleared up. He stood in the doorway of his peeling duplex, his hands shaking as he read the terms. Most of the property had been sold off to satisfy liens and lawyers' fees, but the large country house and six acres remained, along with $28,000. Julian was a thin man of sixty-three, balding, a typewriter repairman who worked out of his spare bedroom and kept to himself. The one time he'd seen the grand old home was when he was eight, riding past it on a gravel road with his mother, back when she could afford a car. The mansion was surrounded on three sides by rows of cracked Doric pillars, its second-floor gallery missing many balusters, its windows patched with cardboard. It had been occupied for many years by a glowering family of squatters who'd slouched on the porches and stared after his mother's black Ford as it crawled past the fence. For all he knew, they were still there.

He went inside, out of the late June heat, and sat in a duct-taped recliner to reread the terms of his good fortune. The only extra money he'd ever had was a hundred-dollar win on a scratch-off ticket. Before his mother died, he'd spent two years at a tiny local college and considered himself at least wealthy in knowledge, more so than the shopkeepers and records clerks he dealt with. Normally, he disparaged people who owned large houses, yet deep in his heart he'd stored the memory of the old mansion as the only grand thing in his family's history. It had shamed him to long for the house, and now he owned it.

The thought of inflicting pain on unlucky people bothered Julian, so instead of personally telling the impoverished family who lived in the house that they would have to leave, he asked the county sheriff to evict them. He spent a month emptying his apartment of derelict Selectrics and Royal 440s, then got into his twenty-year-old Dodge and drove southeast into the scrub-pine flats of northern Mississippi. After an hour, he left the wide state highway for a snaky blacktop road, and deep into the woods he turned left down a gravel lane that ran as straight as a railroad for ten miles. At one point he came up on a five-strand run of barbed wire healed into the bodies of live oaks, and he slowed, took a breath, and stopped the car. The lawn was a weave of waist-high weeds and fallen limbs punctuated by the otherworldly pink domes of thistle blooms, and rising beyond was a mildewed temple. Patches of plaster had fallen away from the main walls, showing an orange, wind-wasted brick. Julian pulled past the end of the fence, got out, and sat on the car's hood. His now-dead mother, whom he'd found hard to bear, pretentious for a poor woman and full of outdated airs, had talked about this house as though it proved something about her ancestors, the God-highs. "They were noble and powerful people," she'd told him the day they'd driven by the place. "And we have their blood." He straightened his back so he could stare over the wiry brush at the soaring columns, the brooding eaves, and suddenly felt that he deserved this inheritance, had deserved it all his life.

He walked up the flag steps, through the unlocked door, and into a broad hall. The house was an echoing series of frighteningly tall rooms that smelled of emptiness and mouse droppings. The place hadn't been painted in many decades, though the last occupants had left it relatively clean. The lightless kitchen, something added a hundred years after the main structure was built, contained a gassy-smelling stove and a badly chipped sink. Upstairs, four vast rooms opened off a wide hall, and a door led up to an attic crossed with naked cypress beams. Above that perched a glassed-in belvedere, unbearably hot, where he could look out over long, flat plots of woods that once were cotton fields. He imagined pickers dragging their bags slowly across the steaming landscape and understood whose labor had paid for the house. The roof was iron and looked to be sound, though storm dented and running with rust. After inspecting the outbuildings, he drove six dusty miles to the town of Poxley, where he bought, on time, a bed, some chairs, a couple tables, and a dinette set. Mr. Chance Poxley, a soft, liver-spotted gentleman in a white shirt and skinny tie, also showed him a small used refrigerator.

"You can't live without no icebox," Mr. Poxley told him. "You'll leave a can of potted meat out too long on the windowsill and think you can eat it the next day. Then you'll get to throwing up all over the place. You'll get the sick headache." Mr. Poxley raised a blue-veined hand to his forehead. "You'll be throwing up things you never seen before."

"All right," Julian snapped. "I'll take the damned thing. When can you deliver it all?"

"Where you live?"

He told him and watched for his reaction.

"Law, is that old place still standing?"

Julian sniffed and raised his chin. "Not only is it standing, I'm going to restore it the way it was."

Mr. Poxley scratched the back of his head and squinted. "What way was it? Ain't nobody alive ever seen a drop of paint on that place."

"That'll change soon," Julian said, plucking his receipt from the old man's fingers.

"You ought to get you a nice little brick house on a half acre, somethin' you can keep up. I don't think you understand how much that place'll cost to fix. How cold it'll be come winter."

"The house is a part of my family's history."

Mr. Poxley seemed to think about this a moment. "Well, I hope history can keep you out of a draft."

The next day, the old man and two high school boys delivered Julian's purchases. Upstairs, Mr. Poxley stared at the sagging bedroom ceiling. "Say, what you do for a livin'?"

"I sell and service typewriters on a business route in Memphis."

"Typewriters," Mr. Poxley repeated, as if Julian had said buggy whips or steam engines. "We threw our last one out ten years ago."

"Some places need reliable old models to fill out forms and such."
Julian spread open a sheet over his new mattress. "Antique shops want
rare old models restored."

The old man gave the house the once-over, looked down the long,
flaking hall, over the warped pine flooring, gazed up at the cloth-covered
wires snaking across the ceiling. "For your sake, I hope typin' comes
back in style."

For the next three weeks, Julian swept down the rooms and galleries
and thinned out the fallen limbs in the yard, the end of each day finding
him tired unto sickness. He bought an electric saw and some lumber to
patch the second-floor gallery, but every time he was halfway through
a board a fuse would blow in the spider-haunted circuit box in the
kitchen. The first time he fired up his double hotplate, the fuse box door
was open and he witnessed a cerulean flash and rat-tail of smoke—the
first of four fuses it took to fry one egg. He had no idea how to upgrade
the wiring, and in the following days he began to eat his food cold.

Every day, he walked through his rooms, calculating how long it
would take to patch the fractured plaster, paint the blotched walls, and
glaze the windows.

Julian understood that he would have to hire cheap help, a broken-
down old carpenter desperate for work or some rehabilitating wino or
mental case, and the idea elevated his spirits, as if such servitude would
echo the history of the place. He thought of the ancient kitchen house in
the backyard, left over from the days when kitchens were built separate
from the main houses to prevent fires, and he figured the hired fellow
could stay there, as part of his salary. The rural living and hard work
would bring the poor man back to health, so giving him the job would
be like granting him a favor.

He drove in to see Mr. Poxley, who as usual was standing at the end of
his counter, his left elbow holding him up. "What can I do for you, Mr.
Typewriter Man?"

Julian frowned at the greeting. "I need to find somebody to do electrical work, simple carpentry, and painting."

Mr. Poxley's eyebrows flew up. "So do I."

Julian crossed his skinny arms. "But I can offer a place to live."

"You say you want this worker to live out there with you? What on earth for? He'll eat you out of house and home and bum money ever' chance he gets. After a few months on the place he'll be the same as a brother-in-law."

"I want an employee, not a relative."

Mr. Poxley flapped his limp hand at him. "You want a sharecropper, son. Them days is over, gone to history."

Julian suspected that Chance Poxley had little grasp of history and was just a desiccated old man who specialized in opinions. Still, he probably knew everyone in the county. So Julian leaned in and lowered his voice. "I thought maybe I could find somebody with a weakness. You know how people go out of circulation because they gamble too much or drink."

"Oh, you want a *drunk* sharecropper," the old man said.

"No, no. Maybe somebody just down on his luck. I could help turn him around."

"Oh, he gets drunk enough he'll turn around plenty." Mr. Poxley slapped his leg and bent over laughing.

Julian had little patience with uneducated people, and started to walk out, but he caught sight of a large corkboard tacked over with hand-printed messages, a community bulletin board. "Can I at least put up a little notice there?"

"Hep yourself." The old man limped off toward the restroom, and Julian searched along the counter until he found a pen and paper.

"Wanted: handyman to live on site and repair house. Ask Mr. Poxley for directions."

Succinct, that was the way to be, Julian thought. He looked back toward the restroom, and added, "No drunks." Choosing a black thumbtack out of the pile in the ashtray, he stuck the note in the middle of the board, next to one offering a free rattlesnake to a good home.

The following Monday, Julian was outside on the lower gallery cleaning up a geriatric Underwood on a plank table he'd dragged from an outbuilding. In each room of the house only a single bulb hung from the ceiling, and the big spaces drank up all the light, so he'd begun to work outside in the morning sun, weather permitting. Around ten o'clock, he sensed movement at the periphery of his bifocals and raised his head to see a man standing in the heat-struck privet lining the road, watching him. Julian called out, and the fellow struggled through the weeds and came up to the house. He seemed about fifty, a lean, fairly tall fellow wearing triple-stitch blue jeans and a matching heavy denim shirt with the sleeves cut to the armpits. His baseball cap was the same material, a plain-billed dome with no inscription. Julian had never seen a cap with nothing written on the front of it. "Where did you come from?" he asked.

"Town. I seen your notice."

"What? Oh, yes." He stood up and began to look him over.

The man's yellowed eyes darted up the side of the building. "I can carpenter good. My name's Obadiah, but people call me Obie. It used to rile me when they called me that, but nowadays I just go along."

Julian studied him, looking for signals. "Can you paint?"

"Your name."

"What?"

"You ain't told me your name."

"Julian Godhigh. Right now it's Smith, but I'm going to change it to my ancestral name when I get a chance."

"Some men can change like a porch lizard switches colors," Obie said, focusing on Julian. "And some cain't." The man listed to the side, and his skin was a cloudy blue gray, as though he were ill in some exotic, interesting way. "I can paint a wall like a artist."

Julian gave him a nasty smirk. "Really? Like Michelangelo?"

Obie looked away. "I reckon. Only I use a roller."

"What about electrical repairs?"

"It ain't nothing I can't pick up. I can do one thing as good as another." He spat off into the grass.

When the man turned, Julian glimpsed part of a tattoo, half a spider crawling out of the collar of his shirt. Again he saw that the skin on his arms was a smudged cyanic color, mottled in incoherent patterns as if the flesh had been cooked all over. "Are you from around here?"

"Over in Georgia."

"Can't find work there?"

"My wife and me been havin' trouble, so I was staying in my cousin's travel trailer. Except now he wants to sell it."

The men walked around to the wasp-haunted kitchen house and forced open the cocked door. Julian said he would buy a cot and the man could sleep there. They would try a working relationship for a few days. The one-room building contained a porcelain-top table and hide-bottom chair, both sitting under an unfrosted lightbulb hanging from the ceiling on a long cord, and Obie went in and scraped dust and fallen dirt-dauber nests off the table with the side of his hand. Julian returned to the big house and brought back a loaf of bread, block cheese, and lunchmeat, and they came to terms.

Obie stepped over to a window. He rubbed a hand against the cloudy glass and cleared a view out toward a collapsing shop. "You ever been married?"

Julian suddenly wanted a drink, and he sat down on the single chair. "One time. It lasted about four years, and then she got unhappy. I could never figure out why."

"They ain't no figurin' out the why of women," Obie said, reaching over his shoulder to scratch his back. "I married a religious woman and did all I could to please her. I even got saved and tithed out of what little pay I made. She run me off even though I done things for her no other man ever would of." He looked down at the floor as though contemplating a scene of great sorrow. "It was a mystery why I did it."

Julian bobbed his head. "Mine asked me to make more money, but I wanted to keep doing what I was doing. Manual typewriters and I were made for each other. I can make the big old Smith Coronas tap-dance like Fred Astaire."

Obie looked up. "You left her or she left you?"

"I think the motions were mutual."

Obie leaned against the beaded board wall. "You traded a woman for typewriters."

At first Julian felt insulted, but the way Obie made the statement suggested that he understood, and that he had made some unusual trades of his own.

"I needed to follow my talent."

Obie nodded. "I know about what a man thinks he needs." And with this he began unbuttoning his shirt. "You think you need to make a statement in life. But it don't seem like nothin' you do gets taken serious."

Julian felt a slight rush of panic as Obie opened his shirt wide to reveal a tattoo of a tailless dragon over his liver and one of a disarmed battleship across his hairless chest. Below the vessel was a dolphin jumping out of the sea, but its fin and eyes were blurred as though by an industrial accident. All the skin from his shoulders down to his waistband was fine-line tattoo work partially eaten away, the flesh abraded and inflamed. "It's a sight, ain't it."

"What in the world happened to you?"

"My tattoo collection. I'm gettin' it burnt off. I got my arms did already. I found a cut-rate Indian doctor to do it over in Poxley, but those treatments still cost like the devil, and I'm about tapped out. It's why I got to go to work."

Julian stood up and looked away. "If you like them, why don't you keep what you have?" The colors, he'd noticed, were garish and mismatched.

"I got my reasons." Obie looked down at himself. "But I realized there's a difference between wantin' and needin'."

Julian looked again at the spider on Obie's neck. "That so?"

Obie splayed five fingers over his wounded chest. "Maybe I don't need 'em no more. Get a little older, you see what you can do without."

Julian pointed derisively at what was left of the dolphin. "Well, there's enough work around here that you can afford to burn yourself white as toilet paper."

The night was warm and Julian turned in his damp sheets, waking briefly at gray dawn and hearing someone walking, inside and out. When he got up at eight and made coffee, Obie came to the big house's kitchen door and waited outside the screen, looking in, as if knocking were beside the point.

"I got a startin' list for you."

Julian looked up from his coffee. "A list of what?"

"Of things to fix the house."

"Come in here." He took the smudged sheet where he sat at the wobbly table. "Good God, this is for over a thousand dollars' worth of stuff. Where'd you get the prices?"

"I borried the phone in the hall."

He shook his head. "That's too much."

"Delivery is free above a thousand. It'll save you seven percent, man said."

Julian saw that he was looking at the ceiling, already working in his mind. "Well, what's on the schedule first?"

"Electric wire. Then low-luster paint for a couple of these rooms." He smiled, showing big, evenly spaced teeth. "Hide the cracks and raise the spirits."

After the Poxley Lumber Company truck left, Obie began work. By Saturday, the difference in the place was palpable. In the kitchen he installed a new gray breaker box, and two walls in Julian's room were patched, sanded, and painted an airy antique white. Julian paid him in cash on the next Saturday morning, then drove him to Dr. Setumahaven's office in Poxley, dropping him off and then going shopping. When he picked him up after the treatments, the expression Obie wore was that of a martyr, his eyes misshapen and dark with pain.

"You look like a boiled lobster," Julian told him.

Obie gently lowered himself into the passenger seat. "I got my money's worth today, all right."

They rode along the dusty road without talking, and Julian imagined he could smell the laser burns.

That day Obie mixed mortar and began patching the ground floor's exterior wall. The next week, he worked on the downstairs bathroom, and the rest of the month he repaired the sewer line out to the septic tank and installed a cheap air conditioner in Julian's room, for he'd complained mightily of the steamy nights. The men tolerated each other and ate supper together on a card table set on the creaking floors of the big dining room. One rainy day, they sat under the wavering glow of a shorting light fixture, and Obie feebly complained about how little Julian was paying him.

"Yeah, but you're getting cheap room and board."

Obie gave a worried glance to the dusty brass disk holding a circle of 25-watt bulbs. "I got to share it with the squirrels and the rats. You ought to charge them half the rent."

Julian motioned to Obie's neck where Dr. Setumahaven's laser had reduced the spider to a dim shadow. "You're still making enough to get rid of your collection."

"You paid me more, I could get 'em burnt off faster."

"I don't understand why you bother at all. I mean, who cares? The doctor's gotten rid of all the ones people can see."

Obie rubbed his narrow face, his whiskers crackling like coarse steel wool. "I used your phone to call my wife. She said she might could take me back if I got rid of all my idols. She calls 'em idols."

"Take you back?" Julian gave him a startled look. "Didn't you tell me that woman beat you with a broom?"

Obie looked down at his plate wearing a faraway smile. "Aw, she's just a woman. Can't hurt no man unless she buys a gun."

Julian stood up and began to clear the table. "Next time you go see Setumahaven, tell him to stick that laser in your left ear and light up your brains."

Obie watched him leave the room and called after him. "Ain't you never lonesome for some company?"

Julian came back in and stood behind his chair. "I've got to the point where I can live alone. I've built up my business, and now I've got this big house to keep me busy and give me a place in the world."

The light fixture made a futzing sound and Obie blinked. "So this here place makes you feel important?"

Julian threw his arms wide. "I *am* important. What do you say to that?"

Obie looked toward the window where the antique glass distorted everything beyond. "I say I need another box of roofin' nails so I can fix the tin on top of your importance."

The work went on through September, and Obie slaved over the corroded wiring and slow-running plumbing. He ran his hands over every board in the building, finding where thousands of square nails had pulled free from the shrunken lumber.

After Julian had gone to bed one night, he heard the back door to the main hall scuff open. Figuring Obie had come in for a drink of ice water, which was all he allowed him to have from the refrigerator, he dropped off to sleep. Soon, he was awakened by talking, just parts of words bouncing up the stairs to his single bed. He crept to the head of the stairway and heard Obie use a soft and rhythmic voice he'd never heard before. Listening hard, he heard him say, "Save me, O God, for the waters threaten my life; I am sunk in the abysmal swamp where there is no foothold." Julian walked down until he could see Obie seated at the old phone table, a flashlight shining down on an open Bible. He wondered if the call was long distance, if he should yell out to stop reading Scripture into the phone at twelve cents a minute.

Someone on the other end of the line must have asked a question, for Obie's voice stopped, and then said, "I'm workin', but I ain't able to save much. He cusses me and charges me for ever thing. Sent me to town in his car to get tar and took the gas out my pay. What? Read Psalm 64? It'll cover him, will it?"

Julian listened for a few minutes and understood that he was speaking to a woman, of all things. He coughed, and Obie shone the flashlight up to the dark landing. "I got to go now. I'll call you fore long." He hung up and raised his face.

Julian's voice sliced down on him. "Was that the Georgia woman?"

"It was."

"You planning on reading the whole Bible to her?"

"No."

"When I get the phone bill, I'll let you know the charges."

Obie turned his head toward the back door and looked as if he might speak, but the only sound that drifted up to Julian was the click of the flashlight and then the invisible creaking of the hallway's boards.

On Wednesday, he drove to Chance Poxley's store to buy a night table. Mr. Poxley was leaning on the end of the counter and watched him walk in the door. The old man screwed up his face as though he smelled carrion.

"Do for you?"

"I need a small, inexpensive table to put beside my bed."

"Uh-huh. That Parker boy still workin' for you?"

"He is, slowly."

"How much you payin' him, anyhow?"

Julian turned his head toward the store's cheap furniture, then looked back. "Has he been complaining to you?"

Mr. Poxley focused on Julian's eyes. "That boy's a good worker. I believe he can fix a broke horse."

"He's all right."

"What you payin' him?"

"That's between me and him. He ought to pay me just to put up with his spooky ways."

"You bring him into town today?"

"He's over at Setumahaven's."

"I heard he had 'em on the bottoms of his feet. Must hurt like fire to have one took off there."

"I don't think about it."

Poxley blinked. "What *do* you think about, Mr. Typewriter Man?"

Julian looked at the old man with a sneer. "What do you think I ought to think about?"

"How about payin' somebody does good work a livin' wage."

"Look, he doesn't have the expenses *I* have. Again, has he been complaining?"

Chance Poxley swung his head away. "That one won't complain."

"Well, by damn, show me a table, then."

· · ·

*H*e finished at Poxley's long before he was supposed to pick up Obie at the doctor's office. He parked his Dodge, angrily mulling over Mr. Poxley's criticisms, and then went into the little red-brick city library, where he found a small Bible and walked into the stacks with it lest someone see him. He turned to Psalm 64 and read:

> *Hide me from the conspiracy of the wicked,*
> *From the noisy crowd of evildoers,*
> *Who sharpen their tongues like swords*
> *And aim their words like deadly arrows.*

He slammed the book shut, holding the cover down as though it might spring open accusingly. Between two musty stacks of dog-eared history books, he waited to see if the words might have some effect, but he felt no change at all, although he couldn't resist touching his tongue to the roof of his mouth.

*W*hen Obie climbed into the Dodge that afternoon, he was bent forward with pain. Julian looked at him sullenly. "I wouldn't give anyone money to hurt me. If I were you, I'd have saved up for an automobile instead."

Obie closed his eyes and leaned his head against the cracked window. "What need do I have of a automobile, with no place to go?"

"Which one did they finish up today?"

"The battleship. Feels like he dug it out of me with a pocketknife."

Julian checked his rearview mirror before backing up. "That'll make a big scab. Will you be able to work on the upstairs porch?"

"Gimme a couple hours. I'll see."

*H*e drove into Memphis the next day, delivering refurbished typewriters and picking up dirty, nonfunctional machines from three behind-the-times businesses and two antique shops. He collected a few accounts and added up his money. The weather had been unseasonably warm, and he considered buying Obie a small electric fan, but then decided it would just make him unhappy if he ever had to live without one again. It was cruel, he thought, to make things too comfortable for someone who was going down in life.

Two weeks later, Obie walked up to where Julian was sweating over an old gray Royal on the front porch and told him that he had an appointment with the doctor on Wednesday.

"I'm not going into town that day."

"It's important. I got to get the big one on my back burnt off."

He put down a slim screwdriver. "You have one on your back? What for?"

"It's a long story."

Julian straightened up in his tin chair. "Let me see it."

Obie unbuttoned his denim shirt, slipped it off, and turned.

Julian put a hand to his chin. "Good Lord, it's Jesus."

"He cost me a lot."

He adjusted his glasses. "It's a good job for such a large image. Too bad I can't skin it off you and frame it or something."

Obie jerked his shirt on and began buttoning it. "Can you take me in on Wednesday or not?"

"I guess. If you pay my gas." Obie stared at him, and Julian wondered how he could expect him to ride him around like a free taxi. "Now, what do you think about that railing up there?"

"I reckon it ought to be changed," he said, tucking in his shirt. "You might lean on it and fall and break your neck."

Julian waited outside the doctor's office, dozing behind the wheel, dreaming of tall gleaming pillars and him standing between them in an immaculate white suit. When the passenger door opened, he woke up feeling sore and sour. He looked at his watch and frowned. "What did your red-dot doctor think about erasing God off you?"

Obie sat with his back away from the seat. "He only took him off the outside," he whispered.

Julian gave him a mean smile. "You sure he didn't replace him with Buddha?"

"Can we go on to the house?"

"Aw, can't you take a joke?"

Obie rolled his burning eyes over toward him. "Do you have any aspirin?"

"There's a tin in the glove compartment. But don't ask me to buy you a Coke."

In late October, the money finally ran out. Julian told him he couldn't pay him anymore, but that he'd let him live on the place for free if he painted the outside. Obie walked out onto the front lawn under the two-hundred-year-old oak and stared back at the house. Julian stood between a pair of cracked pillars, watching him. After two minutes he called out, "What are you thinking?"

"I'm figuring it would take me sixty gallons of primer and paint and a full year to do it myself, what with sandin', washin', and scrapin'. I'd have to live here three years past the end of the job to take the value out in rent."

Julian stepped into the yard himself and looked up at the complex eaves, the paint-sucking galleries. "We can work something out."

"No we can't. I'm finished with my treatments. Setumahaven give me some fadin' chemical, and Monday I'll go to that tannin' parlor by the cornmeal plant."

Julian took a step backward. "What are you talking about? You can't leave."

Obie spread his arms like a gaunt bird ready to take flight. "The old me's gone. The new me's got to move on down the road."

During the next week, Obie's skin changed from an angry mix of blood and ink to a mildly unhealthy skim-milk hue, and after sessions at the Red Bug Tanning Salon, he turned a rosy manila color. One night Julian decided that Obie might stay and work for him if he went into his meager retirement savings and paid him a real salary.

The next morning he got out of bed and fried a ham steak for breakfast, Obie's favorite. After setting the table, he went out into the yard, and his heart skipped a beat when he saw the door to the old kitchen was wide open. Inside, the cot was empty, and Obie's duffel bag, always in the same spot under it, was gone. He began to panic and felt his sickly house looming over him, leprous and crippled. He raced into Poxley, but no one at the bus station had seen Obie, and Dr. Setumahaven's office was closed. After driving around the town's narrow streets for half an hour, he parked and went into Chance Poxley's store.

The old man came out of his office and squinted at him. "What?"

"I can't find my hired man."

"Well."

"He just left without a word."

Mr. Poxley leaned over and pressed the clear button on his adding machine. "That so?"

"Have you seen him?"

The old man shook his head. "It's been a while. He did tell me he'd finished up with the skin doc. I don't think he had much need of your job anymore."

"He told me he used to stay with a cousin. Where's he live?"

"He ain't there. That boy pitched him out to begin with."

Julian stared out the store's broad plate windows emblazoned with shoe-polish lettering—C A S H   T A L K S . "I've got to find him."

"Unless I miss my guess, you can't afford him no more."

"What are you saying?"

Mr. Poxley looked down and his voice softened a bit. "What you need him for, anyway?"

Julian's mouth fell open a bit and he stared at a new gas range to the right of the counter. He could fix a typewriter but nothing else in the world, and he didn't know if he could live in the old mansion, unable as he was to keep it nailed together. But the real problem came upon him as suddenly as thunder. He'd be alone. The house and its canyon rooms would swallow him up, the only sound his own footsteps thrown back in his face, and when he stopped moving, a silence vast as night.

In the middle of November, a freakish weather pattern set in—a howling wind with ice in its teeth. Julian was adjusting a Royal 440 and around sundown his hands began to shake. The single-pane windows and shrunken doors shivered in their frames. There was no insulation anywhere, and what little residual heat there was soon leaked through the ceiling lath. He put on sweaters and two jackets and remembered that the house had no heating system at all. The squatters had used tin trash burners, running the stovepipes out the windows, but all that had been thrown into the yard. Obie had told him that the fireplace flues were no longer safe, that the chimneys were cracking apart in the attic. He climbed in bed under every sheet and spread he owned, deciding that the next night would be warmer.

But instead it brought a whip-cracking gale, and a weatherman on his car's radio announced that a solid week of unusually cold temperatures was on the way. He drove into town and bought an electric heater, but under the fifteen-foot ceilings the device was like a spark at the North Pole. The third night, he slept in his car with the motor running, but he checked the gas gauge on waking and knew he couldn't afford to do that again. He got out of the backseat cursing the oil industry and the whole Middle East and loaded up five repaired typewriters for delivery in Memphis.

The fourth night, he became ill, and for two weeks he suffered through a cold that turned into influenza. After a teasing warm spell, the weather came back mortally cold, and he moved out of the mansion into Obie's little kitchen house. An electric heater and the old wood-burning range together would keep the room at fifty degrees, and he could sleep. But it was a miserable place to stay, its attic full of manic squirrels, its floor a dull smear of ground-in soot and dirt, its walls impregnated with the oily emanations of ten thousand meals.

One day in mid-December there was a knock at the kitchen house door and he found Chance Poxley standing in the tall dead grass, bare-headed, shading his eyes with one hand.

Julian held the door open only a little. "What can I do for you?"

"Can I step in? This wind's goin' to freeze me female."

He backed into the room, and the old man came up the three wooden steps. When his eyes adjusted he looked around. "My God you're livin' like a jailbird in here."

"Next year I'll arrange to keep the big house warm."

Mr. Poxley shook his head. "I hear in the old days it took three servants working full-time to keep all the fireplaces going with coal. You can't even buy coal anymore."

"Did you come out here to discuss my heating problems?"

Mr. Poxley grimaced. "No." He handed him a sheet of paper.

"What's this?"

"You're two months behind on your payments for your appliances and furniture."

Julian reddened. He stood staring at the invoice for a long time as the squirrels began chasing each other above their heads. "Are you sure I haven't paid these?"

"If you can show me the canceled checks, we'll know, won't we."

"I'll examine my records, and if they indicate that I've missed paying you, I'll make it up."

Mr. Poxley held out a hand. "I'd appreciate a check right now."

"But I can't do that. I might wind up paying you twice."

The old man lowered his hand and looked over at the smoking stove. "Let me tell you something. People that take over a place like this have a lot of money. They can afford to hire a bunch of contractors to do a proper restoration."

"My dream is to do just that."

"At the rate you're going, it'll take you a hundred years just to make the place look second-rate. And if you stay out here, this house'll kill you. If that's your dream, then it's a nightmare."

Julian straightened his back. "It's my heritage. Are you suggesting I move back to an apartment in Memphis?"

"There's people that'll pay a bit of money for this property. With what you sell it for, you could get a tight little house with a shop out back."

"And you'd get your money for the refrigerator and air conditioner and the other stuff."

Chance Poxley put out a hand, palm down, and said, in a soft voice, "Look, if you can't pay me, I'll have to put a lien on the place. So will the folks down at the lumber yard, who I hear tell have advanced you considerable supplies on credit."

Julian opened the door and pointed outside. "You'll get your money."

The old man rolled his eyes at the little room. "Well, I got to admit

I've never been throwed out of a worse place than this." He eased down the steps and stopped to survey the property. "You know," he said over his shoulder, "I didn't come here to cause you any trouble. But I got to tell you, when the sheriff found out an owner was on this property, he checked into the tax records and found out you owe on this place back to 1946." The man's thin white hair was torn by the wind. "I didn't want to be the one to tell you."

Julian waved him away as though he were a stray dog. "Get off my property," he yelled. "I can buy and sell every damned one of you." He himself didn't know where this cutting voice had come from, its load of arrogance perhaps conjured up out of the red dirt around him, the dead fields and parched lumber of his inheritance.

Julian sat down that night to balance his checkbook and found that he'd have to transfer money from his tiny emergency fund at the bank in Memphis to hold off his creditors for a week or so. After that, he was bankrupt.

One night of gun-blue sky, the temperature went down to nine degrees. Julian had stuffed the cookstove with scrap wood he'd scavenged, and the stovepipe was glowing red halfway up to the flimsy ceiling. An old Remington manual was set up on the table, and it refused to move when he hit the Tab key, the fresh oil on its parts turned to gum by the cold. At about eleven o'clock, he had to go to the bathroom, so he put on padded slippers and all the clothes in the room and opened the door to the night. The wind was a black punishment, and his bones were rattling by the time he reached the back door of the big house. As soon as he stepped inside, his heart shrank at a splashing sound echoing down the dark hall. His feet began to sting, and when he turned on the hall light he could see water running deep on the floor. He slid over to the foot of the stairs and looked up at a ladder of water coming down, a skin of ice on the edges like a mountain stream. Upstairs, he found that the frozen toilet had shattered and fallen away from the wall, snapping off the feed line at the floor level, and water was jetting up to the ceiling. He had no idea where he could turn the water off. And only one person could tell him.

He sat next to the phone table in the hall and hooked his feet on a chair rung to keep them out of the water, which covered all the floors downstairs and was now pouring through the ceiling above him as well. He pulled out phone bills from the drawer under the phone, studying the columns of calls until he found a number in Georgia. He imagined he had done so much for Obie that the man should at least tell him where a valve was. Looking up, he watched lines of icicles forming where water sluiced through cracks in the plaster.

After many rings, someone in Georgia picked up the phone, and he asked to speak to Obie Parker. "This is his former employer," he shouted into the receiver. "I need to ask him a question."

A woman's reedy voice answered, sounding self-righteous and glad to be so. "Do you have any idea a-tall what time it is?"

"Yes, I'm sorry, but this is important."

"Obadiah is asleep, and a workin' man needs all the rest he's due, so I'm not about to roust him out of a warm bed, mister."

Julian's voice rose in pitch. "But I've got a broken water pipe and—"

"A broke pipe, you say? Mister, there's people in the world got a whole lot worse than that wrong in their lives. They got the cancer, they got children selling dope, they got trailers blown apart by tornado winds that leaves them standin' in the yard starin' up at the stars. But you know what? Ain't a one of them callin' me up at twelve-ten at night to whine about no broke water pipe."

"It's eleven-ten," Julian corrected.

"Mister, you caught up in your own little world so much you think the rest of God's universe is in your time zone. It's twelve-ten in Georgia."

A piano-size raft of plaster detatched from the ceiling and fell at his feet, covering him with a surf of freezing water. "Good Lord, lady, I've *got* to talk to your husband."

"People in hell *got* to have strawberry shortcake, but they don't get it." She hung up.

He lowered the buzzing phone and looked down the long, swamped hall toward the front of the house that was his glory, that told everyone who he was. He knew everything about it, and at the same time, nothing at all. The wind flattened the tall dry grass next to the pillars in a dead shout that told him not a thing that would help. Suddenly he was startled by the jangling phone.

"Hello?"

"Hey. It's Obie. I heard my wife a-talkin' to you."

The voice was like a warm, comforting hand, but Julian could not help shouting, "Where the hell's the water valve to the house? I'm flooded out here."

"If you got water on the floors don't go after that pump switch in the panel box. It'll knock you into the next world. Look under the sink and turn that third valve to the right."

He sloshed through the house and did as he was told, but it was a long time before the system bled down and the water diminished its rattle on the stairs. With a house-shaking crash, the dining room plaster came down all at once. Shivering, he ran back to the phone, wet up to the knees, and climbed onto the chair. "What do I do now, Obie? All the plaster in the place is coming down."

The voice drifted in from Georgia, sleepy and soft. "You can't afford no plaster man, that's for sure." After a pause he said, "Might be time to sell out."

"Never," he yelled into the receiver. "I'll never leave here in a million years."

"One time, I said I'd never give up my tattoos."

"Thanks, but I don't need your moralizing lesson. I need you to come back and fix things."

"I'm sorry, Mr. Smith, but it sounds like things is past fixin'."

Something crashed down in the kitchen like a truckload of gravel. "What can I do about the plaster?"

"That plaster's the least of your problems."

"What do you mean?"

"Well, if you don't know, I can't tell you."

The light fixture above his head filled with water and popped off in a shower of blue sparks, and he dropped the phone. Blind and trembling in the watery dark, he began to struggle down the hall toward his outbuilding, desperate for the warmth of the red-hot stove. When he opened the back door, he saw the old kitchen was now a windblown fireball of lumber, streamers of flame running toward him through the grass. He lurched outside and began stamping at the brush until he understood that with its brick porch and pillars, the house probably would not catch fire. Through a sidelight at the rear door he watched the flames race in the wind, flowing under his car and fanning out to light the corncrib, the smokehouse, and the big sagging barn, which went up in a howl of crackling boards and dried-out hay. At one point he tried to call the Poxley volunteer fire department, but the creosote pole that supported his phone wire had already gone up like a torch, taking his service away. In ten minutes, the fire circled the house, and he climbed up to the belvedere to track its progress as it burned to the ditches surrounding his tract, taking out the pump house, a tractor shed, and incinerating his Dodge, which burned hot and high, killing most of the foliage of the live oak shading it.

At dawn he could see that but for the roadside oaks, everything was gone, burned off the face of the earth as if by a powerful beam of light, the house standing naked and singed in a field of white ash. He stayed up in the belvedere hoping the new sun would warm him, but daylight brought a shrill wind crying like the voices of all the families, wealthy or destitute, who had lived in his house, who, each in turn, had given it up through death or duress and left it to falter. He stood unshaven and burning with fever, dressed in sopping house slippers and several layers of old robes and cotton jackets, waiting—for what, he wasn't sure. But after a few minutes he heard a car on the gravel road, looked down through the bubbled glass and saw them. Even from this distance he could see that Mr. Poxley's mouth had fallen open at the sight of the guttering outbuildings. He and a big deputy stepped out of the police car and walked to the roadside fence. Each man held down his hat with one hand and bore folded papers in the other, liens and tax bills that would take the place away, and Julian felt house and history shrink to nothing under his feet, a void replaced by a vision of himself, dressed in borrowed clothes and defeat, spirited away that very evening on a lurching bus bound for Memphis and sitting next to some untaught, impoverished person, perhaps even another long-suffering and moralizing carpenter.

Attitude Adjustment

*T*wo years had passed since the collision, and now young Father Jim spent a great deal of time lying in a recliner, looking for patterns in the cottage-cheese ceiling. He liked to pretend the flattened globs of Sheetrock mud were ice floes in the Arctic Ocean, and he was in a skiff trying to find a way through them to rescue a stranded person. He could never travel far before his mind just lost track of any direction and wandered back to the starting point at the central light fixture.

The diocese had allotted him this small outdated house on the edge of a North Carolina mountain town, a place with no Catholic church. The bishop told him he was now a pinch hitter, and occasionally he was summoned, as a last resort, to drive to a nearby town and say an early Mass or handle a Bible study session for children. For a long time after the accident, Father Jim felt like a robot he'd seen blown apart in a movie, its many pieces scattered, all still blinking, still functioning, but totally disconnected. Sometimes his nose itched, but he couldn't think of what part of him was supposed to scratch it. Now and then he would feel a sadness rise above the painful healing that he had to endure, but the sad feeling wouldn't quite make it across his brain to the part that could really appreciate it. Sometimes he would close his eyes tight and try to remember what had happened—how, in the heavy forest south of Passion Gap, a train had been trumpeting a monstrous chord of warning through the snow, but Father Jim, driving toward his church while creating a new homily in his head, had failed to hear it. He was proud of his sermons and wanted to get this latest one just right. Suddenly, the road twisted over the tracks, but with no crossing arms or blinking lights to warn him, Father Jim never saw the locomotive of a hundred-car coal train that exploded into his vehicle, shoving it a quarter mile east in a veil of flames and coppery sparks. Upon impact, the priest ascended through a million diamonds of windshield and landed in the middle of Highway 16, his skull fractured like a dropped melon, his hands cut through, both legs broken and bleeding. He lay in the snowy road for an hour waiting for the ambulance crew to come up the mountain through the developing blizzard while the engineer and brakeman crouched over his body trying to stop the bleeding with shop rags.

There were precious few Catholic priests in the mountains, so despite Father Jim's infirmities he was called on to pitch in when a pastor became ill or was called away from his church. He was always the last to be asked, of course, because most of the other priests knew he was forgetful of the most basic things and had developed a horror of giving homilies, a talent he had completely lost after the accident. And then, he was very scary to look at, his forehead and face heavily scarred, one of his eyes fixed and blind; the muscular six-foot-four priest often seemed ready to tumble over because of damage to his feet. He discomfited several adult congregations with his homilies, though when asked to help with children's church, most of the youngest ones liked him a great deal, perhaps thinking he was a reassigned troll from their books of fairy tales. Or maybe they liked his smile, the only facial expression he could still control.

The one rehab he remembered to do was weight lifting, because every morning he'd bang his ankles on the two-hundred-pound barbell next to his bed. Sometimes he questioned why he had to put up with so much discomfort. Now and then he wondered if God had sent a train to run over him. He'd also considered two or three times why God hadn't finished the job, but then he'd forget what he'd been wondering and move on. The doctors said his brain function might gradually improve. Physically, he would have to put up with some malformations. Since the many surgeries, he'd lost most of the hair on his misshapen head, and a rail yard of scars ran diagonally down to where his eyebrows once were. He seemed to have misplaced his sense of humor. His sister, in a failed attempt to make him laugh, told him he resembled a space alien in a set of *Star Wars* action figures.

Early one Saturday, Father Nguyen, up at Bluff Mountain Mission, saw the injured priest's name on a list of retired or partly abled priests. When his phone rang, Father Jim was in his recliner, trying to make sense of CNN and its runway-model announcers. He looked up in the air for the sound, wondering for a moment what it might be. Then on the fifth ring he remembered and picked up the receiver. After a few seconds, he recalled how to say hello. Father Nguyen needed to catch a last-minute flight to attend an aunt's funeral and asked if he would cover the five o'clock vigil service and hear confessions for half an hour before Mass. Father Jim pressed a button on his answering machine, which began to record the call, and then asked for specific directions. The other priest reminded him that Bluff Mountain was only ten miles away and that he'd driven there several times. It was on the same highway as his little house. Father Jim, who for some reason still had a driver's license, told him he would be there on time. He wrote himself a note and placed it under a cheap battery-powered travel clock that he set to ring at three p.m. Later that day, it did, and he followed the sound to the note, got dressed, and went out with his vestments over his arm to sit in his vehicle and try to start it. It was ten minutes before he remembered that the car wouldn't go in gear unless he stepped on the brake. Out on the road, he repeated his destination to himself every minute, and before long he was pulling into St. Timothy's parking lot. He got out and stared down the highway toward where he'd come from, remembering nothing of the trip.

Once in the little reconciliation room, he sat behind a kneeler that was topped with a privacy screen. There was also a plain chair four feet in front of him for penitents who wanted a face-to-face confession, a rare occurrence. Since his accident, Father Jim was embarrassed to hear confessions and felt sorry for the people telling their sins. At one time he'd taken pride in his ability to lend a compassionate ear, to give advice, but nowadays he felt he was no longer any good as a confessor, because he'd lost the talent for saying the right thing. He still tried, but the connection between a penitent's guilt and any remedy he might offer would simply not occur to him. His ideas were like boxcars with no couplers, bumping together and drifting apart.

He heard the scuff of shoes and a woman came in, knelt behind the screen, and confessed that she'd missed Mass twice. Father Jim grew dizzy. He remarked that it was good that she missed Mass.

After a long silence, she whispered, "No, Father, I don't miss Mass, I missed it. I didn't show up."

"Oh," he said. "Then why *don't* you miss Mass? You sound pretty devout and it seems like you would feel incomplete if you let a Sunday go by without attending Mass."

"I don't think I understand," she said.

He thought about this. "That's probably true," he said. "For your penance, you should try to learn to miss Mass."

Five minutes went by and then a man came in confessing a variety of sins. He admitted he had a problem with watching pornography and had visited many sites. Father Jim was struck with fear. He opened his mouth, but no words came out. While he knew he should know what the man was talking about, he didn't. He mentally strained, and the effort made him think of building a church in Rwanda, which he had done as a new priest, physically lifting roof beams in the jungle heat.

"You mean, you visited the sites of pornography, the studios where they film the stuff?"

There was a long pause on the other side of the screen. "Uh, no, Father. I just turned on the computer."

Again, the priest's mind didn't register the words. His imagination had been set in motion in one direction and began to gain momentum. "You know, you really *should* go to those buildings and try to get on the set," he began. "You'd see how young most of the girls are. How a lot of creepy people are standing around working lights and sound, looking bored because they make this stuff every day."

"Father?"

The more he talked, the more he thought he'd stumbled onto a new idea. "The girls are kind of desperate for money to go to college. Maybe they're immigrants forced to work like slaves. They could be your next-door neighbor. Maybe your teenage niece."

The man on the other side of the screen said, in an offended voice, "My niece would never do anything like that."

"Oh, she has enough money to pay for college?"

"Well, no," the man admitted. "She is old enough to work, though."

"Oh yeah? Where does she work?"

"The Burger King down the mountain."

There was some sort of mental impact involving stars behind his eyes. He gave himself over to a thought forming like the tail of a comet. "For your penance, I want you to go watch your niece."

"What?"

"Sure, that's it. Show up and order a meal. Sit behind those plastic ferns where you can see her work. For two hours. Watch the dignity of her work, her service, her efficiency, her mistakes and her successes, how she grows tired but still tries to help people. Compare that to what you see on those sites."

"Aw, can't you just give me a rosary to say or like ten Hail Marys?"

"Nope."

"All right. But this is weird." And the man began saying a grouchy Act of Contrition.

*F*ather Jim sat back in his hard chair and fell asleep. It could happen at any time. Once, after one of his tiny sermons, he fell asleep standing at the pulpit, and an altar boy had to tug at his vestments.

There was the sound of steps, and he opened his eyes. In front of him in the chair sat his gardener, Nestor, a compact, sturdy young man who kept Father Jim's small lawn as neat as a golf course. "Did you remember to weed-eat alongside the front steps?" the priest asked.

"*Sí*, Padre. But I have come for confession."

"Did I remember to pay the last time you did the lawn?"

"You paid twice, and I kept the money. That is one thing I have to confess."

"Oh. Well, just do it next time for free."

"*Está bien.* Now for my other sin, for which I am very ashamed. I wanted some new spinners for my Oldsmobile, but I didn't have the money. I stole my uncle's shotgun and sold it outside the gun show."

For a moment the priest tried to imagine what a shotgun was. Then he remembered he used to rabbit-hunt himself. Yes, his father had several shotguns. Did he still have a father? He would have to check when he returned to his house. "How much did you get?"

SIGNALS

"Five hundred dollars. My uncle found out what happened and he has shamed me to the whole family. He calls me *ratero,* the thief. He even phoned the police. I didn't think he'd miss it. He never hunts anything."

"Would finding him another shotgun settle things?"

"He said I have to buy him a new one just like it. At least a used one in ninety-five percent condition." Here Nestor began to weep. "Nobody in my family will speak to me, Padre. I can't sleep at night. I'd sell my car, but the police have taken it away because of insurance."

"Please don't cry." The one thing Father Jim could not stand, even before the accident, was the tears of other people. He told Nestor to pray for a solution. For his penance he was tempted to ask him to pull the monkey grass out of the flowerbed, but decided on ten Our Fathers instead.

Later, in the vestry, he put his alb on backwards, but Anthony, the altar boy, pointed this out to him. Father Jim was terrified to say Mass. He carried his own big missal with the readings numbered with stick-on notes, 1, 2, 3, 4, for the order of the parts. The congregation, many of whom had heard him say Mass before, watched him very carefully during the ceremony, the way a parent watches someone else's child walk a porch rail.

He made it to the Gospel, read it aloud as best he could, and then everyone sat down for the homily. Father Jim had a special fear of this Gospel passage. It was the one about John the Baptist being beheaded. When he read it to the congregation, it was as if he'd never heard it before, and he was amazed, his good eye roving the page, his blind one fixed on the front pew.

He began haltingly, already sweating, "King Herod must have been knocked out by this dancing girl, right?" He scanned the congregation and saw two people nod, so he was relieved to know he was not speaking Spanish. He had nightmares about waking up in the mornings able to pray only in Spanish, which he didn't understand very well. "Plus, the dancing girl was Herod's stepdaughter, and you always want to support your kids, no matter what. Well, Herod was throwing a big party for the important people in his realm, and he made a promise to this dancing girl daughter of his to grant her a wish if she did a good job. I guess Herod was just desperate to show off for his friends. We all know people like that, don't we?" Father Jim looked out over the many wrinkled brows. He was tempted to just give up, sit down, and maybe wave to the ushers to go after the collection. Looking off to the side, he saw the altar boy give him the "roll on" signal with his fingers, so he said, "Well, she asked him to chop off John the Baptist's head, and he didn't want to do that at all. Herod kind of liked to hear John preach, though he admitted he didn't understand what he said." Father Jim took an enormous breath, his face staining red. "Maybe Herod wasn't a totally bad sort, but, you know, he felt he would lose face if he didn't go through with his promise, so—whack!" Father Jim brought the side of his hand down on the pulpit like an axe, and the women in the front pew sat up stiffly. "And that was it for old John." Father Jim took another tortured breath, closed his eyes a moment, and waited for words to spark a light in his brain. After a while, he said, "I'm not sure what this Gospel means, but then I've known people who do weird things at parties, just to show off. Then they get egged on by their friends. Judging by confessions I've heard, lots of alcohol and marijuana are involved. Country boys like to say things like, 'Hey, watch this,' just before their friends bring them to the hospital. A drunken middle-aged husband will try to fly like a bird if a barmaid asks him to. So I guess you should keep things under control. Think for yourself, or someone else will think for you." He half turned away from the pulpit, but was worried that he hadn't driven the message home. Turning back, he said, "Don't whack people who don't deserve it."

He sat down in a plush walnut chair, and the congregation was as motionless as an unlit candle.

With the help of Anthony, who gave him many cues, he got through the Nicene Creed and the rest of the service. Soon he felt himself reappear in his recliner, nervously watching a *National Geographic* program about endangered lizards in Mexico. The next thing he remembered, he was getting out of bed and banging his ankle on the barbell. Sometimes transpositions happened. He would be one place and then instantly he would be somewhere else the next day. The neurologist at the hospital said these episodes might fade as his brain tried to regenerate. The fact that he was aware of the gaps at all was a good sign, the doctor said. This statement gave him hope; it suggested his brain was like the tail of a porch lizard that had been pulled off by a child and would grow back.

About seven he went to get the newspaper in the driveway and saw Nestor sliding out of his cousin's car, pulling a sling blade after him. *"Hola,"* Father Jim said. *"Dónde está su weed-eater?"* Nestor stood in the gravel and stared after his cousin as he peeled off down the road.

"Father, you don't know how to speak Spanish."

"Yeah, I guess not."

Nestor put the tool on his shoulder. He was strong looking, straight in the back. Normally, he would sing under his breath as he worked; he was a man who smiled easily, but today his eyes seemed worried. "I pawned my weed-eater to start building a shotgun fund. I'm just going to pull grass by hand today and knock the brush down at the edge of the backyard."

Father Jim remembered the stolen shotgun, and the returning thought heartened him. He imagined four or five of his new brain cells lifting weights behind his forehead. "What kind of gun was it?"

"A Browning Auto-Five light twelve of Japanese manufacture," Nestor said. "Nearly a new gun. My uncle wants to beat me up. He called the police on me again. Every time I'm around him he raises his arm like there's a hatchet in it."

Father Jim went inside and wrote down the information about the gun. He felt really sorry for his yard man, who was his friend, who would sit on the back steps on hot days and drink lemonade with him and tell of his parents back in Mexico who lavished praise on him for every cent he sent down across the border. Father Jim sat in his recliner and studied the gun's description in his shaking hand. He remembered very little about firearms. That part of his memory was lying somewhere out beside a mountain railroad. Taking the phone book into his lap, he looked up a local gun shop, wrote down the address and directions from the ad, and went into his room to dress. He thought it would be improper to purchase a firearm dressed as a Catholic priest. Before the accident, he'd owned no casual clothes, wanting to be the type of cleric who wore his collar and black shirt everywhere he went. He stood before his closet and looked in vain for something that seemed secular. Then he ran through his chest of drawers and couldn't even find a white T-shirt to wear. In a box under the bed he found black pants, some black socks, and a joke item his brother had sent him years ago, a black wife-beater undershirt. He put this on and looked in the mirror at his hairy shoulders. He seemed to remember seeing similar attire somewhere. His glossy black lace-up shoes contradicted his clothes, so he removed them along with his socks.

He left Nestor in the yard and drove off toward the gun shop, which was fourteen miles away at a crossroads, far away from the nearest town. The shop bore the name Lead Twilight Guns and Ammo and was perched at the side of the road, cantilevered over a cliff. He got out of his black car and was surprised when his feet pained him as he hobbled over to a heavy door crisscrossed with iron straps.

The six people in the building glanced up when he entered, and they did not look away. The wrinkled clerk behind the counter seemed as if he had met his share of bizarre weapons seekers in his time, but when he saw the scarred, barefoot, three-hundred-pound man wearing a coal-black wife-beater undershirt standing in his door, his mouth began to twitch.

Father Jim walked toward a counter showcase holding Beretta pistols and put his hands palms down on the glass. "I'm looking for a gun," he said, rather too loudly, as his hearing had been damaged in the accident.

The old man swallowed. "I bet you air." His eyes focused on the priest's high, ruined forehead.

"An automatic shotgun."

"What you aimin' to do with that shotgun?" the man asked, taking a step back.

The question seemed odd to the priest, and he thought the salesman wanted the most basic answer. So he intoned, in a priestly voice, "Kill."

The other clerk in the store, a skinny boy dressed in camouflage, slipped in behind the old man and asked, "You ain't lookin' to visit them what messed you up, is you? You know, the feds been watching us gun dealers like red-tail hawks."

The priest looked down at the stainless-steel pistols in the case. The clerk's question began to make sense. And then he forgot it. "I need a Browning Auto-5 in nice condition."

The clerks looked at each other, slightly relieved at the request for a hunting gun. "We got one in nice shape. You want to see it?"

Father Jim took the shotgun they handed him and looked it over as though it were a stick he'd picked up off his lawn, comprehending nothing about it, except that it was shiny and unworn. He gave it back. "How much is it?"

"Seven hundred," the old man said. "Plus tax."

"Okay," Father Jim said.

The young clerk put the shotgun back in the rack, but kept a hand on it. "You mean you want it?"

"Yes."

The boy furrowed his brow and looked closely at the priest, at the still eye, then the roving one, at the trembling fingers. "You ain't never like been in the nuthouse or nothing, has you?"

"Not that I remember."

"We sell to somebody been in the institution," he said more respectfully, "the feds'll send us to Leavenworth for ten years."

"That's a long time, isn't it?" the priest sang.

"You got to fill out a form 4473, then we do a background check on you. You ain't done nothing can keep us from selling you a gun, has you?"

When he heard that, Father Jim became anxious, wondering if there was a statute against clergymen purchasing firearms. "No, no."

The old man narrowed his eyes. "You kind of scary lookin', fella. You ain't planning nothing bad, I hope. We sell you a gun and you do something bad, they'll put us in the same cell with you."

"No, no. I was buying the gun to give to a friend of mine who's in trouble."

The two clerks just stared at him, and one of the customers tugged on the bill of his ball cap and said, "Oh, Lordy," and headed for the door.

The clerks asked him to sit in a chair by the entrance and fill out a form while they set up a phone call for the background check. "You don't know my name," he told them.

"Just you work on the form there, feller," the old clerk said. "We got things under control."

He waited for half an hour, studying the shop, watching other people look at ammunition, bows and arrows. Finally the younger clerk came out from a back room, took the form out of the priest's hand, and told him he'd failed the background check. That he'd have to leave.

"Well, all right," he said, and got to his feet. Then he remembered to ask, "But what failed me?"

The clerk was walking backward. "Uh, we can't sell a gun to somebody who ain't got no shoes."

Father Jim stepped out into the parking lot and was immediately arrested by two sheriff's deputies almost as large as he was, handcuffed, and placed in a cruiser. They told him they were holding him for a federal gun violation. He was taken to Sap Valley, the county seat, where he was sent to a room to meet with an ATF agent who happened to be in the district on other matters.

The agent was a severe little man of about forty, thin as a teenage girl. "So, you are Mr. James Bowman?"

Father Jim smiled. "That's me."

"And you attempted to purchase a Browning semi-automatic shotgun at the Lead Twilight gun store?"

"I sure did."

Here the agent paused and looked at him blankly. "For what purpose?"

For the first time Father Jim felt a little buzz of fear. The feeling was like hearing a distant train whistle when he was about to cross the tracks. The fact that he had been arrested and handcuffed and brought to a dingy room made of dented Sheetrock affected him not in the least. But the little man's voice contained a trace of governmental demon, a connection to knotted regulations more difficult to understand than religious mystery, which at least could be believed through faith, as many arbitrary governmental strictures could not. "I wanted to give it to a friend."

The agent straightened his back. "Why couldn't your friend buy it for himself?"

"Well, he's poor."

"What's your friend's name?" The agent spoke his words so quickly it took a few seconds for Father Jim to comprehend them.

"Nestor Alvarez. He lives about ten miles from here."

The agent's face became a rock. He left the room without a word, and Father Jim began to pray silently, without knowing exactly what to pray for. He had no idea why he had been arrested. For an hour he sat in the room, which was severely air-conditioned. His bare feet stuck to the tile floor.

Finally, the door swung open and the agent held up a handful of papers. "Mr. Bowman, you're under arrest on federal charges."

The priest's still eye tried to move. "Charges? You mean, like a bill? How much is it?"

"Being a straw buyer for an undocumented alien who is also an indicted felon is nothing to joke about. Your young Mr. Alvarez is awaiting trial for felony theft and is out on bail."

Father Jim nodded. "Yes. He'll come by next week to cut my grass. It grows like crazy this time of year." Circuits in the priest's brain were firing like an accident at a fireworks stand.

The agent studied Father Jim's eyes. The left one was starting to roam like a bubble in a spirit level. "Hey, have you ever been diagnosed with mental problems?"

"My brain has been operated on several times."

"But in spite of that, you knew that Mr. Alvarez was an indicted felon?"

"I guess so. He stole a shotgun, after all."

He looked at the agent's face and saw that he was experiencing some kind of incomprehensible happiness.

*F*ather Jim was put in a cell where he had an extended conversation with a toothless meth addict recently blinded in a lab explosion. Father Jim explained how he could get him into a program that would provide false teeth and recommended an eye surgeon in Raleigh who sometimes did free work on accident victims.

The next day the priest was allowed to call his father, who drove over from Charlotte with a lawyer friend. After a long discussion with the sheriff and the ATF agent, the sheriff was willing to let the priest go. The agent, however, insisted on proceeding toward a federal indictment.

The lawyer, a distinguished gentleman whose flowing white hair trembled when he looked at the ATF man, told him, "Surely you have more dangerous individuals to pursue."

"He broke a federal statute," the agent said.

The lawyer shook his head. "As usual, you're going after low-hanging fruit and leaving alone the serious perpetrators who are harder to find." He raised his chin and added, "Or more dangerous."

A mean little smile slid across the agent's lips. "Everybody who breaks the law is a target."

The priest's old father, still straight in the back, said, "Yes, especially those who won't use you as one."

Father Jim then remembered the lawyer, Mr. Randoll, head legal counsel for the archdiocese and a partner in one of the largest firms in the Carolinas. He even recalled one of his famous suits, when his team crucified an IRS agent for dragging an old widow into court. He was amazed that he could call up these details, delighted not only with the memory of the incident, but also with the fact that his brain had reached back into its history and plucked something out of its fragmented darkness. Maybe, as his neurologist had suggested, stress had a beneficial effect on rejuvenation.

After his father arranged for an enormous bail, he drove Father Jim back to his house. While the priest took a shower, he confiscated the wife-beater T-shirt and hid it in the trunk of his car. His father, a former airline pilot, was the size of his son, balding, muscular, smooth faced, and placid. He was sitting on the bed when the priest came back from the shower wearing a set of black pajamas. "How are you feeling, Jimmy?"

At first his son thought this was a puzzling query about his sense of touch. Then he said, "I feel fine." He sat next to his father and the mattress rose up on the other side.

"I'm wondering if you ought to ask the bishop for more leave time. I mean, not totally. But for now, maybe you ought not to drive so much."

Father Jim nodded. "I can get Nestor to drive me."

His father looked away for a moment, then back. "Is he a good man, Jimmy?"

"I think he is."

His father stood up and walked into the little kitchen. "I'm going to fix us some coffee. You want some?"

Father Jim was still thinking about Nestor. "He's just down on his luck."

"You always thought everybody was as good as everybody else," his father said from the kitchen. "Thinking that way can be dangerous."

Father Jim frowned. Something happened inside his head like a cloud drifting clear of the sun. He thought about Jesus palling around with Judas. Sharing food with him. Teaching him things about life. How to get through it. He thought about this a long time.

The next week the bishop, a kindly seventy-five-year-old Irishman, called and had a long conversation with him. The Bureau of Alcohol, Tobacco, Firearms, and Explosives was pressing for an indictment, and the bishop said it would be a good idea if Father Jim would take himself off the Mass and confession availability list, so to speak. And stop driving. However, he could perform other duties, if a pastor needed him.

Father Jim apologized for all the trouble he had caused. "I just stumbled into a world of regulations I didn't know were there," he told him. "It's like getting blamed for walking into a spiderweb at night."

"I know, James," the bishop commiserated. "Sometimes Washington thinks it's the Vatican."

A few days after their talk, Father Jim was still worried but also heartened by his distress, feeling that his brain was reknitting itself because of the pressure of facing jail time. He heard a knock at the door, and it was Nestor, who had been dropped off with a borrowed push mower and some pruning snips.

"*Hola,* Nestor."

"'Sup," Nestor said. He seemed a little drunk, and Father Jim was thankful he hadn't been driving. "Father, I hear you're in a lot of trouble because of me. Some scary government men came by where I stay and tried to say I asked you to buy me a weapon. When they left, my wife was crying. I don't understand what's going on."

"Me neither," the priest admitted. "Come in, I just made coffee."

The two of them sat down at a shaky table in the kitchen, and Nestor described how the ATF had notified Immigration about his presence in the country, and now he and his wife were in danger of being deported.

"You want me to go see someone at that office?" Father Jim asked.

Nestor put up his hands. "No, no, Father. My uncle now feels sorry for me and has asked a man who helps Mexicans with immigration problems to help. Please, don't do anything yourself." The yard man looked distressed.

"*Está seguro?*"

"Father, I can speak English. Lately, better than you," he said, smiling. But then the smile faded, and Nestor looked down at his hands. "You know, none of this would have happened if I didn't steal."

Father Jim poured him a cup of coffee at the stove and sweetened it the way his friend liked, bringing it to the table along with his own. "Well, you've had your shame, and your regret as well, so now it's time to move on."

"I can do that. But what if, you know, they put you in jail?"

The priest experienced a little jolt of alarm and took a long swallow of coffee, hoping it would flow straight to his brain to speed his thoughts. "Don't worry about it. John the Baptist was locked up in jail. Daniel, Saint Paul, Jeremiah—the Bible's full of jailbirds." They sat drinking their coffee in silence, the priest looking through his kitchen window to a storm-damaged tree loaded down with apples. He realized his vision was improving. He closed his good eye and saw a blur of fruit.

Nestor was sent back to Nogales with his wife, and Father Jim's case went to trial. In a three-day ordeal the federal authorities, with the testimony of the gun store clerks, who grudgingly gave their evidence, proved beyond a doubt that he had acted as a proxy gun buyer. His defense lawyer did what he could, but the judge was very rigid in his instructions to the jury, and the next day the group of twelve cranky retirees and habitually unemployed individuals found him guilty.

Father Jim sat in court wearing his Roman collar and for a long moment didn't understand why his father was hugging him and a deputy was carefully putting him in handcuffs. After a moment of panic he realized what was happening to him and said, "I'm glad Nestor isn't here to see the outcome of all this." The statement made sense, and his father studied his son's face a moment, nodding to no one in particular.

Father Jim was sent to jail in a special West Virginia prison filled with politicians, tycoons, confidence men, hedge fund managers, gamblers, and finance company executives, every one of them his least favorite kind of person. The local bishop arranged for him to give services in the cramped chapel, but only two Italian gentlemen regularly showed up, wearing sunglasses in the windowless room. The prison itself was a former county jail with a central hall bordered by rows of barred cells, though the doors were never slid closed unless the occupants wanted them to be. The bunks were wide and held thick mattresses, two to a cell, though some prisoners had the cages to themselves. There was a lounge with books and a television, a small gym, and a large grassy yard with basketball courts painted with fresh green enamel. Father Jim kept working out, getting a bit leaner on prison food.

During the year he was jailed, his mind began to come back to him like a book dropped in the ocean and washed up on shore, all there, but slightly warped. A little hair began to sprout from his tortured scalp. When the two Italian gentlemen went to confession, Father Jim wished he were a judge so he could add years to their sentences. But, still, he transferred forgiveness to them, and all that year they were loyal to him, sweeping the chapel, sharing sausage sent from home, and passing along little hand signals that he never understood when they slid by him in the hall.

One day an over-the-hill professional football player, an ex-kicker, was put into the cell with him. The man liked to wash his hair every day, then blow-dry it for an hour while talking loudly about himself and all the important people he had known in his life. Every day he spoke at length about his significant friends. For many days Father Jim patiently listened to him brag about the things these people owned, how much everything was worth, how smart and influential they were. The third week, Father Jim politely asked him to be quiet so he could concentrate on his prayers. The man, who went by the last name of Sledge, ignored him and began to recount all the objects he had bought in his life, things no one in the building—no one in the whole West

Virgina prison system—could appreciate, and then came a litany of fine cars, cigarette boats, yachts, private rail cars, ritzy watches, diamonds for his many women, swimming pools, horses, engraved machine guns, airplanes. The priest would sometimes walk down the hall, stand by the cell of the old embezzlers, and lean against the wall to read his prayer book.

Eventually, his cellmate began to follow him, decanting his life. One time, Father Jim looked up and told the man to just be quiet. Sledge pulled a comb from his pocket and raised his arms high, combing his well-trained hair in long sweeps. "You make me be quiet," he said.

The priest's brain began to boil like a kettle. His vision cleared. He didn't know how to fight, but something was rising through his neck, some power. "You'll be quiet enough in the grave," he told him, an appropriate thing to say, Father Jim figured, to a person who valued the trinkets of the present life too much. The over-the-hill football player didn't see it that way, and knocked Father Jim down with one punch to the face. When the priest couldn't get back up, Sledge straddled his belly and punched him again, opening up one of the old scars above his eye, which began streaming tears and blood.

As soon as the other prisoners saw that the big priest was not going to get up and defend himself, that he was patiently taking punches, holding his prayer book to his heart, the two Italian gentlemen and a Polish acquaintance pulled the Sledge off and dragged him into the cell with the embezzlers, two cousins who once had worked in New York City government. The priest heard his cellmate holler, then shriek. Next, he called for his mama. The guards bounded in, amazed because they hadn't broken up a fight in many months. They dragged Father Jim down to his cell, where they helped him patch himself up with Band-Aids. Two hours later, Sledge shambled down from the dispensary and showed himself at the cell door, one leg buckled inward, all the buttons ripped off his shirt, and blood seeping through his pants at his knees and crotch.

"Can I go to bed?" he croaked.

Father Jim looked up from his prayers. "Will you try to hurt me again?"

The former kicker blinked through his tumbled hair. "Look what they did to me. Are you crazy?"

Father Jim chuckled. "Used to be," he said. "But come in and lie down."

After his release from prison, the bishop told him it would be a few months, depending, before he would be allowed to handle a large Mass or a complex Lenten observance, though he could fill in for vacationing parish secretaries, bring Communion to the sick, or participate in children's church. Father Jim was disappointed. He wanted to be assigned full duties in a busy church and thought he had come a long way since the accident. At night, after the TV news and one beer, he'd meditate on his unlikely survival. The car he'd driven had been crushed to the size of a motorcycle. The only reason he'd lived was he'd been thrown out of the vehicle because he'd not worn his seatbelt. What made him forget to fasten it? Why was he still here?

One Friday Father Jim was in Charlotte for a doctor's appointment and got a call on his new cell phone from a friend who pastored a large city parish and needed help on the weekend. He said that Father Jim could stay at the rectory, pay a few hospital visits, hear confessions on Saturday afternoon, and then handle the youngest children on Sunday. Father Jim said he'd be happy to help.

On Sunday he found the annex where the children would gather after being excused from the main service. The tall lady in charge couldn't hide her surprise at the sight of him, even though he was wearing a black golf hat to hide as much scarring as he could. She introduced herself and reminded him of what to do. "Father Ralph gives pretty long homilies, so we usually have a brief snack time after you read them a book." And then the children came in. The six- and seven-year-olds regarded him warily, but most of the other children were younger and ran past the legs of this big anonymous adult into the corner of the large room they knew as the story place. He remembered that they were people of the blissful lower regions of life and that nothing above a grown-up's knees was worthy of their concern. Father Jim walked into the carpeted area, looked around for a big person's chair, and, seeing none, sat on the floor

Indian-style. In his lap he spread open a large illustrated book containing the parable of the Good Samaritan.

"We've got a great story today," he announced. At once, the three-to five-year-olds flocked to him. A pair sat on each thigh, three taller children leaned against his back, straining to look over his shoulders at the colorful drawings, and the rest formed a tight semicircle facing him, their bright faces baptizing him with light. Father Jim began to read in an expressive voice, pointing out details in the pictures. He explained that some Jewish people did not especially like Samaritans, and they would not expect a Samaritan to help the Jewish man beaten up by robbers. He looked around him slowly, into each child's morning-clear eyes. He usually thought up a question at this point.

"So who can get this big question right? Here it is. This is a big deal." But he didn't know what the question was. He looked in their eyes for at least five seconds, stalling. Then something popped into his head like an e-mail. "Why did God let the Jewish man get beaten up?" There was silence for a heartbeat or two, then a babble of answers, many answers. One four-year-old girl with blinding blonde hair said the Jewish man got beat up because he was mean to the Samaritans. From her perch on his left knee, a three-year-old with a face like a jewel said maybe the man stole a Samaritan's cookie. That *she* wanted a cookie. A five-year-old with a missing tooth said maybe the Jewish guy was bragging and made somebody mad. A six-year-old, who was in the wrong group, a dour country boy wearing a pearl-button shirt, raised his hand and said, "My name is Bill. God wanted to teach the Jewish guy a lesson."

"Teach him a lesson?" Father Jim's mind still occasionally hit a bump in the road, and the comment jostled his thinking. "I don't know, Bill. That sounds mean."

"I think it's the point," the dour boy said. "I bet the guy who got beat up liked Samaritans and everybody else after he got better. He got a attitude adjustment."

And then the baby girl on his left knee, who had never really ceased talking, asked, "Did *you* get beat up?" She stood on his thigh in her hard Sunday shoes, reached over the child next to her and touched the worst scar on his cheek with her feathery fingers.

"Well, sort of. I was run over by a train."

The children all fell silent, and a treasury of small faces stared at him. "Did somebody come and help you?" a voice behind him asked.

Father Jim frowned. "The ambulance crew. I guess they were like Samaritans on salary."

The children didn't understand the joke, and by the movement of their eyes he saw them study his face and hands.

"Did it hurt real bad?" dour Bill asked.

"Oh, no. Not at first, anyway. They brought me to the hospital and took good care of me."

"Did they give you a cookie?" the baby girl on his left knee asked.

"I don't think so." Other questions followed, and gradually he began to feel like the Jewish fellow on the side of the road must have felt. The children were worried about him, and their concern was like medicine. Even so, his burdened legs were cramping, a thousand needles shooting through them. He started to get up, but the tiny blonde girl on his right thigh keened, "Wait a minute, wait a minute. Who got the big question right?"

Father Jim settled back and realized that no one could know the reason for pain, unless it was that getting hurt was rewarded by visitations like the one around him. He grinned a little. "I'm thinking all of you are right."

The baby girl jumped, landed a hand in his shirt pocket, and smiled in his face. "Snack time," she yelled.

Sorry Blood

The old man walked out of Walmart and stopped dead, recognizing nothing he saw in the steaming Louisiana morning. He tried to step off the curb, but his feet locked up and his chest flashed with a burst of panic. The blacktop parking lot spread away from him, glittering with the enameled tops of a thousand automobiles. One of them was his, and he struggled to form a picture, but could not remember which of the family's cars he had taken out that morning. He backstepped into the shade of the store's overhang and sat on a displayed riding lawn mower. Putting his hands down on his khaki pants, he closed his eyes and fought to remember, but one by one things began to fall away from the morning, and then the day before, and the life before. When he looked up again, all the cars seemed too small, too bright and glossy, more like fishing lures. His right arm trembled, and he regarded the spots on the back of his hand with a light-headed embarrassment. He stared down at his Red Wing brogans, the shoes of a stranger. For half an hour, he sat on the mower seat, dizziness subsiding like a summer storm.

Finally, he got up, stiff and floating, and walked off into the grid of automobiles, his white head turning from side to side under a red feed-store cap. Several angry-looking people sat in hot cars, their faces carrying the uncomprehending disappointment of boiled crabs. He walked attentively for a long time but recognized nothing, not even his own tall image haunting panels of tinted glass.

Twice he went by a figure slouched in a parked Ford sedan, an unwashed thing with a rash of rust on its lower panels. The driver, whose thin hair hung past his ears, was eating a pickled sausage out of a plastic sleeve and chewing it with his front teeth. He watched the wanderer with a slow, reptilian stare each time he walked by. On the third pass, the driver eyed the still-straight back, the big shoulders. He hissed at the old man, who stopped and looked for the sound. "What's wrong with you, gramps?"

The old man drifted up to the window and stared into the car at a middle-aged fellow whose stomach enveloped the lower curve of the steering wheel. An empty quart beer bottle lay on the front seat. "Do you know me?" the old man asked in a voice that was soft and lost.

The driver looked at him a long time, his eyes moving down his body as though he were a column of figures. "Yeah, Dad," he said at last. "Don't you remember me?" He put an unfiltered cigarette in his mouth and lit it with a kitchen match. "I'm your son."

The old man's hand went to his chin. "My son," he said, like a fact.

"Get in." The man in the Ford smiled only with his mouth.

"All right."

"You're having a little trouble remembering."

The old man got in and placed a hand on the chalky dash. "What have I been doing?"

"Shopping for me is all. Now give me back my wallet." The driver held out a meaty hand. The other man pulled his billfold from a hip pocket and handed it over.

In a minute they were leaving the parking lot, riding a trash-strewn highway out of town into the sandy pine barrens of Tangipahoa Parish. The old man watched the can-studded roadside for clues. "I can't even remember my own name," he said, looking now at his plaid shirt.

"It's Ted," the driver said, giving him a quick look. "Ted Williams." He checked his side-view mirrors.

"I don't even remember your name, son. I must be sick." The old man wanted to feel his head for fever, but he was afraid of laying hands on a stranger.

"My name is Andy," the other man said, fixing a veined eye on him for a long moment. After a few miles, he turned off the main highway onto an unpaved road. The old man listened to the unfamiliar knock and ping of rock striking the driveshaft of the car, and then the gravel became patchy and thin, the road blotched with a naked, carroty earth like the hide of a sick dog. Bony cattle heaved their heads between strands of barbed wire, scavenging for roadside weeds. The Ford bumped past mildewed trailers sinking into rain-eaten plots. Farther on, the land was too soggy for trailers, too poor even for grazing the lane's desperate cattle. After two miles of this, they pulled up to a boxy red-brick house squatting in a swampy two-acre yard. Limbs were down everywhere, and cat briers and poison oak covered the rusty fence that bordered the driveway. The old man saw no need for a fence since there was only brush-wracked, cut-over woods running in every direction.

"This is home. You remember now?" Andy said, pulling him from the car. He felt the old man's long arm for muscle.

Ted looked around for clues, but said nothing. He watched Andy walk around the rear of the house and return with a shovel and a pair of boots. "Follow me, Dad." They walked to a swale full of coppery standing water that ran down the side of the property, ten feet from the fence. "This has to be dug out, two deep scoops side by side, from here all the way down to that ditch at the rear of the property. One hundred yards." He held the shovel out at arm's length.

"I don't feel very strong," Ted said, bending slowly to unlace his shoes. He stepped backward out of them and slipped into the oversized Red Ball boots.

"You're a big man. Maybe your mind ain't so hot, but you can work for a while yet." And when Ted rocked up the first shovelful of sumpy mud, Andy smiled, showing a pair of rotten incisors.

He worked for an hour, carefully, watching the straightness of the ditch, listening to his heart strum in his ears, studying the awful plot that was draining like a boil into the trough he opened for it. The whole lot was flat and low, made of a sterile clay that never dried out between thunderstorms rolling up from the Gulf. After four or five yards he had to sit down, the pine trees swimming around him as though laboring to stay upright in a great wind. Andy came out of the house carrying a lawn chair and a pitcher of cloudy liquid.

"Can I have some?" the old man asked.

Andy showed his teeth. "Naw. These are margaritas. You'll fall out for sure if you drink one." As an afterthought he added, "There's water in the hose."

All morning Andy drank from the pitcher, and the old man looked back over his shoulder, trying to place him. The shovel turned up a sopping red clay tainted with runoff from a septic tank, and Ted tried to remember where he had seen such poor soil. The day was still, no cars bumped down the dirt lane; the rattling of the ice cubes and the click of a cigarette lighter were the only sounds the old man heard. About one-thirty he put down his shovel for the twentieth time and caught his breath. He had used a shovel before—his body told him that—but he couldn't recall where or when. Andy drew up his lawn chair, abandoning the empty pitcher in the pigweed against the fence. Ted could smell his breath when he came close, some thing like cleaning fluid, and he closed his eyes, a memory trying to fire up in his brain, but when he opened his lids the image broke apart like a dropped ember.

Andy moved in close and fell back into the chair. "You ever been beat up by a woman?"

Ted was too tired to look at him. Sweat weighed him down.

Andy scratched his belly through his yellow knit shirt. "Remember? She told me she'd beat me again and then divorce my ass if I didn't fix this yard up." He spoke with one eye closed as though he was too drunk to see with both of them at the same time. "She's big," he said to himself. "Makes a lot of money but hits hard. Gave me over a hundred stitches once." He held up a flaccid arm. "Broke this one in two places."

The old man looked at him then, studying the slouching shoulders, the patchy skin in his scalp. He saw that he was desperate, and the old man moved back a step. "She's coming soon, the bitch is. I told her I couldn't do it. That's why I went to the parking lot to hire some of those bums that work for food." He tried to rattle an ice cube in his empty tumbler, but the last one had long since melted. "Those guys won't work," he said. "They just hold those cardboard signs saying they'll work so they can get a handout, the lazy bastards."

Pinheads of light were exploding in the old man's peripheral vision. "Can I have something to eat?" he asked, looking toward the house and frowning.

Andy led him into a kitchen that smelled of garbage. The tile floor was cloudy with dirt, and a hill of melamine dishes lay capsized in the murky sink water. Andy unplugged the phone and left the room with it. Returning empty-handed, he tumbled into a kitchen chair and lit a cigarette. The old man guessed where the food was and opened a can of Vienna sausages, twisting them out one at a time with a fork. "Maybe I should go to a doctor?" he said, chewing slowly, as if trying to place the taste.

"Ted. Dad. The best job I ever had was in a nursing home, remember?" He watched the old man's eyes. "I dealt with people like you all day. I know what to do with you."

Ted examined the kitchen the way he might look at a bizarre exhibit in a roadside carnival. He looked and looked.

*T*he afternoon passed like a slow, humid dream, and he completed fifty yards of ditch. By sundown he was trembling and wet. Had his memory come back, he would have known he was too old for this work. He leaned on the polished wood of the shovel handle and looked at his straight line, almost remembering something, dimly aware that where he was he had not been before. His memory was like a long novel left open and ruffled by a breeze to a different chapter farther along. Andy had disappeared into the house to sleep off the tequila, and the old man came in to find something to eat. The pantry showed a good stock of chili, but not one pot was clean, so he scrubbed the least foul for ten minutes and put the food on to heat.

Later, Andy appeared in the kitchen doorway wavering like the drunk he was. He led Ted to a room that contained only a stripped mattress. The old man put two fingers to his chin. "Where are my clothes?"

"You don't remember anything," Andy said quickly, turning to walk down the hall. "I have some overalls that'll fit if you want to clean up and change."

Ted lay down on the splotched mattress as though claiming it. This bed, it's mine, he thought. Turning onto his stomach, he willed to remember the musty smell. Yes, he thought. My name is Ted. I am where I am.

In the middle of the night his bladder woke him, and on the way back to bed he saw Andy seated in the box-like living room watching a pornographic movie in which a hooded man was whipping a naked woman with a rope. He walked up behind him, watching not the television but Andy's head, the shape of it. A quart beer bottle lay sweating in his lap.

The old man rolled his shoulders back. "Only white trash would watch that," he said.

Andy turned around, slow and stiff, like a sick person. "Hey, Dad. Pull up a chair and get off on this." He looked back to the TV.

Ted hit him from behind, a roundhouse, open-palm swat on the ear that knocked him out of the chair and sent the beer bottle pinwheeling suds across the floor. Andy hit the tile on his stomach, and it was some time before he could turn up on one elbow to give the big man a disbelieving, angry look. "You old shit. Just wait till I get up."

"White trash," the old man thundered. "No kid of mine is going to be like that." He stepped closer. Andy rolled against the TV cart and held up a hand. The old man raised his right foot as though he would plant it on his neck.

"Hold on, Dad."

"Turn the thing off," he said.

"What?"

"Turn the thing off," the old man shouted, and Andy pressed the power button with a knuckle just as a big calloused heel came down next to his head.

"Okay. Okay." He blinked and pressed his back against the television, inching away from an adversary who seemed even larger in the small room.

And then a tall, bony face fringed with white hair drifted down above his own, examining him closely, his features, the shape of his nose. A blistered finger traced Andy's right ear as if evaluating its quality. "Maybe you've got from me some sorry blood," he said, and his voice shook from saying it, that such a soft and stinking man could come out of him. He pulled back and closed his eyes as though he couldn't stand sight itself. "Let the good blood come out, and it'll tell you what to do," he said. "You can't let your sorry blood ruin you."

Andy stood up in a pool of beer and swayed against the television, watching the other man disappear down the hall. His face burned where he'd been hit, and his right ear rang like struck brass. He moved into the kitchen, where he studied a photograph taped to the refrigerator, an image of his wife standing next to a deer hanging in a tree, her right hand balled around a long knife. He sat down, perhaps forgetting Ted, the spilled beer, even his wife's hard fists, and fell asleep on his arms at the kitchen table.

The next morning the old man woke up and looked around him, almost recalling a different room. He concentrated, but the image he saw was like something far away, viewed without his eyeglasses. He rubbed his thumbs over his fingertips, and the feel of someone he'd known was there.

In the kitchen he put on water for coffee, watching his passed-out son until the kettle whistled. He loaded a French-drip pot and located the bread, scraped the mold off four slices, and toasted them. He took eggs and fatty bacon from the refrigerator. When Andy struggled upright, a dark stink of armpit stirred alive, and the old man told him to go wash himself.

In half an hour Andy came back into the kitchen, his face nicked and bleeding from a month-old blade, a different T-shirt forming a second skin. He sat and ate without a word, but drank no coffee. After a few bites, he rummaged in the refrigerator for a can of beer. The old man looked at the early sun caught in the dew on the lawn and then glanced back at the beer can. "Remind me of where you work," he said.

Andy took a long pull on the can. "I'm too sick to work. You know that." He melted into a slouch and looked through the screen door toward a broken lawn mower dismantled under the carport. "It's all I can do to keep up her place. Every damn thing's broke, and I got to do it all by hand." The lawn mower looked as if it had been hammered by lightning.

"Why can't I remember?" The old man sat down to his breakfast and began to eat, thinking, This is an egg. What am I?

Andy noticed his expression and perhaps felt a little neon trickle of alcohol brightening his bloodstream, kindling a single flicker of kindness, and he leaned over. "I seen it happen before. In a few days your mind'll come back." He drained the beer and let out a rattling belch. "Right now, get back on that ditch."

Ted put a hand on a shoulder. "I'm sore." He left the hand there.

"Come on." Andy fished three cans of beer from the refrigerator. "You might be a little achy, but my back can't take the shovel business at all. You got to finish that ditch today." He looked into the old man's eyes as though he'd lost something in them. "Quick as you can."

"I don't know."

Andy scratched his ear and, finding it sore, gave him a dark look. "Get up and find that shovel, damn you."

When Andy drove to a crossroads store, Ted dragged his feet to the ditch and began turning up foul, sopping crescents. The other man returned to sit in the shade of a wormy gum, where he opened a beer and began to read a paper he'd bought. In the police reports column was a brief account of a retired farmer from St. Mary Parish, Etienne LeBlanc, who had been staying with his son in Pine Oil when he disappeared. The son stated that his father had moved in with him a year ago, had begun to have spells of forgetfulness, and that he sometimes wandered. These spells had started the previous year on the day the old man's wife had died while they were shopping at the discount center. Andy looked over at Ted and snickered. He went to the house for another beer and looked again at the photograph on the refrigerator. His wife's stomach reached out farther than her breasts, and her angry red hair shrouded a face tainted by tattooed luminescent-green eye shadow. Her lips were ignited by a permanent chemical pigment that left them bloodred even in the mornings, when he was sometimes startled to wake and find the dyed parts of her flaring next to him. She was a dredge boat cook working her regular two-week shift at the mouth of the Mississippi, and she had told him that if a drainage ditch was not dug through the side yard by the time she got back, she would come after him with a piece of firewood.

He had tried. The afternoon she left he'd bought a shovel on the way back from the liquor store at the crossroads, but on the second spadeful he had struck a root and despaired, his heart bumping up in rhythm, his breath drawing short. He left the shovel stuck upright in the yard like his headstone, and that night he didn't sleep one minute. Over the next ten days the sleeplessness continued and finally affected his kidneys, causing him to get up six times every night to use the bathroom, until by dawn he felt as dry as a cracker. He drove out to buy quarts of beer, winding up in the Walmart parking lot staring through the window of his old car as if by concentration alone he could conjure up someone to take on his burden. And then he saw the old man pass by his hood, aimless as a string of smoke.

For the next two hours, the heat rose up inside Ted, and he looked enviously at the cool can resting on Andy's catfish belly. He tried to remember what beer tasted like, and could sense a buzzing tingle on the tip of his tongue, a blue-ice feel in the back of his mouth. Ted looked hard at his son and again could not place him. Water was building in his little ditch, and he placed his foot once more on the shovel, pushing it in, but not pulling back on the handle. "I need something cold to drink."

Andy did not open his eyes. "Well go in the house and get it. But I want you back out here in a minute."

He walked into the kitchen and stood by the refrigerator, filling a glass tumbler with water and drinking it down slowly. He rinsed the glass at the sink and opened the cabinet to replace it when his eye caught sight of a stack of inexpensive dishes showing a blue willow pattern. A little white spark fired off in the darkness of his brain, almost lighting up a memory.

Opening another cabinet, he looked for signs of the woman, for this was some woman's kitchen, and he felt he must know her, but everywhere he looked was cluttered and smelled of insecticide and was like no place any woman he knew would put up with. The photograph on the refrigerator of a big female holding a knife meant nothing to him. He ran a thick palm along the shelf where the coffee was stored, feeling for something that was not there. It was bare wood, and a splinter pricked his finger. He turned and walked to Andy's room, looking into a closet, touching jeans, coveralls, pullovers that could have been for a man or a woman, and then five dull dresses shoved against the closet wall. He tried to recognize the cloth, until from outside came a slurred shout, and he turned for the bedroom door, running a thumb under an overalls strap that bit into his shoulders.

The sun rose high and the old man suffered, his borrowed khaki shirt growing dark on his straining flesh. Every time he completed ten feet of ditch, Andy would move his chair along beside him like a guard. They broke for lunch, and at one-thirty when they came back into the yard, a thunderstorm fired up ten miles away, and the clouds and breeze saved them from the heat. Andy looked at pictures in magazines, drank, and drew hard on many cigarettes. At three o'clock, the old man looked behind him and saw he was still thirty feet from the big parish ditch at the rear of the lot. The thought came to him that there might be another job after this one. The roof, he noticed, needed mending, and he imagined himself straddling a gable in the glare. He sat down on the grass, wondering what would happen to him. Sometimes he felt that he might not be able to finish, that he was digging his own grave.

The little splinter began to bother him, and he looked down at the hurt, remembering the raspy edge of the wooden shelf. He blinked twice. Andy had fallen asleep, a colorful magazine fluttering in his lap. Paper, the old man thought. Shelf paper. His wife never would have put anything in a cabinet without first putting down fresh paper over the wood, and then something came back like images on an out-of-focus movie screen when the audience claps and whistles and roars and the projectionist wakes up and gives his machine a twist, and life, movement, and color unite in a razor-sharp picture, and all at once he remembered his wife and his children and his venerable 1969 Oldsmobile he had driven to the discount store.

Etienne LeBlanc gave a little cry, stood up, and looked around at the alien yard and the squat house with the curling roof shingles, remembering everything that had ever happened to him in a shoveled-apart sequence, even the time he had come back to the world standing in a cornfield in Texas, or riding a Ferris wheel in Baton Rouge, or in the cabin of a shrimp boat off Point au Fer in the Gulf.

He glanced at the sleeping man and was afraid. Remembering his blood-pressure pills, he went into the house and found them in his familiar clothes. He looked around the mildew-haunted building, which was unlike the airy cypress home place he still owned down in St. Mary Parish, a big-windowed farmhouse hung with rafts of family photographs. He looked for images in the hallway, but the walls were barren. He walked through the rooms wondering what kind of people owned no images of their kin. Andy and his wife were like visitors from another planet, marooned, childless beings barely enduring their solitude. In the kitchen he put his hand where the phone used to be, recalling his son's number. He looked through the screen door at a fat, bald man sleeping in a litter of shiny cans and curling magazines, a wreck of a man who'd built neither mind nor body nor soul. He saw the swampy yard, the broken lawn mower, the muddy, splintered rakes and tools strewn around the carport, more ruined than the hundred-year-old implements in his abandoned barn down in the sugarcane fields. He saw ninety yards of shallow ditch. He pushed the screen door out because something in his blood drew him back into the yard.

His shadow fell over the sleeping man as he studied his sallow skin, the thin-haired, overflowing softness of him as he sat off to one side in the aluminum chair, a naked woman frowning in fear in his lap. Etienne held the shovel horizontally in both hands, thinking that he could hit him once in the head for punishment and leave him stunned on the grass and rolling in his rabid magazines while he walked somewhere to call the police, that Andy might learn something at last from a bang on the head. Who would blame an old man for doing such a thing? Here was a criminal, though not a very smart one, and such people generally took the heaviest blows of life. His spotted hands tightened on the hickory handle.

But then he scanned the house and yard, which would never be worth looking at from the road, would never change for the better because the very earth under it all was totally worthless, a boot-sucking, iron-fouled claypan good only for ruining the playclothes of children. He thought of the black soil of his farm, his wife in the field, the wife who had died on his arm a year before as they were buying tomato plants. Looking toward the road, he thought how far away he was from anyone who knew him. Returning to the end of the little ditch, he sank the shovel deep, put up his hands and pulled sharply, the blade answering with a loud suck of mud that raised one of Andy's eyelids.

"Get on it, Ted," he called out, stirring in the chair, unfocused and dizzy and sick. The old man had done another two feet before Andy looked up at him and straightened his back at what he saw in his eyes. "What you looking at, you old shit?"

Etienne LeBlanc sank the blade behind a four-inch collar of mud. "Nothing, son. Not a thing."

"You got to finish this evenin'. Sometimes she comes back early, maybe even tomorrow afternoon." Andy moved with the difficulty of an invalid in a nursing home, searching around the base of his chair for something to drink, a magazine falling off his lap into the seedy grass. "Speed up if you know what's good for you."

For the next two hours, Etienne paced himself, throwing the dirt into a straight, watery mound on the right side of the hole, looking behind him to gauge the time.

Andy carried another six-pack from the house and once more drank himself to sleep. Around suppertime Etienne walked over and nudged the folding chair.

"Wake up." He poked Andy's flabby arm.

"What?" The eyes opened like a sick hound's.

"I'm fixing to make the last cut." Etienne motioned toward the ditch. "Thought you might want to see that." They walked to the rear of the lot where the old man inserted the shovel sideways to the channel and pulled up a big wedge, the water cutting through and widening out the last foot of ditch, dumping down two feet into the bigger run.

Andy looked back at the middle of his yard where the water was seeping toward the new outlet. "Maybe this will help the damned bug problem," he said, putting his face close to the old man's. "Mosquitoes drive her nuts."

"Is that what bothers her?" Etienne said. Andy took a step back and stared at him.

The next morning it was not yet first light when the old man woke to a noise in his room. Andy kicked the mattress lightly. "Come on," he said. "We're going for a ride."

He did not like the sound of this but got up and put on the clothes he had worn at the discount store and followed out to the driveway. He could barely see anything and was afraid. Andy stood close and asked him what he could remember.

"What?"

"You heard me. I've got to know what you remember."

Etienne made his mind work carefully. "I remember the ditch," he said.

"And what else?"

He averted his eyes. "I remember my name."

Andy whistled a single note. "And what is it?"

"Ted. Ted Williams." He watched Andy try to think that through.

"Okay," he finally said, looking at the gray light beginning to define the lawn. "Get in the car and lay down in the backseat." The old man did as he was told and felt the car turn for the road, then turn again, and he hoped that all these turnings would not lead him back to a world of meaningless faces and things, that he would not forget to recall, for the only thing he was, was memory.

They had not driven a hundred feet down the lane when bright headlights came toward them and Andy began crying out an elaborate string of curses. The old man looked over the seat and saw a pickup truck in the middle of the road.

"It's her," Andy said, his voice trembling and high. "Don't talk to her. Let me handle it." It was not quite light enough to see his face, so the old man read his voice and found it sick with dread.

The pickup stopped, and in the glow of the headlights Etienne saw a woman get out, a big woman whose tight coveralls fit her the way a tarpaulin binds a machine. Her hair was red like armature wire and braided in coppery ropes that fell down over her heavy breasts. Coming to the driver's window, she bent down, pulled a toothpick from her mouth, and asked, "What's going on here, you slimy worm?" Her voice was a cracked cymbal.

Andy tried a smile. "Honey, hey there. I just decided to get an early—"

She reached in and put a big thumb on his Adam's apple. "You never get up before ten. Never."

"Honest," he whined, the word squirting through his pinched vocal cords. Her neck stiffened when she saw Etienne.

"Shut up. Who's this?"

Andy opened his mouth and closed it, opened it again and croaked, "Just an old drinking buddy. I was bringing him home."

She squinted at the old man. "Why you in the backseat?"

Etienne looked into the fat slits of her eyes and remembered a sow that had almost torn off his foot half a century before. "He told me to sit back here."

She straightened up and backed away from the car. "All right, get out. Some kind of bullshit's going on here." He did as she asked, and she looked him over in the dawning light. She sniffed the air derisively. "And who the hell *are* you?"

He tried to think of something to say, wondering what would cause the least damage. He thought down into his veins for an answer, but his mind began to capsize like an overburdened skiff. "I'm his father," he said at last. "I live with him."

Her big head rolled sideways like a dog's. "Who told you that?"

"I'm his father," he said again.

She put a paw on his shoulder and drew him in range of her sour breath. "Let me guess. Your memory ain't so hot, right? He found you a couple blocks from a nursing home, hey? You know, he's tried this crap before." The glance she threw her husband was horrible to see. "Here, let me look at you." She pulled him around into the glare of the head-lights and noticed his pants. "How'd you get this mud on you, pops?" Her big square teeth showed when she asked the question.

"I was digging a ditch," he said.

Her broad face tightened, the meat on her skull turning to veiny marble. She snapped around and hustled back to her truck, pulling from the bed a short-handled square-point shovel. When Andy saw what she had, he struggled from behind the steering wheel, got out, and tried to run, but she was on him in a second. The old man winced as he heard the dull ring of the shovel blade and saw Andy go down in a skitter of dust at the rear of the car. She hit him again with a halfhearted swing.

Andy cried out, "Ahhhhh, don't, don't," but his wife yelled back and gave him the corner of the shovel right on a rib.

"You gummy little turd with eyes," she screamed, giving him another dig with the shovel. "I asked you to do one thing for me on your own, one numbskull job," she said, emphasizing the word *job* with a slap of the shovel on his belly, "and you kidnap some old bastard who doesn't know who he is and get him to do it for you?"

"Please, oh please," Andy cried, raising up a hand on which one finger angled off crazily.

"Look at him, you moron," she shrieked. "He's a hundred son-of-a-bitching years old. If he'd died, you'd go to prison for good, and I'd be sued for the rivets in my overalls." She threw down the shovel and picked him up by the armpits, slamming him down on the car's trunk, giving him openhanded slaps over and over like a gangster in a cheap movie.

The old man looked down the gravel road to where it brightened in the distance. He tried not to hear the ugly noises behind him, tried to remember his farm and family, but when Andy's cries began to fracture like an animal's caught in a steel-jawed trap, he walked around the back of the car and pulled hard on the woman's wrist. "You're going to kill him," he scolded, shaking her arm. "What's wrong with you?"

She straightened up and put both hands on his shirt. "Nothing is wrong with me," she raged, pushing him away, coming after him, but when she reached out, a metal blade gonged down on her head, her eye sockets flashed white, and she collapsed in a spray of gravel.

Andy lowered the shovel and leaned heavily on the handle, spitting up blood and falling down on one knee. "Aw, God," he wheezed.

The old man stepped back, the sound of the iron ringing against the woman's head already forming a white scar in his brain. He looked down the lane and saw her idling pickup. In a minute, he was behind the wheel, backing away in a cloud of rock dust to a wide spot in the road, where he swung around for town, glancing in the rearview mirror at a limping figure waving wide a garden tool. He drove fast out of the sorry countryside, gained the blacktop, and sped up. At a paintless crossroads store, he stopped, and his mind floated over points of the compass. His hands moved left before his brain told them to, and memory steered the truck. In fifteen minutes, he saw, at the edge of town, the cinder-block plinth of the discount center. Soon, the gray side of the building loomed above him, and he slid out of the woman's truck, walking around to the front of the store without knowing why, just that it was proper to complete some type of circle.

The bottom of the sun cleared the horizon-making parking lot, and he saw two cars, his old wine-colored Oldsmobile and, next to it, like an embryonic version of the same vehicle, an anonymous modern sedan. He shuffled across the asphalt lake, breathing hard, and there he found a young man asleep behind the steering wheel in the smaller car. He leaned over him and studied his face, saw the LeBlanc nose, reached in at last and traced the round-topped ears of his wife. He knew him, and his mind closed like a fist on this grandson and everything else, even his wife fading in his arms, even the stunned scowl of the copper-haired woman as she was hammered into the gravel. As if memory could be a decision, he accepted it all, knowing now that the only thing worse than reliving nightmares until the day he died was enduring a life full of strangers. He closed his eyes and called on the old farm in his head to stay where it was, remembered its cypress house, its flat and misty lake of sugarcane keeping the impressions of a morning wind.

Radio Magic

Cliff had a great desire to be famous, if only in a small way. Coming from a long line of people whose only legacy was a grave marker, he figured he could do better. The older he got, the more intense his yen for fame, until at age fifty-two, after his last child left to join the navy, he started taking piano lessons. His teacher, a Miss Deutch, told him he was hopeless and had the worst sense of rhythm in the state of Ohio. He asked if he might be suitable for another instrument and she suggested the ocarina.

Cliff tried art lessons, but his misshapen nudes looked like white cattle that had grazed too long on a nuclear test site. Next he took a creative writing class and tried for two years to get something published, but even a limerick he'd embedded in a letter to the local paper about trash pickup had been cut by the editor. His quest went on through several other episodes before he realized he might have to settle for turning his twins' large bedroom into a man cave, the most famous man cave in the county, a room full of startling objects that his friends down at the waterworks would wonder at and maybe bring to the attention of the regional news media.

The first treasure he installed was a crumbling moose head half the size of a Volkswagen. He purchased it through an ad he heard on the local radio station's *Swap Shop* program, the cheapest way to buy anything manly and grotesque. Every morning he listened at seven while he was eating breakfast with his wife, Tammy, a good woman who tolerated his purchases in silence, suspecting that her sweet-natured and naïve husband could have worse habits. After the moose head, he purchased an electric slot machine with semi-nude Asian cowgirls painted on the glass, and next the trunk section of a 1947 Plymouth that had been made into a neon-green sofa, then a pool table covered with hot-pink felt, followed by two red-glazed cow patty ashtrays, though no one he knew smoked. The collection grew, and his friends came over to play cards on a giant wooden cable spool that had a Lithuanian flag painted in its center. No one said much about all these items, though two from the chemical department cast suspicious glances at the twin dress dummies shaped like overweight women. Cliff liked his collection though he sensed that most of the members of his poker group seemed mildly disturbed by it, especially by the skeleton of a goat hanging over the card table, two blinding bulbs descending from its crotch.

One morning on *Swap Shop,* a man with slurred speech called in to offer five chickens that had been dyed green. The station was in Blue Shaft, West Virginia, a ruined coal-mining town, and the locals would call up and try to sell anything they had just to keep the lights on. The next seller was a woman who was trying to offload a whorehouse piano that had been struck by lightning. Cliff thought the offerings were a good omen, that something special might be coming up. When a young boy came on the air attempting to sell his only pair of pants because he'd outgrown them, Cliff reached to turn up the volume. As the child described his jeans, Cliff took a trip into his young life, about the only kind of travel he could afford, since his wife was an assistant public librarian for the hamlet of Lincoln Foot, Ohio, and he was only the guy at the waterworks who gauged how much came in and went out.

In the middle of the program Tammy got up from the table. "Bye, sweetie," she said as she brushed past. "Don't buy another hornet's nest."

Cliff closed his eyes. "You don't have to keep bringing that up." One of his early purchases from *Swap Shop* was a large nest for $10 from a man down the road. It was an early fall day and the farmer thought the hornets were long dead, and they were. Cliff hung the big nest in his man cave and proceeded to write reports for the water company, not knowing that a few dozen live eggs had been left behind. They hatched more or less all at once when the central heat came on, and the young stingers descended on Cliff's head like tiny syringes of poison. After his eyes swelled shut he figured he'd better go to a doc-in-a-box, but he fell down the side steps, ruining a new sport coat, and when he got into the car, he couldn't see to drive, so he called an ambulance, guessing at the buttons on his phone and calling the Sears washing machine repairman by mistake. By the time he was brought to the hospital, his nose was the size of an adolescent squash. The charge for the ambulance service, emergency room treatment, and injections was monstrous, but what kept him angry for a week was the $109 service bill from Sears.

Swap Shop ran a little longer than usual, and the last item of the day was an antique wooden radio. He remembered his grandfather's Crosley 669, which he was allowed to play when he was a child. Back then, the broadcasts sounded antique, the music muzzled and full of soft pops and windy static, as if there were a fire inside the cabinet, the announcer sounding faintly like Edward R. Murrow even when advertising color TVs. Gramps let him stay up late, and after eleven o'clock Cliff would switch on the police band, which hadn't broadcast police radio since the 1940s, but way down on the left side of the dial, he could tease in a ham-radio operator in Australia who always talked about fishing. He would click a different knob and the set would land on the abandoned shortwave band, but sometimes he could hear what sounded like Chinese, the radio chanting in a far-off and mystical faintness, coming and going like consciousness during a fragmented dream.

He jotted down the seller's number and after many rings he spoke with a creaky-voiced woman named Selma McKeithen, who lived down in nearby Blue Shaft. She wasn't sure about the radio's current condition, only that her deceased son, who had owned an electronics repair shop, had restored it years before, and she wanted fifty dollars for it.

Cliff called in to the waterworks and took the day off.

Blue Shaft, West Virginia, was just twenty miles from Cliff's house. It had been slowly dying over the past six decades, one business closing up per year, ten newly boarded-up houses per annum, fifty young workers moving out in the same time period, until the town felt like a big country house abandoned by its many grown children. The growly old announcer on the radio read his announcements for yard sales and used car lots as if he could barely see the printed text.

Cliff drove past many dusty, empty storefronts. Behind them in the distance hovered mud-colored mountains ribboned with seams of low-grade coal. Mrs. McKeithen lived in a large two-story frame house surrounded by broad, peeling galleries. He knocked and waited a long time, thinking he'd been forgotten or was being ignored because the radio had already been sold. But after six or seven minutes of knocking and waiting, he heard slow, puffy footsteps and saw the white ceramic doorknob turn as slowly as the second hand on a clock.

Mrs. McKeithen was straight in the back and had eyes the color of blue willow china, but she was very old. She apologized for being so slow, explaining, as she motioned him in, that she'd just turned ninety-eight. After she closed the door, she evaluated him up and down. "You're a little thick through the middle, aren't you?"

He didn't know what to say to that.

Putting up a hand, Mrs. KcKeithen said, "My father used to say that a fat, happy dog wasn't happy long." Leading him to a back bedroom over her creaking floors, she pointed to the radio. "It belonged to my oldest son, Vernon." A large mahogany floor model stood next to a tall window. A copper antenna wire snaked through the bottom of the sash and ran, he was told, up to the roof where it was strung between two sticks, one at the front of the house, one at the rear.

"It's bigger than I thought." He turned it from the wall and saw it was a Philco 41-290 that brought in AM, shortwave, and police band. "Does it work?"

She snapped a hand toward the wall. "Plug it in, my boy. It runs on electricity, you know."

"I don't think so. It could go up in smoke."

"Oh, nonsense. Don't you have any courage? It should play just fine."

Cliff gave her a doubtful look. "Can't be too careful."

"Oh, for goodness sake." Mrs. McKeithen slowly bent over to pick up the plug.

"Please don't. Let's just make a deal. Will you take forty for it?"

She straightened up and said, "And what will you do with that extra ten dollars in your pocket? Buy a yacht, perhaps?"

He looked down at the dusty cabinet. With some furniture wax he should be able to see his reflection. "Yeah, okay. Fifty it is."

She held out her hand, wide palmed, not shaking. "My husband says, or said, that Vernon put many new components inside that old dusty thing. He used to make a really good living before his heart went bad."

Cliff pulled out his wallet and frowned into it. "Oh, has your husband passed away?"

She shook her frosty head. "No, we just got divorced last year."

"Really? How long were you married?"

She touched her chin and closed one eye. "Seventy-three years."

Cliff's mouth fell open. "Why'd you get a divorce after seventy-three years?"

She shrugged. "Oh, we wanted to wait until the children were dead."

Later that night, Cliff used a dolly to roll the big Philco into his man cave at the rear of the house, where it joined a mouse-nibbled anteater, part of a broken B-24 propeller, a giant locomotive piston, a jukebox with two bullet holes through the glass, a straitjacket covered with bloodstains, a collage made with twenty red hot-water bottles, and many other oddities, all bought on *Swap Shop* or given to him by friends who were fine judges of bad taste. An acquaintance from work had once given him a plastic donkey whose backpack was filled with cigarettes. When Cliff lifted the donkey's tail the first time, a stale Lucky Strike extruded from the animal's rear end.

Late that night, Cliff pulled the back panel off the Philco and found the insides to be remarkably clean. Nearly every tube, capacitor, and resistor had been replaced, and some modern components seemed to have been added. The plug wire was restoration-grade line sheathed in bronze-colored cloth. Cliff decided to string a temporary antenna wire around the room and fire the set up.

He began his tour on AM with a click and a hum, then a rising whine like a musical saw, so he turned the selector knob and brought in the local country music station. The sound was like his gramps' machine, but cleaner—a big, soft sound with no edges to Taylor Swift. He rolled up on an oldies broadcast and listened while working on a lab report for the county. Then he tried out the police band, which was empty. Cliff found it hard to believe that anything on earth was empty, much less a radio frequency. He turned the tuning knob at a creeping pace, and finally, down at the left side of the dial, he heard a ship call for a bar pilot to come out into the Gulf of Mexico from the mouth of the Mississippi. The conversation was full of depths, currents, and locations and lasted two or three minutes before fading as though the pilot were indeed floating off into the night. Then calypso music drifted in for a moment and left at once, the melody like a supple deer passing through headlights.

For a long time there was nothing, then an old man singing "Dos gardenias para ti," solo in a soft voice, followed by more dead air, interrupted by a tickle of accordion, then more silence. Cliff made himself a whiskey sour and pulled a chair up next to the radio, turning a knob to the shortwave band. From Del Rio, Texas, an amateur station announced its existence and began broadcasting a waterfall of Spade Cooley's western swing music. Much later, tuning farther up the dial, he picked up nothing at all until he hit a steady stream of news in English from the Ivory Coast, and he moved to the sofa. Cliff and his wife had hardly ever left the state, their vacation time of two weeks a year not giving them much latitude for it, but this night, for the first time, he began to understand how vast and varied the world was, and he listened late until he rolled off to sleep in the trunk of the '47 Plymouth.

Tammy woke him up in time to shower and shave. She mentioned that the radio smelled hot, and if he didn't want to burn the house down he might take it over to old man Blumenthal's electronics repair shop to get it checked for safety. He brought the big unit in on the way to work and picked it up when he knocked off, Mr. Blumenthal telling him it was safe.

As he helped load the heavy cabinet the repairman said, "You know, this old gal has been redesigned. I mean, things have not only been replaced, but everything's modified. It's like somebody was trying to make it bring in a specific station more strongly. I've never seen such circuitry, especially in an antique box like this."

Cliff closed his hatchback and took a breath. "I just wanted to know if it's going to catch fire."

"No, no," Blumenthal said. "These things tended to run pretty warm. It's normal. Hope you tune in something interesting."

That evening, Cliff and Tammy sat together in the man cave and watched a football game until the score reached 48–18 and his wife stood up. "No sense in burning time on this turkey. How's your radio working?"

"Blumenthal said it was okay." Cliff turned on the shortwave band and immediately hit a Delta airliner asking for a change in altitude. But that was all, just a shooting star of words and nothing else. Rolling down the dial he found another ship-to-shore broadcast, a tugboat pilot asking for a lineup at a lock on the Ohio River. Then nothing. "Late at night," he told her, "a few more things come on."

She crossed her legs and leaned toward the set. "This is kind of creepy, like we're spying or something. I mean, it's fun."

After two rounds of drinks they discovered a program of belly-dance music from Turkey. Tammy jumped up and swayed her arms and popped her hips until she fell over onto the Plymouth sofa. Around eleven-thirty they gave up listening as the music faded out.

For the next two months Cliff developed a habit of searching the dial right before bedtime, sometimes as late as one o'clock on weekends. He heard marimba music, Cuban club music, Alaskan diatribe, backwoods preaching from three continents, Radio Australia broadcasts to New Guinea in pidgin English, all weak signals except for one bright broadcasting point in the Solomon Islands, from a town, the announcer said, near Gizo.

One morning in December, Cliff got a call from his boss, who said that a pipe had frozen and burst in the attic of the lab and that he didn't need to come in because the place was flooded. He watched the news in the living room for a while, then went into his cave to see if anything was on shortwave. He wasn't having much luck until he reached the spot on the dial for the station in the Solomons, which came in strong. At nine o'clock someone was broadcasting an old recording of a female comedian, originally taped at a nightclub in the Catskills, the announcer noted, in the early forties. Cliff checked his laptop and discovered it was after one a.m. in Gizo. The old Philco had eight preset buttons, and on a hunch he punched each one; four delivered old stations like WWL and WSM, three hit nothing, but the eighth landed the radio back in the Solomons. He listened to the same fast-talking woman deliver a series of vintage barroom narratives. Her bright alto was energy itself sailing over the noise of the club.

One began, "A customer walks into a bar trailed by a big golden retriever. The bartender hollers, 'We don't allow dogs in here.' The customer says, 'But my dog, Jane, can talk.' 'I don't care,' says the bartender. 'I get two talking dogs a week in here.' [*Audience laughter.*] 'Yes, but this dog can do what no other dog can do.' 'What's that?' he asks. 'She can shop. I'll give her a dollar, and I bet you ten bucks she'll bring back what you ask her to.' 'I'll take that bet,' the bartender says. 'Ask her to go out and get the *evening* edition of the city paper.' [*More laughter.*] The customer gives the dog a dollar and sends her out the door. A minute later she comes back with the right newspaper in her mouth and says, distinctly, 'Here you go.' 'Well, that's okay,' the bartender says, handing the owner a ten. 'But let's see if she can do something a little more complicated.' The dog actually speaks up and says, 'Okay, bud. Give me a try.' [*Laughter again.*] The bartender gives the dog a ten and says, 'Hundred-dollar bet. Down the street is Jim's diner. Get me a large hamburger, no mustard or pickles, extra mayonnaise, and a large order of fries.' 'Okay,' the dog says, and bolts out the door. Fifteen minutes later she comes back with a bag in her mouth holding the correct order. The bartender is fuming. 'I'll give her a hundred and we'll up the bet to a thousand dollars. Here's the deal, girlie: Four blocks south of here is the Paradise Liquor Store. I want a quart of Jack Daniel's black label and a bottle of French wine from the Loire Valley, vintage 1926.' Jane takes the hundred-dollar bill in her mouth and trots off. Twenty minutes later, the two men get worried. After an hour, they go out on the streets looking for the dog. Eventually, the customer looks in the window of a beauty parlor and sees his dog lying back in an adjustable chair, her coat perfectly brushed and tinted, a jeweled collar around her neck, her ears getting a permanent wave, and an Asian girl laboring over her glossy pink claws. Her owner runs inside and yells, 'What the hell are you doing?' The dog says, 'I've never had a *hundred dollars* before.'" [*Audience roars.*]

The comedienne delivered two more stories, and then in a crash of nightclub orchestra music she sailed off on a wave of applause. Whoever she was, the long joke had been her stock-in-trade.

The announcer, in an odd English accent, asked the listeners to tune in at 100 hours on Thursdays and Saturdays to hear more comedy recordings from Sally Gruen's 1940s performances. Cliff turned off the set, but the brightness of the comedienne's voice stayed with him. She sounded so happy. The nightclub crowd loved her. She must have been famous.

The following Saturday he caught the whole program, and he had his work hours adjusted so he could listen to the Thursday program as well, which lasted a little over fifteen minutes. The comedienne was a person not even the Internet knew anything about. Into the new year he listened, laughing, captured by the voice and its shining rhythms. Vernon McKeithen might have appreciated the comedienne's work, since the old Philco had been rewired to focus on this one spot on the dial. He wondered about Sally Gruen, when she had died, where she was from. But just as great a mystery was why these tapes were being broadcast from half a world away.

According to his laptop, only one shortwave station was left in the Gizo region. The man he reached there said in wordy English that his station aired no comedy programs, but there was an old Japanese gentleman living on a nearby island who, as a hobby slightly aided by the government, ran renovated World War Two surplus equipment twenty-four hours a day. Cliff got a phone number and reached a Mr. Matsumoto, the third shift announcer and owner, who spoke excellent English and talked at length about his affection for outdated broadcasting equipment.

Eventually Cliff got a chance to ask about the comedy program they aired at one a.m.

Mr. Matsumoto laughed and said, "That's because we have cheapest broadcasting rates."

"I don't understand."

"The programs you mention are a series of forty-eight tapes recorded in the early 1940s in New York, Chicago, and Los Angeles by the comedienne's husband. We get calls from all around the world about them, maybe four or five a week. We've run them over and over for twenty-three years now."

"People don't get tired of them?"

The man laughed again. "We have a widespread audience, mostly by accident. Besides, jokes are like silly friends you can stand to meet at least twice a year."

When Cliff asked how Mr. Matsumoto got hold of the tapes, the phone grew quiet for a few seconds.

"It's kind of odd telling this. About twenty years ago I visited my sister, who lives in West Virginia. She had an old Zenith that she wanted restored, so I found a man named Vernon who ran a local shop. He was a skinny blond guy, very tall, and just as interested in radio history as I was. We met every day the two weeks I spent at my sister's. Years later, Vernon sent me ten thousand dollars in the form of a stock-based endowment to broadcast his mother's comedy routines, and eventually we digitized her old tapes. I tried to reach him a couple years ago and found that he had passed away."

Cliff had to sit down before he could ask, "Really? His mother was the comedienne?"

"Yes. And we'll broadcast these things forever. My son is taking over the station. Who knows how long these jokes will go out from the Copa and the Blue Angel in New York, Chez Paree in Chicago. Even the Concord."

Cliff took a deep breath. "The broadcasts I heard didn't mention the comedienne's real name. It wasn't Selma, was it?"

"Of course. Her stage name was Sally Gruen, but she was Vernon McKeithen's mother, Selma. Where you calling from, by the way?"

"Ohio. Not far from where Selma lives. I met her recently when I bought one of Vernon's radios."

"No. Can't be the same lady. This one was born in 1917."

"That's her!"

Mr. Matsumoto became excited, his voice bounding up and down as he yelled in Japanese to someone else in the studio. "Is she still clear minded? You think she's able to handle an interview? I'd love to speak with her on the phone. Maybe a couple long talks, if she's up to it. We need programming for a VHF station we're starting next year."

"I think she could do it, but I can't guarantee she'd want to."

"You are her acquaintance. If you set it up for us, I'll say who you are in the interview and talk about you a bit. How you met her. I'll run it twice a year."

"I don't know."

"You sure? I can make you famous." Mr. Matsumoto said this as a joke, but Cliff got up out of his chair and turned in a circle.

*H*e tried for several days to phone Selma McKeithen. The following Saturday he drove over to Blue Shaft and parked in front of the old house at ten in the morning. The grass needed cutting, and nothing about the place seemed to have changed, except more paint had peeled away from its weatherboard siding. No one came to the door when he knocked. Sitting in his car for a long time, tapping his fingers on the steering wheel, he grew so increasingly nervous that he decided to go around back, where he stood on a porch hung with rotting mops and rusty galvanized pails. Then he felt foolish. The woman was ninety-eight years old. Maybe she had passed away. A dispiriting thrill of loss trembled through him as he remembered what his own mother had told him when they were at a funeral for his great-aunt, that whenever an old person dies, a library burns down.

But when he came around the house again, a big sedan had pulled up behind his car and a woman about sixty-five years old was helping Selma McKeithen out into the sunshine. The old woman waved at him. "Hello, there," she said. "I hope you don't want your money back for the radio. I lost it all at the horse races."

"No ma'am. I'd just like to visit for a few minutes and ask you some questions about it. The radio works fine, just like you said."

When a rear door of the car popped open, Selma McKeithen put a spotted hand on Cliff's arm. "See if you can help Mr. Bill there get out of that low seat. That's my husband. Once he's upright, he can locomote on his own."

Cliff stepped to the curb and pulled upright a bony old man wearing blue jeans and a heavy sweater. Before he could stop himself, he blurted over his shoulder, "Didn't you tell me you two got a divorce?"

The old man looked at his wife and shook his head. "You told him the one about the old people with the dead children?"

"It was a joke, son," Selma told him. "Don't you know what a joke is? Molly there is my daughter, and I've got two other living children. Vernon's the only one we lost. He had a weak heart all his life."

Once inside the house, Mr. Bill sat in a wing chair and seemed to fall asleep. Selma and Cliff settled on the sofa while Molly went into the kitchen. Later, he explained over his coffee what he'd found out about her routines and how they were broadcast. He figured she'd be surprised to know that her work was still being listened to. He told her how excited Mr. Matsumoto was by the prospect of interviewing her about her career.

As Cliff talked, Selma's blue eyes stayed focused on his own, but her expression didn't change. She shook her head and said, "Son, we listened to those programs for about ten years on Vernon's special radio. It took a year for that boy to modify the thing and then two more to find someone to put me on the air, longer than I was in the business. Listening to his radio was fun, but then it got old. When Vernon passed on, I didn't need to hear any more. Me and Mr. Bill still know those routines by heart. But Vernon, he loved me so much he'd play those tapes late at night, and we could hear him laughing to himself from all the way upstairs. All his life he'd ask me things like why I quit the show, and he'd tell me I could have been rich and renowned and all that stuff. Finally, I told him the truth: that he came along, and I liked him so much, I decided to make Annie and Chuck and Molly."

Cliff sat back on the flowered sofa. "He wanted to make you famous."

"I guess so." Then her voice softened. "He told me one time how radio signals bounce around in the sky, and that I was landing all over the world. He said it would keep happening for years. Oh, he got so serious one night, he leaned into me like when he was a baby." Here she moved her head over toward Cliff and drew closer, her pale and wrinkled face at odds with her youthful eyes. "He told me some signals go straight out into space, toward the planets. How someday one of my jokes would scratch past Pluto and keep going to God knows. Way out to whatever's past all we can see. Sometimes I think about that, how the sounds we make never really stop, and then I believe all of us are famous but just don't know it yet."

"What do you want me to tell the radio station operator?" he asked.

Selma turned to her husband, who opened his eyes and winked at her. "You can tell Mr. Matsumoto," she said, "that he's got enough already, though not the best of me."

Cliff's face darkened and he studied the floor. "He said he'd mention my name in the interview. He'd tell about how I found you and made the connection."

Selma pulled back and patted him on the shoulder. "Mr. Cliff, if you want to be well known, go out in your backyard and say your name to the sky."

When he got home, he was angry. There was a note from his wife on the table, telling him she was spending the night with a sick aunt in the next town over. He wandered through the house for a while feeling like he was catching the flu, so he went into the man cave to take a nap. But the space he'd given so much time to now seemed to accuse him, and he couldn't bear to look at it. Suddenly he punched the moose head to the floor and shoved it out the back door and down the steps into the yard, where it landed with a puff of dander and loose hair. The table with its tribute to Lithuania was next, followed by the disgusting donkey, which he threw overhand into the dark, then the terrible manikins and everything else, until after an hour, the room was bare except for the radio. He retrieved a bottle of furniture wax from the kitchen and rubbed the cabinet all over, then he tuned in an accordion festival in France, standing there listening stone-still until his legs ached. After raising the volume, he turned and walked through the back door, past the hill of embarrassments, and all the way to the fence, where he stopped in pitch-dark shade at the edge of the woods, the radio, from here, just a dancing tingle. He looked straight up at stars massed like schoolfish, a current of silver signals.

"Hello," he called out. "My name is Cliff."

The Furnace Man's Lament

The wind started out of the northwest, and the snow came sideways, running like a train past my windows. I stayed inside and played spades with the kids, and now and then I went to the front window and looked out at a sky wrestling with itself. I saw the snowplow sail by and knock down the mailbox again. That time of year.

After lunch, the phone jittered back in the hall, and I was afraid it would be a service call. I'm the furnace man, and it could be the end of the world out there and still somebody would call and bug me about their thermostat. I live in Minnesota with my wife and two kids, and it comes with the territory, these calls.

The voice on the phone was high-pitched, like a very old man's. He said his name was Swenson and he lived in Sauerville, about six miles away. Our place is out in the country, and sometimes I wish we'd moved to town, especially when the drifts get up to the eaves. I told the Swenson guy he wasn't a regular customer, so I wouldn't come out in a storm. The phone got quiet, and then the voice said there was an old person in the house who might get real sick if the furnace stayed off. I thought about that. My wife, Linda, tells me I have a starched and ironed heart, whatever that means, and I was remembering that at the moment. Just then, she came into the hall, put an imaginary receiver up to her ear, and mouthed, "Who is it?"

I put my hand over the mouthpiece. "Some guy I never worked for before. Said his heater's on the fritz."

She came close and gave me a jab in the ribs. "It's gonna be way below zero tonight. Way below." Two more jabs. "You go fix it, Mel."

"Are you crazy? You hear that wind out there?"

Then she crossed her arms. That means I'm done for, starched heart and all. "What's the address?" I droned to the voice on the line.

So I pulled on my storm gear, and it took about ten minutes to get all the zippers and snaps done, all the layering, the special gloves, and then I bulled out into the wind. There was only about a foot of new snow in the drive, so I put the pickup in four-wheel and backed to the road. Then I had to climb out and unstick the iced-over wipers. While I was futzing with them, Mrs. Shannon came along the highway, saw me, and slammed on the brakes, her old white Dodge sliding fifty yards like a puck and giving my bumper a rap. There was no damage I could see, so I apologized for being in the road, and she rolled down her window and waved me off. "Go about your business, Mel, before you blow away," she yelled. "Not a car around here escapes winter without a dent or three."

By the time I got into Sauerville the wind was going like a siren, and a basketball was rolling ahead of me down the street faster than I was driving. I could barely make out Mr. Swenson's house number. I'd driven by the place many times. It was in the middle of a block of old two-stories, built maybe in the First World War when the metal-stamping plant was set up. I knocked on the door and the thing rattled in its frame. About as heat efficient as a piece of gauze. A boy, maybe sixteen years old, kind of small for his age, a kid with an old face, held the door open against the wind, squinting.

"Come in, whoever you are," he keened in the voice on the phone.

"I'm the furnace man."

"Come in quick." He grabbed my coat and pulled.

The house was pretty chilly, I guess. About fifty. The boy, who introduced himself as Jack, wore baggy jeans and sweatshirts over sweaters.

"Where's your dad, son?"

He looked surprised by the question. "They never told me." I looked at him closely then, deciding that yep, this is an odd one, a kid who chooses to say things that mean a lot more than what you hear on the surface. I run into more and more of them each year. I gave him another look, up and down. His face was dirty, and no parent would dress him in those lumpy hand-me-downs. He reached up and scratched his straight dark hair. I decided not to ask about his mom.

"So, you're living here with your grandparents, eh?"

"Granma died last year. Gramps is taking care of me." He nodded toward the stairs.

"Why don't you go get him?"

"He's asleep right now."

I looked up the steps and noted the sooty wallpaper. "Where's the door to the basement?"

"Under the stairs. I'll show you."

The minute I'd stepped in the front door I could smell partially burned fuel oil. It was in the air, and I guess in the furniture, walls, and carpets. Sometimes people get used to the smell and live with an unregulated furnace for years, the odor getting stronger and stronger— petroleum in their bones, practically. Down in the cellar, the smell was tough, and I wasn't surprised to see the furnace, an old coal-eating tin man that had been converted to burn oil.

The boy flicked on the lights, then folded his arms and looked at me hopefully. "I hope you can fix it quick."

I did the usual, pressed the reset switch, which did nothing, checked the transformer, the blower motor, the fuses. Old furnace men called this one an octopus, I guess because of all the ducts rising like silver arms from the heat exchanger. The wiring was a mess, and the whole thing looked like it had been worked over by a dozen different amateurs in the past seventy years. I got down on my knees and opened the inspection door and flicked on my flashlight. Right away I saw the burner was the wrong one and caked with wet crusts of oil. The heat exchanger was perforated, which explained the fumes.

"Aren't you going to light it?" the boy asked.

"Let's go see your grandpa."

He made a face. An old face that was figuring all the angles. "We'll have to wake him up. You can talk to me about it."

I stood up and stared at him for a bit. I imagined that if I got close enough, I could smell oil fumes on his breath. "No, I can't. Let's go find Gramps."

"I can handle it. I can handle everything."

"Look, you're a kid. You can't take an estimate and pay my bill." I started up the steps, and back in the upstairs hall he slid past me and up another flight.

"Okay. Come on, then."

I followed him up the shoe-dished steps, and behind a paneled door on the second floor was Gramps, a white-haired fellow asleep in a wing chair next to an unmade bed. The boy stood beside me and didn't make a sound. "Mr. Swenson?" I said loudly.

"His name is Harry." The boy went to him and shook his shoulder.

"What?" the old man said, and judging by his lost eyes and the way he said it, I knew it was the *big what*. Like "What are you?" or "What decade is it?"

"The heat man's here, and he wants to talk to you about the furnace."

"Why?"

The boy raised his voice a notch. "The furnace repairman. I called him. He wants to talk to you." Jack pointed, and the old man looked my way.

"Hello. My, it's cold in here."

It was true. The storm was rumbling down from Canada, and I could hear gusts bowling metal trash cans down the street. "Yes sir," I said. "I checked out your furnace, and you really need a new one. It's been hanging in there a long time and's finally wore out."

"You better talk to my wife. She takes care of things, you know."

The boy gave me a look.

"I can't legally work on it because it's leaking fumes up through the registers."

Old Harry Swenson nodded. "You know, she pays the bills. These heavy curtains, she bought those."

From the looks of them, that had been during the Eisenhower administration. I guess it was forty-eight degrees upstairs. "You folks will have to go somewhere tonight. The temp's dropping like a stone."

The old man nodded slowly. "Is that so?"

I waited a minute for him to say something more. The room was painted green, and the bed frame was an old coming-apart thing made back in the Depression. I watched the window curtains move from the wall like ghosts, then settle back. When I glanced at the old man, he was asleep. I motioned to Jack and we went downstairs into the hall again.

I looked the kid in the eye. "Who else lives here?"

"It's just me and Gramps."

"How do you pay for things?"

"He has a credit card, and a pension or something puts some money in his checking account so's we can pay the bills."

I shook my head. "I can't take a credit card." I began to think about all the hard luck locals who'd stiffed me on a bill.

"I know how to write a check." He seemed to study my expression, which to be honest was probably pretty doubtful. "I can carry it upstairs for him to sign."

"He still can sign his name, eh?"

The kid looked away. "After I give him his bath he's awake enough to do a few things."

"Well, you better bundle him up and get him to the Motel 6 on the edge of town."

The boy put his chin up at me, kind of pushy all of a sudden. Surprised me. When he grew up he wouldn't take any crap from anybody, I could see that. "Hey, the furnace kind of worked until day before yesterday."

I noticed my breath floating in the room. Back home, my wife would ask me what I'd done on the call. "Ah, let me go check something out in the truck."

As soon as I opened the door the wind tore my toboggan off, and I had to go chasing the damn thing through the side yard. I saw the rusty oil tank on stilts by a window and gave her a knock. Not too much in there. In the truck I called the sheriff and found out the nearest homeless shelter was twenty miles away in Elbo. I asked if there was an emergency fund to pay me for the repair if Gramps couldn't, and he said nope, though maybe I could get a local church to pony up something.

I looked at the old place, the scaling paint, the warped little porch. It wasn't too big of a house, kind of plain. By two a.m. all the pipes in it would start to split. By dawn, the toilets would break open and all the P-traps would bust under the sinks. The boy and his grandfather could stay under blankets and quilts, but they couldn't come out to eat without getting sick. Maybe the old guy'd get frostbite. The high forecast for tomorrow was six. I looked at the house again. I knew *I* wouldn't want to die in it. I started the truck, cursing the fact that the kid's check might be no good, that I might wind up busting my ass and not making a dime. I shouldn't be so negative, but that's how I'm wired. Me negative, wife positive.

Across town in an old asbestos-siding building was Abe's Plumbing and Heating. Abe was about eighty, tough as a two-dollar steak, one of those die-hards who, if they found out somebody froze to death because he didn't maintain his furnace right, would only nod and say, "Yah, there's no cure for stupid!" I convinced him to root through his old parts in a shed out back of his business, and he found the right burner. Charged me like hell, he did.

I got back to the house, and the kid followed me down to fight the octopus. He watched everything I did, like he was really interested. My own fifteen-year-old wants to be a lawyer. That'll cost like flaming hell, so I used to bring him out with me on service calls, to see if he'd fall into my line of work. But he was unimpressed with what I did every day to feed his face. I could tell he'll never be a furnace man, that's for sure.

The old burner was corroded in place, and it took forever to get it off. About seven or eight other problems had to be fixed. The only thing that worked at first was one fuse, and that because somebody had put a penny under it. But right at dark I got a fire, and the ducts above me began to tick and ping with the rising heat.

Young Jack watched everything I did and asked a million questions. By the time I left, he knew as much about that furnace as I did. He paid me with a ragged check he had in his pocket, and I was on my way. At the door, though I was anxious to get home to dinner, I took time to sit on the stairs and re-lace my boots.

"Jack," I said, "do you have any relatives other than your grandfather?"

"Nope."

"A mom somewhere?"

He picked up his head and looked at me for a second. "I'm kind of alone."

"How long have you lived here?"

"Since I was born." He said it quick.

I thought about what he'd just said. "You never saw your mother?"

"Nope. Granma told me she went over to Minneapolis and never came back. I don't remember her."

The wind was screaming across the porch, but the shiver running along the top of my shoulders wasn't because of the cold. "What was her name, son?"

"Doris. Doris Evelyn Swenson." He recited his mother's name as if it was a brand of cereal. No pang of longing there, and who could blame him? He never saw his mother. Not once. But I had, years ago, right out front of this house. The woman was my age. I'd seen her around when I was in high school, but I didn't tell the kid that.

"Doris Evelyn Swenson, eh? You ever try to find her?"

He shrugged. "How do you find somebody like that?"

"Oh, yeah." I nodded. "Your Gramps, he have any brothers or sisters?"

"He used to talk about that, how he and Granma were the youngest in their families, how almost everybody had died. There's one brother."

I looked up from my boots. "Where's he live?"

"Germany. He moved over there a long time ago, Gramps said."

"Germany?" I looked at him hard, but he seemed to be drifting away from me in the dim light. "You must have some cousins, eh?"

He closed one eye, as if that might help him remember. "Well, yeah. A lady in a nursing home over toward Fargo."

"She's that old?"

"Granma said she had something wrong with her brain. I don't know."

"Did you ever meet these people?"

"No. I think the lady in the home sent Gramps Christmas cards, but he stopped writing back. He told me one time it made him sad to write her."

I stood up and settled in my boots. "You go to school?"

He rolled his eyes. "Of course. Fourth Precinct. I'm a junior."

"You get along all right with your grandpa?"

Here his face fell a bit. "He was a real good joke teller. Worked in the tin plant and knew how to make anything out of metal. Until a couple years ago when his talking slowed down. Most of the time now he just sleeps. He says he doesn't understand the TV anymore."

I zipped up my coat. "Well, bud, I patched up the old furnace as best I could. You're going to have to get a new one, though. She won't last long." The kid braced his foot against the door and let me slip out.

When I stepped through the opening, I was sucked into a black wind. The porch had iced up, and I slid across and down the steps into a drift, my tool kit banging open. I had to dig for wrenches and sockets on my knees for five minutes. The howl was racketing and complex, tearing through the trees for miles around. Snow was flying so thick I couldn't see my white truck from twenty feet away, and even in first gear it could barely push away from the curb. Out on the county road, though the plow had made another pass, the truck fishtailed this way and that, and I started to feel drunk. Coming down Needham Hill I stood on the brakes, and the truck rattled on like a block of ice and took out the Pulaskis' old wooden mailbox.

Before supper I was in the den resting up when Ted, my youngest, came through.

"Hey, kid."

"Dad." He kept on toward the kitchen, but I grabbed his arm.

"I met a boy today about your age. Goes to Fourth Precinct. Jack Swenson. You know him?"

Ted sniggered, shaking his blond hair out of his eyes. "Yeah, he's in the other homeroom. We call him Stinky."

"Stinky?"

"It's just a joke. He doesn't mind. Sometimes he smells like oil is all. Or a little sour. He told me one time his bathroom was on the fritz."

"Is he an okay fellow?"

"He's cool. Not too dumb and real good at PE. A guard on the basketball team."

"He in your Boy Scouts or anything?"

Ted put his thumbs in his jeans pockets and bit his lip, which meant he was pretending to think. "He hasn't shown up in a long time. A real old lady used to drop him off at the VFW for the meetings last year." He glanced into the kitchen. "Mom's about ready."

"All right."

"Where'd you meet Jack?"

"I fixed his furnace today."

"Jeez. In the nick of time." And he lurched into the kitchen in that rubber-jointed way sixteen-year-olds walk.

After supper and a shower, I got in bed and turned on the laptop. I tried a few different search engines and turned up Doris Swensons who were presidents of corporations in Alaska or were ninety years old, but nobody around the Twin Cities. My wife came in and went to bed. I told her what I was looking for, and she said to try newspaper police reports and obituaries. I wished she hadn't said this, because after I turned off the computer, I lay there thinking about it. And why did I care? I mean, I fixed the kid's furnace, took his risky check, and went out in a storm to do it. What else was I supposed to do? Linda sensed I wasn't asleep in two seconds like I usually am, so she said in this tiny little wife voice, kind of whispery, "If you use the computer, it won't keep me awake."

So I sat up and surfed, and pretty soon I found out that four years ago, in a dried-up little factory town outside of Minneapolis, a thirty-seven-year-old Doris Evelyn Swenson had died of burns incurred in a meth-lab explosion. She was a native of Sauerville and was survived by her parents.

Turning off the laptop, I listened for a long time to the wind tearing through the eaves. I was glad I had a metal roof over my head and two feet of insulation in the attic, but I wondered how Jack and his grandfather were doing, alone as they were in the world. I had my kids, my wife, my brother two houses over, both of my cranky old parents, aunts and uncles, and a drawerful of cousins spread over the near counties. How would I feel if I had only one blood relative to help me in the whole freakin' world?

A gust slammed the house like a locomotive trying to couple up. I pulled the covers up to my chin, and my wife gave me a little pat.

The next morning the phone rang me out of bed at seven, and it was Mrs. Puderer, a couple miles east.

"Mel, can you get out?"

"What's wrong?"

"The heat pump's making a noise when it cycles. It's still heating. Just making that noise."

"It's probably just loading up. Let me look out the window." I went into the front room, and the damned plow hadn't come at all. I'd never seen that not happen before. In the middle of the highway there was something like a large flat boulder. "Honey," I called. "What the hell's that in the road?"

From the kitchen she said, "It's Old Lady Canaby's Buick. It gave up right there."

"Where is she?"

"In the back bedroom with Ted. She knocked on the door about four-thirty, and I put her up."

"I didn't hear anything."

"You were snoring."

I went back to the phone and told Mrs. Puderer that with three or four feet of snow in the road I couldn't get out until the plow came, if it ever did. She was satisfied with that, having lived here every day of her life.

So we played Scrabble all day, and the weather girl on TV told us the blizzard wasn't going to stop, was a double-barreled freak with more wind and snow coming. Mrs. Canaby got spunky and launched the family into a cribbage marathon, playing for money until about eleven when we all turned in. I was asleep, dreaming of a handful of sevens and eights, when the phone rang at three a.m. It was Jack Swenson, and he sounded upset.

"Mr. Todd, the furnace stopped working about noon. I tried all day to restart it myself, but it just won't go."

"Aw, we're covered up out here, boy." There was no way I was going out. It was a killer storm.

"Gramps won't wake up. I can't get him to move at all." He started yelling and begging me to come start his furnace. "I tried to make him some tea, but the water stopped running."

I looked at the floor, scared to go out, maybe. But my wife would never settle for me not helping a kid in trouble. Let's see, he's six miles away, the roads are closed, the wind's blowing like a jet engine. Maybe I could try to get to town on my lawn tractor. Nope. Then there's my brother's snowmobile. "Look," I said, "I'll give it a shot, but I can't promise I'll get there. Meanwhile, call the fire department and 911."

"I did that," and here he began to cry, holding back as much as he could. "Nobody can come because of the blizzard. The emergency people say they're evacuating a nursing home ten miles from here."

"Hang on. All I can do is try."

I called up Butchie, and without a pause my brother said he'd take me on his snowmobile. As if I'd asked him to take me to the hardware store on a sunny day. Last year I made fun of him for buying that rig, told him it was a waste of money. But he enjoys wearing white camo and deer hunting with a bow in winter. He likes to ice-fish at night. I think he has antifreeze in his brain. At any rate, after suiting up, I heard this racket at the back door, so I opened the kitchen window and stepped up onto the snow, dragging my toolbox after me. He had to yell, the wind was so bad. He said we had to go cross-country.

"Why?" I hollered.

"If we cave in a car roof out on the road, we're liable for the damage. Besides, it's shorter."

So off we went, zipping up a drift and shooting over the back fence.

He's got halogen headlights, but they lit up the ice in the air so much it was like driving in a snow globe. We cut across the rear of his property and along the barbed wire bordering the Pudlewskis' dairy farm. We got in their back field, which was clear of boulders and machinery, and buzzed west at a good clip through the dark. I didn't know about

Butchie, but everything on me began to hurt with the cold. At the Trask farm we banged up over a big lump of something that spilled me off into the snow. He righted the machine and came back to me on his snowshoes.

"What the hell did we hit?" I asked.

"I'm afraid I know," he said, scraping snow until he hit a layer of furry ice. Then we saw it was a big milk cow that got caught out.

We started again, headed up a hill, the engine whining, the wind about to tear my nose off, and then we got hung in a chain-link fence. All the way to Sauerville, we wandered over the outlines of things, hunting gaps in the fences, squeezing through windbreaks, at one point scraping over a snow-swamped hay baler. Finally we hit the railroad where a big wedge plow had just shoved through, and we rode the snow ridge it made all the way into town. We buzzed up the kid's street, steered around a fallen cottonwood, and stopped on his lawn.

It was cold as hell in the house, let me tell you. Jack began pulling me upstairs, and I told Butchie to go whack on the furnace. When I got up to the old man's bed, I couldn't feel anything by touch because my own hands were dead. I lifted the covers and moved his arms. Or at least I tried to.

I didn't want to turn around and face the boy. How do you tell someone that the last person in the world who could care for him was dead? It struck me, as I covered up his grandfather, how alone Jack was now, coming from someplace he didn't understand the history of—and going where? I put an arm around his shoulders and told him what had to be said. Jack walked to the old man, pulled the covers down, and gave him a long hug. Then he went to the door and laid his head against the narrow edge of it with his eyes held shut.

"Come on," I told him, and made him walk downstairs, where he called the sheriff himself, and put his disaster at the tail end of all the bad stuff happening that night.

Butchie was already taking the heater apart in the cellar, and the boy sat down on a wooden box and watched us work. At one point he began sobbing. I guess the reality hit him then.

I kept working because I didn't want to fool around in his pain. But he cried on and on, and though I was pretty sooty, I decided to go over, squat in front of him, and chuck him on the shoulder. "Hey, it's gonna be all right."

"He was a great old guy," the boy said. "Granma was great too. I used to talk to the mailman about them, and he said they don't make people like them anymore."

"I know."

"She was forty-one when she had my mom," Jack said. "She used to tell me how happy she was to have her. They'd tried for a lot of years. But she said my mom was never happy, and nobody ever knew why." Here the boy looked me right in the eyes. "What could make her so unhappy?"

Man, oh man, what was I supposed to say? A psychiatrist or mind reader I'm not. I started to give him some cliché bull, like, life's a mystery, or who knows, but at this time, in this situation, I figured I'd give a real explanation a shot. So I said, "You know, one time I bought a load of transformers for furnaces. The first one only lasted a week and the customer gave me hell on the phone about that. The next one I installed caught fire in my hands as I was wiring it in. The company I got them from overseas said they couldn't help me. I was stuck with twenty-four of these things, so I took one apart on the workbench. It was wired wrong. One of the fields was wound with mostly uncoated wire, making the whole thing a big short circuit. It would never work right."

Jack had stopped crying and was staring at me, breathing through his mouth. "You're saying my mom was wired wrong?"

I thought he was quick, but now I knew it for sure. I gave him a look. Lowered my voice. "Maybe it wasn't her fault. Each baby comes from the factory different from the next. Different circuits, different wires."

"But why wasn't she like Granma?" he sobbed.

"I don't know, bud. Genes don't control everything. We just don't know why people do or don't do things."

He seemed to think about that. Nodded and straightened up. He wiped his eyes on his shirtsleeve. "Now what's gonna happen?"

I had to tell him something. "There's social workers and judges that'll take care of you. Unless there's a relative or a family you're close to that can help."

He looked over to the furnace. "It'll be a judge, then," he said.

Eventually we fired up, sending heat rising through the pipes and registers, kind of bringing the house back alive at least. Then we heard the crunch of the deputies' boots above us on the porch.

The coroner made it out later that morning. Butchie was good about hanging around, tinkering with the dampers. Everyone was talking to me like I was in charge, and I kept telling them, "I'm just the furnace man." The more I said it, though, the more I felt that I'd somehow become part of the kid's family by default. Finally, Butchie came up and gave me the "So?" look. Then I packed my tools and left, leaving the deputies and firemen and one old neighbor man to sort things out. Butchie and I got on the snowmobile and buzzed off toward home. The wind had died down, and the snow had slacked off. The temperature had come up to about zero, and the ride home wasn't exactly a pleasure, but it felt like an escape from an awful scary place.

The funeral was late the next week. Me and my wife went. There was a good crowd of neighbors and creaky folks the grandfather had worked with at the tin-stamping plant. The boy was seated up by the coffin, his eyes red, acting brave and saying what he could to people who paid their respects. Normally a wife or daughter does that, not a teenage boy. The minister gave a nice devotional, and we walked across the street to the Lutheran graveyard and stood among the gray, weather-leaned stones. The ground was hard, and it must have taken a hell of a big backhoe to dig the grave. We settled at the edge of things, and I asked Deputy Toller if Jack was in child services or what.

"Yep," he said. "The Maxy family on the west edge of town has him and a couple others."

"That's kind of sad," my wife said. "I mean, to be uprooted like that."

Toller leaned in close. "Minnesota law says sometimes a kid can live by himself if he's able and a judge okays it. But the boy didn't want to stay in the house."

(87)

"I don't know what to think about that," I said.

The deputy shrugged. "Child services says he's been taking care of himself for two years already, him and the old man. But he wanted out. Looks to me like he wants to move on, that one."

I shivered at what I would have done. No family of any sort, alone in a rambling place that needed all kinds of repairs. "Was there an estate?"

"Well, there was a will, Sheriff said to me this morning. The boy'll get a decent bank account, the house, and some life insurance. Probably some other stuff as well, like a town lot or some antiques in the attic. All the accounting hasn't been done. The old man was working back in the fifties when making money was easy as falling off a log."

Linda stood on her tiptoes to see them lower the coffin. She watched the boy during the rest of the prayers and then gave me one of her hard-to-figure-out looks. What in the world was she thinking? I glanced over at Jack as the minister handed him a little scoop of dirt to throw down in the crypt. He tossed it and then stared into the hole as if he was hoping the old man would climb back out.

When the funeral party had pretty much dispersed, he came up to me. "Hey, Mr. Todd."

I wanted to squeeze him on the shoulder, but I held back. "We're sorry for you, Jack," I told him. "It's always tough to lose a grandpa."

"If there's anything we can do to help, let us know," Linda said.

He looked back at the grave and fastened the top button on his coat. "Thanks. The minister brought me. He'll take me back out to the Maxys', I guess."

"Oh, we'll give you a ride," my wife said. She's the kind who always goes out of her way to help. Sometimes I think she does it just to make me feel selfish. "Go tell the minister you're going out there with us."

So I have to drive down the old farm road west of where the mill used to be, and it's rutted and half rock salt. Then we turn off toward the north a couple miles, and right after the one-lane bridge with no guard rails is the Maxy place. I give it the eye as I slide into the drive. Needs paint. Boxy place built in the late forties and sided with asbestos. Big lot, fenced with hedges that hadn't been trimmed I bet in twenty years. I turned to the boy, who was in the back. "You been here, what, since last week? How's it going?"

"It's all right. Mrs. Maxy's okay. Kind of old, like Granma."

"And the other kids?"

"Two guys. They kind of mind their own business."

The front door opened and a starved-looking old gent, Mr. Maxy, I guess, stood out on the front steps and looked at us. "Thanks for the ride," Jack said, popping open the door and kicking snow up through the drive.

"We could do that," my wife said, kind of dreamy sounding.

"Do what?"

"Be foster parents."

"Hey, I can hardly handle the ones I got now." I tried to make it sound like a joke, and it was, actually, because my kids never gave me any trouble to speak of, and I made good money. She didn't say any more about it on the ride back home. I kind of expected her to, but she didn't. Maybe she figured if she didn't say anything, I'd think about it. And she was right. Foster parents in these parts were poor folks who needed the money from the state. I didn't exactly fit into that category. I was the furnace man. I didn't have to take in strays. Orphans, I guess. Though poor Jack was a stray if ever there was one. Aw, hell.

About a month later, my daughter, who was home from the little college two towns over, we call her Bunny, was reading the newspaper at breakfast. Her habit was to scan the police reports to see if any of her old high school chums had been picked up for DWI or speeding. "Uh-oh," she said, drawing the paper close to her face.

"Uh-oh, what?" her mom asked.

"Dad's buddy Jack got arrested for underage possession of alcohol."

"What do you mean, *my buddy*?" Bunny's gonna make a hell of a sadistic wife someday. "Where's it say that?"

"Right there in the paper."

I took it from her and found the right column. "Damn."

So why should I care? But that afternoon, when I finished with the mayor's new steam heat system, I was anxious to get out to the Maxys'.

Get back out in the cold, anyway. His honor has four feet of insulation in his attic, and he keeps his house like a sweat lodge.

When I got out there I asked Jack to put his coat on and come sit with me in the truck awhile.

After he climbed in, I said, "I see you got your name in the paper."

He pushed back his hoodie. "Yeah. I got a citation when I bought some beers for Marv."

"Marv live here with the Maxys?"

"Yeah."

"Well, why'd you do it?"

He looked off toward the plain, plain house for a long time. "I was tryin' to get along with him."

I tapped him on the shoulder and he turned to me. "Did he threaten you?"

"Let's just say I have to live here until I'm seventeen or eighteen, depending on what judge controls my case."

The wind began gusting out of the north and my truck started to rock. Felt like it was trying to start and drive off someplace better than where we were. "And then what?"

"I think about that. To start, I could fix the old place so's it was good enough to live in, then sell it off and go to college."

"I don't know. A house goes down fast in this part of the country when nobody's living in it."

Jack didn't look at me. "Last thing I did before the sheriff picked me up was to drain the pipes and flush the toilets dry." He bobbed his head and snickered, once. "The heater stopped again. I checked the fuse box and number two went out. The blower motor shorted, I guess."

I stared across my hood where some dry snow was bouncing like soap powder. We talked for a good while. A long time, in fact, until most of the light was gone. He told me he missed playing basketball for his school. The Maxys didn't want to drive him to the games. "I wish that was different," he said, with the only really sad note I'd heard in his voice. Then he smiled and said, "I wish I lived with you instead of these people."

"Yeah," I said, pretending to agree, but looking away and knowing that he saw how I felt about that. "I wish I could afford to." I hated to tell him that. It wasn't true, but when you take over somebody else's life, it's not a casual thing.

"You don't have to say nothing about it," the boy said. "What would be nice and what will happen are usually two different things."

"I guess so," I said. I couldn't look at him.

He opened the door to the truck, then, but before he could slide off the seat my arm went out and grabbed his elbow. I didn't do it. My arm moved by itself. Funny how those little motions take place that aren't connected to my brain.

"What?" Jack said, surprised.

"When do you get off school?"

"Quarter to three in this county."

"Sometimes I need a gofer or somebody to hold up pipe or pull a wire. You got time for doing a little work? If things go right, you could work all day on Saturdays."

So that's what we did, the cold months. I scheduled jobs so he could fit in around three and work till six, six-thirty. I picked him up, or the wife did, or one of the Maxys. First thing I noticed is he didn't waste time as a worker. Learned how to wire thermostats and check freon levels, and with his pay he bought some books on electronics and heating systems. Saturdays he put in a full day, just like me, installing ductwork, replacing burners. I paid him what I usually had to pay a grown helper.

Summer rolled around and he worked full-time, then cut back in the fall when school cranked up. I could see a change in him. Jack paid even more attention to his work. And he always looked like he was thinking. Sometimes I asked what was on his mind, but he never would tell, just kind of gave me a slow smile and rolled those nut-brown eyes of his. All I knew was that he didn't piss off his money on handheld games and junk, though he did have an old-man cell and a better multimeter than I carried. He gained a little weight. Got taller all of a sudden. Strong jaw for a boy.

.   .   .

*T*he next year he graduated right under valedictorian. I didn't go to the ceremony, but a few days later I called him for a job in the new subdivision. I picked him up at the Maxys' and saw right away he had a black eye and a few scuffs on his cheeks. I grabbed the top of his head and turned his face toward me. It felt good in my hand.

"What happened to you?"

He blinked slowly and gave me a grimace, but it was kind of comic the way he did it. "Marv's going through a rough time" was all he said.

"Well, you'll be away from him as soon as you reach eighteen."

He smiled big-time, then turned away and gazed out the windshield over the farm next door as if he owned it and everything he could see for miles.

*J*ack's birthday was July 23, a Wednesday. He'd asked for a couple days off. I didn't see him until Friday, and I asked him that afternoon if Mrs. Maxy had baked him a cake, and he just snickered and kept shoving duct at me. Didn't say much the whole job. On Monday I called him for a thermostat install, but his cell didn't answer, so I rang up old man Maxy, who said he wasn't in. I went out and did the job myself and didn't get home until seven-thirty. After supper and a bath I called him again, and Maxy said he hadn't seen him yet. I tried his cell again and got nothing, so I was a little bit worried. The next day we were supposed to start on an apartment building over in Frost Falls. I told Maxy to have him call me, but by the time I fell asleep I hadn't heard anything. I figured maybe he and Marv went out and did something crazy, like I did on my eighteenth birthday. Maybe he climbed a water tower or something. So I laid off calling him the next day. I went down to Abe's Plumbing for a part, and when I passed the kid's old house I saw a sold sign in front. *Whoa.* I called Oscar at Sauerville Realty and asked him about it.

"Yeah," Oscar said, out of breath like always. I pictured him squeezed behind his secondhand teacher's desk, a cigarette rolling between his fat fingers. "I closed that on Wednesday last. I hope you weren't interested in it."

"No, no. I just know the kid who inherited it. He works for me."

"Jack? Yeah. That's some kid. Old school, huh? Got manners."

"What'd he get for it?"

"He cleared about $89,000. Not bad considering the exterior. The appraisal was $119, but he wanted to sell quick."

"I didn't think it was worth near that."

"Well, he'd installed a new heating and air-conditioning system, redid all the plumbing and much of the wiring. I'd seen him over there early mornings before school working away, carrying supplies up the street in a wheelbarrow from Abe's."

My mouth fell open a bit at that news. "What'd he do with the money?"

"I don't know. We gave him a cashier's check."

I smelled a rat, so I went down to Abe's and asked about it. The old man told me Jack had bought a lot of stuff on my contractor discount.

I had to ask. "Did he charge anything to me?"

"Hell, no," Abe said. "He paid cash for everything. I thought maybe you were trying to sneak a cash job by to save a little tax money. He ain't in trouble, is he?"

"I don't think so. He was just fixing his old house on his own, I guess."

"Branching out, eh? Taking a chance. Well, I'd give that young 'un a discount if he goes into his own business. He's a worker, that one. Reminds me of you, a little."

I was turning for the door, but when he said that I did a one-eighty. "What?"

"Likes what he's doing, and he's good at it."

"That's a good thing, all right."

Abe pursed his lips in thought. "But it looks like he'll take a chance. That's *not* like you."

When I drove back down the street, someone had backed a truck up to the porch of Jack's house and was already loading furniture. I pulled to the curb and met a tall older man coming out carrying a box of silverware. "Hi, is Jack Swenson here? He's an employee of mine."

The guy said nope, that he was from Antique Gold Mine and Estates over in Frost Falls. He'd bought everything in the house from basement to attic.

I gave him a look. "You paid him a good price?"

The man put down the box and whistled. "He had a few nice things mixed in with the junk. His grandpa had a small coin collection and a few nice Winchester rifles. I had to pay full retail for the guns, but they're a big draw at the auctions." The man frowned, like he realized I was suspecting him of something fishy. "He wasn't a sucker, let's put it that way. He pretty much knew what everything was worth. It's that damned Internet. Everybody's an expert nowadays."

Next, I stopped at the bank, and, sure enough, he'd cleaned out his account. The teller, Sadie, my first cousin, whispered that Jack had told her he was going to use an Internet bank to hold his money. I didn't need to go to the lawyer who handled the estate because by then I knew Jack must have harvested the whole kit and caboodle. His grandfather's stocks, an old brick warehouse and lot on the poor side of town, the family car, and everything else had been changed into electrons and deposited in a place where he could access funds from anywhere in the country.

*F*or months and months I tried every way I knew to find where Jack was. It got to be a hobby. The cops sort of looked, and the Maxys, but he was gone. Right into thin air. Between jobs I searched for clues on the Internet, and when my son went off to Arizona to college in the fall, taking my laptop with him, I haunted those fast machines in the library, just looking. I don't know why I did. Maybe for the mystery of things. Where does someone who's totally disconnected go to connect?

I kept focusing on the damaged cousin the boy had said was in a nursing home in Fargo. I needed a name. One day I called my cop friend, Deputy Toller, and asked who the oldest lady in Mr. Swenson's neighborhood was.

"Bud, why do you want to know?" He sounded kind of grouchy, but I guess I'd be too, coming off a shift of trying not to get shot at.

"What are you, a cop or somethin'?"

"Ah, shut up."

"I'm still on Jack's trail."

"Yeah, well I wish you luck. As far as old ladies who'll talk to you, try Ms. Salmen at 900 Charles Street. Big yellow house on the corner, about a block from the Swensons'."

"Thanks."

"Hey."

"What?"

"Why're you so hot to find that kid? He owe you somethin'?"

"I don't know. I'm wondering if he'll ever come back. I need the help."

There was a pause on the other end of the line. "Look, I know Ms. Salmen. She taught me in first grade. Next time I get a chance I'll drop in on her and see what she knows about the Swensons' family connections. If you show up on her porch she might think you're from the government or something and clam up."

"Good man," I said.

I got busy and kind of let Jack slide out of my mind for a while. I guess I thought someone else was worrying for me. Before I knew it, two weeks had gone by. Then a month. Me and Linda began missing our kids. Sure, we had the relatives, but when we went to the house at night and ate supper, we were alone.

A couple three years went by and one afternoon I ran afoul of a 220-volt line in an old machine shop that was upgrading its system. I shoved in the big two-handed plug that led to their welder, and a long blue arc came out alongside that plug like a fire hose squirting electricity. I was thrown off a catwalk and broke two vertebrae in my back. I was messed up for about three months. When I got out to work again, it took me forever to creak around and get things done. My hands were damaged as well as my back. I needed a helper but couldn't find anybody other than old guys who thought they knew more than I did, or dopehead kids. Nobody I tried worked out, and the upshot of the accident was that my income was cut in half.

One day I was in the kitchen, sitting at the table, dizzy from the pain pills and stiff as a poker. The wife wasn't home yet, and I started thinking about Jack. I remembered that conversation we had outside the Maxys' house years before, the day we'd talked for so long. When he was close to tears and asked me to be his guardian so he could live with us for a year. I remembered turning him down. Well, I gave him a job. How far do you have to go, anyway? That job was something, and I didn't understand why he used it to bankroll his getting out of town. I still didn't know how I felt about that. Kind of cheated, I guess.

I got up and went out into the yard to get some fresh air in my lungs. It wasn't too cold, just a few spits of snow tapping the tin roof on the garage. I heard a jet plane high up, a quiet mumble above the clouds, and wondered if Jack was living so close that he could hear the same plane somewhere on its route.

I started to think about Jack's mother. My only connection to Doris Evelyn Swenson was when I was a senior in high school. A friend got me a blind date with this good-looking blonde who he said went to the private school in Frost Falls. I remembered driving over to the Swensons' street all prepared to go in and meet the folks, but she was out by the mailbox, shoulders hunched like a hitchhiker desperate to get on down the road. She was a big, fair-haired, loud girl, pretty, all right, and first thing she asked me was could I get her a drink. She never stopped talking about how lousy Sauerville was, how stupid all her teachers were. After a movie in Frost Falls, she showed me a place to go park and make out. Right away she gave me two shark-attack kisses. I felt more like a meal than a date, and just when she began to push me down a local deputy came and parked behind us with his brights on. I wound up taking her for a burger, which she ate in about four bites like it was life itself. I took her home, and all the way there she had her window down like she was hoping to be blown out into the darkness. She was a scary girl, so I never called her again. The point of this is that if things had maybe gone different, I could have been Jack's dad. I might have run away and joined the navy for four years, and Jack would have had the exact same life he's had. At the moment, I was having a little trouble telling the difference between a kid I might have made and Jack himself. I folded my arms and looked up at the now-empty sky. I mean, kids are kids. Suddenly it seemed like a thin line between what made one mine or not mine.

I thought about Deputy Toller and turned for the house, and his wife gave me his cell. He was on duty, but he answered, and when I asked him about some old lady he'd told me about, at first he acted like I was crazy.

"Yah, yah, now I remember you asking me about Mrs. Salmen. I'm pretty sure I called you about that and left a message on your machine, but you never got back to me. That was quite a while ago, bud."

"Well, did she know about the cousin in Fargo?"

"I can't recall what she said."

"Can you phone her again?"

"I don't think so. She died last year."

"Well, damn. Don't you remember anything?"

"Got a few things on my plate myself, buddy. I remember talking to Donna about it, though. Call her back. She's got a mind like Velcro. *Whup,* that guy just ran the stop. Gotta go." I heard a chirp of siren before the line went dead.

I called his wife back. She's from the South, so I had to be nice for a few sentences, asking about the kids and all, before I got down to business.

"Oh yeah, I remember Jimmy telling me about Mrs. Salmen. She was friends with Jack's grandma. The cousin was on old Harry Swenson's side of the family. And her married name was Schoen, same as my mother's grandma's maiden name. Elsa Schoen."

So the next day I got Jimmy Toller to make some official police-type calls, and after three days he found out that Elsa Schoen was still alive, not in a nursing home but in a high-end village for "limited people" in Plotkin, this side of Fargo. The manager of the facility told him that since Elsa never had company, she'd be glad to see me. No, she couldn't talk on the phone because of her hearing.

When the wife got home that Friday, I followed her into the kitchen and told her I was driving over by Fargo the next day, early, and explained why.

She got that little warning tic in the corner of her mouth. "What can she tell you?"

"I don't know. Maybe Jack contacted her and she has some idea where he is. I kind of doubt it, but then maybe she knows the other guy, Jack's great-uncle."

"The weather's supposed to turn nasty."

"I like nasty weather. Money for the furnace man." I gave her a grin she didn't return.

Linda settled her rear end against the stove and folded her arms. "Baby, is this a guilt thing?"

"Guilt thing? Hell, no. What are you talking about? I'm just wondering what happened to the guy. If he's all right. He worked with me a fairly long time."

"Okay, don't get steamed at me." She got this expression like she had something more to say but was holding back.

"What?"

She gave me a look, then, like she could see right through me into the next county. "What yourself," she said, and walked into the hall, out of my sight.

So the next day I got in her Buick to drive to North Dakota, about two and a half hours away. I was up real early, so it was dark, but the weather didn't look too bad. Cold as a cube, but no snow. I was kind of excited, like I was finally going to find out something that would lead me to Jack. Not that I wanted to see him or anything. Maybe get a little phone time with him, wherever the hell he was. See if he needed some advice or something. If he was ever coming back.

At dawn it was cloudy, and about an hour later, before I hit the border, here came the snow, so much of it that I knew it was a mistake not driving my truck. The wind blasted out of the northwest and the light wasn't coming up, like the sun got stuck to the horizon.

I got to the village of limited people around eight-thirty, and it looked like a nice place, with a few hardy trees and old Chicago brick veneer. Inside at the desk the attendant told me to speak loudly when I met Elsa Schoen, that she was awake and well enough to see me. I walked along a hall and found her apartment. Elsa was only about forty-five but suf-

fered, she told me, from a rare type of epilepsy. She was in storage, she
joked, waiting for a cure. She didn't know Jack even existed, but she did
give me a phone number and e-mail for his great-uncle, Ewe Brot Swenson, in Germany. I was let down, but figured the lady deserved some
small talk. After I had been visiting for twenty minutes, the wind started
to sound like a pack of wolves, so I thanked her for her time, held her
shaky hand awhile, then headed down the hall.

Outside, the wind pushed me like a forklift, skidding me over to
the car. I had to break the floppy wipers loose on Linda's old sedan and
scrape off the ice. On the highway the wind seemed to die down, but
the snow came curling like a dense migration of moths. I drove over
the flat area toward the Minnesota line, and pretty soon traffic thinned
to where I was the only one left moving, creeping along at twenty-five
miles an hour, past a couple stopped cars with their emergency flashers
glowing under a glaze of sticky snow. Then the wind came up again, and
I could feel my rear tires slide sideways a little. I was stupid for coming
away from home with no chains in a two-wheel-drive sedan. Being out
in the storm made me wonder about my judgment in general. About
my whole life, maybe.

When I hit a slight downgrade I felt all four tires lose it. I remembered not to mash on the brakes and tried to accelerate out of the skid.
I went on like this, like a cat on slick ice, until right after I crossed the
state line. The snow suddenly got so heavy that the wiper on the passenger side snapped off and blew away. I saw a cow standing by a roadside
cell tower looking like a powdered éclair, no legs showing, just this big-
headed tube on top of all that white. After a while, a gust blew me in
a circle and spun me down into a ditch, a pretty deep and wide swale
full of chunks of ice. I knew better than to get out. A plow or cop would
find me, and I had warm clothes and lots of gas. It was about eleven
o'clock, and I called the house, but Linda wasn't there. I called the highway patrol and they said they'd find me, eventually. And then I sat, my
windows turning to milk glass as the snow covered me up.

I hated being idle like this, because I'd begin thinking about things.
My memories attacked me, and after a half hour I realized how seldom I did this, this going over my own history, the things I did that I

was proud of and the ones maybe not so proud of. I'm never without something to occupy my time, and now here I was barreling down a chute of self-examination that was as scary as the storm outside. I called Butchie, and evidently his cell was off. I wished I could've called my father, who'd passed away last year. He wouldn't have answered anyway, because right now was his naptime. I began to think of all the dead people I wish I'd talked to.

I got desperate for something to do, so I started going through the glove box, rounding up all the expired proofs of insurance. Then I opened my wallet and threw away all the old AAA cards, fishing licenses, phone numbers with no faces to them, and like that. Then I saw Uwe Swenson's phone number. In high school I did a science project about time zones, so I figured it was around eight p.m. in Germany. It was something to do, so I went through the rigmarole of making a call to Europe. Pretty soon a man picked up the phone and said something I didn't understand.

"Uh, hi, this is Mel Todd in the U.S.," I said.

"Okay," the voice said. "I'm good with English."

"That's great. Look, I have a young friend by the name of Jack Swenson, and I was wondering if by some chance he'd contacted you? I think he's your great-nephew or something."

"Well, no," he said, and my heart sank. "Not since this morning. Is something wrong?"

I was speechless. He couldn't be talking about the same kid. "No, no. But just to be sure, is this the same young man who used to live in Minnesota?"

"Yes, it is. And now I recall that he mentioned he used to work for you, Mr. Todd."

"Sure. That's right. Is he at home? Can I talk with him a minute?"

"Oh, I'm sorry, no. Jack is still in the next town estimating a job."

"He's found work over there, eh? He always was a smart kid."

Mr. Swenson laughed at this. "He's not exactly a kid anymore. He's twenty-three years old and owns his own heating company."

I looked at my lap. "He was a go-getter," I said, my voice flat, feeling like I'd lost some sort of lottery.

"I'm sorry he's not here to speak with you," Uwe Swenson said. "He mentioned you several times. What he learned from you. Call back any-time, maybe on a Sunday."

I began to feel short-winded but had to ask, "Did you have to help him out?"

"Well, I took him in. I used to be an architect, so I could help him find work. He took German lessons and at the same time spent two years at a technical institute. He's started to do quite well. Jack and his new wife live in a house just down the road. He's a big help to me and my wife, as we're getting on a bit."

I felt that the air in my car had run out of oxygen. "Very generous of you. I mean, to take in a stranger like that."

"Well," Mr. Swenson said, "sometimes you have to gamble."

We talked a little longer, then I hung up and watched the inside of the car get darker and darker. I turned off the engine to save gas and but-toned my jacket up to the neck, swung my arms against my chest, and stomped my legs. About four o'clock, I began to get afraid and started thinking about all the people caught out in the storm, people like me who were marooned, slowing down, going over everything. I thought about what life would be like if Jack was still around. I tried to start the car but it wouldn't turn over. After full dark, I began to feel sleepy and sick. Why hadn't my wife tried to call? When my phone did ring, it was the state police.

"Mr. Todd?"

"Yes?"

"You still stuck, eh?"

"Stuck as I've ever been."

"Well, we're coming east from the North Dakota line on High-way 10. Where are ya?"

"Maybe five miles on the right side, off in a ditch. About a mile past where some cows are milling against the fence."

"Are you completely covered?"

"Buried." I could imagine him moving slow, behind a plow or tow truck, craning his neck. In a half hour I heard the noise of an engine go past, then nothing. Right then I wished I could have reached my brother. Nobody looks out for you like family, people you've gone to bat for in the past and are used to returning the favor. Now even the wind was fading away, sound itself forgetting me.

My phone rang again. "I can't find you, bud," the trooper said.

For the first time, I felt the cold all the way inside me. "Aw, no. Please."

"You say you're at the bottom of a ditch?"

"The very, very bottom," I said.

"You have people with you, or are you alone?"

My fingers were dying, my toes. I couldn't bring myself to say that word.

Deputy Sid's Gift

I'm going to tell you about the last time I went to confession. I met this priest at the nursing home where I work spoon-feeding the parish's old folks. He noticed that I had a finger off, and so he knew I was oil field and wanted to know why I was working indoors. This priest was a blond guy with eyes you could see through and didn't look like nobody inside of two hundred miles of Grand Crapaud, Louisiana. He didn't know that when sweet crude slid under $12 a barrel, most oil companies went belly-up like a stinking redfish, and guys like me had to move out or do something else. So I told him I took a night class in scrubbing these old babies, and he said I had a good heart and bull like that and invited me to come visit at the rectory if I ever needed to.

One day I needed to, yeah. Everybody's got something they got to talk about sometime in their life. I went to the old brick church on LeBlanc Street on a Saturday morning and found him by himself in his little kitchen in the old cypress priest house, and we sat down by the table with a big pot of coffee.

So I told him what had been going through my head, how I used to have a 1962 Chevrolet pickup truck, a rusty spare I kept parked out by the road just to haul off trash. It was ratty, and I was ashamed to drive it unless I was going to the dump. One day after Christmas my wife, Monette, told me to get rid of the tree and the holiday junk, so I went to crank the truck. Well, in a minute I'm standing by the road with a key in my hand, looking at a long patch of pale weeds where the truck used to be. I'm saying to myself that it coulda been gone a hour or a week. It's just a thing you don't look at unless you need it.

So I called Claude down at his little four-by-four city jail and he said he'd look for it the next day, that he had more expensive stuff to worry about. Ain't that a hell of a note. Then I called the sheriff's office down at the parish seat, and when I told them the truck's over thirty years old, they acted like I'm asking them to look for a stole newspaper or something. It was my truck and I wanted it back.

The priest, he just nodded along and poured us our first cup of coffee from a big aluminum Drip-o-Lator. When he finished, he put the pot in a shallow pan of water on the gas stove behind his chair and stared down at his shoe, like he was hearing my confession, which I guess he was. He even had his little purple confession rag hanging on his neck.

I told the priest how the cops searched a lil' bit, and how I looked, but that old truck just disappeared like rain on a hot street. Monette, she was glad to get it out the yard, but I needed something for hauling, you know? So after not too long I found a good old '78 Ford for a thousand dollars and bought that and put it right where the other one was.

One day my little girl Lizette and me, we was at the nursing home together because of some student-visit-the-parent-at-work deal at her school. She was letting the old folks hug her little shoulders and pat her dark hair. You know how they are. They see a child and go nuts to get at them, like the youngness is gonna wear off on their old bodies. At the end of my shift, one of the visitors who was there to see his dried-up wife—I think he was a Canulette, kind of a café au lait dude from out by Prairie Amère—his truck won't crank, so me and Lizette decided to bring him home. Me in my smocky little fruit uniform and Lizette with her checkerboard school suit went off in my shiny thirdhand Buick, old man Canulette sitting between us like a fence post. We rolled down the highway and turned off into the rice fields and went way back into the tree line toward Coconut Bayou. We passing through that poor folks' section on the other side of Tonga Bend when Lizette stuck her head out the window to make her pigtails go straight in the wind. Next thing I knew, she yelled, Daddy, there's your truck, back in the woods. I turned the car around in that little gravel road and, sure enough—you couldn't hardly see it unless you had young eyes—there was my old Chevy parked up under a grove of live oaks maybe 150 yards away.

We walked up on it, and judging from the thistles that had growed up past the bumper, it'd been there maybe three months. I held back and asked Monsieur Canulette if anybody lived around there, and he looked at the truck and said the first word since town: Bezue. He said here and there in the woods a Bezue lived, and they all had something wrong in they heads. I told him I'd put me a Bezue in jail if he stole my truck, but he just looked at me with those silver eyes of his in a way that gave me *les frissons.* I brought the old man to his little farm and then came back to Tonga Bend Store to call the deputy, who took most of an hour to get out there.

They sent Sid Touchard, that black devil, and he showed up with his shaggy curls full of pomade falling down his collar, the tape deck in his cruiser playing zydeco. He got out with a clipboard, like he knows how to write, and put on his cowboy hat. He asked me if I was the Bobby Simoneaux what called, and even Lizette looked behind her in the woods for maybe another Bobby Simoneaux, but I just nodded. He looked at the truck and the leaves and branches on it and asked me do I still want it. *Mais,* yeah, I told him. Then Sid walked up and put his hand on the door handle like it was something dirty, which I guess it was, and pulled. What we saw was a lot of trash paper, blankets, and old clothes. I looked close, and Lizette stepped back and put her little hands on her mouth. The air was nothing but mildew and armpit, and by the steering wheel was a nappy old head.

He's living in it, Deputy Sid said. His eyebrows went up when he said that. Even he was surprised, and he works the poor folks of the parish. He asked again do I still want it. Hell yeah, I said. He spit. He's a tall man, yeah, and it takes a long time for his spit to hit the ground. Then he reached in to give him a shake, and he sat up and stared at us. He was black—back-in-the-country black. He wasn't no old man, but he had these deep wrinkles the old folks call the sorrow grooves, and he looked like he was made out of Naugahyde. His eyeballs was black olives floating in hot sauce, and when Sid tried to get out of him what he was doing in the truck, he took a deep breath and looked over the rusty hood toward the road.

Finally he said, I'm Fernest. Fernest Bezue. My mamma, she live down that way. He pointed, and I could see he been drunk maybe six years in a row. The old cotton jacket he had on was eat up with battery acid and his feet was bare knobs. Sid give me that look like he got on bifocals, but he ain't. Hell no, I told him. I want my truck. He stole it and you got to put him in jail. So Sid said to him, you stole this truck? And Fernest kept looking at the road like it was something he wasn't allowed to see, and then he said he found it here. When he said that, I got hot.

Deputy Sid tugged Fernest out into the sunlight, slow, like he was a old cow he was pulling from a tangle of fence wire. He put him in the cruiser and told me and Lizette to get in the front seat. He said where Fernest's mamma lived, my Buick can't go. So we rolled down the gravel a mile, turned off on a shell road where the China ball and sticker bushes about dragged the paint off that beat-up cruiser. Lizette, she sat on my lap, looking at Deputy Sid's candy bar wrappers on the floor, a satsuma on the seat, and a rosary around the rearview. The road gave out at a pile of catbrier and we turned left into a hard-bottom coulee full of rainwater next to Coconut Bayou. The water come up to the hubcaps, and Lizette wiggled and told Deputy Sid we on a ferryboat for sure, yeah.

There's this little shotgun shack up on brick piers with the tar paper rottin' off it, stovepipe stub sticking out the side wall, no steps to the door, cypress knees coming up in the yard, egg cartons and water jugs floating around on the breeze. Deputy Sid leaned on the horn for maybe fifteen seconds till the front door opened and a woman look like a licorice stick stood there dressed in some old limp dress. He rolled down the window and asked if it's her son in the backseat. She stooped slow, squinted a long time. That Fernest, she said to the water. She sure wasn't talking to us. Sid stepped out on a walk board and told me to follow. I jacked up my legs, slid over all the junk, and brought out that satsuma with me. Can't leave this with Lizette, I told him. She loves these things. Sid took it from me, give it a toss, and she caught that with one hand.

While he talked to the woman I looked in the house. All this while, my shoes was filling up with water. The first room had nothing but a mattress and a kerosene lamp on the floor and some bowls next to it. The walls was covered with newspaper to keep the wind out. In the second and last room, the floor had fell in. The whole place was swayback because the termites had eat out the joists and side beams. It didn't take no genius to tell that the roof rafters wasn't gonna last another year. A wild animal would take to a hole in the ground before he lived in a place like that.

Deputy Sid asked the woman did she know about the truck, and she said he was living in it. He turned to me and said, look around. You want me to put him in jail?

Hell yeah, I told him, and Sid looked at me hard with those oxblood eyes he got, trying to figure a road into my head. He told me if I file charges and put him in jail, that'd cost the parish. My tax money was gonna pay to feed him and put clothes on him. He said let him stay with his mamma. The old woman stooped down again, and Fernest stared at her like maybe she was a tractor or a cloud. I looked at the house again and saw that putting him in jail would be a promotion in life, yeah.

Sid took off the bracelets and walked him to the steps. The old lady said he could stay. Then we left, that cruiser bottoming out and fishtailing from the yard, its mud grips digging down to the claypan. Back at my truck I threw all his stuff in a pile, old coats with cigarette holes burnt through, medicine bottles from the free clinic in town, dirty drawers I handled with a stick, fried chicken skin and bones, a little radio with leaking batteries. I put my key in but the engine didn't make a sound. When I opened up the hood, all I saw was a pile of a thousand sticks and three long otter-looking animals that took off for the woods. The sheriff's tow truck brought the thing back to my house and that was that. My wife took one look at it and one smell of it and told me it had to be gone. I already had me a truck.

A rainy spell set in and the Chevy sank down in the backyard for a couple weeks with the crawfish chimneys coming up around it till I got a nice day and scrubbed it inside and out. Down at the home we got five new poor, helpless folks from the government without nobody dying to make room for 'em, so another week passed before I got to the hardware and bought me a nice orange FOR SALE sign.

Now this was when the priest kind of leaned back against the window frame and made a faraway smile and looked out to the rose garden Father Scheuter put in before they transferred him to Nevada. Priests try not to look you in the eye when you telling stuff. Scared maybe you won't tell it straight, or tell it all. So I told him straight. The second night that old truck was parked back out on the street wearing that sign, it got stole. I called up Deputy Sid direct this time and let him know what happened. He said, you want me to look for that truck again? I told him hell yeah. He said, don't you got a truck already? I think that pomade Sid been smearing on his head all these years done soaked in his brain, and I told him that. He said, you got a nice brick house, a wife, three kids, and two cars, you might could quit at that. Anyway, he said, he didn't feel like burning fifty dollars' gas looking for a forty-dollar truck. I told him I was gonna talk to the sheriff, and he said okay, he'd look.

I wound up at the home helping out for music day, when Mr. Lodrigue brings his Silvertone guitar and amp to play songs the old folks recognize. Man, they love that rusty stuff like "As Time Goes By," "The Shrimp Boats Is A-Coming," and such 78 rpm tunes they can tap a foot to. I get a kick out of them people—one foot in the grave and still trying to boogie. And Mr. Lodrigue, who has wavery silver hair and kind of smoky gray eyes, he looks like Frank Sinatra to them old gals.

I got through with music day and went out to where my car was at behind the home, and there was Sid sitting on the hood of his muddy police car, big as a hoss. I walked up and saw his arms was crossed. He said, I found it. I asked where it was, and he said, where it was before. I said, you mean Fernest Bezue got it back in Prairie Amère? Man, that made me hot. Here I let him go free and he comes back on me like that. I cursed and spit twice. Deputy Sid looked at me like I was the thief. I asked him why didn't he haul him in, and he looked away. Finally, he said, he's alcoholic. That got me hotter. Like *I* could go down to Generous Gaudet's used-car lot drunk and steal me a car and somebody would let *me* off. Deputy Sid nodded, but he said, Simoneaux, you play with those old people like they your own *grandpère* and *grandmère,* yet you don't know what *they* ever done wrong in they time. I sat down next to him when he said that. The hood metal popped in and shook loose a thought in my head that kind of got me worried. About the folks in the home. Maybe I was nice to 'em because I was paid for that. Nobody was paying me to be nice to a drunk Bezue from Prairie Amère. I spit on the sidewalk and wondered if Deputy Sid's really as dumb as I thought.

Then I remembered Fernest Bezue out under the oaks, staring at the road like crazy. So I said, okay, get the tow truck to pull it in, and he says, no, I can't make a report because they'll pick him up.

What you think about that? I got to go get my own stole truck, yeah. That's my tax dollars at work.

The pot on the range gave a little jump like a steam bubble got caught under its bottom, and the priest turned and got us another cup. He was frowning a little now, like his behind's hurting in that hard-bottom chair, but he didn't say anything, still didn't look.

I went on about how I wanted to do the right thing, how me and Monette got out on the gravel past Prairie Amère, trying to beat a big thunderstorm coming up from the Gulf. When we got to where the truck sat in the mud, the wind was twisting those live oaks like they was rubber. Monette stayed in the Buick and I walked up to the old red truck, and in the bed was Fernest, sitting down with a gallon of T&T port between his legs, just enjoying the breeze. You stole my truck again, I told him. He said he had to have a place to get away. He said it like he was living in a vacation home down on Holly Beach. He was staring up into the black cloud bank, waiting for lightning. That's how people like him live, I guess, waiting to get knocked down and wondering why it happens to them. I looked at his round head and that dusty nap he had for hair and started to walk off. But he had what was mine and he didn't work for it, and I figured it would do him more harm than good to just give him something for nothing. I said if he could get two hundred dollars he could have the truck. I didn't know where that come from, but I said it. He said if he had two hundred dollars he wouldn't be sitting in the woods with a $5 gallon of wine. I wondered for a minute where he wanted to go, but just for a minute, because I didn't want to get in his head. So I looked in the cab where he'd hot-wired the ignition, and I sparked up that engine. I pulled out his blankets and some paper bags of food and threw them in a pile. Then I jumped into the bed and put down the tailgate. I had to handle him like the real helpless ones at the home, he was that drunk, and even in that wind he smelled sour, like a wet towel bunched up in the trunk. I put the truck in gear and left him in the middle of that clearing under them oaks, him that wouldn't pay or work. When I rolled up on the road ahead of Monette in the Buick, the rain come like a water main broke in the sky. I looked back at Fernest Bezue and he was standing next to his pile of stuff, one finger in that jug by his leg and his head up like he was taking a shower. Then a big bolt come down across the road and the rain blew sideways like busted glass, and I headed back for town.

All that night I rolled like a log in the bed. I thought the weather would blow over, but the storm was setting on Grand Crapaud like a flatiron and dropped big welding rods of lightning almost till dawn. On the way to work I got tempted to drive back to Prairie Amère, but I didn't, and all that day I was forgetting to change bed linen and was slopping food on the old babies when I fed 'em. It took me a week to relax, to get so I could clean the truck some more without seeing Fernest looking up at the sky, waiting. I got it ready and put it on the lawn, but this time I took out the battery and left it in the carport. Nobody looked at it for about a week. One morning Lizette, she kissed me bye and went out to wait for the school bus. A minute later I heard the screen door open and Lizette said the old truck was trying to run. She said it was making running noise. So I went out and looked through the glass. Fernest Bezue was in there snoring on his back like a sawmill. When Lizette found out it was a big drunk man she yelled and ran for the house. She was scared, yeah, and I didn't like that. I opened the driver door and it took me five minutes to convince him I wasn't Mr. Prudhomme, a cane farmer he used to work for ten years back. When he sat up, his left eye capsized, then come back slow, and it was weak, like a lamp flame at sunup. He stared out the windshield at a place I couldn't see.

I told Fernest I ought to pull him out and turn the hose on him for scaring my little girl like he did. He mumbled something I didn't catch, and I told him to get the hell away. But he just sat there in the middle of that old sprung bench seat like he half expected me to get in and drive him somewhere to eat. Finally he told me the house had fell in and his mamma went off somewhere and didn't tell him. Man, I let him have it. Told him to stop that drinking and get a job. He said that his drinking was a disease, and I told him yeah, it was a lazy disease. He said if he could help it, he would. That his daddy was the same way and died in a wreck. I told him he was having a slow wreck right now. I looked back at my house and them wilting camellias Monette planted under the windows. Then I told him if he could stay dry for a week I'd see if I could get him a mopping job at the rest home. He could save up and buy my truck. Then he put his head down and laughed. I can't stop, man, he told me. That pissed me off so bad I went in and called the cops. After a while Claude come up in the town's cruiser, took one look at Fernest, then looked over where I'm standing by my Japan plum tree. How they made a gun belt skinny enough for that man, I don't know. He asked me, *Mais*, what you 'spect us to do with him? Claude is real country, can't hardly talk American. He said Fernest can't do nothing to that truck he can arrest him for. If he steal it again the mayor gonna give him the town beautification award. I said arrest him, and I could see in Claude's eyes that nobody was on the night shift to keep a watch on Fernest down at that one-cell jail. Do something, I told him. He's scaring Lizette sleeping out here.

What Claude did is put Fernest in the squad car, stop by Bug's Café and buy him a ham sandwich, and drop him off at the town limits, by the abandoned rice mill. They told me that when I called the station later on.

This was when the priest got up and stretched. He pointed to my cup and I shook my head. He fixed himself one more with lots of cream, got a glass of water from the tap, and sat down again, looking at me just once, real quick.

That made me feel like I could keep going, so I told him how that night and a couple nights more I couldn't sleep without dreaming something about that no-good drunk. I mean, lots of people need help. My one-legged uncle needs his grass cut, and I'd do it, but he says he don't want me to mess with it. Says I got better things to do with my time. Other people deserve my help, and Fernest didn't deserve nothing, but every time I went to sleep, there he was in my head. When I read a newspaper, there he was in a group picture, till I focused real good. But after a while he started to fade again, you know, like before. I settled into business at the home, putting ointment on the bald men's heads, putting Band-Aids on the old ladies' bunions so they can wear shoes, even though there ain't no place for them to walk to.

Then one morning here come Fernest's mamma, all dried up like beef jerky, with three other poor folks the government paid us to take. She had herself a stroke out on Mr. Prudhomme's farm, where she was staying for free in a trailer, and one side of her wouldn't work. I stayed away from her for three days, until it was time for Mr. Lodrigue, the music man, when everybody gets together in the big room. I was just walking by to get Mr. Boudreaux his teeth he left in the pocket of his bathrobe when her good arm stuck out and grabbed my fruity little uniform. I didn't want to look in her eye, but I did. She slid out her tongue and wet her lips. The mailbox is the onliest thing standin', she told me. The house fall in. I told her it's a shame and wanted to walk away, but she got hold of my little smock and balled it up in her fist.

She said his government check come in the mailbox, then he walk five mile for that wine. She told me he was gonna die of the wine and couldn't I help. I looked at her and I felt cold as a lizard. I asked her why me. She said, you the one. I told her he was past all help. He had the drinking disease and that was that. I pulled away and went and got old man Boudreaux's choppers, and when I come back I saw her across the room, pointing at me with the one finger what would still point. You the one, that finger said. I laughed and told myself right then and there I wasn't going to help no drunk truck thief that couldn't be helped.

The priest, he made to swat a mosquito on his arm, but he changed his mind and blew it away with his breath. I didn't know if he was still listening good. Who knows if a priest pays a lot of attention. I think you supposed to be talking to God, and the man in the collar's just like a telephone operator. Anyway, I kept on.

I told him how after work I used the phone out in the parking lot to call Deputy Sid to help me find Fernest. Yeah, I was ashamed of myself. I didn't know what I was going to do if Sid found him for me, but I had to do something to get the old lady's pointing finger out my head. I went home, and about a hour before sundown Deputy Sid pulled up in my front yard and I went out to him carrying Lizette, who had a cold and was all leechy like a kid gets when she's feeling bad. Sid had him a long day. His pomade hair hung down like a thirsty azalea. He said we got to go out to Prairie Amère, so I put my little girl down, got in the old truck, and followed him out.

We went through the pine belt and past the rice fields those Thibodeaux boys own and by them poor houses in Tonga Bend, then we broke out into Prairie Amère, which is mostly grass and weed flowers with a live oak every now and then, but no crops. The old farmers say everything you plant there comes up with a bitter taste. All of a sudden the cruiser pulled off into the clover on the side of the road, so I rolled up behind. There ain't a thing around, and I walked up and Deputy Sid said over his shoulder that empty land's a sad thing. He stretched and I could hear his gun belt creaking. I asked why we stopped and he pointed. Maybe a hundred yards out in the field, eat up by weeds, was a little barn, the kind where a dozen cows could get in out of the sun. We jumped the ditch and scratched through the buttonbush and bull tongue. Deputy Sid stopped once and sneezed. He said I told him to find Fernest and he did. It wasn't easy, but he did. He asked what did I want with him, and I said his mamma wanted me to check, but that wasn't it, no. It was the people at the home what made me do it. I was being paid to be nice to them. I wanted to do something without getting paid. I didn't give a damn about some black truck thief, but I wanted to help him. I couldn't tell Deputy Sid that.

We got to the tin overhang on the barn and wasn't able to see much inside. The sun was about down. We stepped in and waited for our eyes to get used to the place. I could smell that peppery-sweet cypress. A building can be a hundred years old—if it's made of cypress, you going to smell that. Along the side wall was a wooden feed rack three feet off the ground, and sleeping in there was Fernest, his face turned to that fine-grain wood. Deputy Sid let out a little noise in his throat like a woman would make. He said Fernest was trying to sleep above the ground so the ants couldn't get to him. He said one time, two years before, Fernest passed out on the ground and woke up with a million fire ants blazing all over him like red pepper in a open wound. He stayed swole up for three weeks with hills of pus running all over him, and when his fever broke, he was half blind and mostly deaf in one ear.

I went over to the feed trough and shook him. It took him five minutes to open his eyes, and even in the dark you could see 'em glowing sick. I asked him was he all right, and he asked me if I was his mamma, so I waited a minute for his head to get straight. Deputy Sid came close and picked up a empty bottle and sniffed it. I reached through the slats and bumped Fernest's arm and asked him why he drank so damn much when he knew it would kill him. He looked up at me like I was stupid. He said the booze was like air to him. Like water. I told him maybe I could get him in the home with his mamma, and he stared up at the tin roof and shook his head. I asked Sid if maybe his mamma could get him picked up and put in the crazy house, and Sid told me no, he's not crazy, he's just drunk all the time. The state thinks there's a difference. Fernest sat up in the trough, hay all stuck in his hair, and he started coughing deep and wet like some of the old folks do at the home late in the evening. Night shift is scary because them babies sail away in the dark. Anyway, Fernest's face got all uneven, and he asked what I wanted. That stopped me. I opened my dumb mouth just to see what would come out, and I told him that Deputy Sid bought my truck and was giving it to him so he could stay in it sometime. I held up the key and handed it to him. He nodded like he expected this, like people wake him up all the time to give him cars. I looked at Sid and I could see a gold star on a tooth, but he stayed quiet. Then I told Fernest I knew he couldn't drive it, and I was going to take the insurance off anyway, but he could use it to sleep out of the weather like he done before. He looked past me at Sid and reached out and gave him some kind of boogaloo handshake. In a minute I had the truck up in the grass by the barn, and I pulled the battery out just in case, and Deputy Sid drove me and the battery toward home. We pulled away from all that flat, empty land, and after about five miles Sid asked why I told Fernest *he* gave him the truck. I watched a tornado-wrecked trailer go by and said I didn't want nothing for what I did. The cruiser rattled past Tonga Bend, and Sid tuned in a scratchy zydeco station. Clinton Rideau and the Ebony Crawfish started pumping out "Sunshine Can't Ruin My Storm," but I didn't feel like tapping my foot.

I went home and expected to sleep, but I didn't. I thought I did something great, but by two a.m. I knew all I did was give away a trashy truck with the floor pans rusting out and all the window glass cracked. I gave up the truck mostly to make myself feel good, not to help Fernest Bezue. And that's what I told the priest I come there to tell him.

The priest looked at me in the eyes, and I could see something coming, like a big truck or a train. Then he leaned in and I could smell the soap on him. He told me there's only one thing worse than what I did. I looked at the floor and asked, what's that? And he said, not doing it.

I like to fell out the chair.

About a month later Fernest's mamma died in the night, and I called up Deputy Sid at dawn. He went out to look but couldn't find Fernest nowhere. Sid brought his big black self to my house, and I saw him bouncing up my drive like he got music in his veins instead of blood. He got on a new khaki uniform tight as a drumhead, knife creases all over. He told me the liquor store past Coconut Bayou said they ain't seen him. The mailbox at the old place been eat down by termites. None of the farmers seen him. I said it's a shame we can't tell him about his mamma, and Deputy Sid looked at me sidewise and kissed his lips like he's hiding a smile. I told him to come inside, where Monette fixed us all a cup of coffee, and we sat down in the kitchen and cussed the government.

Summer come and the weather turned hot as the doorknob to hell. The old babies at the home couldn't roll around outside, so we had to keep 'em happy in the big room by playing cards and like that. I had to play canasta with six ladies who couldn't remember the rules between plays, so I would spend three hours a day explaining rules to a game we'd never finish.

I guess it was two months after Fernest's mamma passed. I got home and sat in my easy chair by the air condition when Lizette come by and give me a little kiss and said Deputy Sid wanted me on the phone. So I went in the kitchen, and he told me he's in his cruiser out at Mr. Thibaut's place in the north end of the parish, west of Mamou. He found Fernest.

I couldn't say nothing for half a minute. I asked him was he drunk, and he said no, he was way past that, and I asked when, and he said he died about yesterday in the truck. I got a picture of Fernest Bezue driving that wreck on the back roads, squinting through the cracked windshield, picking his spot for the night. I told Deputy Sid I was sorry and he said, don't feel like that. He said, we couldn't do nothing for him, but we did it anyway.

Gone to Water

The dawn seemed more like a sunset, the horizon a luminous peach-colored line, and above it, gray commas of cloud with copper bottoms, each the size of a small town. The old man came onto his back porch holding a cup of coffee and looked east over the sound, his great-grandson dawdling behind, hands in his pockets, a willowy boy of nine. Claude Ledet was eighty-eight, his skin a sun-eroded fabric of pale craters and burgundy spots. He looked down to his little wharf hugging the island.

"We goin' fish today, down to the mouth of the river," the old man said.

"The river?" The boy's voice sailed high with the question.

"The Mississippi," his great-grandfather snapped. "Don't you know nothing?"

The boy grinned, goofy and sweet. "I know it's a long way off, Pa Claude. For your boat."

The old man turned west, looking for weather. Sometimes he would see what was there; other times his mind would layer memories over the present, and he would see what was there last year, or ten years before that, or sixty years earlier when he'd built his little frame house high up on pilings. The day before, he'd watched the big wooden oyster lugger *The Two Sons* go by, loaded down, and he'd waved to his cousins Henry and Rene where they sat on the deck sorting what they had dredged up from their lease, even though Henry and Rene had been dead of old age for many years and *The Two Sons* lay sunk and rotting in Lake Borgne. Sometimes he saw things from several different decades at once, steam tugs, coastal sailboats, brand-new Chris-Craft mahogany yachts, Jet Skis carrying windblown children racing above the swells, time-wandering images overlapping like a bowl of shucked oysters.

Claude looked down at the boy. "Why you here?"

"Aunt Brenda couldn't come stay with you today. She's at the doctor with the flu."

"That oldest girl couldn't come?"

"Suzie?"

"That's right. So many come around to visit with me I can't keep 'em straight."

The boy gave him a long look. "Great-aunt Suzie's your daughter."

The old man nodded west. "Get two rods off the porch and my box. I'm goin' bail the skiff."

"Her friend's husband got killed in that rig accident about three weeks ago. It's a big mess out in the Gulf."

"My radio's burnt out, and that damn television don't make no sense to me at all."

"Everybody's talking about it. You haven't heard?"

Claude put a hand to his stubbly chin. "We need some crackers and potted meat and a jug of water."

The boy settled a baseball cap down on his curls. "I didn't know we were going fishing."

Soon the two of them were in a plank skiff being pushed east by Claude's five-horse Champion, a smoky old outboard he had to pull on ten times before it would even pop, the first tugs on the rope making only the noise of a startled hen. The twelve-foot boat rattled and wandered but managed after a while to get up to ten miles an hour as it cut between the big shrimp company dock and an incoming corporate trawler.

The boy looked back at the vessel as the wheelman leaned out of the cabin to watch them tumble into his wake. "Pa Claude, you sure you want to go all the way to the river?"

The old man didn't answer as he watched for the pass that led to the Gulf, which he saw after a minute and turned into, and then two minutes later turned back out of when three-foot rollers caused the skiff to buck and sway. They began to follow the grassy back of the island where there were no houses, still headed east, a longer but calmer route.

Several miles on, they began to pass oil company canals cut into the marsh on both the left and right, and the motor hit a stump, hard, jumping up and puttering in open air until Claude could find the kill switch. While he replaced the propeller's shear pin with a cut nail, the boy asked him what a stump was doing out in open salt water.

"Aw, Jackie, this used to not be water."

The boy brushed dark hair under his cap. "What was it?"

"Ha. Land, you little fool. You see how what we in now looks like a lagoon? Years ago it was a long, narrow cut, not a hundred feet wide." He looked up from his work. "All this was land. Over there was camps, but they fell in the water every one. A farmer grew sugar cane in a sure-enough field over there. I remember a road." He squinted into memory. "The world's meltin' away on account of all these rig canals."

"Maybe you ought to stay off the shore and out of these stumps," the boy said quietly.

"Yah." The old man lowered the motor back into the water. "I'll go out farther, take the old way."

In another five miles the island fell away to the right and they stopped in a wide sound. "The chop ain't too bad." Claude pointed at a long, concave shore a mile off to the northeast that had been cut into with five canals. "We can head over there and then skin down that long bank south of it and around past the jetties at the mouth. We can anchor in a little hook inside the rocks where it'll be calm. That's where them redfish hide." He looked across the water again. "This used to be cypress trees, here. Even a little high ground."

As the motor idled, they studied a broad, whitecapped channel they would have to cross. A smell other than bitter marsh hung in the air. The great-grandfather pushed a lever on the motor and the skiff slid east. They rocked through a rough place, shipping only a couple gallons of water because the old man still knew how to play the swells.

Close to the crescent of marsh and out of the big currents, the boat cut into rusty water topped with an engulfing stench like that of a steaming refinery. "What the hell," the old man yelled over the racket of the motor.

"Pa Claude, what's that stink?" The boy leaned over and saw a glossy slime.

"I don't know, baby. We run up on a little oil, I guess."

But as the skiff slid along, they saw they were going through a broad, deep pool of reddish crude that had blown against the shore and was turning the marsh grasses into tarred pretzels. They saw pelicans trembling along the bank like bronze ghosts. The slathered skiff seemed lost in a vast storage tank of crude oil thick as glue. Looking overboard, Claude saw that the engine's water pump was pulling pure oil and spitting it up in a fuming stench. He killed the outboard, fearing that the sea itself could erupt into flames.

"This must be some of that blown-up rig's stuff," the boy said.

"What? What rig? The steam plant by North Pass?" The old man was dizzy, afraid, and his mind suddenly went many years off track. To the east he saw more water than he remembered, open Gulf running all the way to the orange triangle at the eroded mouth of the river. He wondered what had happened to the land, its fish-filled inlets, the shrimp-spawning marsh, the oak groves, the hummocks overrun with white egrets, how a place that fed so richly whoever sailed through it could dissolve, history and church and graveyard and home.

They waited, the sun straight overhead; it was May, and the Louisiana heat was cooking the oil to fumes as the skiff stuck in place. After an hour the boy began to vomit overboard. Claude stuck his arm into the water and it came up covered with a black-and-red batter halfway to his elbow. The boy retched again, and the old man himself felt headspun and sick. He pulled the starter rope, figuring they should try for open water to the south. Doddering up to speed, the boat dragged through the oil until the bow suddenly rose up on, what, a thousand-year-old cypress stump, or one of a million abandoned pipelines? The hull ramped high and rolled off to the right, dumping Claude Ledet into the terrible slop, and as he went under, his mind came back to a splintered version of the present, and he knew at once that he had to get back to the surface because the boy, he felt sure, would jump in after him. A news account he'd read thirty years before suddenly bloomed into his head, of a grandfather and grandson gone fishing and not coming back at the appointed time, and when the sheriff's men dragged the canal the next morning, the hooks brought up together the grandfather and a four-year-old boy wrapped tightly in his arms. Sweet Jesus, the old man thought, give us a hand.

He twisted to get his bearings but could not tell up from down until he felt ten narrow fingers pulling on his arm and he knew with a pang that Jackie was in the water with him, driven by that blood-kin urge that nobody understands, but now the old man knew which way was up, so he spread his arms, cupped his hands, and pulled for the sky. He remembered not to take a breath too quickly once his head broke the surface. His great-grandson he knew to be a weak swimmer, and the boy had taken in a large amount of oil, now jetting from his nostrils as he coughed and spat. The old man took him by the collar and struggled fifty yards toward shore, slow as a giant water bug. Reaching his depth, he walked them in the rest of the way where they fell onto a thin shell reef and coughed and puked burning red streamers of oil until they were nearly unconscious with the strain of it. They sat like oiled birds and longed after the skiff, which had beached far across the open water. In another hour the boy began to cry that his skin was burning all over and he couldn't breathe. Claude had pulled his handkerchief and mopped the thickest sludge from Jackie's face and eyes, but the white skin itself would not come clean and kept the color of thin-smeared tar. The old man stood and walked off the ledge of shells into the grass, but all he could see was the great flat marsh spreading north. Miles away, a ship seemed to navigate on land as it followed the river toward the Gulf. A helicopter chopped over at two thousand feet. They would just have to wait.

Claude sat next to Jackie, but it hurt the boy to be touched, so the old man just watched and slept, dozing now and then, rousing with a start and forgetting what had happened, who this weeping person next to him was, why his own neck and back flamed and blistered. Around four o'clock they saw a sports fisherman, and Claude stood and waved his bony arms. They were taken into a smudged new boat and brought to the landing on the island, where an ambulance sped them up Highway 1 to the hospital. The old man spent one night there because it took that long for the nurses to scour him and test his blood over and over. Against all prohibitions he walked down the hall past the priest, through a crowd of relatives and friends, or people he guessed were such, to see Jackie, who was on a ventilator, his eyelids blue, his beanlike fingers cold. Claude waited long to see if the boy would at least open one eye to discover that his Pa Claude was in good shape. But he didn't. The nurses had cleaned Jackie up, but the smell of oil hung in the room like an unwelcome spirit.

A week later, the relatives took Claude's boat away from him, and then his car, which he had not driven in three years anyway. On a Tuesday he woke up and dressed for work at the fish plant, which had been closed twenty years, and his daughter had to tell him to go sit on the little porch and drink his coffee. He walked down to his wharf instead and stood at the very end, remarking to no one how the land had dissolved all around him just since yesterday. So much water and no place to go. He turned for a moment and saw his graying daughter seated on a rush chair on the porch, her head down in her hands.

An engine throbbed in his ears, and looking again at the water he saw his old uncle, Monsieur Abadie, from all the way over in Tiger Island, going out in his long skiff propelled by a one-cylinder inboard. On the north side of his uncle raced the freshly painted *Aztec,* the sailing lugger owned by the Czechs who lived on the river, and knifing between the boats, but coming in, was *The Two Sons,* its decks piled high with sacks of oysters, Jackie standing at the very bow, raising his arms and waving with big sweeps of his sun-brightened hands.

The Bug Man

*I*t was five o'clock and Felix Robichaux, the Bug Man, rolled up the long, paved drive that ran under the spreading live oaks of the Beauty Queen's house. He pulled a one-gallon tank from the bed of his little white truck and gave the pump handle five patient strokes. When a regular customer was not at home and the door was unlocked, the Bug Man was trusted to spray the house and leave the bill on the counter. Her gleaming sedan was in the drive, so he paused at the kitchen door and peered through the glass. A carafe of steaming coffee sat near the sink, so he knew Mrs. Malone was home from the office. When he tapped on the glass with the shiny brass tip of his spray wand, she appeared, blonde and handsome in her navy suit.

"Mr. Robichaux, I guess it's been a month? Good to see you." He always thought it funny that she called him *Mr.,* since he was five years younger, at thirty-one the most successful independent exterminator in Lafayette, Louisiana.

He gave her a wide smile. "You been doing all right?"

"You know me. Up's the same as down." She turned to place a few dishes in the sink. He remembered that a touch of sadness lingered around the edges of nearly everything she said, around the bits and pieces she had told him about herself over the years, about her dead husband. Why she told him things, the Bug Man was not sure. He had noticed that most of his customers eventually told him their life stories. He began to walk through the house, spraying a fine, accurate stream along the baseboards. He treated the windowsills, the dark crack behind the piano, her scented bathroom, the closets hung with cashmere and silk. Soon he was back in the kitchen, bending behind the refrigerator and under the sink.

"Would you like a cup of coffee?" she asked. Then, as he had done off and on for five years, he sat down with her at the walnut breakfast table and surveyed her fine backyard, which was planned more carefully than some people's lives, a yard of periwinkle beds skirting dark oaks, brick walks threading through bright, even St. Augustine, and in the center an empty cabana-covered pool. The Beauty Queen had been a widow for four years and had no children. He called her this because she had told him she once won a contest, he forgot which—Miss New Orleans, maybe. Each of his customers had a nickname he shared only with his wife, Clarisse, a short, pretty brunette who worked as a teacher's aide. She liked to be around children, since she couldn't have any of her own.

"Hey," he began, "have you seen any bugs since the last time?"

She turned three spoons of sugar into his cup and poured his cream. He stirred. "Just a couple around the counter."

"Little ones, big ones, or red ones?"

"Red ones, I think. Those are wood roaches, aren't they?" She looked at him with her clear, cornflower-blue eyes.

"They come from outside. I'll spray around the bottom of the house." He put a hairy arm on the table and raised the cup to his mouth, sipping slowly, inhaling the sweet vapor. "You don't have newspaper piled up anywhere, do you?"

She took a sip, leaving a touch of lipstick on the ivory cup. "I quit reading the newspaper. All the bad news bothers me more than it should."

Felix looked down into his coffee. He thought it a waste for such a fine woman to live an empty life. Clarisse, his wife, kept too busy to be sad, and she read every word in the newspaper, even police reports and the legals.

"I'd rather read sad stuff than nothing," he said.

She looked out the large bay window into one of her many oaks. When she turned her head, the natural highlights of her fine hair shimmered. "I watch TV, everybody's anesthesia. On my day off, I shop. More anesthesia." She glanced at him. "You've seen my closets."

He nodded. He had never seen so many shoes and dresses. He started to ask what she did with them all, since he guessed that she seldom went out, but he held back. He was not a friend. He was the Bug Man and knew his place.

In a few minutes he finished his coffee, thanked her, and moved outside, spraying under the deck, against the house, even around the pool, where he watched his reflection in a puddle at the deep end, his dark hair and eyes, his considerable shoulders rounding under his white knit shirt. He saw his paunch and laughed, thinking of his wife's supper. Turning for the house, he saw the Beauty Queen on her second cup, watching him in an uninterested way, as though he might be a marble statue at the edge of one of her walks. He was never offended by how she looked at him. The Bug Man lived in the modern world, where he knew most people were isolated and uncomfortable around those not exactly like themselves. He also believed there was a reason that people like Mrs. Malone opened the doors in their lives just a crack by telling him things. He was a religious man, so everything had a purpose, even though he had no idea what. The Beauty Queen's movements and words were signals to him, road signs pointing to his future.

After Mrs. Malone's came Felix's last job of the day, the Scalsons'; he had nicknamed them the Slugs. As the Bug Man, he had seen it all. Most customers let him wander unaccompanied in and out of every room in the house, through every attic and basement, as though he had no eyes. He had seen filthy sinks and cheesy bathrooms, teenagers shooting drugs, had sprayed around drunken grandfathers passed out on the floor, had once bumbled in on an old woman and a young boy having sex. They had looked at him as though he were a dog that had wandered into the room. He was the Bug Man. He was not after them.

Even so, he faced the monthly spraying of the Scalsons' peeling rental house with a queasy spirit. Father Slug met him at the door, red faced, a quart bottle of beer in his hand. "Come on in, Frenchie. I hope you got some DDT in that tank. The sons of bitches come back a week after you sprayed last time."

"I'll give it an extra squeeze," Felix told him. But he knew the entire house would have to be immersed in a tank of Spectracide to get rid of the many insects crawling over the oily paper bags of garbage stacked around the stove. When he opened the door under the sink, the darkness writhed with German roaches.

He finished with the kitchen, then walked into the cheaply paneled living room, where Mr. Scalson was arguing with a teenage son, Bruce.

"It wont my fault," the son screamed.

Mr. Scalson grabbed the boy's neck with one of his big rubbery hands and slapped him so hard with the other that his son's nose began to bleed. "You shoulda never been born, you little shit."

Felix sprayed around them as though they were a couple of chairs and went on. Glancing out the window he saw Mrs. Scalson burning a pile of dirty disposable diapers in the backyard, stirring them with a stick. In an upstairs bedroom, he found the round-shouldered daughter playing a murderous video game on an old television surrounded by half-eaten sandwiches and bowls of wilted cereal. In another room, the sour-smelling grandfather was watching a pornographic movie while drinking hot shots of supermarket bourbon.

The tragedy of the Scalsons was that they didn't have to be what they were. The grandfather and father held decent jobs in the oil fields. Their high school diplomas hung in the den. Yet the only thing the Bug Man ever saw them do was argue and then sulk in their rooms, waiting like garden slugs dreaming of flowers to kill.

Felix Robichaux lived on what was left of the family homestead outside of Lafayette. The white frame house was situated a hundred yards off the highway, one big pecan tree in front and a live oak out back between the house and barn. Rafts of trimmed azaleas floated on a flat lake of grass. He thought the shrubs looked like circles of children gossiping at recess. He ate his wife's supper, a smoky chicken stew, and helped her clear the dishes from the Formica table. While she washed them under a noisy cloud of steam, he swept the tile floor and put away the spices. Then they went out on the front porch and sat on the yellow spring-iron chairs that had belonged to his father.

Clarisse and Felix lived like a couple whose children had grown and moved out. They felt accused by the absence of children, by their idleness in the afternoons when they felt they should be tending to homework or helping at play. They had tried for all their married life, ten years, had gone to doctors as far away as Houston, and still their extra bedrooms stayed empty, their nights free of the fretful, harmless sobs of infants. They owned a big Ford sedan, which felt vacant when they drove through the countryside on weekends. They were short, small-boned people, so even their new motorboat seemed too large the day they first anchored in a bayou to catch bream and talk about where their lives were going. Overhead, silvery baby egrets perched in the branches of a bald cypress, and minnows flashed in the dark current sliding around the boat's hull like time.

From the porch Clarisse stared at the pecans forming in the tree in their front yard. She slowly ran her white fingers through the dark curls at the back of her neck. Felix watched her pretty eyes, which were almost violet in the late-afternoon light, and guessed at what she would say next. She asked him whose house he had sprayed first, and he laughed.

"I started out with Boat Man."

"That's Melvin Laurent. A newer one?"

He nodded. "Then Fish, Little Man, Mr. Railroad, the Termite Twins." He stared high into the pecan tree and flicked a finger up for each name. "Beauty Queen and the Slugs."

She put a hand on his arm. "You ought to call them Beauty Queen and the Beasts," she said.

"I spray the Beasts tomorrow."

She laughed, a tinkling sound. "That's right." Clarisse crossed her slim legs and held up a shoe to examine the toe. "It's too bad Mrs. Malone doesn't get married again. Just from the couple times I saw her working down at the bank, I could tell she's got a lot to offer."

Felix pursed his lips. "Yeah, but she needs a lot, too. You ought to hear all the droopy-drawers talk she lays out in the afternoon. Everything's sad with her, everything gets her down. She lost too much when her husband got killed." He thought of the Beauty Queen's eyes and what they might tell him.

"You think she's good-looking still?"

"Talk about."

She stared off at the highway, where a truck full of hay grumbled toward the west. "Too bad we can't fix her up with somebody."

He rolled his eyes at her and put his hand on hers. "We don't know the kind of people she needs. What, you gonna get her a date with Cousin Ted?"

"Get off your high horse. Ted's all right since he's going to AA and got his shrimp boat back from the finance company." She pulled her hand away. "I could call names on your side, too."

As the lawn disappeared in shadow, they brewed up a playful argument until the mosquitoes drove them inside, where their good cheer subsided in the emptiness of the house.

For the rest of the month he sprayed his way through the homes of the parish, getting the bugs out of the lives of people who paid him no more attention than they would a housefly, and on the thirty-first, in the subdivision where the Beauty Queen lived, he visited a new customer, a divorced lawyer named McCall. Even though it was his first time spraying there, Felix was left alone by the tall, athletic attorney, who let him wander at will through the big house he had leased. Felix took his time in the living room so he could watch McCall and size him up. He sprayed in little spurts and stopped several times to pump up. The lawyer smiled at him and asked if he followed pro football.

"Oh yeah," the Bug Man said. "I been following the poor Saints since day one."

The other man laughed. "Me too. You know, I handled a case for a Saints player once. He sued a fan who came into the stadium tunnel after a game and bit him on the arm."

"No kidding?" Felix was fascinated by the story of a human insect, a biting football fan. He stayed a half hour and drank a beer with Dave McCall, discovering where he was from, what he did for fun, what he didn't do. After all, why wouldn't the lawyer tell him things? He was someone who might not ever come around again. In his invisibility he listened for things that might have significance.

"You should meet Mrs. Malone," he found himself saying. He had no idea why he said this, but it was as if a little blue spark popped behind his eyes and the sentence came out by itself, appearing like a letter with no return address. "She's a former beauty queen and a real nice lady." The lawyer smiled, seeming to think, What a friendly, mean-ingless offering. His smile was full and shining with tolerance, and Felix endured it, knowing he had done something important, had planted a seed, maybe.

On the fifteenth, he watered that seed when he had coffee with Mrs. Malone. She seemed empty, gray around the eyes, offering him only a demitasse, as though trying to hurry him off, though she was not brusque or distant.

"You know," he began, delivering his rehearsed words carefully, "you ought to get out more."

She showed him a slim line of wonderful teeth. "I guess I do what I can."

He took a sip of coffee. "There's a single man your age who just moved in down the street. I met him the other day and he hit me as being a nice guy. He's a lawyer."

"Are lawyers nice guys, Mr. Robichaux?"

The question derailed his train of thought. "Well, not all of them. But you know . . . uh, what was I talking about?"

"A new man in the neighborhood."

"Single man." He had run out of coffee; he tilted his cup to stare into it and then looked at the carafe. She poured him another sip. "I sprayed Buffa—I mean, Mrs. Boudreaux—this morning, and she said there was gonna be a neighborhood party at the Jeansonnes' tomorrow. This guy's supposed to be there."

"So you think I should check him out?" She wiggled her shoulders when she said this, and Felix worried that she was making fun of him.

"He's an awful nice man. Good-lookin', as far as I can tell."

"Would your wife, Clarisse, think he was good-looking?"

He bit his lip at that. "Clarisse thinks *I'm* good-looking," he said at last, and the Beauty Queen laughed.

That night Clarisse and Felix sat on their porch and listened to the metallic keening of tree frogs. The neighbors had just gone home with their two young children, and Felix put his hand on a damp spot near his collar where the baby had drooled. He caught the cloth between his fingers and held it as though it contained meaning. Clarisse sat with her left arm across her chest and her right fist on her lips. "If we had had a little girl, I wonder who she would've looked like."

"Dark, curly hair and eyes deep like a well," he said. The frogs in the yard subsided as he spoke. They sometimes did that, as though wanting to listen.

After a long while she said, "Too bad," a comment that could have been about a thousand different things. One by one the frogs commenced their signals, and the moon came out from behind a cloud like a bright thought. Across the road a door opened and a mother's voice sang through the silvery light, spilling onto the lawn a two-note call— "Ke-vin"—playful but strong, and then, "Come out of the dark. You've got to come out of that dark."

The next week he showed up off-schedule at Mrs. Malone's house, later than usual, and found her in the backyard looking at the empty pool.

"Since the weather's been so damp, I thought I'd give a few sprays around while I was in the neighborhood."

She nodded at him as he walked by her and began squirting the cracks in the pool apron. "I appreciate the service," she told him, a hint of something glad lingering around her mouth.

"Uh, you been goin' out any? You know, chase the blues away?" He drew a circle in the air as if to circumscribe the blues.

"Thinking about it," she said, hiding her mouth behind a pale ringless hand.

"Yeah, but don't think too long," he said. "Might be time to check it out." He wiggled his shoulders and blushed. The Beauty Queen bit a nail and turned her back on him slowly.

When he sprayed the lawyer's house, he spent an hour with him, marveling at both Mr. McCall's charm and two bottles of imported beer.

Three weeks later the Bug Man went down to LaBat's Lounge after supper. As he was driving down Perrilloux Street, he passed the Coachman Restaurant, an expensive steak house. He saw a BMW parked at the curb, and sweeping out of it smoothly were the long legs of Mrs. Malone. The lawyer was holding her door and looking like he had been cut with scissors out of a men's fashion magazine. In the short time he had to look, Felix strained to see her face. It was full of light, and the Beauty Queen was smiling, all unpleasant thoughts hidden for the night, at least. Her blonde hair spilled over her dark dress, and at her throat was a rill of pearls. The Bug Man drove on, watching them in his rearview as they entered the restaurant's brass doorway. When he reached LaBat's old plywood barroom, he drank a Tom Collins instead of a beer, lost three dollars in the poker machine, won four in a game of pool with two cousins from Grand Crapaud, and for the rest of the night celebrated his luck.

The next day was the fifteenth, and Mrs. Malone served him coffee and no sad talk, but not one morsel of what was going on between her and the lawyer. And the Bug Man could not ask. He was satisfied with the big cup of strong coffee she fixed for him and the sight of the new makeup containers on the vanity in her bedroom. He finished his work carefully and went to spray the next customer. Even the visible stench of the Slugs' bathrooms could not dampen a deep, subtle excitement Felix felt, almost the hopeful anticipation a farmer feels after planting, a patient desire for a green future.

Mr. and Mrs. Scalson were having an argument as Felix was trying to spray the kitchen. She got her husband down on the floor and beat at him with a flat-heeled shoe. Her lip was split and her brows and cheeks were curdled and swollen. Mr. Scalson broke away from her, grabbed a pot of collard greens from the stove, and slung it, splashing her on the legs. The screaming was a worse pollutant than all the rotten food stacked against the stove. Felix watched the greens fly across the floor, the water spattering the cabinets, a hunk of salt meat coming to rest under the table, where he knew it would stay for a week. Their young daughter ran into the kitchen, a headset tangled in her hair, and began pulling ice from the refrigerator for her mother's burns. The Bug Man left without waiting to be paid, jogging down the drive toward his scoured and shiny white truck.

The summer months rolled into August, and Felix Robichaux mixed his mild, subtle concoctions, spraying them around the parish in the homes of good people and bad, talking to them all, drinking their coffee, and seeing into private lives like the eye of God, judging but invisible. He began using a new mixture that was nearly odorless and, unlike the old formula, left no cloudy spots or drips, and now there was even less evidence that he had passed through these people's lives, which bothered him a bit, because everyone wants to leave something of themselves behind, more, anyway, than an empty coffee cup and a bill.

He became even more curious about Mrs. Malone, and during one visit he stepped over the implied boundary between them by asking about Mr. McCall with a directness that made her eyes flick up at him. There was no doubt that for weeks she had been happy, asking about Clarisse, telling him about plans for putting her pool back in service, since she'd found out that the lawyer liked to swim.

But suddenly there was a change. In mid-August she let him in without speaking, going to the sink and doing dishes left over from the day before. While he was spraying the living room, he heard her gasp and drop one of her Doulton plates to the tile floor. He put his face in the kitchen doorway and said, "Let me clean that up for you. I know where the dustpan's at."

"Thank you. I'm a bit shaky today." Her color was good, he noticed, but there was a worried cast to her usually direct, clear eyes. He knelt and carefully swept the fragments into a dustpan then wet a paper towel and patted the floor for splinters of china.

"You want me to make you some coffee?" he asked.

She put her head down a bit and shaded her eyes. "Yes," she said.

The Bug Man set up the coffeemaker, then sprayed the rest of the house while the machine dripped a full pot. When he came back, she had not moved. He knew where the cups and the spoons were in dozens of houses, and the first cabinet he opened showed him what he wanted. "What's gone wrong?" he asked, pouring her a cup and taking his seat.

"Oh, it's nothing. I'm just not myself today." She crossed her legs slowly and pulled at her navy skirt.

"Mr. McCall been around?"

"Mr. McCall has *not* been around," she said sharply. "And he tells me he never will be."

The Bug Man shook his head slowly. Mrs. Malone and the lawyer looked like the elegant, glittering stars on the soap operas his mother watched, people he could never figure out. He was not an educated man and had never set foot in a country club unless it was having a roach problem, but he guessed that many wealthy people were complicated and refined, qualities that made it harder for them to be happy. But he had no notion of why this was so. He thought of Clarisse and felt lucky. "I'm sorry to hear that" was all he could think of to say. "I thought you two were hitting it off real good."

The Beauty Queen then grabbed a napkin from the table and began crying.

Embarrassed, he looked around the kitchen, raised his hands, then dropped them.

"Yes," she said, and then looked at him with such intensity that he glanced away. He could have sworn that she really *saw* him. "We've been hitting it off very well. I thought David was a little like my late husband." She looked toward the backyard, but her gaze seemed to waver. "I thought he was a man who carried things through."

"Aw, Mrs. Malone, these things have a way of working out, you know?"

"I'm pregnant," she told him. "And David wants nothing to do with me."

Felix took a swallow of hot coffee, opened his mouth to say something, but his mind was blasted clean by what she had told him. A light seemed to come on in the back of his head. "What are you going to do?" he said at last.

"I'm not sure, exactly." She narrowed her gaze and watched him carefully. "Why?" He scooted his chair back and ran his left hand down his white uniform shirt, his fingers pausing just a second on the green embroidery of his last name.

"I mean, do you think you'll keep it, or give it up for adoption?" His eyes grew wide and he slid his round bottom to the edge of the chair.

Her voice chilled a bit with suspicion. "I shouldn't be discussing this with you." She looked down at the glossy floor.

"Mrs. Malone, Clarisse and me, we've been trying for years to have a baby, and if you're going to give up the one you got, we'd be happy to get it, let me tell you." The Bug Man was blushing as he said this, as though he were trying to be intimate and had no idea how to proceed.

The Beauty Queen straightened up in her chair. "We're not talking about a cast-off sofa here, Mr. Robichaux."

"Mrs. Malone, don't get mad. You know I'm just a bug man and can't talk like a lawyer or a businessman." He opened his thick palms toward her. "Just think about it, that's all."

She stood and pulled the door open for him, and he picked up his tank and walked outside. "I'll see you in a month," she said. When she closed the door, the smell of her exquisite perfume fanned onto the stoop. For a moment, it overcame the smell of bug spray in Felix's clothes.

For the next month he made his rounds with a secretive lightness of spirit, not telling Clarisse anything, though it was hard in the evenings not to explain why he held her hand with a more ardent claim, why he would suddenly spring up and walk to the edge of the porch to look in the yard for something, maybe a good place to put a swing set. The closer the days wound down to the fifteenth of the month, the more hopeful and fearful he became. When he sprayed the lawyer's house, McCall let him in without looking at him, disappearing into the garage, leaving him alone in the expensive, empty house. The Bug Man decided to name him Judas.

Finally, at a little before five on the fifteenth, the Beauty Queen let him in, and he went about his business quickly, finishing as usual by spraying under the kitchen sink. He noticed that she had not made coffee. He looked for her in the hall and in the living room, retracing his route, giving embarrassed little shots into corners as though he were going over a poor job. He found her in the bedroom, with her back against the headboard, reading a book.

"I left a check for you on the counter," she said.

"I saw it. How you doin', Mrs. Malone?"

"I'm fine." But the stiffness of her mouth and the deep-set hurt in her eyes said otherwise. She rested the book on top of her dress, a dark print with lilies against a black background. "Is there something you forgot to spray?"

"Yes, ma'am. Usually I mist under your bed. Every now and then you leave a snack plate and a glass under the edge." He got down on his knees, adjusted the nozzle of his wand, and sprayed. "You decided what to do about the baby yet?" He wondered if she sensed the wide gulf of anticipation behind the question.

"I'm having an abortion tomorrow," she said at once, as though she were reading a sentence from the book in her lap.

His thumb slipped off the lever and he froze on his knees at the foot of her bed. "It would be such a fine baby," he said, straightening his back and staring at her across a quilted cover. "You, a beauty-contest winner, and him, a good-looking lawyer. What a baby that would make." He began to say things that made his face burn, and he felt like a child who had set his heart on something, only to be told that he could never have what he wanted. "Clarisse would be so happy," he said, trying to smile.

Mrs. Malone drew up her legs and glared at him. "Mr. Robichaux, what would you do with such a baby? It wouldn't be like you and Clarisse. It would look nothing like you."

He stayed on his knees and watched her, wondering if she had planned out everything she was saying. He reflected on the meanness of the world and how for the first time he was unable to deal with it. "It'd mean a lot to us" was all he could tell her.

"It would be cruel to give this child to you. Why can't you see that?" For a moment her face possessed the blank disdain of a marble statue in her backyard. "Would you please just get out," she said, looking down at her book and balling a fist against her forehead.

The Bug Man left the house, forgetting to close the door, feeling his good nature bleed away until he was as hollow as a termite-eaten beam. In twenty minutes, as he pulled into the littered drive of the Scalsons', his feelings had not improved. He was late, and the Slugs were seated at their hacked table arguing bitterly over pieces of fried chicken. Felix stood in the door, pumping up his tank, looking into the yellowed room at the water-stained ceiling, the spattered walls, the torn and muddy linoleum, the unwashed and squalling Scalsons. The grandfather dug through the pile of chicken, cursing the children for eating the livers.

The mother was pulling the skins off every piece and piling them on her plate while the children gave each other greasy slaps. They tore at their food like yard animals, spilling flakes of crust and splashes of slaw under the table. "Gimme a wing, you little son of a bitch," Mr. Scalson growled to his son.

"It doesn't have to be like this," Felix said, and everyone turned, noticing him for the first time.

"Well, I'll be damned. It's the Frenchman. You must have water in that tank of yours, because the bugs have been all over us the past month. What'd I pay you good money for anyway, shorty?"

Ever since he had opened the door the Bug Man had been pumping his tank, five, ten, twenty strokes. He adjusted the nozzle to deliver a sharp stream, pressed the lever, and peeled back Mr. Scalson's left eyelid. The heavy man let out a yell and Felix began drilling them all with streams of roach killer—in their faces, across their chests, the grandfather in the mouth. The family sat stupidly for several moments, sputtering and calling out when they were sprayed again in the eyes as though being washed clean of some foul blindness. One by one the Scalsons scampered to their feet. The father swung at the Bug Man, who ducked and then cracked him across the nose with his spray wand. When the grandfather came at him with an upraised chair, he snapped the brass wand across the top of his head, leaving a red split in the hairless meat on his skull.

*T*he next evening the weather was mild, and at dusk Felix and Clarisse were sitting in the yellow spring-iron chairs, whose backs were flattened metal flowers. He had told her everything, and together they were staring at a few late fireflies winking on the lawn like the intermittent hopes of defeated people. Across the road a mother called her child for the second time, and they watched him bob up out of a field.

In the house the telephone rang, and Felix got up slowly. It was Mrs. Malone, and she sounded upset.

"What can I do for you?" he asked. He twisted the phone cord around his fist and closed his eyes.

"I was in the clinic's waiting room this afternoon," she began, her voice stiff and anesthetized, "and I read the local paper's account of the attack."

He winced when she said "attack" and stared down at the dustless hardwood of his living room. "I'm real sorry about that." He thought of the expression on his wife's face when she had brought the money for his bail.

"And you did it right after you left my house," she said, her voice rising. "I didn't know what to think."

"Yes, ma'am." He listened to her breaths coming raggedly over the phone for at least a half minute, but he didn't know what else to say. He wasn't sure why he had hurt the Scalsons. At the time, he had wanted only to keep them from damaging the world further.

"I don't want you to work for me anymore. I just can't have you in the house."

"I wouldn't bother you again, Mrs. Malone."

"No." The word came back quick as a shot. "You'll stay away."

And that was it.

The Bug Man went back to his work at dawn, and for that day and every workday for the next ten years he walked through houses and lives. His business expanded until he had to hire three easygoing local men to spray bugs with him. He erected a small building with a storage area and office, hiring a young woman to manage appointments and payments. Clarisse attended the local college, became a first-grade teacher, and labored in her garden of children. In his spare time he began attending a local exercise club and soon lost his bulky middle, though much of his hair left with it.

Felix had been thirty-seven when the other independent exterminator in town decided to sell the business to him. These new routes were profitable, and Joe Brasseaux, Felix's best sprayer, tended them religiously, never missing an appointment for two years, except for one day when he called in sick. Felix looked over Joe's route for the afternoon, and when he saw the addresses, he decided to treat the houses himself.

About four o'clock, he pulled into the long drive that led to the Beauty Queen's house. Getting out of the truck, he looked up at the oaks, which had changed little, and at the pool in back, which swirled with bright water. The plantings were mature and lush, rolling green shoulders of liriope bordering everything.

The driveway was empty, but in the door was a key with a pair of small plastic dice hanging from it. He rang the bell and bent down to pump up his tank. When the door opened, he looked up, and standing there was a young boy with sandy hair, blue eyes, a dimpled chin, an open, intelligent face and, Felix noticed, big feet.

"Yes, sir?" the child said, adjusting the waistband on what appeared to be a soccer uniform.

For a moment Felix couldn't speak. He wanted to reach out and feel the top of the boy's head, but he pointed to his tank instead. "I've come to spray for bugs."

"Where's Joe? Joe's the one takes care of that for us."

The Bug Man looked inside hopefully. "Is your mother Mrs. Malone?"

"She's not here. And I'm sorry, but she told me not to let in anyone I don't know." The boy must have noticed how Felix was staring, and stepped back.

"You don't have to be afraid of me." Felix gave him his widest smile, all the while studying the child. "I'm the Bug Man."

The boy narrowed his bright eyes. "No sir. Not to me you aren't. You'd better go away."

At once he felt shriveled and sick, like a sprayed insect, and wondered whether he should tell the boy that he knew his mother, that he knew who he was, but the Bug Man was by now a veteran of missed connections and could tell when a train had left the station without him. He scanned the child once more and turned away.

Pulling out of the drive, he saw in the rearview a small fair-skinned figure standing on the steps, looking after him, but not really seeing him, he guessed. He allowed himself this one glance. One glance, he decided, was what he could have.

Wings

Marissa was a member of a small accounting firm, a short woman with straight black hair falling only to her chin, and dark, terrier eyes. It was now a week since her husband had been buried, a Saturday, and she examined the contents of his workbench for only a moment before raking all of it into a trash can. There were a few tools she had no use for and some rusty gizmo he'd been tinkering with the day he had a heart attack. He owned so much stuff, and not much of it fit onto her balance sheet.

Later, she walked into the backyard and glanced around at the too-tall carpet grass and shaggy boxwoods waiting to be trimmed, their gardener lying across town working a lawn from the underside. She bent down and pulled a single weed, unable to think of what to do with it.

Her cell phone rang and it was Alice, the retired and disabled flight attendant who lived across the street. She said how sorry she was to hear about Brad's death and then seemed to run out of things to say. She ended the brief conversation by reminding Marissa that she'd left her garage door open. Alice wasn't really disabled, but Marissa liked to think of her that way. She had a barely noticeable limp.

"Garage?"

"I hate to be a nag, but your whole house looks so much nicer with that broad door closed. It's why the subdivision made the rule, Marissa."

"I guess I left it open when I put the car up." She was generally polite to the woman across the street, a once willowy beauty with whom she had nothing in common, especially once willowy beauty.

Alice had lived over there at least twenty years, a widow, still single and good-looking, though going gray and soft around the edges. When asked, she would say she'd been a stewardess, using the old term as if to freeze herself in a younger time. She sported through the neighborhood in her little red Mercedes, driving more carefully each year. The summer Marissa and her husband had moved to Green Oak subdivision, Alice seemed to flirt with him at a newcomers' party, and Marissa felt like throwing her Bloody Mary into her lap.

"Oh, and I wanted to tell you I was so sorry I couldn't come to the funeral."

Marissa's little mouth grew smaller. "But mainly you wanted me to hide the plastic junk in my garage, right? That's more important than a dead husband."

There was a little gasp on the other end of the line. "I'm sorry. I shouldn't have mentioned it. You know—"

Marissa hung up, angry with herself for being angry. Alice, after all, was like most of her neighbors in the subdivision, people who would mail a personal note about a peeling board on the side of a house, but not about a wedding or funeral. She didn't know much about her, having chosen to avoid the wide lake of her beautiful presence whenever she'd come over to ask Brad a question.

She dropped the weed she was holding on the lawn. What would be the point of losing patience with everyone? Someday she might need help, since she was alone now; her daughter, who was in graduate school, had left an hour before, desperate to get back to her library carrel.

She went in and rang the office to say she would show up Monday morning to deal with the tax accounts, but it was May, and taxes were no longer a burning issue. In the kitchen she sat and stared across the breakfast table at her husband's chair. The one next to it was missing a screw. She saw a phantom Brad bent over it with a screwdriver, so she got up, grabbed her purse, and walked through the house quickly, past his engineering degree hanging on the wall, past her daughter's graduation photo, heading for the garage.

She found Alice waiting for her, standing under the big open door, and just for an instant Marissa wished she had the remote control in her hand.

Alice folded her arms and said, "Look, I know I seem a bitch about this door thing. I know it."

Marissa stepped back. The other woman had seldom come across the street to talk to her directly. Her husband had been another matter, and Alice was always plying him with questions about lawn plants and air conditioner maintenance. "I was just going to bring the door down."

"And I know I should've come to the funeral, but I just can't take them. I went to my father's last year, and it almost killed me."

She knew that Alice had been to one other burial, her husband's. He'd been an airlines pilot. Marissa had never known the man who went down in a wind-shear accident somewhere over Iowa with forty-seven passengers, but she thought she would have liked him if for nothing else than his last words, picked up by the cockpit's voice recorder: "Oh, well . . ."

She stepped around Alice to make sure her Lexus was clear and then noticed that her husband's shiny pickup wasn't all the way in. Fishing keys out of her purse, she walked over and sat in the truck's leather seats, pausing now, for what, she wasn't sure, maybe a whiff of him, some residual touch from his fingers. She ran a palm slowly over the arc of the steering wheel. Alice walked up to stand at the open window. "You should go for a long drive." The statement sounded as though there was some experience behind it.

"You think?" She stared straight over the hood.

"Yeah." She crinkled her nose. "Sadness is kind of like cigarette smoke that sticks in your clothes. Air it out. Lose it."

Marissa studied the tall woman in the smart peach sundress. What right did she have to look so good at midday in this Louisiana humidity? "There's a lot to lose."

"I know it."

"He didn't pay much attention to me. Just his tools and his toys."

Alice bit her lip for a moment. "He had a lot of them, all right."

"Yes. Well, here I go."

Alice didn't step back from the window. She seemed to be waiting for something. "Where are you going?"

"I don't know. Maybe just down the road for ten minutes and back." She put a hand on the shift lever.

"Oh. Can I come along?"

It would have been rude but understandable to say no, and Marissa opened her mouth to do just that, but instead the word *okay* came out of her mouth, startling the both of them. She had no idea where the word came from and was reminded of the time her English teacher gave her the assignment to write a poem, something she'd never done before or since. She remembered sitting in front of her old Apple word processor and staring as letters formed on the screen like ants in a line. It was a poem about shades of light in her empty campus mailbox. When she finished, she had absolutely no clue where the words had come from.

Alice's eyes widened and she gave her long hair a toss. "Pull over to my drive while I get my purse."

Marissa backed into the street, considered pulling the remote out of the glove box to close the garage, but didn't, finally moving across the way to pick up Alice. She glanced at her ice-blue eyes and wondered what her neighbor was thinking, but she was unreadable, just like a stewardess walking a plane's aisle during a thunderstorm.

Marissa turned right toward the subdivision's wisteria-haunted guardhouse and rolled through onto the bright, open highway beyond. She would drive west for a bit, that's all, and think about what to do with Brad's things. He was a collector, and in the attic display room were arrays of metal toys as old as a hundred years, antique guns, porcelain store signs, not to mention walls of tools—a lifetime of bought history. Brad had trained in the knowledge of objects, dragging her along on forays into antique shops and flea markets all their married life. She never understood what he'd seen in any of it, though he'd tried to explain why he'd chosen this truck or that sign, and why it was important to preserve them. Even the toys were forms of art, he'd told her. Now, who could tell her how to get rid of it all? She gave Alice a sudden look of appraisal. "Did my husband ever talk to you about his collecting?"

Alice stared ahead down the sun-crazed road and waited a moment before answering. "He was in the garage working on a little toy gas tanker once and said he had a lot more. He took me upstairs and showed me about twenty Texaco trucks from different eras."

Marissa pictured the little wheeled city of painted steel vehicles in the attic, the miniature running boards and radiator cowlings limed with dust. "I don't know how I'm going to get rid of it. If it was up to me, I'd throw it all out. But my daughter called an appraiser to come over and look at it."

"I'm not surprised she's not interested in that stuff either. It's a man's thing, gathering piles of iron or brass. Hard stuff, mostly. Coins, antique barbed wire. Stuff with an edge. They compete with one another for it."

Marissa sped around a pickup with two expensive motorcycles tethered in its bed. She looked over at the man and woman in the cab, who both waved at her. "Your better half, what did he collect?"

Alice seemed a bit startled at the question. "Nothing." She turned her face away. "He never made it to that stage. It took me maybe ninety minutes to clean out everything he owned."

The new crew-cab truck rode like an old lady's sedan, its cushioned motion carrying Marissa's spirit along and up, promising some vague escape or roadside vision that might hint at why her husband had to die in his early fifties. She drove to the first little town and was over its bridge and into the woods beyond so quickly she couldn't remember if she'd driven through at all. "How much time do you have to spare?" she asked. "This feels better than I thought it would."

Alice shook out her hair and put on white-framed sunglasses. She looked fresh. "Whatever. I'm the retired one. I've got the obligations of a preschooler. Brad used to tell me how envious he was."

Marissa tightened her grip on the wheel as she swung up the on-ramp to the westbound interstate, and said nothing until twenty miles later, when the next hamlet, Pine Oil, came and went. Then she asked what she should do with Brad's suits.

"I gave my husband's to Goodwill. It felt odd, but that's what I did."

Marissa nodded. "I was moving one of Brad's this morning. I felt for him inside a sleeve. Isn't that pathetic?"

Alice gave her a worried glance. "How far are we going?"

"Baton Rouge is only forty minutes farther. There's a store in the new mall that carries really comfortable retro shoes, kind of like Peter Fox pumps."

Alice remained silent, so Marissa drove on, reluctantly grateful for the company. Already she had noticed that Alice knew when and when not to talk.

But by the time she saw the light standards of the mall south of the interstate, she was seduced by the smooth current of traffic and remembered the snarled, glaring parking lots. She raced past the exit, the truck swinging around a cloverleaf like a bug caught in a whirlpool.

Alice glanced at her watch. "You're kidnapping me."

"I don't know where I'm going," she cried. "I thought I wanted some shoes."

"It's all right. Calm down. You know, they sell those same shoes at the big flea market down Airline Highway a few miles. Seconds, but you can't tell." She tilted her head and looked at Marissa. "Quarter-price, sometimes."

"Oh, I don't know."

"Well, we've got to go somewhere."

On an overpass they rode above the boiling exhausts of a smoking tanker truck, and Marissa felt a quick lightness in her stomach, as though she were escaping all forty-six years of her life. She hoped that if someone curious to see what grief was like rang her doorbell tomorrow, no one would be there to answer.

She followed Alice's directions. Five miles south of Baton Rouge, she was in a new country. "What say we stay out as long as we can stand it?"

Alice bent forward and studied her eyes a long moment. "You're all right?"

"Yes."

She folded her arms. "Well, no one's exactly holding their breath for us to come home."

Marissa considered the statement and then accelerated, glad she'd left her garage door wide, her wastebaskets, hose racks, and other plastic sins plain and bright for her neighbors to gape at in despair. The subdivision had so many rules, and Brad had followed every one, swept the pine straw off the roof, avoided putting up a Christmas decoration that was over forty-eight inches tall, bought only apple-green trash cans.

She stole a glance at Alice, whose pretty face was holding that unreadable stewardess expression she must have habitually turned on a cabin full of passengers intent on seeing in her features the meaning of the sudden plunge in altitude, the sickening lurch.

They came at last to the sprawling flea market, a series of long, open-sided sheds scintillating under the sun. The parking lot was a long plane of clamshells, and Marissa charged through its bleached light while collarless dogs swirled in the dust spooling behind the truck.

They stopped next to a dealer selling antiques, tools, and what appeared to be stolen highway signs. Right in front of them was a dented six-foot green panel proclaiming S H R E V E P O R T.

Alice gave out a short, bitter laugh and said, "I crashed there once."

"What?"

"At the airport. One of my first flights ever. I was working for Mid-South Lines and we came down with no landing gear in the last DC-6 in commercial service anywhere." She put a hand to her throat.

"Were you hurt?"

"It was a *crash*, Marissa. We skidded into a hangar, knocked the place down, and blew up. The blast killed the copilot and ten passengers. Hell yes I was hurt. My pelvis was crushed and everything inside as well."

Marissa put the truck in park and stared at the road sign. "My God, how did you keep flying after that?"

Alice looked her in the eye. "The pilot and I were in the same little hospital for a month, and that's the man I married. He said there was no way one of us would ever get killed in a plane crash. It would be celestial double jeopardy. That's what he said. It was like we were insured against disaster." She popped her door open. "He was a super guy but not much of a fortune-teller."

"I'm sorry I never knew your husband." She wondered if he and Brad would have become friends, would have talked about cars and planes, gone swimming. "How long has it been since you lost him?"

"Twenty years, nine months." Alice stood in the clamshells and straightened her sundress. "Two weeks, two days." She looked at her watch and said quietly, "Fourteen hours, fifteen minutes, and nine seconds."

·   ·   ·

*T*hey found that every flat space was covered with old dresses, new wrenches, Navaho blankets, guitars, stuffed elk heads, gold chains, perfumes, rings, incense, dead batteries, and live ducks.

"This is some place," Alice said. "These pickers come from as far away as Colorado. Let's start walking. The shoe man is around here somewhere."

"I don't know. It's pretty hot." Marissa put a hand up to shade her eyes.

Alice tugged at her arm and pointed. "Those shoes are way at the end of this shed, I think. I see something down at the other end I want to check out first. I'll catch up with you." They walked in opposite directions, Marissa through rafts of shotguns, hand tools, shiny table lamps, wagon wheels, truck fenders, and corroded oscillating fans. Alice limped toward bright racks of formal clothing, price tags spinning from sleeves in the hot wind like tethered butterflies.

Marissa approached a table and picked up a toy metal sedan and had the momentary urge to call her husband about it. Then she put it down, wondering, if he were still alive and she'd bought this for him, would it have carried any meaning for him? Under the table, listing on an army blanket, a leprous metal clock shaped like a horse looked up at her with coppery eyes, and she remembered an identical monstrosity on her dead uncle's mantel along with other glinting knickknacks—a brass paperweight shaped like the Empire State Building, a tiny ceramic hula girl with a real grass skirt. He'd offered it to her when she was six or seven, but Marissa had just shrugged, looked blankly at him, and said no thank you. She couldn't remember when he'd died. George was his name, and his trinkets were sold to the four winds. She suddenly felt that the old man was like one of her favorite books that her mother had thrown away. She missed it years later with a sense of violation, of theft. She walked on, considering the value of keeping objects that belonged to dead people. Maybe some were links to the self, keeping the former owners, who'd formed her in small ways and large, tacked onto her history. She looked ahead at the many thousands of orphaned items. "Oh, boy," she sighed.

She searched her way down to a table of stout, elegant shoes, new stock, still in original boxes. They were pliant yet substantial in her hands, so she slipped on a pair of navy-and-cream spectator pumps and knew at once that she could stand for days in the things, could float down the long halls of the office. She paid for the shoes and stepped out into a grassy field, the pumps in a box under her arm, and spotted a Gibson guitar exactly like the one Brad kept in the attic and, farther on, a Communion dress like her grandmother's, an Allis-Chalmers tractor like her grandfather's. She kept walking through disparate items large and small washed up into the sprawling market from estate sales and attic cleanings all over America, a tide of obsolete loot showing the conscious choices of dead people, their green glass teacups, black ceramic panthers, bulbous aluminum coffeemakers, and inlaid wooden clocks, all their treasures and tastes dragged down to Louisiana and spread out like a big incoherent novel that mocked what people both cherished and needed. Marissa walked on through so much merchandise she became lost and had to stop at a booth selling neckties to ask directions.

Heading back to her truck she saw, through the abraded Lexan of a shallow display case, a pair of metal flight attendant's wings for the airline Alice had worked for, probably the type she wore when she first took to the sky. They were dusty and tagged fifty cents. Maybe, she thought, if she gave them to Alice she'd lay off about the garage door. Maybe, like that poem she'd written, the wings might bring out something new in herself as well. She might even be able to talk more easily to Alice. Find out why she'd watched Brad all the time. What she saw in him. Go over for coffee and spend some of her new free time. She purchased the silvery wings and looked around, almost embarrassed. Then she began to feel very tired, very aware of how big the flea market was and how exciting all these treasures would have been to that tinkering ghost in her attic.

She spotted Alice a hundred yards away and began walking toward her, sweating in the heat. Alice had several bags at her feet and was turning something over in her hands. Marissa strained to see what it was as she replaced it on the counter and then picked it up again, putting her finger on it as though testing an apparatus. From fifty feet away Marissa saw it was a yellow toy, a rusted metal truck.

At two o'clock they got back on the interstate, and Baton Rouge began shrinking in the truck's oversized rearview mirrors like something over-cooked. Marissa had a faint headache and her stomach was growling. Alice was quiet, her eyes narrowed as though she was worn out by all the shopping. At Denham Springs they stopped at a restaurant and to escape the crowd sat outside despite the wind and western flash of heat. They ordered sandwiches and watched the interstate traffic.

Alice crossed her legs slowly and bent down to rub her right calf. "What I couldn't believe is that it was Brad's heart that gave out. He always outswam me down at the club."

Marissa glanced at her sharply, recalling that she was a member of the subdivision's country club, a posh and leisure-wracked place she had been to only twice. The slow, liquored civility of the club's patrons made her feel ill. "Maybe it was the stress. After the truck plant closed, he wasn't the same. We had to cut back. He was worried about his retirement." She studied her companion's lotioned skin, her cornsilk hair. "You spend a lot of time on your hair, don't you?"

"At my age most of my money goes for maintenance. I need more upkeep than my house does."

"I see you spend a lot on your yard. Your azaleas, your fence. Do you know how many times you've painted that fence?"

Alice shrugged. "Got to keep up with the neighbors."

Marissa looked away. "Yeah. Brad was a slave to our yard."

"He enjoyed it."

"He enjoyed everything. Like swimming with the neighbors." The comment was nearly an accusation. She wondered how Alice had looked, scissoring through the country club's jeweled waters. She shifted in her chair, looked down at her plain white walking shoes, and balled up her napkin in a fist. "With Brad I could be young, because, you know, I was young with him once. I don't feel that way today."

The cloth awning popped in the breeze, and a teenage waitress lolled out and freshened their drinks. Alice took a swallow, then stared at the glass. "I'm sorry about your losing him. At least you had a good husband a lot longer than I did."

The statement surprised and embarrassed her. Marissa turned and pretended to look into the restaurant. "You ran into him at the club a lot?"

"He'd come in all by himself and look for someone to pace him in the pool."

Marissa felt a subtle light-headedness, a sensation she'd known as a predecessor to panic. "I never learned to swim. The water always went up my nose."

"Sometimes he told me you were too tired to even talk to him at night when you got home from work. That you didn't want to learn to play golf."

Marissa suddenly imagined Alice in a one-piece swimsuit, springing out of the pool, a running gloss on her long body, and she turned to her with her face's question.

When Alice saw that look, her own expression changed, as though a lightning bolt had just zinged past her plane's windows. "The two of us would swim a couple laps, until my foot started hurting, and he'd keep going for maybe an hour."

"I knew he played golf with you a few times, in a group," Marissa said, still focused on Alice, who was, she remembered, still a stranger to her.

"I guess you could say we were pals," Alice said, her voice growing smaller as though she was biting the inside of her cheek.

"Pals," Marissa repeated, drawing the word out. "Pals and what else?" she asked rudely.

Alice straightened up in her chair. "Well, you never did a damn thing with him. Every afternoon that you worked late, he'd come back from his job and roam around the neighborhood like a stray dog, then settle in at his workbench. And on Saturdays at the club, when most of the men were golfing or gambling in the bar, he exercised. Killing time, he called it."

Marissa's face flushed and she put both feet on the concrete. "Look, maybe I spent too much time with the accounts now and then," she said, "but the money I brought home made it easier for him to buy his junky little toys." She looked into Alice's eyes, trying to read some signal of how things really were. "Maybe sometimes he wasn't so good for me as well."

Alice tried to show nothing, then said, "He was better to you than you thought he was."

At that moment, the waitress came out, took one glance at the two of them, and said, "Jeez, is it that hot out here?"

On I-12 East, she began burning up the lanes. Outside of Walker, a state patrolman chased her down and wrote her a ticket, which she took with a nod, putting only one overpass between her truck and his radar before pushing her speed back over ninety. She was as angry as she'd ever been, at losing her husband, at wasting time on this trip, but most of all at Alice. For saying what she'd said. It was a half hour before she could stand to ask, "How the hell well did you know Brad?"

Alice turned in her seat. "Why are you upset?"

"I don't know. Maybe because I don't know you, and Brad does. Did." She made a face. "It's my fault, I know. I haven't been much of a neighbor, but my God, you've done all these things with him, and I've hardly looked at you all these years."

"Marissa, nothing went on between us, if that's what you're worrying about." Alice sounded disappointed, as if the whole day had boiled down to a single cliché.

Marissa was upset that she was jealous. As the miles ticked by, she replayed in her mind every stewardess joke she could remember, but nothing gave her the least relief. At last she pulled into the subdivision and drove straight into her open garage. Alice gathered her purchases and crossed the street without a word, her back bent over from the ride. Marissa did not close the garage door.

Later that night she picked up a framed photograph of Brad, looked carefully at his smirk, and understood there were many things she didn't know. She frowned at him and ran her fingertips over the glass, something she imagined widows do all the time, hoping to read the Braille of loss. But the image gave her no signals, and then she had the startling vision of the frame forty years in the future, sitting on a dusty table at a roadside flea market a thousand miles away, a young housewife buying it for a quarter and discarding the stranger inside. She slammed the picture down on her dresser. "Aw, crap," she said. "It's all crap if you don't know anything about it."

The next morning, the bedside phone rang and it was Alice. "I can imagine what you're going through," she said. "How're you making out, anyway?"

"I am making out just fine," she snapped. "How are you making out?"

"Listen, I want you to come over right now."

In the dresser mirror, Marissa watched the straight line of her mouth. "Why don't we just leave things as they are?"

"In about fifteen minutes?"

"No."

There was a sigh on the line. "You've never been over here. If you don't come I'll go over there and drag you kicking and screaming."

She let her head fall back and looked at the ceiling, growing angry again. "Oh, all right, already."

"And Marissa, you must've been really tired when we got back yesterday, because you forgot to close the garage door."

She was speechless, and for an instant wanted to scream *bitch* and *insensitive, soulless tramp,* but then realized. Alice was making a joke. "Damn it, for a minute I thought you were serious. I didn't know how to take you."

"You've got a problem like that," she said, hanging up.

She kicked around the bedroom getting ready, throwing her nightgown at the dresser, brushing her short hair straight back as though trying to tear it out. She left the house through the garage, crossed the street, and went into Alice's kitchen without knocking. The room was luminous, many windows laden with light.

Alice came in looking freshly showered, her legs flashing tan below her short bathrobe. Her smile was nervous, a little forced. Marissa took a chair at the breakfast table but couldn't keep her eyes off her, wondering what Brad had thought of all this skin and movement.

Finally, Alice sat down and put a hand on the table, palm up. "You doing okay, sweetie?"

She sounded as if she were dealing with an airsick passenger, and Marissa said, quietly, "No, I am not okay."

Alice pulled back her hand. "I don't know what to say to make you feel any better. But I want you to look across the street through my windows."

"What?"

"Turn around and look at your house."

She swung and squinted into the light, examining the triple set of windows and then focusing through the glass to the scene across the street. She viewed with sudden shame and alarm the cluttered maw of her open garage, where Brad's dust-haunted motorcycle leaned against the back wall, his fishing rods floated below the rafters, his golf clubs shone above an oiled leather bag, and his wrenches and pliers winked silver against the Peg-Board. She saw the workbench where he'd spent hours, the open garage door giving him light, tinkering with his brittle tin cars, repairing her blender, oiling the hinges on her briefcase. Marissa imagined the life Alice had watched unfold across the street, Brad setting up the ladder to clean the gutters, washing the cars, taking their daughter to her music lessons—levelheaded Brad, sober, singing under his breath the jukebox songs of their youth, waving to the neighbors. In short, the future Alice had lost a long time ago.

"Wow. I didn't realize" was all she could say. "It was like watching a movie, wasn't it? A years-long movie."

"It's my view," Alice said. "Morning, noon, and night."

Outside, a dusty mail truck squealed to a halt, and Marissa watched the postman slip the short envelopes of sympathy cards into her box. A pregnant cat waddled past her open garage, looked in a moment, and padded on. Alice fixed her a cup of coffee and a roll, and the two of them ate quietly. The conversation was brief and careful, each word chosen like a berry from a bush. Later, she walked across the street and pressed the button that brought the door down tight.

Marissa spent the rest of the week cleaning house after work, waxing floors, dusting the tops of picture frames, scrubbing bathrooms, boxing up her husband's clothes for Goodwill, and it was a wild cleaning where the abrasive was not in her cleanser but in her motion.

On Saturday the doorbell rang, and it was the appraiser her daughter had asked to evaluate her father's collection. A big ex–pro football player named Clint, he filled her doorframe.

"Hi, you Mrs. Marissa? Your daughter asked me to come up from New Orleans."

"Uh, yes. She told me about you. Come in. It's mostly upstairs, though there are things in the garage as well." He walked past her, and the backwash of cologne cut her breath. She'd never seen so many teeth in a human. Hair swept back like a wolverine's.

Clint carried a tablet, and a huge wallet protruded from the back pocket of his khakis. She led him upstairs and turned on the lights. "Well, here it is. Be sure to check the cabinets under the display counters, and there are a lot of antique guns back there in that closet."

Clint pointed a big finger at the rafters. "All the old signs go as well?"

"Everything." She looked around and saw a phantom Brad painting pin stripes on a toy farm wagon. "It's not that I hate the stuff. I just don't know much about it."

Clint put up a hand, palm out. "I know. It's my business to deal with husbands' estates. Usually I can leave behind some prime thing. A family remembrance, you know?"

From downstairs she listened to him thump around for over three hours. When he came down his knit shirt was dusty. He asked to see what was in the garage, and after fifteen minutes he came back in and she offered him a cup of coffee and a donut. Clint tapped and fretted over his tablet at her dinette table, then sat back. She was afraid the old chair was going to explode.

"I'm an appraiser, but I also have a collectables company and auction house. I can charge you for the appraisal and head on out. But if it's okay, I'd like to make an offer on the whole shebang."

The accountant in her perked up. Well, here it comes, she thought. He'll try to skin me in some complicated deal. The shebang probably won't net a couple thousand dollars, but so what? It's just stuff, she told herself, picking up her napkin and twisting it. Brad's stuff. "What do you have in mind?"

"I can write you a check for the toys, guns, the Harley and sports equipment in the garage and have it all out of here in two days. I can only pay wholesale, but your alternative is selling it piece by piece online for years and years." He gave the screen on his tablet a final tap. "It comes to just over a hundred and eighty-six thousand."

She swallowed once, slowly, unable to think, stunned at the figure, thinking this must be her daughter's idea of a joke.

Clint saw her distress and misinterpreted it. "But of course," he began, "that's just a starting number. Would you feel better if I evened the offer out at two hundred thousand?"

She took a breath. "That would be fine," she said quietly, feeling somehow shamed.

Clint nodded and pulled out his checkbook. "Your husband had a top-notch eye for rarity and quality. But there's one thing upstairs I won't buy."

"What is it?"

"I left it in a large box on the center table up there. It's a big metal train set in nearly new condition."

She blinked and shook her head. "I don't really remember it."

"Did you know there's a handwritten note in the box? It said your husband got it for Christmas when he was nine years old. I can tell, even back then he knew how to take care of things. It's real clean and all the little parts are there. Even the original cardboard boxes. It takes character to take care of something like that. He must've been quite a guy." Clint took a long swallow of coffee and studied her face.

Marissa looked away. "How do the other widows feel when you buy their husbands' belongings?"

Clint handed her the check and stood up. "Most people feel the way they're able to."

The last thing she did that day was clean the truck. She backed it out near the street, took off her shoes, hand-washed the pearly paint, then dried it with a cloth. While cleaning the interior, she found the supple new shoes and the flight attendant emblem she'd bought. She stood in the driveway holding her hand high to make the wings come alive in the light and imagining a young Alice swinging down the aisle of a rumbling DC-9, twenty pounds lighter, not a wrinkle under an eye or a single worry that life would ever be less than a sky-high ride to whatever she really wanted. It could have been like that. For the both of them. Marissa considered crossing the lane and giving her the wings. She knew they belonged with Alice, because they were part of her history. Instead, she shoved the emblem deep into the pocket of her slacks and made a fist around it until the metal feathers stung her palm, branding her with the memory of the days after Brad's death, and at once she began to understand the importance of objects. It was all about connections. She wanted the wings, but at the same time she needed the link to Alice.

Out of nowhere came the thought that she should put on the wonderful shoes. She slipped her feet into leather as soft as lips, and then she was standing in a new, comfortable world. She seemed to be floating as she took three long steps down to the curb, looked up and down the empty street, and was carried across.

The Piano Tuner

The phone rang Monday morning while the piano tuner was shaving, and he nicked himself. The strange lady was on the line, the one who hardly ever came out of her big house stuck back in the cane fields south of town. The piano tuner told her he would come out, and then he wiped the receiver free of shaving cream and blood. Back at the lavatory he went after his white whiskers, remembering that she was a fairly good-looking woman, quite a bit younger than he was, in her midthirties. She also had a little money, and the piano tuner, whose name was Claude, wondered why she didn't try to lose some of it at the Indian casino or at least spend a bit cheering herself up with a bowl of gumbo at Babineaux's Café. He knew that all she did was sit in a hundred-fifty-year-old house and practice pop tunes on a moth-eaten George Steck upright.

Claude gathered his tuning kit, drank coffee with his wife, then headed out into the country in his little white van. He made a dozen turns and got on the clamshell road that ran by Michelle Placervent's unpainted house, a squared-off antique thing set high up on crumbling brick pillars. Behind it were gray wood outbuildings, and beyond those the sugarcane grew taller than a man and spread for miles, level as a giant's lawn.

As he pulled his tool kit out of the van, Claude recalled that Michelle was the end of the line for the Placervents, Creole planters who always had just enough money and influence to make themselves disliked in a poor community. Her mother had died ten years before, after Michelle had graduated with a music degree and come home to take care of her.

He looked up on the gallery, stopping a moment to remember her father, a pale, overweight man with oiled hair, who would sit up there in a rocker and yell after cars speeding in the dusty road, as though he could control the world with a mean word.

The piano tuner remembered that Mr. Placervent began to step up his drinking after his wife died, and Michelle had to tend him like a baby until he dropped dead in the yard shouting at the postman about receiving too many Kmart advertisements. From that point on, it was just her and the black housekeeper on the home place, with a thousand acres the bank managed for her. Then the housekeeper died.

It had been a year since she had called him for a tuning. He stopped under a crape myrtle growing by the porch, noticing that the yard hadn't been cut in a month and the spears of grass were turning to seed. The porch was sagging into a long frown, and the twelve steps that led to it bounced like a trampoline as he went up. He knocked and Michelle turned the knob and backed into the hall, waving him in with a faint hand motion and a small smile, the way Placervents had been doing for two hundred years to people not as good as they were, but Claude didn't hold it against her because he knew how she had been raised. Michelle reminded him of one of those pastries in the display case down at Dufresne's Bakery—pretty, but when you tried to handle them, they fell apart and your fingers went through to the goo inside. She was bouncing on the balls of her feet, as if she expected to float off at any minute. He saw that she'd put on a few pounds and wasn't carrying her shoulders well, but also that there was still a kind of graceful and old-timey shape to her hips and breasts. Her hair was dark and curly, and her eyes were the brown of worn sharps on an old upright piano. A man could take an interest in her as long as he didn't look in those eyes, the piano tuner thought. He glanced around the house and saw that it was falling apart.

"I'm glad you could come so soon," she said. "C above Middle C is stuck." She pointed over to an ornate walnut-cased vertigrand, and he remembered its rusty harp and dull, hymning soundboard. It would take three hours to get it regulated and pulled back up to pitch. He saw an antique plush chair with the imprint of her seat in its velvet, and knew she would sit there until he was finished. Claude usually talked while he did regulations, so he chatted as he unscrewed the fall board, pulled off the front, and flopped back the lid. After a little while, he found an oval pill wedged between two keys and fished it out with a string mute. When she saw what it was, she blushed. "This one of yours?" he asked, putting it on a side table. Her eyes followed his hand. "You remember Chlotilde?" He nodded. "She sure could cook, I heard."

"She called it a happy pill. She told me that if things got too much for me to handle, I could take it." She glanced up as though she'd told a secret by accident, and her eyes grew round. "I never did, though, because it's the only one."

Claude stole a look at her where she sat in front of the buckled plaster wall and its yellowed photographs of dead Placervents. It occurred to him that Michelle had never done anything, never worked, except at maintaining her helpless mother and snarling old man. He remembered seeing her in town, always in stores, sometimes looking half-dead and pale, sometimes talking a mile a minute as she bought food, medicines for the aged, adult diapers, coming in quick, going out the same way, enveloped in a cloud of jasmine perfume.

"You know," he said, "you could probably go to a doctor and get another pill or two."

She waved him off with two fingers. "I can't stand going to doctors. Their waiting rooms make me want to pass out."

"There," he said, running a trill on the freed ivory. "One problem solved already."

"It's good to get rid of at least one," she said, folding her hands in her lap and leaning forward from the waist.

"What problems you having, Michelle?" He put a tuning hammer onto a pin and struck a fork for A. His tuning machine was being repaired at the factory, so he'd gone back to listening, setting temperament by ear.

"Why, none at all," she said too brightly and breathlessly. Claude thought she spoke like an actress in a 1940s movie, an artificial flower like Loretta Young who couldn't fish a pill from between two piano keys to save her soul.

He struck the tuning fork again, placing it to his ear and tuned A440, then the A above that, and set perfect reference notes in between, tuning by fifths and flatting strings until the sounds in the wires matched those in his head. He then tuned by octaves from the reference notes, and this took over an hour. Michelle sat there with her pale hands in her lap as though she'd bought a ticket to watch. The piano's hammers were hard, so he gave them a quick grind with his Moto-Tool, then massaged the dampers, which were starting to buzz when they fell against the strings. He went over the tuning pins again. "I don't know if this job will hold perfect pitch, Michelle, but if a note or two falls back, give me a call and I'll swing by."

She nodded. "Whenever you're out this way, you can stop in. If something's wrong with the piano, I'll be glad to pay to get it fixed." She smiled a little too widely, like someone desperate to have company, which the tuner guessed she was. He sat down to play a little tune he tested instruments with, but then stopped after half a minute.

What the tuner remembered was that he'd never heard Michelle play. Judging from the wear on the hammers, she must have practiced all the time, so he asked her. She stood, fluffed her skirt, and walked over with a goosey step. Claude expected she might wring the notes out more or less in time, the way most players do, but after about ten measures of "As Time Goes By" he could hear that she had a great natural touch, laying the hammers against the strings like big felt teardrops and building note words that belled out into the room. Claude was moved by what she was doing with his work, for the notes were hers, but the quality of the notes was his, all the more recognizable when she began playing Bach.

Claude had hung around recitals long enough to know a little about classical music, though he'd seldom heard it out here in the cane fields. He leaned against the velvet chair and watched her long fingers roll and dart.

When she began a slow, fingertippy introduction to "Stardust," he had to sit down. He'd heard the song played by everybody and their pet dogs, but her touch was something else, like Nat King Cole's voice made from piano notes, echoing and dusty. She used the old bass sustain pedal to milk the overtones out of the new tuning, lifting each note from the page to give it wings, and Claude closed his eyes to watch the melody float slowly around the room.

The piano tuner was the kind of person who hated for anything to go to waste and thought the saddest thing in the world was a fine instrument that nobody ever touched, so it made him uneasy that someone who could play like this lived alone and depressed in an antique nightmare of a house ten miles from the nearest ear that knew what the hell her fingers were doing. When she finished, he asked, "Michelle, how do you spend your time?"

She folded her music and glanced at him out of the corner of an eye. "Since my father's gone, there's not much to do," she said, turning on the bench to face him. "Sometimes the people who lease the land come by to talk. I have television." She motioned to a floor-cabinet model topped by an elaborate set of rabbit ears.

"Lord, why don't you get a satellite dish?"

She turned over a hand in her lap. "I really don't watch anything. It just keeps me company when I can't sleep at night." She gave him a kind of goofy, apologetic smile.

He began to slip his tools into their felt pockets. "As good as you play, you ought to get a decent piano."

The corners of her little mouth came down a bit. "I tried to get Lagneau's Music to bring out a new upright, but they said the old steps couldn't hold a piano and moving crew." She placed an upturned hand on George's yellowed teeth. "They told me they'd never get this big thing off the porch. We're seven feet above the ground here."

"You can't take it out the back?"

"The steps are worse there. Rotted through." She let the fallboard drop over the ivories with a bang. "If I could get a new instrument, I'd push this out of the back door and let it fall into the yard for the scrap man." She passed a hand quickly above her dark hair as though waving off a wasp.

He looked up at the rain-splotched plaster. "You ever thought about moving?"

"Every day. I can't afford to. And, anyway, the house . . . I guess it's like family."

Claude picked up a screwdriver. "You ought to get out more. A woman your age needs . . ." He started to say she needed a boyfriend, but then he looked around at the dry-rotted curtains, the twelve-foot ceilings lined with dusty plaster molding, and then back at her trembly shoulders, realizing that she was so out of touch and rusty at life that the only man she should see was a psychiatrist, so then he said, "a job," just because he had to finish the sentence.

"Oh," she said, as though on the edge of crying.

"Hey, it's not so bad. I work every day, and I'm too busy to get blue."

She looked down at his little box of mutes and felts. "I can't think of a thing I know how to do," she said.

At supper, Claude's wife was home from her little hole-in-the-wall insurance office, and he asked if she knew Michelle Placervent.

"We don't carry her," she said, going after a plate of red beans and rice and reading a pamphlet on term life.

"That's not what I asked you."

She looked up and the light caught in her bottle-brown hair. "Is she still living out in that little haunted castle?"

"Yeah. The whole place shakes just when you walk through it."

"Why'd they build it on such tall piers? Did the water get that high before they built the levees?"

"Beats me. You ever hear anything about her?" He handed her the hot sauce and watched her think.

"I heard she was depressed as hell, I can tell you that. Boney LeBlanc said she had a panic attack in his restaurant and had to leave just as the waitress brought her shrimp étouffée." Evette shook her head. "And Boney makes dynamite étouffée."

"She can play the hell out of a piano," he said.

"Seems like I heard that." Evette turned the page on her pamphlet. "Sings, too."

"She needs to get a job."

"Well, she knows how to drive a tractor."

"What?"

"I heard her father forced her to learn when she was just a kid. I don't know why. Maybe he was mad she wasn't born a boy." Evette took a long drink of iced tea. "I heard if a field hand left a tractor by the gate and a rain was coming up, he'd send Michelle out to bring it under the shed. Wouldn't even let her change out of her dress, just made her climb up on the greasy thing and go."

"Damn, I wouldn't have thought she could operate a doorbell," Claude said.

His wife cut her eyes over at him. "It might surprise you what some people can do," she told him.

Two weeks later, Claude was sitting in his recliner, his mind empty except for a football game playing in it, when the phone rang. It was Michelle Placervent, and her voice struck his ear like the plea of a drowning sailor. She was crying into the receiver about how three notes on her keyboard had soured and another key was stuck. The more she explained what was wrong with her piano, the more she cried until she began weeping, Claude thought, as if her whole family had died in a plane crash, aunts and cousins and canaries.

"Michelle," he interrupted, "it's only a piano. Next time I'm out your way, I'll check it. Maybe Monday sometime?"

"No," she cried, "I need someone to come out now."

Uh-oh, he thought. He hung up and went to find his wife. Evette was at the sink peeling onions, and he told her about Michelle. She banged a piece of onion skin off her knife. "You better go fix her piano," she said. "If that's what needs fixing." She looked up at his gray hair as though she might be wondering if Michelle Placervent found him attractive.

"You want to come along for the ride?" he asked.

She shook her head and kissed him on the chin. "I've got to finish supper. When Chad gets home from football practice, he'll be starving." She picked up another onion and cut off the green shoots, her eyes flicking up at him. "If she's real sick, call Dr. Meltier."

Claude drove out as quickly as he could, sorry he'd ever tuned the worn-out piano in the first place. Giving a good musician a fine tuning is always a risk, because when the first string starts to sag in pitch, he gets dissatisfied and calls up, as if one little note that's just a bit off ruins the whole keyboard, the whole song.

She was dressed in faded stretch jeans and a green sweatshirt, her hair unbrushed and oily. The house was as uncombed as she was. Claude looked at her trembly fingers and her wild eyes, then asked if she had any relatives or friends in town. "Everybody is dead or moved far away," she told him, her eyes streaming and her face red and sticky.

He watched her, feeling suddenly tired and helpless. He tried to think what Evette would do for her, and then he went into the kitchen to make some hot tea. The cabinets looked as though someone had thrown the pots into them from across the room. The gas stove was an antique that should have been in a museum, and it was listing, the floor sagging under it. The freezer was full of TV dinners, and the pantry showed a few cans of Vienna sausages and beanie-weenies. Claude realized he'd be depressed himself if that's all he had to eat.

When he brought the tea, she was in a wing chair, leaning to one side, her shoulders rounded in. Sitting on the bench, he carefully checked the keyboard by unisons and fifths but found nothing out of pitch, no stuck key. At that moment, he knew that when he turned around he would have two choices: to say there's nothing wrong, get in his van, and go on with his life, or to deal with her. He inspected the alligatored finish on the George Steck's case for a long time, examined the sharps for lateral play. Even while he was turning on the satiny bench, he didn't know what he was going to say. Then he saw her eyes, big with dread of something like a diagnosis. Claude felt as though he were slipping off into quicksand when he opened his mouth.

"Michelle, who's your doctor?"

Her eyes went to the dark, wax-caked floor. "I'm not going."

"You got to. Look at yourself. You're sadder'n a blind man at a strip show."

"I just need a little time to adjust. My father's been gone only six months." She put a hand on her forehead and hid her eyes from him.

"You need a little something, all right, but it ain't time. You got too *much* time on your hands." Then he told her what her doctor could do for her. That her depression was just a chemical thing. That she could be straightened up with some medicine.

He said many things off the top of his head and convinced her to make an appointment with Dr. Meltier. He talked with her a long time in that cold living room. When a thunderbolt lit up the yard and a storm blew in from the west, he helped her put out pots to catch leaks. He held her hand at the door and calmed her down so she wouldn't call him out of his warm bed in a few hours, telling him that her piano had gone up in pitch or was playing itself.

A month or so passed, and Claude was cutting grass one afternoon when he saw Michelle's old black Lincoln charging up the drive. She got out, smiling too widely, wearing a navy cotton dress that was baggy and wrinkled. He asked her to come in for coffee and listened to her talk and talk. The doctor had given her some medications to test for a couple of months, and her eyes were bright. In fact, her eyes showed so much happiness they scared him. She asked if he could help her find a job playing the piano for somebody.

"When you're ready, I'll help." For years Claude had tuned pianos for places that used lounge pianists, and he knew all the managers.

She put four spoons of sugar in her coffee with a steady hand. "I'm ready right this minute," she said. "I've got to make my music go to work for me."

The piano tuner laughed at that, thinking the poor thing was so cheery and upbeat he should call Sid Fontenot, who managed the lounge in that big new motel over in Lafayette. "Sid's always trying out pianists," he told her. "I'll give him a call for you."

When he got off the phone, she asked, "How do you play in a lounge?" and Claude tried to keep a straight face.

"There's nothing to it," he said, sitting down with her and frowning into his coffee cup. "You must know a thousand show tunes and ballads."

She nodded. "Okay. So I play requests. Whatever they ask me to." She adjusted a thin watchband and then looked him in the eye.

Claude got up and put their cups in the sink. "Sid asked me if you can sing. You don't have to, but he said it would help. You get a lot of requests for old stuff in a classy motel lounge."

"I was good in voice," she said, clasping her hands until they went white. And then he thought he saw a weak mood flash through her eyes, a little electrical thrill of fright. "How do I dress?"

He lathered up a dish cloth and studied her short coffee-brown hair, dry skin, the small crow's-feet around her eyes. "Why don't you go to Sears and buy a black dress and some fake pearls. Get a little makeup while you're at it. You'll be the best-looking girl in the lounge. Sid says he'll try you tomorrow night in the bar at nine o'clock. It's the big new motel on the interstate."

Claude's wife had often told him that he invented reality by saying it, and he was thinking this as he talked to the medicated hermit-like woman seated in his kitchen. He was also thinking that the last place on earth he would want to be was in the piano bar of a Lafayette motel at nine at night. And naturally, the next question to come out between Michelle Placervent's straight white teeth was, "Can't you please come with me this first time?"

Claude took a breath and said, "I'd be glad to," and she clapped her hands like an organ grinder's monkey. He wondered what she was taking and how much of it.

*H*e almost convinced Evette to come along, but their seventeen-year-old boy came down with the flu, and she stayed home to nurse him. She made Claude wear a sport coat, but he refused to put on a tie. "You want to look good for your date," she told him with a smirk.

"Get out of here." He turned red in the face and went out on the porch to wait in the night air.

Michelle picked him up, and he had to admit that she looked blue blood sharp. He imagined she must have bought a girdle along with her velvety black dress. On the way to Lafayette, as the Lincoln drifted above the narrow flat highway through the sugarcane fields, Claude got her to talk about herself. She told him that she had been engaged twice, but old man Placervent was so nasty to the young men, he just ran them off. Her grandfather had wanted to tear the old house down "from bats to termites" and build a new one, but her father wouldn't hear of it. She said he'd worn the building like a badge, proof that he was better than everybody else. "The only proof," Michelle said. "And now I'm trapped in it." The piano tuner didn't know what to say, other than that she could always look forward to hurricane season, but he kept his mouth closed.

The lounge was a long room, glass walls on one side, a long bar with a smiling lady bartender on the other. He introduced Michelle to Sid, the manager, a bright-looking man, savvy, dressed in an expensive suit. Sid smiled at her and gestured toward the piano, and the next thing Claude knew, she was seated behind a rebuilt satin-black Steinway playing "Put on a Happy Face," her high-heeled foot holding down the soft pedal. After a while, the room began to fill with local oilmen and their glitzy women, plus the usual salesmen sprawling at the tables, and even a couple of cowboys who lit like dragonflies at the bar. A slim, tipsy woman wearing tight white jeans and spike heels approached the piano and made a request, putting a bill into a glass on the lid. Michelle stared at the money for a moment and started "Yesterday," playing for a full six minutes.

Claude sat at a tiny table next to the glass wall overlooking the swimming pool and ordered a German beer. He'd never done anything like this and felt out of place. When he did frequent a bar, it was a place with Cajun music on the jukebox and a gallon jar of pigs' feet on the counter. Michelle finished the tune, looked over at him, and he gave her the okay sign. She smiled and sailed into another, then tickled off a half dozen more over the next forty-five minutes. At one point, she walked to Claude's table and asked how she was doing. Even in the dim light he could see that her eyes were too intense, the way a person's eyes get when they're having too much fun.

The piano tuner wanted to say, Lighten up on the arpeggios. Slow your tempo a bit. But she was floating before him as fragile as a soap bubble, so he gave her the thumbs-up and said, "Perfect. Sid told me you can have a hundred dollars for four hours, plus tips."

"Money," she squealed, bouncing back to the piano and starting the "Pennsylvania Polka," playing with a lot of sustain pedal. A brace of oilmen looked over briefly, possibly annoyed, but most people just leaned closer to talk, or patted their feet. Claude signaled her to quiet it down a bit.

For an hour and a half he watched as Michelle played and grinned at people coming to her tip glass. She sang one song through the microphone over her keyboard and drew a moderate wave of applause. She was a good-looking woman but had never learned how to move around people, and Claude got the feeling that folks who studied her close up thought she was a little silly. He sat there wishing there was an adjustment button on the back of her head that he could give just a quarter turn.

Eventually, the piano tuner became drowsy and hungry in the dim light of the lounge, so he walked across the lobby to the restaurant and treated himself to a deluxe burger basket and another cold bottle of beer. He sat there next to the plant box full of plastic flowers and worried about Michelle and whether he'd done the right thing by turning a Creole queen into a motel lounge pianist.

As soon as he left the restaurant, he could tell something was not exactly right. A young couple walked out of the lounge with quick steps, and then he heard what she was playing: Hungarian Rhapsody no. 2. Sid appeared at the lounge entrance and waved him over. "Michelle's really smoking our Steinway," he said, yelling to be heard over the music. "You know, this crowd thinks classical music is something like Floyd Cramer's Greatest Hits." Claude looked into the room where customers seemed to bend under the shower of notes like cows hiding from a thunderstorm. Some of the loud salesmen had stopped selling mud pumps and chemicals to listen, and the two drunk cowboys had picked up women and were trying to jitterbug.

The manager put a hand on Claude's shoulder. "What's going on? She's got to know that's not the right music for this place."

"I'll talk to her."

Sid watched the performance. "She's smiling a lot. Is she on something?" Sid knew musicians.

"Depression medicine."

He sniffed. "Well, I guess that music'll drive you off the deep end, all right."

After the big rumbling finale, the drunk cowboys let out a rebel yell, but no one applauded. Claude walked over, bent down, and put his hand on her back. "That was good, Michelle." What else could he say to her?

She looked up at him and her eyes were wet, her skin flushed and sweating. "You don't fool me. I know what you're thinking. But I couldn't help it. I just got this surge of anger and had to let it out."

"What are you mad at?" He felt her shoulders tremble.

She didn't say anything at first, then she shrugged. "I've been sitting here thinking that I'd have to play piano five nights a week for over twenty years to afford renovating my house." She straightened up and looked over the long piano at the bartender, who had both hands on the bar, watching her. "What am I doing here?" She ran a palm down her soft throat. "I'm a Placervent."

Claude pushed her microphone aside. "Your medications are maybe a little out of adjustment," he said in a low voice, wishing he were anyplace on earth other than where he was. He glanced over at Sid. "You ought to finish this set, though."

"Why? I can survive without the money. I mean, I appreciate you getting me this job, but I think I'm ready to go home." She seemed confused and out of control, but she didn't move.

He was sure his face showed that he was getting upset himself. She stared down at the keys until finally, one of the cowboys—really just a French farm boy from down in Cameron Parish, wearing a loud shirt and a Walmart hat—came up and put a five in her tip glass. "Hey, lady, can you play any Patsy Cline?"

An injured little smile came to her lips. She straightened her back and started to say something to him, but instead she looked at Claude, at his embarrassed and hopeful face. Her mouth closed in a line, and her right hand went down and began picking out an intro. Then, to his amazement, she started to sing, and people looked up as though Patsy Cline had somehow come back to life, but without her country accent, and the whole room went quiet to listen. "Crazy," Michelle sang, soft as midnight fog outside a bedroom window, "crazy for feeling so lonely."

*H*e didn't see her for a long time. At Sid's lounge, someone spilled a highball into the Steinway, and when Claude was over there to straighten it out, the manager told him she was still playing there on weekends, and off and on at the Sheraton, and a little at the country club for the oil-company parties. He said that she'd gotten her dosage pretty regulated and was playing well, except toward the end of the night when she would start singing blues numbers and laughing out loud between the verses as though she were telling jokes in her head. Laughing very loudly. The piano tuner wondered if she could ever get on an even keel. People like Michelle, he thought, sometimes their talent helped them fix themselves. Sometimes not. Nobody could predict.

*I*n the middle of December she called him to come tune a new console she'd bought. She'd finally gotten a carpenter to put knee braces under the front steps so Lagneau's Music could bring a piano into the house. They'd told her they didn't want the George Steck as a trade-in, though, and wouldn't move the big vertigrand down into the yard for a million dollars. It was built like a wooden warship and weighed nearly eight hundred pounds.

When Claude got there, the entry was open, so he stepped around the dark giant of a piano at the head of the long hall that led to the back porch. He noticed the new piano in the parlor, a cheap, ugly blond-wood model he couldn't believe she'd chosen.

Michelle appeared at the far end of the hall looking wild-eyed, her hair falling in loose, dangling ringlets. She was wearing rust-smudged tan slacks under a yellow rain slicker and was lugging the end of a half-inch cable in her cotton gardening gloves.

"Claude," she said, shaking her head, "you wouldn't believe the trouble I've had this morning. I asked Lagneau's crew to push the old piano into the hall, but the rollers on the bottom locked up. Just look what they did to the floor." She swept a hand low. The floors were so covered with two-hundred-year-old divots brimming with cloudy wax that he couldn't spot much new damage. "They managed to get it up on this old braided rug, and I figured I could tow it off the back porch and let it fall into the yard."

He looked in her eyes to see what was going on. "You gonna skid this thing down the hallway on this rug? We can't just push it ourselves?"

"Give it a try."

He leaned on it, but the piano tuner was not a muscular man, and the instrument didn't budge. "I see what you mean." He looked down the hall to the open rear door. "I thought you said this would fall through the back steps?"

"They need to be replaced anyway. Mr. Arcement said he would cart away the mess next week." She ran the cable under the keyboard and around the back through the handholds, completing a loop and setting the hook. When she passed by the piano tuner he smelled gasoline in her clothes, and he walked to the back door to see what she would hook the cable to. Idling away in the yard was a John Deere 720, a big two-cylinder tractor blowing smoke rings.

"God almighty, Michelle, that tractor's the size of a locomotive."

"It's the only one out in the barn that would start," she said, tossing the cable into the yard.

He looked out at the rust-roofed outbuildings, their gray cypress darkening in the drizzle. She began picking her way down the porous steps, which didn't look like they'd support his weight, so he went out the front door and walked around to the back. He watched Michelle set the cable hook to the tractor's drawbar and then climb up on the right rear axle housing. She faced backward, looking at the piano in the hall while the machine's exhausts thudded like a bass drum. He recalled that older John Deeres have a long clutch lever instead of a foot pedal, and she was easing this out to take up slack in the cable when a front tire strayed onto the septic tank lid, causing the tractor to veer sharply. Claude didn't know exactly what she was trying to do, but he offered to help.

"I've planned this through. You just stand there and watch." She sat in the seat, found reverse gear, backed the tractor off the lid, snugged the steering wheel with a rubber tie-down so it wouldn't wander again, then eased forward in lowest gear until the cable was taut. Then she put the lever all the way forward, and the machine began to growl and crawl. Claude walked way out in the yard, stood on tiptoe, and saw George skidding down the hall, shifting from side to side, but looking as though it would indeed bump out of the house and onto the back porch. However, about three feet from the door, the piano rolled off the rug and started to turn broadside to the entryway. Michelle stopped the tractor and yelled something he couldn't understand over the engine noise, but she might have been asking him to go inside and straighten the piano. She stepped out onto the axle again, leaned forward to jump to the ground, and the piano tuner held his breath because there was something wrong with the way she was getting off. Her rain slicker caught on the long lever and he heard the clutch pop as it engaged. Michelle fell flat on her stomach, the enormous tractor moving above her. Claude ran over and when she came out untouched from under the drawbar, he grabbed her arm to pull her up. Meanwhile, the tractor had drawn the piano's soundboard flat against the entryway to the house, where it jammed for about half a second. The big machine gasped as its governor opened up, dumping gas into the engine, and *chak-chak*, the exhaust exploded, the big tires squatted and bit into the lawn, and George came out with the entire back wall of the house, three rows of brick piers collapsing like stacks of dominoes, the kitchen, rear bed-room, and back porch disintegrating in a tornado of plaster dust and cracking, wailing boards. A musical waterfall of slate shingles rattled down from the roof, the whole house trembled, nearly every window-pane tinkled out, and just when Claude thought things had stopped collapsing, the hall tumbled apart all the way to the front door, which swung closed with a bang.

The tractor kept puttering away toward the north at around four miles an hour, and the piano tuner wondered if he should run after it, but Michelle began to make a whining noise deep down in her throat and hung onto his arm as if she was about to pass out. He couldn't think of a word to say, and they stared at the wreck of a house as though hop-ing to put it back together with airplane glue, when a big yellow jet of gas flamed up about where the stove would be in all the rubble.

"A fire," she said breathlessly, tears welling up in her eyes.

"Where's the closest neighbor?" he asked, feeling at least now he could do something.

"The Arcements. About a mile off." Her voice was tiny and broken as she pointed a thin white arm to the east, so he gathered her up and walked her to the front, putting her in his van and tearing out down the blacktop toward the nearest working telephone.

. . .

*B*y the time the Grand Crapaud Volunteer Fire Department got out to Michelle Placervent's place, the house was one big orange star, burning so hot it made little smoke. The firemen ran up to the fence but lost heart right there. They began watering the camellias at the roadside and the live oaks farther in. Claude had rescued Michelle's Lincoln before the paint blistered off, and she sat in it looking like a World War Two refugee he'd seen on the History Channel. Minos LeBlanc, the fire chief, talked to her for a while and asked if she had insurance.

She nodded. "The only good thing the house ever had was insurance." She put her face in her hands then, and Claude and Minos looked away, expecting the crying to come.

But it didn't. In a minute she asked for a cup of water, and the piano tuner watched her wash down a pill. After a while, she locked her Lincoln and asked Claude to take her into town. "I have an acquaintance I can stay with, but she won't come home from work until five-thirty."

She ran her eyes up a bare chimney rising out of the great fire. "All these years and only one person who'll put me up."

"Come on home and eat supper with us," he said.

"No." She inspected her dirty slacks. "I wouldn't want your wife to see me like this." She seemed almost frightened and looked around him at the firemen.

"Don't worry about that. She'd be glad to loan you some clothes to get you through the night." He placed himself between her and the fire.

She ran her fingers through her curls and nodded. "All right," but she watched him out of the corner of her eye all the way into town. About a block before Claude turned down his street, she let out a giggle, and he figured her chemicals were starting to take effect.

Evette showed her the phone, and she called several people, then came into the living room, where Claude was watching TV. "I can go to my friend Miriam's after six-thirty," she said, settling slowly into the sofa, her head toward the television.

"I'll take you over right after we eat." He shook his head and looked at the rust and mud on her knees. "Gosh, I'm sorry for you."

She kept watching the screen. "Look at me. I'm homeless." But she wasn't even frowning.

The six o'clock local news began on channel 10, and the fifth story was about a large green tractor that had just emerged out of a cane field at the edge of Billeaudville, dragging the muddy hulk of a piano on a long cable. The announcer explained how the tractor had plowed through a woman's yard and proceeded up Lamonica Street toward downtown, where it climbed a curb and began to struggle up the steps of St. Martin's Catholic Church, until Rosalie Landry, a member of the Ladies' Altar Society who was sweeping out the vestibule, stopped the machine by knocking off the tractor's spark plug wires with the handle of her broom. As of five-thirty, Vermilion Parish sheriff's deputies did not know where the tractor had come from or who owned it and the battered piano.

Claude stood straight up. "I can't believe it didn't stall out somewhere. Billeaudville's at least four miles from your house."

Michelle began to chuckle, her shoulders jiggling as she tried to hold it in. Then she opened her mouth and let out a big, sailing laugh, and kept it going, soaring up into shrieks and gales, some kind of tears rolling down her face.

Evette came to the door holding a big spoon, looked at her husband, and shook her head.

He reached over and grabbed Michelle's arm. "Are you all right?"

She tried to talk between seizures of laughter. "Can't you see?" she keened. "It escaped too." On the television a priest was shaking his head at the steaming tractor. She started laughing again, and this time Claude could see halfway down her throat.

A year later, he was called out for four tunings in Lafayette on one day.

September was like that for him, with the start of school and piano lessons. On top of it all, Sid wanted him to fish a bottle of bar nuts out of the lounge piano. He got there around five-thirty, and Sid bought him supper in the restaurant before he started work.

The manager wore his usual dark-gray suit, and his black hair was combed straight back. "Your friend," he said, as if the word *friend* held a particularly rich meaning for them, "is still working here, you know."

"Yeah, I was over at her apartment last month tuning her new Steinway console," Claude said, shoveling up pieces of hamburger steak.

"You know, there's even some strange folks that come in as regulars just to hear her."

Claude looked up at him. "She's a good musician, a nice woman," he said between chews.

Sid took another slow drink, setting the glass down carefully. "She *looks* nice," he said.

The piano tuner recognized that this is how Sid talked, not explaining, just using his voice to hint at the unexplainable. The manager leaned into him. "But sometimes she starts speaking right in the middle of a song. Saying strange things." He looked at his watch. "She's starting early tonight, for a convention crowd—a bunch of four-eyed English teachers."

"What time?"

"About eight." Sid took a drink and looked at the piano tuner. "Every night I hold my breath."

The room was cool and polished. A new little dance floor had been laid down near the piano, and Michelle showed up wearing round metal-frame glasses and an expensive black dress. The grand piano was turned broadside to the room, so everyone could watch her hands. She started playing immediately, a nice old fox-trot Claude had forgotten the name of. Then she played a hymn, then a ragtime number. He sat a couple of tables away, enjoying the bell quality of his own tuning job. Between songs, she spotted him, and her eyes ballooned. She threw her long arms up and yelled into the microphone, "Hey, everybody, I see Claude from Grand Crapaud, the best piano tuner in the business. Let's give him a round of applause." A spatter of clapping came from the bar. Claude gave her a worried glance, and she made herself calm, put her hands in her lap, and waited for the applause to stop. Then she set a heavy book of music on the rack. Her fingers uncurled into their ivory arches, and she began a slow Scott Joplin number with a hidden tango beat, playing it in a way that made the sad notes bloom like flowers. Claude remembered the title—"Solace."

"Did you know," she asked the room during the music, "that Scott Joplin played piano in a whorehouse for a little while?"

Claude looked out at all the assembled English teachers, at the glint of eyeglasses and nametags and upturned, surprised faces. He understood that Michelle could never adjust to being an entertainer. But at least she was brave.

"Yes," she continued, "they say he died crazy with syphilis, on April Fools' Day, 1917." She nodded toward the thick music book, all rags, marches, and waltzes. "One penicillin shot might have bought us another hundred melodies," she told the room. "That's kind of funny and sad at the same time, isn't it?"

She pulled back from the microphone and polished the troubling notes. Claude listened, feeling the hair rise on his arms, and when she finished, he waved at her, got up, and walked toward the lobby, where he stood for a moment watching the ordinary people. He heard her start up a show tune, and he turned and looked back into the lounge as three couples rose in unison to dance.

The Review

An afternoon thunderstorm dropped a bolt into Sidney Landry's backyard, incinerating a pine sapling against the rear fence, but Sidney didn't blink, even though he was at the window where he could have seen the smoldering stub. He was checking Amazon for reviews about his new novel. A handful of three-star reviews had appeared and one four-star written by his brother. He personally knew everyone who'd written the summaries, had even solicited a couple, but the comments still pleased him. He told himself that he was a small fish in a small bowl, but still, here he was on Amazon at last. Twice a day he checked for a new review, hoping for his first five-star fan. But today, along with the lightning and thunder, came a dreaded one-star review from someone who gave a first name, Zeno, and his hometown, Stamp, Indiana.

At the age of fifty-one, after many years of fantasizing about being a published novelist, Sidney had written about a kidnapping, a topic he figured was a surefire investment of time. The book was set in south Louisiana and was about a farmer whose son had been taken and then rescued by family members—not an ambitious or unusual story, Sidney realized. Many novels on Amazon he found to be neither ambitious nor unusual, so he figured he was in good company. He was a big, balding, obsessive man, occasionally sour-tempered and always unable to forget perceived slights. His thin skin was indeed like a dermatological condition, a case of emotional shingles, not at all his fault. Writing fiction relaxed and distracted him from his job as a low-level accountant. But the writing and columns of numbers never blended well. His office manager often complained that Sidney's reports were both literary and lengthy, even containing an occasional disdainful metaphor about a client's expense account.

His publisher was the Nutria Press, formed the previous year at a local printer's office. His book drew a pair of lukewarm reviews in the Baton Rouge and New Orleans papers, and two regional bookstores invited him to read from *The Farmer's Stolen Son* and sign copies. About a month after the novel came out, Amazon listed it, and, according to the publisher, sold about four copies a week. Sidney was satisfied with his success and dropped back to part-time status on his job to begin working on a second novel and a group of short stories. His wife, who was a nurse, a small woman with a long-suffering face, made enough to keep the family afloat, and his daughters, who never came around much, made more money as realtors than he did.

When Sidney noticed the single-star Amazon review, every part of his body seemed to turn to stone. Only his eyes moved as they scanned the first sentence, which was, "Oh boy, what tree died for this book?" He looked down the long, wide column of print and began to sweat. He labored through half of the review, each word like a thrown knife, down to the sentence that began, "The author has invented a world based on ignorance of his subject. I can tell he has never suffered through any type of kidnapping, because the characters show no sign of such trauma and go about their business not as if a member of the family has been stolen away, maybe never to return, but as if their brick ranch house has been wrapped in toilet paper by neighborhood children. And the prose reads like an owner's manual for a 1951 Studebaker. The choppy sentences, chapter after chapter after chapter, made me seasick. I didn't care about any of the characters, especially the decidedly unreal kidnapped boy, who seemed like a sitcom prig, too snotty even to be afraid of his insane captors. The author hails from the Bayou State, and his story line meanders at an oozy pace, lost in a swamp of details about the father's employment history, about how the mother applies her makeup, but nothing about their agony of losing a child—yawn! These people are as tedious as a Kansas interstate. I've never returned a book in my life, but tomorrow I'll make a special trip into town to mail this turkey back. From now on I'll stick with my local bookstore in the mall.

The scenes on the father's farm were painful to read. The author knows nothing about farm animals, and judging from his novel, knows little about humans and how they feel. Overall, the story's emotional load is that of a dollar greeting card. Why a publisher would waste ink on this word-junk is disorienting to the point of mystery."

Sidney sat immobile, his face white, his fingers gradually closing into fists. He feared that everyone he knew was going to see the review: his wife, his daughters, his friends in accounting, his boss, his mother, half the people he knew in Louisiana. He tried to tell himself it didn't matter, that idiots were writing reviews 24/7 all over the Internet. He remembered that another reviewer had once given Milton's *Paradise Lost* two stars. Said it was too damned long.

At supper that night, his wife seemed to sense that something was wrong. She asked him if he had a fever, and he said he didn't think so, being indefinite so she'd walk over and feel his forehead. He thought her caress would help, for he loved his wife, but it didn't work this time. Lately, when she touched him, her hands were cold and felt as though she were testing for dust. And sooner or later she would find out what the folks in Stamp, Indiana, thought of him. He hoped she wouldn't agree. Sidney pushed his green beans around his plate and looked out into the backyard, wishing the reviewer were trapped inside his cedar fence while he approached him with a golf club. His instinct was to lash back, as he once had when an eBay dealer sold him a wristwatch that didn't work. After trading a series of snarky e-mails with the man, he'd driven two hundred miles to a southern Texas town to berate the seller, who stood shirtless on his front steps and glared at him, incredulous, refusing to refund a penny.

The next day at work, Gilman Raider, who had a talent for saying the wrong things, caught Sidney's arm as he came into the office. "Sid. I guess you checked Amazon last night?"

Sidney's jaw clenched. So this is what he would have to face for a few very long days. "Yep."

"The guy's a real cutie, right? Though you got to admit, the first sentence was funny."

Sidney slid through his door and began to close it. "Yeah, he's a riot," he said. "Got to work."

He avoided his fellow accountants all day. At supper he could tell that his wife had checked Amazon by the look she gave him, an expression he couldn't figure out, something like, Why do you want to write stuff if you don't make any money to speak of and some nobody in the Midwest comes after you with three nails and a hammer? At least that's what he thought the expression meant. Over the years he could figure her out less and less while he sometimes got the feeling she could see through him like an X-ray machine.

The next day while Sidney was driving to work, a stranger in the next lane gave him a studying look and Sidney imagined the man knew who he was and what the reader in Indiana had written. Alone in his office, checking the figures for a local foundry, he began to feel like one of their heavy castings, an overheated engine block for a locomotive, tons of hot rage for a stranger who had a choice of all the evils in the universe on which to vent his disdain—terrorists, dictators, inducers to evil, late-night talk show hosts, politicians, telemarketers, pedophiles, famine and plague—but had decided instead to come down with two feet on a first-time novelist who'd written a tame whodunit and had sold all of 487 copies, mostly out of his trunk. Why couldn't he have gone up against Grisham or Anne Rice? he wondered.

Sidney spent that afternoon and much of the next day at his fast office computer trying to find the identity of the reviewer. It wasn't hard to check. He read Zeno's other reviews, which were generally positive, and extracted another reference to a mall bookstore in Stamp. A city directory listed one mall and two bookstores. With such an odd name as Zeno to go on, he figured a phone call would be worth a shot. At the first store an old man with hearing problems shouted into the phone that he didn't know anyone named Zeno, but that he was having a half-off sale on all used Harlequin paperbacks. Sidney thanked him anyway and called the second store, where a girl picked up the phone.

"Hi, this is Michelle at Bland Books," she chirped.

"I'm looking for a fellow book lover who might frequent your store."

There was a sticky noise on the phone, as if someone were chewing three pieces of gum, and then the girl said, "What's his name?"

Sidney's heart gave a leap. "Zeno."

"I don't recognize him. Mr. Bland will be back in fifteen minutes. You could call back. Is this an emergency?"

"No. Not really. Is there maybe another staff member there who might know him and if he's been in today or yesterday?"

More sticky sounds, and then a yell that made him jerk the receiver away from his ear. "Tri-shaaa, do you know a customer by the name of Zeno?"

Sidney could hear a response in the background. "Is he that overweight man who teaches at the junior college? The one that buys books and then returns them for refunds?"

"I don't know," the girl with the phone said. "There's a guy here wants to know if he's been in."

"If it's the customer I'm thinking of, tell him no."

"Sorry," Michelle said. "We haven't seen him."

Sidney rattled the keys on his computer, soon finding Jason Polinski Community College in Stamp. A scan of the faculty listings revealed Zeno Bardol, who taught language arts. This was a disappointment because Sidney had hoped the reviewer was an angry bartender or an unemployable misfit, but the fact that he taught English gave him a bit of credibility. He felt a gloom envelop him, and he got up to go home, walking quickly past fellow workers in the hall as though on an urgent mission.

For the next week, he prayed for new reviews to be posted, something to buffer the terrible report, to get in the way of a reader's attention, and he even imagined ordering a book himself and writing a review under an alias, giving himself four stars and saying, "Well, it ain't so bad as the last guy says." Sidney began to mope around the house until his wife snapped at him, "Dammit, if it's bothering you so bad, just call the guy up. You've got to get over this. Work on the new book. Stop drooping around. I hate it when you get like this. My patients die on me all the time, but I just go on to help the next one. *I* could write a book if I wanted to."

This last comment bothered him because his wife indeed led an interesting life as a trauma nurse and had a lot of narrative stored up in her.

Despite her warnings, he didn't snap out of it. What he did do was download a route to Stamp, Indiana, gas up the Prius, and take off on a Tuesday morning without telling anyone. He decided that he just wanted to see the reviewer, maybe figure out how to talk to him without the man knowing who he was. The truth is, he didn't know what he wanted, other than maybe he had been wronged and he should do something about it. He was tempted to let the whole thing drop, but he also knew he didn't want to. Speeding north through the cypress swampland, he made it into the pine belt and soon rolled into a thunderstorm at the Mississippi border. Lightning bolts bombed the woods at the edge of his vision, a roadside tree brightening like tungsten. He felt sorry for anyone hiding from all the white-hot rods spearing the forest and pastures around him. He couldn't stop himself from thinking of the strikes as bad reviews on Amazon—random and pointless attacks. He couldn't become angry at static electricity building in clouds, but the fact that a human had singled out his novel for a literary thunderbolt made his jaw clench.

That night, in a mildewed motel outside of Cairo, he called his wife.

"You're where?" she shrilled.

"I'm going up to meet the guy."

Her voice came like a rifle shot. "You're an idiot. I didn't know what to think when you weren't home for supper. I was about to call the police." She was screaming at this point.

He was surprised at her anger and sat up straight in bed. "Look, relax. I just have to figure out how to talk to the guy about things, and then I'll come home."

"Yes, like you talked to that man about the used car he sold you five years ago. You were almost arrested for what you put that salesman through."

"Why do you have to bring that up?"

She made her voice calm. "Sid, do you have your pistol with you?"

"I left it upstairs, though let me tell you, I thought about bringing it along."

There was a long silence on the line. Finally his wife said, "You have no idea how hard you are to live with, do you?"

"I'm all right this time. Keep the light on for me?"

All he heard was a click and a heartless dial tone. Sidney bit his lip, wondering if he should get drunk or something, punch the wall a couple times, then drive back to Louisiana. But he just could not let things drop. He realized this about himself, but blamed it on genetics, though his parents were calm people, really good tax accountants.

On the hunt now, he fired up his laptop and began mining it for information on Zeno Bardol. He bought an online report for $18.75 that yielded much information, telling him Zeno had no police record, no traffic offenses, was sixty years old, and lived at 670 Sesame Lane in a house he'd purchased thirty-five years ago. Included in the report was an interview that a Canadian student, Marie Labat, had done with him years before, about teaching writing. The site promised updates if their Internet crawler found more records. Sidney closed his laptop, turned on his rusty bedside lamp, and reread a short story he had written and printed out the week before, looking for opportunities for revision, but finding none. Then he made plans.

Stamp was a town of about four thousand people, many of them employed at a stamping and forging plant where giant presses slammed sheet steel into truck bumpers and 30,000-pound hammers crushed glowing billets of steel into crankshafts in one shot, a ka-thump that traveled a mile or more in all directions, vibrating the whole town. He ate a breakfast of soggy hash browns and tasteless bacon at a café full of old men wearing feed-store caps. Though he couldn't hear the stamping plant, he could see vibration lines in his coffee, each circular wave a huge gear hammered into being.

He drove out to the junior college, asked a department secretary where and when Zeno Bardol's class was meeting, and stood outside the classroom door with a manila folder in his hand until a bell rang like a fire alarm. When the last student left, he walked into the room, smiling.

"Mr. Bardol?"

The face that looked up was all bulldog. The dove-gray eyes seemed almost blind. "You're not from the dean's office, are you?"

Sidney smiled wider. "No, I'm Bob Carnisky. I know a former student of yours, Marie Labat."

"Who?"

"She's a girl from Canada who interviewed you a few years ago."

"Oh yeah, the little Frenchie." Zeno Bardol straightened up in his flimsy chair, and Sidney saw that he was a big man, a little bent and overweight, but still able looking.

"Well, she called me the other day and I asked her if she knew someone I could pay to examine a short story I'd written. She said I might check with you."

Zeno picked up a pile of handwritten freshman themes and let them drop back to the desk. "I've no lack of things to read. And I teach three other sections just like this one."

Sidney leaned in. "It'd mean a lot to me. You know how hard it is to find someone to mark up creative work."

Zeno looked up at him, and Sidney saw in his eyes some sort of damage, maybe from reading freshman essays for several decades, the same clichés, the same mistakes. Maybe he would welcome something different to read.

"You don't sound like you're from around here," Zeno said suddenly.

"I used to live in east Texas. A long time ago."

He nodded. "Hard to break old speech rhythms, I guess." He stood up. "Well, you're not a student, so how much are you willing to pay for an evaluation of your story there?"

"Would fifty dollars work?"

Zeno's eyebrows went up. "Like a cop on Saturday night. Come on to the student center and I'll let you buy me a cup of coffee. If we go to my office, whiny kids will come in asking for everything under the sun."

So for twenty minutes Sidney had Zeno to himself. He handed over his story and said he'd been trying to get better at writing for twenty years, which was true. Zeno read the first sentence and sniffed, closing the folder. "Tell me about it. I try to make myself look productive around here, so I put down the words that remind me of what language can do. I've had some success in literary magazines. Gave me some cred as a writing teacher. Now and then they let me teach the advanced fiction-writing course."

"I haven't published anything yet," Sidney told him. "My wife said I should ask someone's opinion to see if I'm wasting my time."

Zeno nodded and mentioned that his wife had told him something similar, long ago. Like most people who have to talk to strangers for any length of time, he began to summarize parts of his life, mentioning that he had two daughters and a son, that his wife had left him many years before. He waved his hand as though brushing away a large insect. "That's all in the past, I guess. And now I've finally had a book accepted for publication."

Sidney nodded slowly and took a sip of coffee. He couldn't believe his good fortune. Old Zeno would have a book on Amazon, a big target for him to bomb with a weapons-grade review. "So this book, when's it coming out?" His right hand began to shake, so he covered it with his left.

"Pretty soon. Maybe two months. It's being published by a small press in New York owned by Random House." Zeno pushed away his Styrofoam cup of coffee. "Well, got to go." He tucked Sidney's folder under his arm. "I can have this marked up for you by Friday morning. You want to come by the office after my first class? Nineish?"

"Sure. You going home?"

"I stop off at a bar and put down three cold ones. No offense, but I like to be kind of alone. Unwind a bit and get away from some of the creepy people I work with."

"I understand."

"Friday, right?"

"Friday at nine."

Sidney drove back to the motel, a faded-out place with exterior doors that had been recoated so many times the paint dripped in thousands of jellied tears. He lay in the creaking bed feeling that his mission had been partially accomplished. However, he still wondered why a man like Zeno would write such a cruel review. He didn't seem to be the type. No doubt the man had an edge to him. But he didn't seem to be the vicious dullard he'd hoped he might find, someone petty, small-minded, weak.

He had a day and a half to kill, so he tried to find a decent place to eat. At a meat-and-three diner surrounded by trucks, he ate the most tasteless hamburger steak he'd ever had. He could feel the slug of the stamping machine come up from the floor through his stool and into his pelvis. The next morning he went to an antique engine show where motors idled in a field by the hundreds, their pop, splut, whoosh, and bang drowning out the thunder of the stamping plant right down the road. He bought a pastry from a stand touting local foods and it tasted like chilled lard. The exhibitors at the show were friendly, corn-fed people open to talking about their displays, and he wandered among them until lunch, when he bought an abomination the locals called a loose meat sandwich. After one bite he slammed it into a trash barrel and bought a rib-eye special from the local Shriners' food wagon. As he chewed and chewed through the gummy white bread, he thought about the source of the meat, the sickly cow, a species of living jerky, eating brambles all its life, leaning against a fence one morning and looking so pitiful that the owner decided to shoot him and sell him to the Shriners before he died on his own. The steak was increasing his anger, and he sat in the sunshine at a splintery picnic table imagining a food review he might write that was filled with images from an infernal kitchen run by a ghoul wearing a fez.

Thursday night he rode up and down the highway and spotted the area's only Mexican restaurant. Surely he could get a meal with some zing to it, at least a little peppery burn, a rotella surprise, a garlicky guaco. The only Mexican decoration in the dining room was a plain sombrero nailed to the wall behind the register. The salsa that came with the chips was pure tomato catsup, and every entrée came with a side of fries. He went back to the hotel and felt the jump of the stamping plant in the mattress. That night they must have been making ship anchors with one stroke because the bedside lamp was winking. He fell asleep wondering if Zeno Bardol had felt the ka-thump all these years. If every ounce of his compassion had been hammered out of him.

The next morning, he was waiting at Zeno's office door. The teacher showed up looking hungover, his eyes tinted yellow. He brushed past Sidney and plopped in his chair, but not before giving him an annoyed glance. "You know," he began, "not everyone is cut out to be a writer of literary fiction."

Sidney shivered as though he'd received a costly court judgment. Zeno Bardol began to tell him how his short story didn't really have an ending. His voice was courteous but firm as he explained that the main character was flat and the plot seemed borrowed from television, as was the New York setting. He leaned back in his chair, stopped speaking for a moment, and looked out through a very small office window, really just a glass hole in the cinder-block wall. Sidney pondered the critique and was glad he'd left his gun in Louisiana. But he also felt foolish because he'd driven eight hundred miles to meet what seemed to be the one man in the world who really hated the way he wrote. So he just asked questions as if he were interested in the answers, watching the man's face for clues.

When Zeno handed over the story at the end of their discussion, Sidney saw that there were more comments handwritten on each page than there was text. "You have a good critical eye," Sidney mumbled, trying carefully to control his voice. "Do you ever write reviews of books?"

Zeno looked at him suspiciously. "Yeah, I do. Mostly in literary magazines and, I'm ashamed to admit, now and then on Amazon."

Sidney pretended to be surprised. "Oh, yeah? I bet you've written about some losers."

Zeno folded his hands on his desk and leaned forward. "Not really."

"Well, I'm glad you take it easy on people, then." He looked down at the highways of red lines traversing his story.

"I do. But sometimes, maybe when I've had a few, or I read work by someone who has absolutely no idea what he's writing about, no heart, you know, I can get surly. If he had heart, he wouldn't write about things he had no experience with. Readers deserve better than that." Here he made eye contact. "Sometimes a guy writes about war or loving someone, and I can tell that he's a coward or a loveless person. It's just an attitude that infects every word, and then almost any reader can see he's a phony."

Sidney swallowed hard. Trying to keep his voice from trembling, he asked, "What do you like about books, you know, the ones you like?"

Zeno frowned. "I like most of them, really. Even pretty bad ones, bad detective books, novels with all sorts of historical mistakes. I respect the effort, I guess. Writing a book asks for sacrifices, takes a writer away from his or her spouse sometimes." He shook his head. "Did you say you have a wife?"

"Yes."

"That's nice. It must be nice to still have a wife. Same wife as always?"

"Yes."

"I envy you." Zeno sat back in his chair. "Well, do you have any questions?" He opened his hands as if to receive something.

Sidney wanted to tear off his mask and ask why Zeno had written such a terrible review about his book. But he held back, because he was ashamed and already knew why. Instead, he asked, "Does the vibration from the stamping plant bug you?"

Zeno was quiet. Then he said, "Sometimes at night I can feel it in my back, and I think, That machine doesn't stop, and I can't either. You've got to keep at it. If something bad happens, ignore it and keep on producing. The machine doesn't whine when it bangs out a bad refrigerator door."

A class bell echoed down the tiled hall. Zeno stood and picked up a stack of essays and moved for the door.

"Wait, here's your money." Sidney followed him into the hall and held out an envelope.

"What? Oh, heck. Just keep it." And he was gone, his rubber-soled shoes lisping off toward one of the building's many overheated rooms.

Driving back to Louisiana, he tried to relish the thought of waiting for Bardol's book to appear, but all he could think of was similar trips he'd made about three times a year. Several to spy on his daughters, one to a telemarketer's house in Florida, another to an eBay seller in Mississippi who'd sold him a lousy used laptop, one to an IRS agent in Atlanta, enough visits to keep him awake and remembering all the way home. The trips were joyless adventures, but there was something inside that made him want to get even with people. Or maybe something that wasn't inside him. At the time he had found it thrilling to insult the IRS agent to his face, but now he remembered the man's pained, embarrassed expression. The elderly gentleman in Mississippi grudgingly gave him another used laptop and a little gas money, but Sidney remembered with a pang that he lived in a small rusty trailer. As the interstate rattled under his car's wheels he wondered what he had gotten out of Zeno Bardol other than more criticism. Almost automatically, he began to plan his review, forging razory words into murderous sentences.

He pulled into his driveway, exhausted, his back aching like a sore tooth, and was surprised that no lights were on in the house. Bulling into the kitchen, he fumbled the switch on and saw a single sheet of paper on the table. It was a note from his wife stating, in the declarative tone of someone reminding him to take out the trash, that she was leaving him. He went to the phone and called her, but no one answered, and neither did his daughters, so he suspected they all were looking at their caller IDs, biting their lips, waiting for him to give up. He called her friends, but they didn't know where she was. Her sister and brother were reserved with him, telling nothing. He called an old uncle of hers and he said she was probably at her mother's house. Her parents had been dead a few years, but the family had never gotten rid of the outdated house or most of its furniture. He tried there, but the land line had long been disconnected.

Practically starving, he got something to eat out of the refrigerator. Twenty minutes later he went back to look for dessert, and the phone rang.

"There's pie on the second shelf, in the back."

He held the phone with both hands. "Why'd you take off?"

"Sid, I need some time away from you. Maybe forever."

"What the hell? I don't know what's happening."

"That's the problem."

"You're trying to hurt me?"

"Sid, nobody is trying to hurt *you*. That you believe everybody's out to get you is your biggest problem." And she hung up.

She wouldn't meet him. He thought she'd be gone three days, but she didn't return his calls for the many days he left messages. Over the next month, he learned to cope with the empty house. Then one week she called twice, around eight in the morning, and he tried to argue with her. At work, his associates would ask about his wife, but never about him. It killed him that they knew. Gilman Raider passed him in the hall and said, over his shoulder, "Kind of lonely in the house, eh?"

Every day he'd check Amazon at least four times, his sense of expectancy growing as the weeks slid by. And then, two months after he had returned from Indiana, there it was, a new novel titled *The Summer of No Returns,* by Zeno Bardol, associate professor of English at Jason Polinski Community College. He ordered it at once and paid extra to have it sent overnight. The next afternoon, it was sitting on his side porch, and he tore the package apart like an excited child and went in to sit with the hardback at his kitchen table, a red pen in his hand, ready to slash through passages, to attack. He wanted to be the first to comment on the novel, to set the tone for anyone else who might want to take a crack at old Zeno. He read the first two sentences carefully, the way a clinician might study a biopsy. The novel began: "At false dawn, the boy appeared in the farm lot and placed a pail next to his animal. It was a three-winters cow, its silky coat the color of red mahogany, and it submitted to slender white fingers pinned deep in its fur as the boy pulled the huge head around to baptize the soap off it with the hose. After a short time, they stood still together in the scanty fall snow, the red Charolais now steaming and clean for the fair and breathing a silver crown above the child's head."

Sidney read thirty pages and couldn't mark a word. He fixed himself a sandwich and a beer, then took the book into the den and sat in his leather lounger, reading another fifty pages, never letting go of the red pen. Around eight, he reluctantly put the book down and went upstairs to turn on his laptop to check his mail.

The $18.75 records check on Zeno Bardol had sent a bonus report, and some bot crawling through the world's records added newspaper content. Sidney looked for something that would make him hate the guy, write him off as a loser, but all he found was a long series of articles about Zeno Bardol's nine-year-old son, a Boy Scout, science-project winner, altar boy, a blond, green-eyed kid who had been kidnapped years and years before, held for ransom, and murdered. There were ten articles in the state paper. The description of what the kidnapper had done to the child made Sidney suddenly press the off button on the machine and pull his finger back as if it had been burned. He understood why Zeno and his wife had decided not to stay together. It was because they had created this child who was delivered to such a dark fate. Each look at the other would remind them of that fate for the rest of their lives.

Sidney went back to his chair and resumed reading. It wasn't a long novel, barely three hundred pages, and he read carefully until first light, the red pen forgotten on the table next to the chair. When he closed the book, he was agitated and confused. There wasn't one bad sentence anywhere. There was dark tragedy, there was light, there was understanding that could only be drawn from living through it all. He dropped the book to the floor. It was time to write the review.

In his upstairs office he turned on his laptop, logged on to Amazon, and set up the evaluation. First the customer had to click from one to five stars. With the mouse in his hand he felt the power to hurl meteors at all the people who had hurt him down through the years. He floated the cursor above the first star and set his jaw. At that moment, the desk phone next to his left hand began to ring. He picked up the receiver and heard his wife ask if he'd like to meet her for breakfast. To talk.

He was drowsy and disoriented. "Talk about what?"

"Sid, please."

He didn't know why, but he was able to recognize an attempt at connection in her voice, something that must have always been there. "You want to talk about me?"

"Yes," she said, and he slid the cursor over the second star, wondering if his wife really wasn't who he'd thought she was, someone always trying to get his goat, to make him feel small.

"I'm pretty tired, but . . . well, sure, I'd be glad to have breakfast with you."

"That's good, honey. We have to try something different."

"Something different," he repeated, remembering his wife's eyes, how she had looked at him back when they were first married. The cursor slid above the fifth star, his forefinger trembling over the mouse as if paralyzed by a lifetime of bad decisions and trying to break free from the shadow of all of them at once. "Different's good," he said at last.

Easy Pickings

*H*e drove into Louisiana from Texas in the stolen sedan, taking the minor roads, the cracked and grass-lined blacktop where houses showed up one to the mile. The land was overrun with low crops he did not recognize, and was absolutely flat, which he liked because he could see a police car from a long way off. He was a short man, small of frame, tattooed on the neck and arms with crabs and scorpions, which fit his grabbing occupation of thief. In the hollow of his throat was a small blue lobster, one of its claws holding a hand-rolled cigarette. He thought of the woman in Houston he'd terrorized the day before, coming into her kitchen and pulling his scary knife, a discount Bowie he'd bought at the KKK table at a local gun show, and putting it to her throat. She wept and trembled, giving him her rings, leading him to her husband's little stash of poker money. The day before that, he'd spotted an old woman in Victoria returning alone from the grocery store, and he'd followed her into the house, taking her jewelry, showing the knife when she balked, and getting the cash from her wallet. He'd robbed only these two women, but it seemed that he'd been doing it all his life, like walking and breathing, even though he'd just got out of jail the week before after doing two years for stealing welfare checks. He looked through the windshield at the poor, watery country. Anyone who would live out here would be simple, he thought, real stupid and easy pickings.

His name was Marvin, but he called himself Big Blade because the name made him feel other than what he was: small, petty, and dull.

He noticed a white frame house ahead on the right side of the road, sitting at the edge of a flooded field, clothes on the line out back. Big

Blade had been raised in a trashy Houston subdivision and had never seen clothes dried out in the open. At first he thought the laundry was part of some type of yard sale, but after he stopped on the shoulder and studied the limp dresses and aprons, he figured it out. Across the road and two hundred yards away was a similar house, an asbestos-siding rectangle with a tin roof, and after that, nothing but blacktop. Big Blade noticed that there were no men's clothes on the line, and he turned into the driveway.

Mrs. Arceneaux was eighty-five years old and spoke Acadian French to her chickens because nearly everyone else who could speak it was dead. She came out into the yard with a plastic bowl of feed and was met at the back steps by Marvin, who pulled out his big knife, his eyes gleaming. Mrs. Arceneaux's vision was not sharp enough to see the evil eyes, but she saw the tattoos and she saw the knife.

"Baby, who wrote all over you? And what you want, you, wit' that big cane cutter you got? If you hungry, all I got is them chicken *labas,* and if you cut off a head, throw it in the bushes at the back of my lot and pluck them feather over there because the wind is blowin' west today and—"

"Shut up, and get inside," Big Blade growled, giving the old woman a push toward her screen door. "I want your money."

Mrs. Arceneaux narrowed her eyes at him and then hobbled up the back steps into her kitchen. "Well, I be damn. Ain't you got nobody better to rob than a ol' lady whose husband died twenty-nine years ago of a heart attack in a bourrée game holding ace, king, queen of trumps? The priest told me—"

Big Blade began to seethe, his voice aspirate and low. "I will kill you if you don't give me your jewelry and money. I'll gut you like one of your chickens."

The old lady stopped speaking for just a second to bring him into focus. "You with the crawfish drew on your throat, you trying to scare me wit' a knife? Like I ain't use to death? I break a chicken neck three time a week and my brother he got shot dead next to me at the St. Landry Parish fair in 1936 and all my husband's brother got killed in that German war and that Lodrigue boy died with his head in my apron the day the tractor run over him, 'course he was putting on the plow with the damn thing in gear and even the priest said it wasn't too bright to get plowed under by your own plow and—"

"They call me Big Blade," Marvin thundered.

"My name's Doris Arceneaux, I used to be a Boudreaux before—"

He slapped the old woman, and her upper plate landed on the Formica dinette table. With no hesitation she picked up her teeth and walked to the sink to rinse them off. Grabbing the incisors, she slid her dentures back in place. "Hurt?" she yelled. "You want to hurt a old lady what had seven children, one come out arm-first? Look, I had eight major surgeries and a appendix that blowed up inside me when I was first marry, made me so sick I was throwing up pieces of gut and the priest gave me extreme unction nine time."

"Shut up," Big Blade yelled, raising his hand over her puff of hair.

"Oh, you kin hit me again, yeah, and then I'm gonna drop on the floor and what you gonna do with me then?"

"I can kill you," he hollered.

"But you can't eat me," Mrs. Arceneaux shrilled back, wagging a knobby finger in Big Blade's befuddled face.

In the other house on that stretch of road old Mrs. Breaux realized with a gasp that she was not going to take a trick in a bourrée game and would have to match an $18 pot. The third trick had been raked off the table when Mrs. Breaux turned up her hearing aid with a twist of her forefinger and began begging, "Oh, please somebody don't drop you biggest trump so I can save myself."

"I can't hold back, *chere*," Sadie Lalonde told her. "I got to play to win. That's the rules." Mrs. Lalonde's upper arms jiggled as she snapped down a trump ace.

Mrs. Breaux's eyes got small as a bat's, and her mouth turned into a raisin. "You done killed my jack," she yelled, following suit with her card. "I'm bourréed."

Mr. Alvin crossed his legs and sniffed. "You bourréed yourself, girl. You should know better to come in a game with the jack dry." Mr. Alvin

SIGNALS

shook a poof of white hair out of his florid face and carefully led off
with a four trump followed by Sadie's ten and a stray diamond by Mrs.
Breaux, whose little cigarette-stained mustache began to quiver as she
watched the money get raked off the table.

"You done it!" Mrs. Breaux hollered. She shrank back in her wooden
chair and searched over her ninety years of evil-tempered earthly existence for the vilest curse words she'd ever heard, and none of them
packed the power she wanted. Finally she said, "I hope you get diabetes
of the blowhole!"

The other three widows and one never-married man laughed aloud
at her exasperation and fidgeted with the coins in their little money
piles, digging for the next ante. Mrs. Guidroz pulled her aluminum cane
off the back of her chair to get up for a glass of tap water.

"There's ice water in the fridge," Sadie offered.

Mrs. Guidroz shook her tight blue curls. "I wasn't raised to drink
cold water. That stuff hurts my mout'." As she drew a glassful from
the singing tap, she looked out the window and down the road. "Hey.
Doris, she got herself some company."

"If it's a red truck it must be her son, Nelson," Sadie said. "Today's
Tuesday, when he comes around."

"Non, this is a li'l white car."

"Maybe it's the power company," Mr. Alvin suggested.

"Non, this is too little for a 'lectric company car. Where would they
put their pliers and wire in that thing?"

Sadie Lalonde hoisted herself off the two chairs she was sitting on
and wobbled to the window, putting her face next to Mrs. Guidroz's.
"That's either a Dodge or a Plimmit."

"What's the difference?"

"I think they the same car, but they label the ones with ugly paint
Plimmets." Sadie looked over her glasses. "Doris don't know nobody
drives a car like that."

Mr. Alvin came to the window and wedged into the women. "You
sure it ain't a Tyota? One of her two dozen granddaughters drives one
like that."

"Nanette. I think she sold that, though."

Mr. Alvin shook his head. "Oh, no she wouldn't. You know, them

little yellow fingers make them Tyotas and they don't never wear out."
He looked through the window. "But that's one of them little Freons."

"Is that a Chevrolet?"

"No, it's a cheap Dodge with a rubber-band motor. Only a Jehovah
Witness would drive something like that."

"Aw, no." Mrs. Guidroz stamped her cane on the linoleum. "You
think we ought to call over there and see if she needs help runnin' them
off. Them Jehovah Witness like cockleburs on corduroy."

From the card table behind the group at the sink rose Beverly Per-
riloux's voice. She had lit up a Camel and was talking out the smoke.
"Y'all come back and play some cards before Mrs. Breaux catches herself a little stroke." She took another intense drag, all the tiny warts on
her face moving in to the center.

"Damn right," Mrs. Breaux complained. "I got to win my eighteen
dollar back."

Mrs. Guidroz gulped two swallows of water while Sadie reached for
her wall phone.

Big Blade looked around Mrs. Arceneaux's kitchen at the plywood cabinets, the swirling linoleum that popped when he stepped on it, at a
plastic toaster that was a clock and out of which a piece of plastic toast
slowly arose every ten seconds. It occurred to him that he was trying to
rob the wrong woman.

"I want your wedding rings," he announced.

She held her hand out toward him. "I stopped wearin' one when
Authur told me to."

Big Blade wiggled his knife. "Arthur?"

"Yah. Arthur-ritis."

"Where is it?"

"It wasn't but a little silver circle and I gave it to a grandbaby to wear
on her necklace. Oh, I had a diamond up on some prongs, too, but it
used to get plugged up with grandbaby shit when I changed they diapers, so I gave that away."

The phone rang and Big Blade stepped toward it. "Answer and act
normal. One false word and I'll cut you open."

She gathered her arms vertically in front of her, her fists under her chin, feigning fright, and tiptoed to the wall phone.

"Hallo," she yelled. Then turning to Big Blade she told him, "It's Sadie Lalonde from down the road." Speaking back into the receiver she said, "No, it ain't no holy-rolly, it's some boy with a sword trying to rob me like the government."

Big Blade reached out and cut the phone cord with a swipe. "I ought to kill you where you stand," he said.

Mrs. Arceneaux grabbed the swinging cord and gave him a savage look. "And then what would you have?"

He blinked. "Whoever called better not cause no trouble."

She put a thumb over her shoulder. "Sadie and that gang playing bourrée. You couldn't blow 'em out that house with dynamite."

He looked around, perhaps wondering if the worn-out contents of her kitchen would fit into the stolen car he'd left idling out front. "You got to have some money around here somewhere. Go get it."

She raised a hand above her head and toddled off toward the hall. "If that's all it takes to get you out my hair you kin have it, yeah." Abruptly she turned around and walked toward the stove. "I almos' forgot my chicken stew heatin' on the burner."

"Never mind that," he growled.

Mrs. Arceneaux rolled up an eye at him. "You hungry, you?" She lifted a lid, and a nimbus laden with smells of onion, garlic, bell pepper, and a medium nut-brown roux rose like a spirit out of the cast-iron pot.

"What's that?" Big Blade sniffed toward the stove, his knife drifting.

"Chicken stew. You eat that over some rice and with potato salad and hot sweet peas." She looked at the boy's eyes and stirred the rich gravy seductively. "You burglars take time to eat or what?"

"Oh, Jesus, Mary, and Joseph," Mrs. Lalonde sang, holding the dead receiver to her ear and looking out of her little kitchen window with three other worried card players. "I don't know what to think."

"She's probably just being nasty to us," Mrs. Guidroz said, tapping her cane against Mr. Alvin's big, soft leg. "She wants us to worry."

"That woman says some crazy things," Beverly agreed. "She spends so much time cooking I think she's got natural gas on the brain."

At the table, Mrs. Breaux lit up a Picayune with her creaky Zippo. "Hot damn, let's play cards. Ain't nobody can put nothin' over on Doris Arceneaux."

"Somebody's over there intrudin'," Sadie protested.

Mrs. Breaux sniffed. "She'll talk the intrudin' parts off their body, that's for true."

"Well, her phone won't answer back. Somebody ought to go over and see who's there with her."

The old women turned toward Mr. Alvin, a tall, jiggly old man with pale, fine-textured skin, and built like an eggplant. His pleated gray trousers hung on him like a skirt on a fat convent-school girl. "Why me?"

"You a man," Mrs. Guidroz exclaimed.

Mr. Alvin's eyes expanded as though the information was a surprise. "*Mais,* what you want me to do?"

Sadie turned him toward the screen door. "Just go look in her kitchen window and see if everything is all right."

"I shouldn't knock first?"

Mrs. Guidroz shook her tiny head. "If there's a bad man in there you gonna tip him off."

Mr. Alvin hung back. "I don't know."

"Dammit Alvin," Mrs. Guidroz said, "I'd go myself but it's been raining and last time I walked to Doris's from here my stick went down in her lawn a foot deep, yeah, and I couldn't get it unstuck and Doris wasn't there so I had to limp all the way back and call my son to come pull it out."

"Go *on,* Alvin," Sadie said, putting a shoulder to his back and nudging him out the door.

Mr. Alvin looked down the road to Mrs. Arceneaux's house as he walked the clamshell shoulder trying to seem inconspicuous. An old pickup truck passed by driven by what seemed to be a twelve-year-old boy, and Alvin did not return the child's wave. He walked the grassy edge of Mrs. Arceneaux's driveway and took to the spongy lawn, circling around to her kitchen window. He stooped and walked under it, the way he'd seen detectives do in the movies. When he raised his eyes slowly past the window ledge, he saw a strange man at Mrs. Arceneaux's table waving a murderous-looking knife at the old woman while chewing a big mouthful of chicken stew.

"You don't watch out I'm gonna put you in that stewpot," the man said.

Mr. Alvin lowered himself slow as a clock's hand and began slogging through the deep grass toward the highway. He heard something like a steam engine puffing as he walked along, then realized that it was his own breath. He thought about running and tried to remember how to do it, but his heart was pounding so hard that all he could do was swing his arms faster and paddle the air back to Sadie's house.

The women were at the window watching him hurry back. "Oh, *mon Dieu*," Mrs. Guidroz sang, "look how fast Alvin's moving. What's it mean?"

Mrs. Breaux cackled. "It's probably just his Ex-Lax working."

They opened the door and pulled him into the room by his flabby arms.

"There's someone there holding a knife on Doris," Mr. Alvin gasped.

"*Ai, yai, yai,*" Sadie shouted.

"Call Deputy Sid," Beverly announced from the card table, where she was refilling her butane lighter from a miniature canister of gas.

Sadie shook her head. "It'll take him a half hour to get out here." She straightened up and looked around. "Maybe one of us ought to go over there with a gun."

Mr. Alvin put up his big hands. "Oh, no, I went already." He walked over to the phone and dialed the sheriff's office.

Mrs. Breaux threw down a pack of cards in disgust. "What kind of gun you got?"

Sadie reached into the next room to a little space between an armoire and the wall, retrieving a double-barreled shotgun with exposed hammers. "This was Lester's daddy's gun."

Mrs. Breaux walked over and figured out how to open the action. "They ain't no bullets in this thing."

Sadie walked over to her dresser, her perfume and lotion bottles clinking against each other on the vanity, and pulled out the top drawer. "Does this fit?" She handed Mrs. Breaux a tarnished .38-caliber cartridge. She dropped it into the gun, but it rattled down the barrel and tumbled out onto the linoleum.

"It's not the right size," Mrs. Breaux complained, peering into Sadie's outstretched hand and plucking two high-brass cardboard shells labeled with double 0s. "Here you go." She plunked in the shells and snapped the gun shut.

*T*he parish had only one settlement to the south, Grand Crapaud, and south of that the highway came to an end, its center line leading up to the steps of a twelve-by-twelve plywood building on piers, the office of the South-End Deputy.

Deputy Sid was a tall black man wearing a cowboy hat with a gold badge on the crown and an immaculate, freshly ironed uniform. He sat at his little desk filling out a report about Minos Blanchard letting his Dodge Dart roll overboard at the boat ramp next door. The phone rang and it was the dispatcher from the parish seat.

"Sid, you there?"

"I'm here all right."

"Mrs. Lalonde out by Prairie Amère called in that Doris Arceneaux has an intruder in her house right now."

"That's those peoples always playin' cards?"

"And the one that's always cooking."

"How does Mrs. Lalonde know they's somebody in there?"

"There's a strange car in the yard."

"Did she say what kind it was?"

"She said it was a Freon."

"They ain't no such thing."

"I know that. Mr. Alvin looked in the window and saw the intruder."

Deputy Sid pushed back his hat. "What's Mr. Alvin doin' lookin' in a *woman's* window?"

"Can you get out there?"

"Sho." He hung up and in one step was at the door.

Mrs. Arceneaux watched Big Blade finish one overflowing plate of chicken stew, and then she fixed him another, providing him all the while with French-dripped coffee laced with brandy.

"You better think where you put your money," Big Blade said through a mouthful of potato salad.

"You ain't had some dessert yet," Mrs. Arceneaux cooed. "Look, I foun' some bread pudding with whiskey sauce in the fridge."

Big Blade took a tentative taste of the dessert, then a spoonful, eating slowly and with one eye closed. By the time he'd eaten everything on the table, he was stunned with food, drowsy, dim-witted with food. He had been eating for half an hour. When he saw movement at the screen door, he ignored it for a moment, but when the form of a uniformed black man imprinted itself on his consciousness, he jumped up holding his knife in one hand and the old lady's bony arm in the other.

Deputy Sid stepped in smiling, moving easily as though he'd lived in the kitchen all his life and was walking through his own house. "How you doin', Mrs. Arceneaux?"

"Hey yourself, Deputy Sid. They's fresh coffee on the stove."

"Freeze," Blade barked.

Deputy Sid stopped the motion of his hand above the range. "I can't have no coffee?"

The little plastic slice of toast peeked out of the clock, and surprised, Blade yelled, "Ahhh."

"What?" Deputy Sid looked to the clock, checked his wristwatch.

"It's just that damn clock," Mrs. Arceneaux said. "Crazy thing scares the hell out of me, too, but my sister give it to me and what can you do? I come in here at night sometime and that little toast come up like a rat stickin' its head out a cracker can and—"

"Never mind." Big Blade was looking at the staghorn-gripped, nickel-plated revolver that was angled toward him on the policeman's narrow hip. "Give me your gun or I'll cut the old lady's throat."

Deputy Sid considered this for a moment. "Okay, man. But hold on to Misres Doris 'cause she fixin' to take off." The deputy popped his safety strap, lifted his revolver with two fingers, and laid it on the table. Blade held on to the old lady with one hand, reached to the table, still holding the big knife, and realized that he would have to put it down to retrieve the gun. The second he put his finger into the trigger guard of the pistol, Deputy Sid moved his hand over and picked up the knife.

"Hey," Blade said, pointing the shiny pistol at his head.

"You don't need this no more." Deputy Sid dropped the knife behind the refrigerator.

"I want my knife."

"You better get on out of here while you got the upper hand."

Big Blade glanced through the screen door. "Yeah. I bet you got buddies outside just waiting."

Deputy Sid shook his head. "No, man. It's just me. But let me give you some advice. You on a dead-end parish highway. The open end got a roadblock right now. South of here it's all marsh and alligators."

"And then what?"

Deputy Sid screwed up an eye to think. "Cuba, I guess."

"Shit. What about north?"

"Rice fields for five miles."

"That little car I got will get me through the roadblock."

"I don't know. You left the motor runnin' and it idled out of gas. You can get in it, but it won't go nowhere."

Big Blade's eyeballs bounced back and forth for a few seconds. He waved the gun. "Handcuff yourself to that oven door and give me the keys."

Mrs. Arceneaux pointed. "Careful you don't scratch nothin'. The last thing my husband did before he died is buy me that stove and it got to last me a long time. He told me—"

"I'm taking her with me. So if you got partners outside, you better call to them."

"I'm the onliest one back here," Deputy Sid told him, cuffing himself to the stove's door.

"Is your cruiser idling?" Big Blade asked with a wicked smile.

The deputy nodded slowly.

"Hah, you people are dumb as dirt," he said, backing out of the kitchen with the old lady in tow.

Deputy Sid watched them walk out of his line of vision. He looked at the stove, felt the side of the coffeepot, and then stretched to the cabinet to get himself a cup.

The cruiser was eight years old, and Big Blade had to clean out clipboards, a digital adding machine, dog-eared manuals on report writing, apples, candy bars, chewing gum, magazines, and empty cans of mace before his hostage would fit into the front seat. She buckled her seat belt, and he climbed in on the driver's side. The old white Dodge's transmission slipped so badly that it would hardly back out onto the road, but soon they were spinning along the highway, going west. After five miles, he could see one police car in the distance parked across the flat road, and he knew he could make the escape work. All he had to do was hold the pistol to her head and let the officers see this. They'd let him roll through like a tourist.

Just then Mrs. Arceneaux crossed her hands over her breastbone and announced in a strangled voice, "I'm havin' me another heart attack."

Big Blade stopped the car and watched the old woman's face turn red. She coughed once, and her arms fell limp at her side, her upper plate tumbling from her mouth and bouncing on the floor mat. He looked ahead to what he could now see were two police cars waiting with their flashers swatting the flat light rolling off the rice fields. Feeling with great dread the flesh of the woman's neck, he could find no pulse, and suddenly everything changed. He imagined himself strapped to a gurney in a Louisiana prison waiting for the fatal charge to come along the tube into his arm. He looked into his rearview and then turned the car around, the old woman's head rolling right. Maybe there would be a boat at the end of the road and he could escape in that.

The Dodge stuttered and groaned up to thirty, forty, forty-five as he headed in the other direction. Soon Doris Arceneaux's house was rolling up on the right, and on the left he watched the only other house in the area, with a mailbox out front and a bushy cedar growing next to it. As soon as he passed that mailbox his peripheral vision snapped a picture of five old people crouching in a line, hiding behind the cedar. At once he heard a huge detonation and the car began a drunken spin, metal grinding on the blacktop, the tires howling until the cruiser stopped sideways in the road. Big Blade shook his head and fell out of the front seat, holding Deputy Sid's revolver. He saw a skinny old woman in a print dress walking up and holding a shotgun toward his midsection. One hammer on the gun was down, and the other was up like a fang ready to drop. He stood and raised the nickel-plated revolver and pulled the trigger, aiming at her legs, but all the weapon did was go tik-tik-tik-tik-tik-tik.

"Get on the damn ground," Mrs. Breaux hollered in her creaky voice, "or I'll let the air out of you like I did that tire, yeah."

As Big Blade lay down in the road, he heard a cackle from the front seat of the cruiser as Mrs. Arceneaux unbuckled herself and climbed out with her upper plate in her hand. "Ha, haaaa, I foolt him good. He tought I was dead and run from them other cops."

Along the shoulder of the road came Deputy Sid, a sea-green oven door under his arm. He bent down, picked up his revolver, and loaded it with six shells dug out of his pocket. "I got him now, ladies, Mr. Al."

Mrs. Arceneaux sidled up to him. "You got some more police comin'?"

"Yeah. I called 'em from your bedroom phone. Then I called your neighbors here."

Mrs. Breaux lowered the hammer on the shotgun. "Hot damn. Now we can get back to the game. Doris, you want to play?"

She waved her hand above her white hair as if chasing a fly. "Naw, me, I got to go clean up my kitchen."

"What about you, Deputy Sid?"

He rested the bottom of the oven door on the asphalt and studied his blasted front tire and the pellet holes in the fender. "It gon' take me a week to write all this up. Maybe next time ya'll play you can give me a call."

Sadie lumbered up out of the grass, followed by Mr. Alvin. "Don't bring that gun into the house loaded," she said.

Mrs. Breaux opened the action and plucked out the good shell, chucking the empty into the ditch. She handed the weapon to Mr. Alvin, who took it from her with his fingertips, as though it might be red-hot. Mrs. Breaux grabbed a handful of his shirt and let him tow her off the road and across the soft lawn. Suddenly, she wheeled around. "Hey you," she called to Big Blade, who was squirming under the barrel of Deputy Sid's revolver.

"What?" He had to look through the window of the oven door to see her.

"If you ever get out of jail, I want you to come play cards with us." She threw back her head and laughed.

"Why's that?" He twisted his head up. "What you mean?"

"Just bring lots of money, boy," Mrs. Breaux called as she turned to look down the road at an approaching parade of flashing lights and the warbling laugh of a siren sailing high over the simple rice fields.

Signals

When his cherished stereo receiver died, giving off a spiral of white smoke through its top, Professor Talis Kimita knelt before it and placed his hands on the walnut case as one might console a relative who had suddenly become ill. He'd bought the instrument new in 1976 for many lats on the black market in Riga, and even connected to his terrible East German speakers it made him the envy of his intellectual friends because of its dreadnought power and long arm of reception that brought in noncommunist news and classical music from all over Europe. It bore the brave name Pioneer, which made him think of wagon trains and the endless western prairies he'd read of as a child. The seller let him have it for a good price because it wouldn't operate on Latvia's 220-volt current. Talis painted a public toilet in Ogre by himself to earn enough money to buy a high-end voltage converter.

In 1979 he graduated from university and managed to leave Latvia on a student visa, bringing the seventy-pound music box with him to graduate school in New York. Connected to better speakers, the rumbling Pioneer SX-1250 became his Mozart-seeping companion morning and night, more of a partner than his new and younger American wife. Marlena was a statuesque woman of severe beauty, a philosophy student from Illinois, who was at first attracted but later repelled by his brooding and isolated nature. She began calling him a cold fish, declaiming in their little apartment kitchen that he was an icicle of logic despiritualized by Russian thought. He called her names as well, announcing during more than one argument that her stylish American clothes made her excessively provincial. She claimed he was too used to small-breasted women wearing soot-colored wool sweaters and blanket-like skirts to protect their fat legs from frostbite. He told her she smelled like a tart and should take up smoking.

His first teaching job in New York had lasted two years. He lost his position because of low student evaluations; his pupils didn't accept his condescension, his lack of tolerance. He found a job at a smaller school in Minnesota, where he liked the climate, and then, after his marriage failed, he taught in a half-occupied college in Oregon, a failing Episcopal school in Connecticut made of drafty stone buildings, a computer-based university in tumbleweedy west Texas, a community college in Eatabuga, Mississippi, beginning a long train of non-reappointments until he'd been through ten schools in all, each less prestigious than the previous. He finally wound up at Marshland Community Junior College and Trade School in Grand Crapaud, Louisiana.

And so on a Tuesday night, ungraded freshman history tests spilling from his lap, Talis Kimita hovered over his venerable machine, twisting its many silver knobs and clicking its bright levers up and down to no effect. His house fell silent for the first time, for the machine had been turned on every minute he was awake since he'd owned it, giving him classical music, the BBC, and the polite outrage of public radio commentators. In a panic, he read through his phone directory searching for repairmen, but soon discovered that there was no local technician who worked on old high-end audio equipment, and even on the Internet the closest place he could find was in central Texas, and they would repair it at a cost of $750, plus an absurd shipping charge. He had doubts the receiver would be safe in the mail, but the next day he called the Texas business, and a man who sounded like a parody of a cowboy told him cheerfully, "Hell yeah, ol buddy, we'll have that unit a-singin' like Willie Nelson in no time." Talis distrusted cheerful Americans, suspecting they were out to trick him, that their good cheer was a cover for incompetence. Good cheer reminded him of his father, a minor Communist official in charge of lubricating oil consumption in Riga. His father had a round head, a black mustache, and a little shock of dark hair oiled down straight across his skull. He used to say, when a young Talis would come to him for advice on the big truths of existence, that nothing was of any

significance unless it stopped your breathing. Then he would laugh and
light a cigarette.

On Wednesday night, he walked around his quiet house, a renovated cypress cottage in the middle of an overactive Louisiana lawn, and
mourned the loss of music. The machine was his heart, his thought, an
ever-flowing well of Bach and Sibelius that buoyed him along through
his bitter life. But with the music turned off, his thoughts turned into
sheep escaping their pasture, and Talis became annoyed by his own
mental activity. It occurred to him that the stereo receiver had insulated
him from things to which he should have paid more attention.

For the remainder of the week he was grumpy with his colleagues,
even more distant than usual at the coffee machine in the teachers'
lounge. He was big and round-shouldered, every hair on his body silver as Latvian frost. His fellow professors taught in short-sleeved shirts
and tennis shoes, but even in the Gulf Coast climate Talis continued to
dress in somber wool suits and glossy leather lace-ups. The smothering humidity of the region was a daily mystery he chose to ignore, as
though the heat were a meteorological mistake that would disappear at
any moment, to be followed closely by snow. No one had told him that
it hadn't snowed in Grand Crapaud since 1949. After work on Friday,
he sat in his house and sweated in silence, as he loathed American television and had depended on the radio broadcasts to keep him informed
of the world's disasters, the daily history, as he termed the news.

On Saturday morning came the noise that always made him think
of Russian helicopters trembling above his little childhood home in
Lielvārde. It was Janice LeBlanc cutting the grass on his tiny lawn with
her roaring, wheeled disk of a machine she steered by levers. A Dixie
Chopper, he believed it was called. Janice came once a week because the
St. Augustine of the front and back yards rose daily like slow green fire
around his house. When she had finished edging the walk, she stepped
up onto the porch, and Talis opened the door to hand her a check.

"Is a good job," he said, glancing past the glistening middle-aged
woman in a denim shirt.

"Thanks, doc. You got any other work to do, just let me know. Your
porch could use pressure washing."

Talis looked over at a rocking chair he had never used. He was unaware of what to do on a porch, since where he was raised people did not sit out enjoying the blizzards. "No, thank you, Janice."

"All right. If you need a tune-up on that Volvo, I can do that too. There's nothing I can't fix if I set my mind to it." She pulled off her leather gloves, and Talis saw that she had surprisingly nice hands, younger looking than his.

"The Volvo never gives me trouble. But thank you."

Janice threw a backward glance at the old brick-red automobile parked against the curb. "Yeah, those cars are like defensive linemen. You can run into them, but you won't hurt them much."

The lawn lady, Talis noticed, personified her various machines. The complex and rumbling lawn mower sported a man's name painted on the side in art deco script next to a tiny stick-on image of the Blessed Virgin. The tiny chainsaw she used to cut back the azaleas she referred to as Termite. He imagined she was a simple person who liked symbols, saw meanings in objects.

After Janice left, Talis ate lunch and checked his watch. It was time for the opera broadcast from a New Orleans station, and he stared at the old Pioneer receiver longingly, then walked over and for the hundredth time wiggled its electrical cord, its antenna, worried its bright buttons, knobs, and levers to no good result. He ran the station-indicator needle back and forth under the glass dial and gave the side of the cabinet several affectionate slaps. Finally, he sat back and stared. The lights inside the dial were on, but the machine was as soundless as one of his sophomores when asked about the causes of the Sino-Russian war. So he began to replay in his head some of the music that the box had given him in the past, but merely imagining a Puccini opera was no match for hearing the oiled and glossy walnut speakers sing through his bones.

Talis began to think it odd that he didn't have any friends. The one speaking acquaintance he'd made at Marshland Community Junior College was an electrical engineer, Modred Stallings. So the next time they were seated at adjacent tables in the faculty lounge, not speaking, Talis leaned over and mentioned his failed stereo receiver.

Modred was a scientist, a Canadian, a man who understood the pointlessness of wasting time. He didn't stop chewing as he spoke. "Buy a new stereo and throw the old one in the trash," he told him.

"No, no. The new models don't have the richness of sound. They are covered with nearly invisible black buttons in their black frames. With my old unit I can nurse along a weak station." His hands sprung open like a bird's wings. "It brings in music from all over."

Modred's Adam's apple jiggled in his thin, pale neck. "The thing's what, thirty-five, forty years old? It's worn out. In America, we discard things that are worn out."

Talis gave him a cold look. "Don't talk to me as though I just passed through Ellis Island."

Modred took another large swatch of sandwich into his mouth. "Seems like that old box is awfully important to you. Is that all you do? Just listen to it?" He swallowed, blinking hard. "Why don't you come to the faculty parties on Fridays? Just for a beer."

He shook his head. "I don't know any of those people."

"You might if you were less distant with them."

"You're saying I am cold?" An image of his wife of long ago flashed in his mind, a thin hand on a long hip, ebony hair sailing off to one side as she patiently berated him.

Modred seemed about to say something, but closed his mouth.

Talis leaned closer and clasped his hands. "Look, I was wondering if you would examine the receiver."

Modred shook his head. "There are a thousand old components in that box of yours, and just about any of them could fail and stop your machine from working. It just doesn't make sense to fix it."

He sat back again. "I could pay you."

"Not enough. That system's before my time."

Talis put his forehead down on the silly plastic table. He'd forgotten that Modred was only thirty and he was sixty. The young man had never lived through the deep-canyon sound of seventies audio and probably listened to nothing more complex than that Britney Spears person. "I've called around in Baton Rouge and New Orleans but can't find anyone I'd trust to work on it."

"The fact that there's no one left who works on such equipment should tell you something." Modred rose to leave, crumpled up his lunch bag, tossed it toward the trash can and missed.

By himself in the faculty lounge Talis scowled at his cooling coffee, pondering the lack of compassion among his colleagues. Modred could have volunteered to come by, drink a cup of tea, and at least make a symbolic examination of his receiver, but instead Talis had to endure his shallow ridicule. In the next few days he stopped colleagues he hardly knew to ask for advice about his problem, but no one seemed able to help.

At least once a day for the next week he turned the large silver knob that ran the glowing needle along the station numbers behind the glass front of the machine. Gently he exercised the filter buttons, the balance control, the muting switch, the stereo lever. The machine had been playing a piece by Melngailis the night he made love for the first time in his college hovel in Riga. It played Gershwin in New York and Chopin in Iowa after his divorce and was more of a companion than most people he had known in life. Its silence was like a death.

Saturday morning Janice parked her pickup at the curb on Delaune Street and backed her mower off the trailer. Talis watched her carefully through his kitchen window as he leaned over the sink, drinking black coffee. He had never paid much attention to the woman. That graying ponytail suggested she might not be as able as he hoped, but her eyes were steady with ability. She was not quite matronly, still quick moving. Always moving, as a matter of fact. Maybe fifty years old. When she came up on the porch after she'd finished his lawn, he asked her to come into the house. As she walked by, he took in a whiff of gasoline and soap.

He cleared his throat. "Janice, you mentioned that you can repair things?"

She blinked, adjusting her eyes to the dark room. "The Volvo's acting up?"

"No, no. My Pioneer stereo receiver." He motioned across the small living room as to a corpse. "Perhaps you know of someone who can examine it?"

"Hell, I'll take a look at it."

His eyebrows flew up in alarm. "You have experience in electronics?"

"They trained me in the army to test out circuit boards in tanks."

"Yes, but this is audio and rather old."

"I work on my son's guitar amps and they have vacuum tubes. Trust me, I know about this stuff. It's all made out of the same types of parts." She pulled a red screwdriver from her back pocket and walked to the stereo. "Hey, a 1250. This thing's got some thump in it, I bet."

She had the wooden case off in less than a minute. Pulling a floor lamp over the machine, she peered in.

"Aren't you going to turn it on?"

"Not yet."

He watched her bring the light closer, shifting her head this way and that. She sniffed at the works. She flipped the power switch and turned her ear down to listen while holding her ponytail out of the dusty insides. Looking past her, he could see hundreds of pill-like electrical parts soldered down in soldierly groups to a green circuit board. He gazed on with no comprehension, as though he were examining brain tissue without a microscope. "Is no good," he said, gesturing dismissively. "Nobody can make sense of that mysterious stuff."

She glanced up at him. "There's ways to deal with mysteries. You see these black things with two silver wires coming out? Now, look in here. The ones about the size of peanuts? Those are capacitors. They store and release electricity. There's bigger ones and smaller ones, and they're the first thing to go in these old sets. Here's a big one with a drop of fluid running down its leg, so it's leaking and not doing its job. And you see these guys the size and shape of Chiclets chewing gum? Those are the driver transistors. They run the show in here. And the forty-leven flat-sided cylinders wandering all over the board are smaller transistors, and those rows of three-quarter-inch-long things about the diameter of spaghetti are resistors. The little colored bands around them tell how much electricity they control." She pointed with her screwdriver tip and explained the potentiometers, relays, fuses, and protection circuits, and as she did, Talis drifted close to her in the lamplight.

"If one thing goes out, everything stops working?" he asked.

"At least things'll change. When this set was new, Frank Sinatra's voice came through with a sharp edge to it." She placed her screwdriver on a thumb-sized capacitor. "When this fellow gets weak, the voice's edge goes. When that gray transistor over there loses a bit of control, Frank starts to sound gritty, like Rod Stewart."

Janice sat back for a moment and stared into the case. "It's like a big family in here. Every single thing affects everything else. When an uncle's dying, the whole family's blue about it. Mealtimes on Sunday just aren't the same." She gave him a sad smile.

Talis stared over her head for a moment, wondering where his ex-wife was. He hadn't really thought of her in years. When they were first married, she had smiled at him like this simple woman did, indulgently, patiently. She could have smiled lovingly, and he began to question himself why she didn't.

Janice continued checking the electronics, tapping with the screwdriver. "Do you have family?" she asked.

"No. I had only a brother and he was killed in Afghanistan."

She looked up, out the front window. "No family. I can't imagine it."

Talis nodded toward the mechanism. "Now, I'm really alone. For the first time this machine has broken down."

"Aw, it's nothing I can't fix."

He straightened up. "Really?"

"Sure. But my computer got eat up by a virus, so I don't have access to an online manual. I'll write down the address of a website with all the specs on it, and you can download and print out the schematic for this particular model."

"I can have it for you tomorrow afternoon."

She reassembled the cover. "I'll stop by to pick it up after church." She looked at him. "Do you ever go to church?"

He moved his head and looked at the wall for just a moment.

"I thought not," she said. "Most history professors are atheists."

He raised his chin. "How do *you* know that?"

She slid the screwdriver back into her jeans. "I went to college for a couple of years. Long enough to know that you guys focus on the bad stuff—wars, famine, and dictators. That'll mess you up, thinking that's all the world's about." She glanced around the room as if looking for human failure.

"But those three things are history."

She grinned and reaching out, poked his chest with a finger. "Yeah, what do you know about history, Mr. Loner Schoolteacher who doesn't even own a TV? To me, history is what happens *between* famines as well. It's about what people ate on holidays, what songs they sang after a day in the fields."

He put a hand over the place she touched and could not resist frowning, as though it hurt. "Well, if you solve the tragedy of my stereo, I'll sing you a peasant song."

On Monday, Talis spread electrical schematics before Modred as if they were photos of his family.

Modred spat on his eyeglasses, rubbed them with a paper napkin, and put his face down close to the diagram. He nodded. "So. Many redundant systems. Interesting. It must've taken ten pounds of solder to put this thing together."

"My yard woman says she can repair it. Should I trust her?"

"Hmm. If she's had any electronics training she can do it. Everything's so big a blind man could replace the parts." He put a finger down on the page and frowned. "Warn her about those two big capacitors there. They'll blow her across the room if she touches the terminals with a screwdriver."

"She's a careful person."

Modred looked up at him, his eyes shrunken in his thick glasses. "Is she your age?"

Talis straightened up. "Younger. I mean, not too young." His fair skin turned red up to his forehead.

"Does she interest you?"

"Don't be silly. She's a grass cutter."

"But you'll be in love if she brings Haydn back into your life?"

Talis scraped up the schematics in a noisy crinkle of paper and began walking backward toward the lounge door. "Thank you for looking at these."

"No problem. Keep me posted," he said with a smirk.

Back at his quiet house that afternoon, Talis began to reminisce, something he rarely did as there was usually no room in his head for such activity, every minute between lecture preparation and paper grading filled by music or intelligent commentary. He actually closed his eyes and tried not to think, but the machine's absence caused his brain to take on tasks other than listening. He recalled that it had been twenty-two years since he'd seen his wife, and he began to go over the old intimacies he and Marlena had shared. They liked the same food, the same composers; they both liked to sit Indian-style on the sofa and listen to opera, following along in the same libretto. They differed, however, in what they read. She liked American fiction, and he read mostly biography and historical research. Their marriage lasted six years, his wife's enthusiasm for compromise shriveling until one day she looked at him at the kitchen table and said, "Nothing is happening."

He looked up from a new book on Nazi Germany. "What do you mean?"

"Between us. You read, I read, we summarize to each other what we read."

He waved a hand at her. "You're tired," he said.

"I'm not tired enough." And she looked at him accusingly. "I'm not doing anything."

"You are an editor. You help people get published."

She sniffed. "People with no tastebuds who write cookbooks. Love-less people who write about love." He recalled the look that came over her face then, an expression of abiding emptiness.

Marlena, his dark-haired beauty, returned to upstate Indiana to work for Notre Dame. Talis, for a while at least, was ashamed that he enjoyed being alone, that he could play Bartók until his apartment trembled. He dated different women, but none would stay with him for long. He was a historian who repeated his own history, learning nothing in the process. And now, in the limitless silence of his tiny house, he began to wonder what his options were.

Janice stopped by about five in the afternoon, and they spread out the schematic and manual on the coffee table. She pulled a small spiral pad from her breast pocket and began writing down numbers from the parts list. It was a long list, and he watched the tanned back of her neck as she wrote. He knew her husband had been killed in Iraq, that she had two almost grown boys. He needed something to replace his music, and when she'd finished writing and told him she'd order the many parts, that they were cheap, he looked into her eyes and asked if she would go out with him.

She glanced at him, head to toe. "Thank you, but that wouldn't be a good idea," she said.

"Oh, just a friendly meal someplace. I am, perhaps, past courting age."

She smiled at him. "No."

"All right." He smiled back. "But why not?"

"No offense, but I don't believe we're cut from the same bolt of cloth."

"You're holding my education against me?"

She looked around the room, at the plain walls, the shrine to the old stereo. "Where has your education brought you, doc?"

"You don't know anything about me," he told her.

"I know a train wreck when I see it."

Talis forced his smile now. "As the students say, that's cold."

She folded her tablet. "I'll pay for these parts and you can reimburse me when I send you the bill for the labor."

As he held his front door open for her and gave a small bow, she turned her face next to his. "Doc, I favor people who are going somewhere, anywhere. I think you're stuck in one spot. You don't seem to want to change things. You're scared of watching TV," she glanced down at his black wing tips, "or wearing a pair of loafers. It's like you don't have a lot of trust for this old world. You can't even give up a worn-out radio."

He took a step back into his house and latched the screen as though protecting himself from mosquitoes or from some more subtle inoculation. "Good night."

Janice stopped at the edge of his porch. "Hey, I bet you never heard this old one in Latvia."

"What?"

"What do you call an atheist in his coffin?"

He put his nose against the screen. "My ex-wife told me that one."

She stepped off onto the firefly-haunted lawn. "Well, what's the answer?"

He sighed, "All dressed up and no place to go."

On Sunday he usually listened to at least one full opera. He finished marking tests from his vast sophomore class and, as it was a warm, pleasant day, stepped out onto his front porch, standing for a long time with his hands in his pockets and staring at the white oak rocker. He nudged it with a black shoe as if testing its function, then sat down. The street in front of his house was lined with modest frame houses better than his own. He'd been told that they were all made of cypress, and he imagined the primitive and brutal life of the lumbermen cutting away in the steaming swamps a hundred years before. An old corner grocery lay two blocks to his left, and Talis thought of the great wealth the owners had bled out of the neighborhood in the past century with their high prices. One block to his right, an AME church pointed its rusting spire skyward. He heard loud singing and rhythmic hand clapping, shouts of praise springing out into the sunshine, and all he could think of was how these people rhapsodized in a fog of delusion. Maybe it was anesthetic for African Americans to convince themselves that they were happy, that their kidnapping, persecution, and slavery had never happened. Singing flowed up his street, and Talis began to rock in time to "When I Rose This Morning," not realizing what he was doing. His fingers tapped the arms of the rocker. Around noon his stomach growled, and he decided to walk down to the old store, Macaluso's, which opened at twelve on Sundays. The storefront had a generous wooden awning above the sidewalk, and he walked up three steps and pushed the door open, its wood worn concave where hands had shoved at it a million times. Inside he smelled apples, and toward the back, freshly cut meat. He asked the butcher to slice him thin pieces of a smoked ham already in the slicer, to go with a creole tomato and a small loaf of French bread he'd already chosen.

"Hey, you makin' yourself a sandwich?" the man asked.

"Yes, I'm preparing lunch."

The butcher ran the slicer, then pulled the ham out of the machine and threw in a block of Swiss cheese. "Lemme cut you just one slice of this for the sandwich. No charge. You gonna like it."

"Well." Talis didn't know what else to say.

On Monday he returned home early, and in his silent house he actually thought of buying a television. His wife had always demanded one, and he'd argued against it, but he realized now that she'd probably needed the company. He'd been thinking a great deal about his wife in recent days, and that night, for the first time, he dreamed about her, that she was sleeping soft and quiet like a breathing pillow in his bed. When he woke, her presence was still in the dark, and he remembered how at breakfast she'd watch him with her careful eyes while he read a book. For years she observed him with incredible patience. What was she looking for?

At dawn he gave up trying to sleep, rose, and mixed himself a glass of chocolate milk, enjoying the music of the spoon against the glass as he stood in the kitchen, stirring, stirring.

On Tuesday morning, preparing his lesson plans about French royalists slaughtering the population of a Huguenot town, he was struck with a craving for smoked eel. He hadn't thought of the dish in many years and wondered if he was going a bit daft. All the silence was opening strange windows in his head. That same day, after his usual supper of cold cuts and milk, he turned on his computer and searched half the night for some trace of his ex-wife, finding not one electron of evidence that she existed. He did find her sister's phone number.

He remembered Camille as a fiercely practical, athletic version of his wife, attractive in a leathery, overexercised way. She answered the phone, her voice a snap of certainty, and for a moment he was afraid to speak.

"Hello, this is Talis." He tried to sound friendly but had no idea what the woman's reaction would be.

There was a telling pause before she spoke. "Well, bud, I've got to admit, I'm surprised to hear from you. You've truly dropped off the radar. Years ago, we tried to contact you."

"Really. For what reason?"

"That's water under the bridge now. What can I do for you?"

"I was wondering if you could give me Marlena's phone number."

There was a snort on the other end of the line. "You don't want to talk to her. She remarried a long time ago, has three kids. Why stir up ancient history?"

"Well."

"In short, I won't tell you how to contact her. It won't do anybody any good, in my estimation."

He spoke with the sister a few more minutes, trying his best to make a connection, finally crying out, "She loved me once."

The sister came back with, "I don't know, bud. Now that I'm standing here thinking about it, I don't think she loved you as you were, but as you could've *chosen* to be."

"Still," he persisted, "it would be nice to talk to her."

The sister took a breath. "Hey, Talis, boat has sailed. No tickee, no washee. By the way, you still worshiping the big zero in the sky?"

This was an old joke between them. "I'll take a look tonight and see what's up there," he told her.

On Wednesday he went to Walmart and bought a portable stereo and several classical CDs. He also bought a case of beer, a brand he'd discovered that carried a hint of kvass. He imagined the music and drink would kill some of the silence.

But the boom box gave out a tinny sound and made Bach sound inconsequential and repetitive. He thought, for the first time in his life, that Bach was perhaps a little crazy, playing no great music but only silly variations of scales. The beer, especially the seventh one, made him feel old and blatantly down. By midnight he'd had enough music and drink and turned off the stereo, poured out his last open beer, and put on woolen pajamas. After he had covered up and turned off his light, he leaped from bed and switched the lamp on again, staring at the mattress, realizing for the first time that he had slept all these years on one side, on the edge, on one pillow. He never journeyed to the other side or sprawled over the middle. He crept again under the covers, but in the dark he lay on his back and stared toward the ceiling. Once, before daylight, he put his arm out into the wasteland beside him.

On Friday afternoon, Janice showed up carrying plastic bags of electrical components bright and rattling like a child's candy, and a toolbox. She placed the receiver on the kitchen table and unsoldered capacitors and installed new ones until Talis went out and came back with a bag of hamburgers and sodas. "You see, we are sharing a meal after all," he said, clearing a space for them among the pliers and spools of rosin core solder.

"Just for the record, Talis," she said, "this is not a date."

He bit into his hamburger and said nothing, and soon she was back at it, working quickly, taking the circuit boards apart and finishing the capacitors, searching out blackened transistors. While she studied the schematic and made decisions, he told her about his life in Latvia, his father, a small-time politician, and his mother, who worked in a foundry throwing specially measured chemicals into the giant ladles of molten metal. He waited for her to ask him questions, but she didn't talk while she worked, her eyes lost among the spindly legs of resistors.

On Saturday she showed up early to mow the lawn. Coming in later, she began replacing components at once, filing relays, repairing solder cracks she found with a magnifying glass. Talis pretended not to watch her, but on one pass through the kitchen he said, "It's amazing how you understand all of that."

"I don't really understand any of it," she told him.

"I mean how all that apparatus pulls sound from the air and delivers it to our ears, working invisibly." He stood over her and took a sip of tea. "What do you mean you don't understand it?"

"I can replace parts that will make the sound come back, but I'm not the engineer who designed it."

"Ah, then the engineer understood it."

"Probably not. His know-how was made of little pieces of info borrowed from a bunch of engineers working through a lot of years." She glanced up. "History, as you would say."

"Surely someone understands it completely."

"I don't know," she said. "Even the guy who invented the foundations of audio might not understand this here battleship. It'd be a mystery to him."

Talis went into the kitchen and made another cup of tea. He began thinking of both the day he was married and the day he received the divorce papers, and how he once thought he understood the two events. But the circuit between those points in his life was too complex, now that he had time to think of it. He wondered if he were the faulty component in the mechanism of their marriage, the one little part that took the music out of their love.

Around nine that night, after she had cleaned the control contacts, reassembled the faceplate, but left off the case cover, she connected an FM antenna, dragged the speakers over, and plugged in the unit. Talis hovered behind her as she struggled to turn the receiver upside down on the kitchen table.

"Now what are you doing?"

"I have to take some voltage readings on the bottom to recheck these big capacitors." She pointed at four black cylinders the size of tomato paste cans.

Janice lowered the silver power switch. First there was silence, then a relay ticked and the speakers gave off a serpent's hiss. She rolled the dial to the low end of the band toward classical music, watched the signal-strength needle, and landed dead center on a Dvořák string quartet. Talis closed his eyes to listen. After a full minute he nodded solemnly. "The high range is very crisp," he said. "And the cello, I can hear not only the strings but even the instrument's body." He blinked as though regaining consciousness. "Let's feed the CD player through the set. I'd like to hear voice. Do you listen to opera?"

"I only heard one in my life," she said, running the wires for the CD player. "In music appreciation we listened to *La Bohème* and followed along with the translation."

He raised a forefinger. "I have that. The old production by Sir Thomas Beecham. Jussi Björling was the tenor, and I'm always amazed by his singing."

In a moment the introduction to Puccini's opera rumbled out of the set, and Talis listened like a hawk hunting for mice.

Janice began to pack her tools and wire. "Well, does it sound okay?"

He turned down the music a bit. "It sounds different. I'll have to listen to it for a while."

"It is a little different. The voices are being formed through new electronics." She tilted her face and looked up at him. "Eventually, it might even sound better to *you*."

He seemed to notice her for the first time in several minutes. "Of course. You've done a wonderful job. Music is back for me at last."

"Oh, I'm not finished yet. The readings are way off on these old main capacitors. And there's a low hum. The new ones are in the bag here, and I can come back after lunch tomorrow and change them out. I don't like fooling with those without rubber safety gloves. I'll leave my tools and put the cover on later. Then we'll let the components burn in for a couple hours to make sure we're all set." She turned the receiver off.

"Thank you, Janice. And if you want to come in tomorrow morning, feel free."

"Well, me and my boys are going to Mass at St. Ben's down the street. Then we usually go out to eat seafood at Babineaux's Café."

"Do you think you could finish tomorrow? There's a wonderful opera program in the evening."

"I don't know. You might have to wait a bit longer to hear the fat lady sing," she told him, showing him a little smile as she turned for the door.

.   .   .

*A*fter she left, he turned on the set, but the hum increased in volume, so he snapped the switch off and began drinking. He sat in the den and tried to prepare a lecture on the Battle of Austerlitz, contemplating the suffering of the 9,000 French casualties as if they were somewhere outside his house, lying in the street and yard. Janice, he knew, would point out that 58,000 in that army were unhurt and returned to France to live as heroes for the rest of their lives. After another five beers he'd finished his preparations for class. He wondered again where his wife lived. If she ever told her children about him.

*T*he next morning he dressed and walked down the street to St. Ben's, intending to meet Janice and her boys when they came out. He'd thought the service began at ten, but everyone was showing up close to eleven, so he drifted in and sat in the last pew of the fairly crowded church. The building was very large and old for an American church. As Mass proceeded he examined the stained-glass depiction of Adam and Eve being driven out of Paradise, images of Christ's crucifixion, statues of his mourning mother, and the many otherworldly patterns of color and light. He couldn't see Janice and imagined she was sitting close to the front. With all the depictions of patient suffering in her church he wondered why she was always choosing the bright side of things. Was there really a cheerful side to getting bayoneted at Austerlitz or fed to the lions in Rome?

Talis stood, sat, and moved as those around him did, enjoying the air-conditioning and even the mild strain in his back as he kneeled.

He greeted Janice and her tall sons on the many steps outside the church and asked if he could go to the restaurant with them. The boys weren't particularly interested in who he was, and from this he gathered that she had not mentioned him to them at all.

"I was inside too. For the service, I mean."

"You went to Mass?"

"Yes."

She looked at him directly, then. "Well, do you have any questions?"

He watched her boys move ahead of them down to street level. "What happened to your husband?"

She shrugged, the big final shrug that says it all. "He was in a bomb disposal unit in Iraq."

"I'm sorry for you," Talis said.

"Well, as my dad used to say, when it wears out its welcome, sorry is pretty sorry. You want to go eat some crawfish?"

He put his hands in the pockets of his suit. "Will this be a date?"

"No."

*T*hat afternoon he opened a beer to quench the salt from all the sea-food. He had never seen so many crawfish in his life. He rocked on the front porch for a long time, watching the street between the AME church and the store. Eventually, Janice drove over. She was wearing her hair in twin braids. These always caught his eye, especially when a mature woman wore them, mocking her age. She came in and changed out the large capacitors, turned things right side up, and attached the case. "Check it out," she said, standing back against the kitchen wall.

He flipped the switch and the CD of *La Bohème* bloomed into the room. Bending over the set, he meditated on the little civilization of circuits shuttling its resident electrons, reforming them on a thousand anvils of silicon. The heat of interdependent electrical community rose into his face as it devoured and performed the invisible signals on the disk. He switched to FM and the set drew from the fabric of the air around him a Chopin étude, and it made his head swim to think of all the cell phone, television, radio, shortwave, and computer signals piercing every cell of his body with him unable to hear any of it. He pushed a button to bring back the first act of *La Bohème* and raised the volume for the beautiful aria in which Rudolfo defines himself to Mimi. He raised the volume again and the sound was both clear and fathoms deep.

He looked over at her and smiled.

"Doc," she said, "you're back in the saddle again. You can sit and listen as much as you can stand."

He touched the volume knob again and listened as the receiver thundered toward the end of act one, the tenor singing so hard Talis wondered how such intensity could be possible. The character he was playing was, after all, addressing a woman he had just met, no one very important on the world's stage, a suffering soul who, at the end of the act, gives in to his pleading and sings *"Io t'amo,"* and it's all over, for they are both enthralled, and the tenor, who was known to have a very bad heart, sings out over her ringing soprano as powerfully and earnestly as ever man sang, giving the last note as if determined to sacrifice his health, singing the great mystery, *"Amor! Amor!"*

He clicked the set off and turned to her. "You've done a perfect job. Let's celebrate and go to a really nice restaurant sometime this week."

She looked into the small living room at shelves filled with many thick textbooks. "No." She shook her head. "You stay home and be a good listener."

He put his hand on the machine and looked it over carefully. Suddenly he began tearing out its speaker wires. He picked it up with a grunt and walked to the front door, struggling through it.

"Hey, doc, where're you going with that?" she called. "It's fixed."

He didn't answer but plodded down the steps to the little cement walk that lead to the street. Unsure if he could do it, Talis raised the receiver over his head, his face reddening. He turned and faced Janice, who was standing with her arms crossed just outside the door.

"What are you doing? Are you nuts?"

"Will you go out with me?"

She shook her head, and her braids whipped her shoulders. "Won't do that. We're just too different."

It was then that Talis threw the receiver down to the walk, where it hit on one of its corners and broke apart in a shower of bright buttons, a flash of glass, and a splintering of wood. He raised his eyes to the porch, where Janice had covered her open mouth with a bright hand. Talis gestured operatically to the wreckage. "And now?"

Janice watched, incredulous, as the capacitors unloaded and a crooked spirit of smoke rose from the shattered receiver. Her arms fell to her sides, palms forward. "It'll never make another sound," she said in a small voice.

"I don't care," Talis told her.

She raised her hands a bit, and said, "In that case, yes."

Good for the Soul

*F*ather Ledet took a scorching swallow of brandy and sat in an iron chair on the brick patio behind the rectory, hemmed in by walls of ligustrums stitched through with honeysuckle. His stomach was full from the Ladies' Altar Society supper, where the sweet, sweet women of the parish had fed him pork roast, potato salad, and sweet peas, filling his plate and fussing over him as if he were an old spayed tomcat who kept the cellar free of rats. He was a big man, white-haired and ruddy, with gray eyes and huge spotted hands that could make a highball glass disappear. It was Thursday evening, and nothing much ever happened on Thursday evenings. The first cool front of the fall was noising through the pecan trees on the church lot, and nothing is so important in Louisiana as that first release from the sopping, buggy, overheated funk of the atmosphere. Father Ledet breathed deep in the shadow of a statue of Saint Francis. He took another long swallow, glad the assistant pastor was on a visit home to Iowa, and that the deacon wouldn't be around until the next afternoon. Two pigeons lit on Saint Francis's hands as if they knew who he was. Father Ledet watched the light fade and the hedges darken, and then looked a long time at the pint of brandy before deciding to pour himself another drink.

When the phone rang in the rectory, he got up carefully and moved inside among the dark wood furnishings and dim holy light. It was a parishioner, Mrs. Clyde Arceneaux, whose husband was dying of emphysema.

"We need you for the anointing of the sick, Father."

"Um, yes." He tried to say something else, but the words were stuck back in his throat, the way dollar bills sometimes wadded up in the tubular poor box and wouldn't drop down when he opened the bottom.

"Father?"

"Of course. I'll just come right over there."

"I know you did it for him last week. But this time he might really be going, you know." Mrs. Arceneaux's voice sounded like she was holding back tears. "He wants you to hear his confession."

"Um." The priest had known Clyde Arceneaux for fifteen years. The old man dressed up on Sunday and came to church, but stayed out on the steps, smoking with three other men as reverent as himself. As far as he knew, he'd never been to confession.

*F*ather Ledet locked the rectory door and went into the garage to start the parish car, a venerable black Lincoln. He backed out onto the street, and when the car stopped, he still floated along in a drifting crescent, and he realized that he'd had maybe an ounce too much brandy. It occurred to him that he should call the housekeeper to drive him to the hospital. It would take only five minutes for her to come over, but then the old Baptist woman was always figuring him out, and he would have to endure Mrs. Scott's roundabout questions and sniffs of the air in the car. Father Ledet felt his old mossy human side take over, and he began to navigate the streets of the little town on his own, stopping the car too far into the intersection at Jackman Avenue, clipping a curb on a turn into Bourgeois Street. The car had its logical movement, but his head had a motion of its own.

*P*atrolman Vic Garafola was parked in front of the post office talking to the dispatcher about a cow eating string beans out of Mrs. LeBlanc's garden when he heard a crash in the intersection behind him. In his rearview he saw that a long black sedan had battered the side of a powder-blue Ford. He backed his cruiser up fifty feet and turned on his flashers. When he got out and saw his own parish priest sitting wide-eyed behind the steering wheel, he ran to the window.

"You all right, Father?"

The priest had a little red mark on his high forehead, but he smiled dumbly and nodded. Patrolman Garafola looked over to the smashed passenger-side door of a faded Crown Victoria. A pretty older woman sat in the middle of the bench seat holding her elbow. He opened the door and saw that Mrs. Mamie Barrilleaux's right arm was obviously broken and her mouth was twitching with pain. Vic's face reddened because it made him angry to see nice people get hurt when it wasn't their fault.

"Mrs. Mamie, you hurtin' a lot?" he asked. Behind him, the priest walked up and put his hand on his shoulder. When the woman saw Father Ledet, her face was transfigured.

"Oh, it's nothing, just a little bump. Father, did I cause the accident?"

The patrolman looked at the priest for an answer.

"Mamie, your arm." He let his hand fall and stepped back, and Vic could tell that the priest was shocked. He knew that Father Ledet was called out to give last rites to strangers at gory highway wrecks all the time, but this woman was the vice president of the Ladies' Altar Society, which dusted the old church, put flowers on the altar, and knitted afghans for him to put on his lap in the drafty wooden rectory.

"Father, Mrs. Mamie had the right of way." Vic pointed to the stop sign behind the priest's steaming car.

"I am dreadfully sorry," Father Ledet said. "I was going to the hospital to give the anointing of the sick, and I guess my mind was on that."

"Oh," Mrs. Barrilleaux cried. "Who's that ill?"

"Mrs. Arceneaux's husband."

Another cruiser pulled up, its lights sparking up the evening. Mrs. Mamie nodded toward it. "Vic, can you take Father to the hospital and let this other policeman write up the report? I know Mrs. Arceneaux's husband, and he needs a priest bad."

Vic looked down at his shoe. He wasn't supposed to do anything like that. "You want to go on to the hospital and then I can bring you back here, Father?"

"Mamie's the one who should go to the hospital."

"Shoo." She waved her good hand at him. "I can hear the ambulance coming now. Go on, I'm not dying."

Vic could see a slight trembling in Mamie's iron-gray curls. He put a hand on the priest's arm. "Okay, Father?"

"Yes, that would be fine."

They got into the cruiser and immediately Vic smelled the priest's breath. He drove under the tunnel of oak trees that was Nadine Avenue and actually bit his tongue to keep from asking the inevitable question. But once they were in sight of the hospital, he could no longer stop himself. "Father, did you have anything to drink today?"

The priest looked at him and blanched. "Why do you ask?"

"It's on your breath. Whiskey."

"Brandy," the priest corrected him. "Yes, I had some brandy after supper."

"How much?"

"Not too much. Well, here we are." Father Ledet got out before the patrol car had completely stopped. Vic radioed his location, parked, and went into the modern lobby to find a soft chair.

The priest knew the way to Clyde Arceneaux's room. When he pushed open the door, he saw the old man in his bed, a few strands of smoky hair swept back, his false teeth out, his tobacco-parched tongue wiggling in his mouth like a parrot's. Up close, Father Ledet could hear the hiss of the oxygen through the nasal cannula strapped to his face. He felt his deepest sorrow for the respiratory patients.

"Clyde?"

Mr. Arceneaux opened one eye and looked at the priest's shirt. "The buzzards is circlin'," he rasped.

"How're you feeling?"

"Ah, Padre, I got a elephant standing on my chest." He spoke slowly, more like an air leak than a voice. "Doris, she stepped out a minute to eat." Clyde motioned with his eyes toward the door, and Father Ledet looked at his hands, which were bound with dark veins flowing under skin as thin as cigarette paper.

"Is there something you'd like to talk about?" The priest heard the faint sound of a siren and wondered if gentle Mrs. Barrilleaux was being brought in to have her arm set.

"I don't need the holy oil no more. You can't grease me so I can slide into heaven." Clyde ate a bite of air. "I got to go to confession."

The priest nodded, removed a broad, ribbon-like vestment from his pocket, kissed it, and hung it around his neck. Mr. Arceneaux told the priest he couldn't remember the last time he'd been to confession, but he knew that Kennedy was president then, because it was during the Cuban Missile Crisis when he thought for sure a nuclear strike was coming. He began telling his sins, starting with missing Mass "damn near seven hundred fifty times." Father Ledet was happy that Claude Arceneaux was coming to God for forgiveness, and in a very detailed way, which showed, after all, a healthy conscience. At one point the old man stopped and began to store up air for what the priest thought would be a new push through his errors, but when he began speaking again it was to ask a question.

"Sure enough, you think there's a hell?"

Father Ledet knew he had to be careful. Saving a soul sometimes was like catching a dragonfly. You couldn't blunder up to it and trap it with a swipe of the hand. "There's a lot of talk of it in the Bible," he said.

"It's for punishment?"

"That's what it's for."

"But what good would the punishment do?"

The priest sat down. The room did a quarter turn to the left and then stopped. "I don't think hell is about rehabilitation. It's about what someone might deserve." He put his hand over his eyes and rubbed them for a moment. "But you shouldn't worry about that, Clyde, because you're getting the forgiveness you need."

Mr. Arceneaux looked at the ceiling, the corners of his flaccid mouth turning down. "I don't know. There's one thing I ain't told you yet."

"Well, it's now or never." The priest was instantly sorry for saying this, and Clyde gave him a questioning look before glancing down at his purple feet.

"I can't hold just one thing back? I'd hate like hell to tell anybody this."

"Clyde, it's God listening, not me."

"Can I just think it to God? I mean, I told you the other stuff. Even about the midget woman."

"If it's a serious sin, you've got to tell me about it. You can generalize a bit."

"This is some of that punishment we were talkin' about earlier. It's what I deserve."

"Let's have it."

"I stole Nelson Lodrigue's car."

Something clicked in the priest's brain. He remembered bits of this event himself. Nelson Lodrigue owned an old Toronado that he parked next to the ditch in front of his house. The car had no mufflers and a huge eight-cylinder engine, and every morning at six o'clock sharp Nelson would crank the thing up and race the engine, waking most of his neighbors and all the dogs for blocks around. He did this for over a year, to keep the battery charged, he'd said. When it disappeared, Nelson put a big ad in the local paper offering a $50 reward for information, but no one came forward. The men in the Knights of Columbus talked about it for weeks.

"That was around ten years ago, wasn't it? And isn't Nelson a friend of yours?" Nelson was another Sunday morning lingerer on the church steps.

Mr. Arceneaux swallowed hard several times and waited a moment, storing up air. "Father, honest to God I ain't never stole nothin' before. My daddy told me thievin' is the worst thing a man can do. I hated to take Nelson's hot rod, but I was fixin' to have a nervous breakdown from lack of sleep."

The priest nodded. "It's good to get these things off your chest. Is there anything else?"

Mr. Arceneaux shook his head. "I think we hit the high points. Man, I'm ashamed of that last one."

The priest gave him absolution and a small penance.

Clyde tried to smile, his dark tongue tasting the air. "Ten Hail Marys? That's a bargain, Father."

"If you want to do more, you could call Nelson and tell him what you did."

The old man thought for just a second. "I'll stick with them little prayers for now." Father Ledet got out his Missal and read a prayer over Mr. Arceneaux until his words were interrupted by a gentle snoring.

Vic sat in the lobby waiting for the priest to come down. It had been twenty minutes, and he knew the priest's blood-alcohol level was ready to peak. He took off his uniform hat and began twirling it in front of him. He wondered what good it would do to charge the priest with drunk driving. Priests had to drink wine every day, and they liked the taste in the evening, too. A ticket wouldn't change his mind about drinking for long. On the other hand, Father Ledet had ruined Mrs. Barrilleaux's sedan that she had maintained as if it were a child for twenty years.

A few minutes earlier, Vic had walked down the corridor and peeked into the room where they were treating her. He hadn't let her see him, and he studied her face. Now he sat and twirled his hat, thinking. It would be painful for the priest to have his name in the paper attached to a DWI charge, but it would make him understand the seriousness of what he had done. Patrolman Garafola dealt with too many people who never understood the seriousness of what they were doing.

The priest came into the lobby and the young policeman stood up. "Father, we'll have to take a ride to the station."

"What?"

"I want to run a Breathalyzer test on you."

Father Ledet straightened up, stepped close, and put an arm around the man's shoulders. "Oh, come on What good would that do?"

Vic started to speak, but then motioned for the priest to follow him. "Let me show you something."

"Where are we going?"

"I want you to see this." They walked down the hall and through double doors to a triage area for emergency cases. There was a narrow window in a wall, and the policeman told the priest to look through it. An oxygen bottle and gauges partially blocked the view. Inside, Mrs. Barrilleaux sat on an examining table, a blue knot swelling in her upper arm. One doctor was pulling back on her shoulder while another twisted her elbow. On the table was a large, menacing syringe, and Mrs. Barrilleaux was crying, without expression, great patient tears. "Take a long look," Vic said, "and when you get enough, come on with me." The priest turned away from the glass and followed.

"You didn't have to show me that."

"I didn't?"

"That is the nicest woman, the best cook, the best—"

"Come on, Father," Vic said, pushing open the door to the parking lot. "I've got a lot of writing to do."

*F*ather Ledet's blood-alcohol level was twice what the patrolman needed to write him up for DWI, to which he added running a stop sign and causing an accident with bodily injury. The traffic court suspended his license, and since he'd banged up the Lincoln before, his insurance company dropped his coverage as soon as their computers picked up the offenses.

A week after the accident, he came into the rectory hall drinking a glass of tap water, which beaded on his tongue like a nasty oil. The phone rang and the glass jumped in his fingers. It was Mrs. Arceneaux again, who told him she'd been arguing with her husband, who wanted to tell her brother, Nelson Lodrigue, that he'd stolen his car ten years before. "Why'd you ask him to talk to Nelson about the stealing business? It's got him all upset."

The priest didn't understand. "What would be the harm in him telling Nelson the truth?"

"Aw, no, Father. Clyde's got so little oxygen in his brain he's not thinking straight. He can't tell Nelson what he did. I don't want him to die with everyone in the neighborhood thinking he's a thief. And Nelson, well, I love my brother, but if he found out my husband stole his old bomb, he'd make Clyde's last days hell. He's just like that, you know?"

"I see. Is there something I can do?" He put down the glass of water on the phone table next to a little white statue of the Blessed Virgin.

"If you'd talk to Clyde and let him know it's okay to die without telling Nelson about the car, I'd appreciate it. He already confessed everything anyway, right?"

The priest looked down the hall toward the patio, longing for the openness. "I can't discuss specific matters of confession."

"I know. That's why I gave you all the details again."

"All right, I'll call. Is he awake now?"

"He's here at home. We got him a crank-up bed and a oxygen machine and a nurse to sit with him at night. I'll put him on."

Father Ledet leaned against the wall and stared at a portrait of John the Baptist, wondering what he had done to deserve his punishment. When he heard the hiss of Clyde Arceneaux's mask come out of the phone, he began to tell him what he should hear, that he was forgiven in God's eyes, that if he wanted to make restitution, he could give something to the poor or figure out how to leave his brother-in-law something. He hung up and sniffed the waxed smell of the rectory, thinking of the sweet, musky brandy in the kitchen cupboard, and he immediately went upstairs to find the young priest and discuss the new Mass schedule.

On Saturday afternoon, Father Ledet was nodding off in the confessional when a woman entered and after she'd mentioned one or two venial sins, she addressed him through the screen. "Father, it's Doris Arceneaux, Clyde's wife."

The priest yawned. "How is Clyde?"

"You remember the car business? Well, something new came up," she whispered. "Clyde always told me he and the Scadlock kid towed the car off with a rope and when they got it downtown behind the seawall, they pushed it off the wharf into the bay."

"Yes?"

"There's a new wrinkle."

He removed his glasses to rub his eyes. "What do you mean?"

"Clyde just told me he stored the car. Been paying thirty-five dollars a month to keep it in a little closed room down at the U-Haul place for the past ten years." She whispered louder, "I don't know how he kept that from me. Makes me wonder about a few other things."

The priest's eyebrows went up. "Now he can give it back, or you can give it back when your husband passes away." As soon as he'd said this, he knew it wouldn't work. It was too logical. If nothing else, his years in the confessional had taught him that people didn't run their lives by reason much of the time, but by some little inferior motion of the spirit, some pride, some desire that defied the simple beauty of doing the sensible thing.

Mrs. Arceneaux protested that the secret had to be kept. "There's only one way to get Nelson his car back like Clyde wants."

The priest sighed. "How is that?"

Mrs. Arceneaux began to fidget in the dark box. "Well, you the only one besides me who knows what happened. Clyde says the car will still run. He cranks it up once every three weeks so it keeps its battery hot."

The priest put his head down. "And?"

"And you could get up early and drive it back to Nelson's and park it where it was the night Clyde stole it."

"Not no," the priest said, "but hell no!"

"Father!"

"What if I were caught driving this thing? The secret would get out then."

"Father, this is part of a confession. You can't tell."

The priest suddenly sensed a plot. "I'm sorry, I can't help you, Mrs. Arceneaux. Now I'm going to give you a penance of twenty Our Fathers."

"For telling one fib to my daughter-in-law?"

"You want a cut rate for dishonesty?"

"All right," she said in an unrepentant voice. "And I'll pray for you while I'm at it."

After five o'clock Mass on Saturday, Father Ledet felt his soul bang around inside him like a golf ball in a shoebox, something hard and compacted. He yearned for a hot, inflating swallow of spirits, longed for the after burn of brandy in his nostrils. He went back into the empty church, a high-ceilinged gothic building more than a hundred years old, sat in a pew, and steeped himself in the odors of furniture oil, incense, and hot candle wax. He watched the insubstantial colors of the windows flowing above him, and after a while these shades and smells began to fill the emptiness inside him. He closed his eyes and imagined the housekeeper's supper, pushing out of mind his need for a drink, replacing the unnecessary with the good. At five to six he walked to the rectory to have his thoughts redeemed by food.

The next evening, after visiting a sick parishioner, he was reading the newspaper upstairs in his room when the housekeeper knocked on his door. Mrs. Mamie Barrilleaux was downstairs and would like to speak with him, the housekeeper said.

The first thing Father Ledet noticed when he walked into the study was the white cast on the woman's arm.

"Mamie," he said, sitting next to her on the sofa. "I have to tell you again how sorry I am about your arm."

The woman's face brightened, as though being apologized to was a privilege. "Oh, don't worry about it, Father. Accidents happen." She was a graying brunette with fair skin, a woman whose cheerfulness made her pretty. One of the best cooks in a town of good cooks, she volunteered for every charity event involving a stove or oven, and her time belonged to anyone who needed it, from her well-fed smirk of a husband to the drug addicts who showed up at the parish shelter. While they talked, the priest's eyes wandered repeatedly over the ugly cast, which ran up nearly to her shoulder. For five minutes he wondered why she had dropped in unannounced. And then she told him.

"Father, I don't know if you understand what good friends Clyde Arceneaux's wife and I are. We went to school together for twelve years."

"Yes. It's a shame her husband's so sick."

Mrs. Barrilleaux fidgeted into the corner of the sofa, placed her cast on the armrest, where it glowed under a lamp. "That's sort of why I'm here. Doris told me she asked you to do something for her and Clyde, and you told her no. I'm not being specific because I know it was a confession thing."

"How much did she tell you?" The priest hoped she wouldn't ask what he feared she was going to, because he knew he couldn't refuse her.

"I don't know even one detail, Father. But I wanted to tell you that if

Doris wants it done, then it needs doing. She's a good person, and I'm asking you to help her."

"But you don't know what she wants me to do."

Mrs. Barrilleaux put her good hand on her cast. "I know it's not something bad."

"No, no. It's just . . ." He was going to mention that his driver's license was suspended but decided he didn't want to tell her that.

Mamie lowered her head and turned her face toward him. "Father?"

"Oh, all right."

*H*e visited Mrs. Arceneaux on a Wednesday, got the keys, and late that night he sat outside on the dark rectory patio for a long time, filling up on the smells of honeysuckle, until the young priest walked up to him and insisted that he come in out of the mosquitoes and the dampness. Upstairs, he changed into street clothes and lay on the bed like a man waiting for a firing squad. Around midnight his legs began to ache terribly, and the next thing he knew they were carrying him down to the kitchen where the aspirin was kept, and as his hand floated toward the cabinet door to his right, it remembered its accustomed movement to the door on the left where a quart of brandy waited like an airy medicinal promise. The mind and the spirit pulled his hand to the right, while the earthly body drew it to the left. Somewhere in the sky above, he heard the drone of an airplane, and he suddenly thought of an old homily about how people were like twin-engine planes, one engine the logical spirit, the other the sensual body, and that when they were not running in concert, the craft would run off course to disaster. The priest supposed he could rev up his spirit in some way, but when he thought of driving the stolen car, he opted to throttle up the body. One jigger, he thought, would calm him down and give him the courage to do this important good deed. As he took a drink, he tried to picture how glad Nelson Lodrigue would be to have his old car back. As he took another, he thought of how Mr. Arceneaux could gasp off into the next world with a clear conscience. After several minutes, the starboard engine sputtered and locked up as Father Ledet lurched sideways through the dark house looking for his car keys.

At one o'clock he got into the church's sedan and drove to a row of storage buildings at the edge of town. He woke up the manager, a shabby old man living in a trailer next to the gate. Inside the perimeter fence, Father Ledet walked along the numbered roll-up doors of the storage areas until he found the right one. He had trouble fitting the key into the lock but finally managed to open the door and turn on the light. The Oldsmobile showed a hard shell of rust and dust and resembled a million-year-old museum egg. The driver's door squawked when he pulled on it, and the interior smelled like the closed-in mausoleum at the parish graveyard. He put in the key, and the motor groaned and then stuttered alive, rumbling and complaining. Shaking his head, the priest thought he'd never be able to drive this car undetected into the quiet neighborhood where Nelson Lodrigue lived. But after he let it idle and warm up, the engine slowed to a breathy subsonic bass, and he put it in reverse for its first trip in ten years.

The plan was to park the car on a patch of grass next to the street in front of Nelson's house, the very spot where it had been stolen. The priest would walk into the next block to Mrs. Arceneaux's house, and she would return him to his car. He pulled out of the rental place and drove a back road past tin-roofed shotgun houses and abandoned cars better in appearance than the leprous one that now moved among them. He entered the battered railroad underpass and emerged in the nicer part of town, which was moon washed and asleep. He found that if he kept his foot off the accelerator and just let the car idle along at ten miles an hour, it didn't make much noise, but when he gave the car a little gas after stop signs, the exhaust sounded like a lion warming up for a mating. The priest was thankful at least for a certain buoyancy of the blood provided by the glasses of brandy, a numbness of spirit that helped him endure what he was doing. He was still nervous, though, and had trouble managing the touchy accelerator, feeling that the car was trying to bound away in spite of his best efforts to control it. Eventually, he turned onto the main street of Nelson's little subdivision and burbled slowly down it until he could see the apron of grass next to the asphalt where he could park. He turned off the car's lights.

One of the town's six policemen had an inflamed gallbladder, and Patrolman Vic Garafola was working his friend's shift, parked in an alley next to the Elks Club, sitting stone-faced with boredom when a shuddering and filthy Toronado crawled past in front of him. He would have thought it was just some rough character from the section down by the fish plant, but he got a look at the license plate and saw that it bore a design that hadn't been on any car in at least five years. Vic put his cruiser in gear, left his lights off, and rolled out into the empty streets, following the Toronado at a block's distance past the furniture store, across the highway, and into the little Shade Tree subdivision. He radioed a parish officer he'd seen a few minutes earlier and asked him to park across the entrance, the only way in or out of the neighborhood.

Even in the dark Vic could see that the car's tires were bagged out and that it was dirty in an unnatural way, pale with dust—the ghost of a car. He closed in as it swayed down Cypress Street, and when he saw the driver douse his lights, he thought, Bingo, somebody's up to no good, and he hit his headlights, flashers, and yowling siren. The Toronado suddenly exploded forward in a flatulent rush, red dust and sparks raining backward from underneath the car as it left the patrolman in twin swirls of tire smoke. Whoever was driving was supremely startled, and Vic started the chase, following but not gaining on the sooty taillights. Shade Tree had only one long street that ran in an oval like a racetrack. At the first curve, the roaring car fishtailed to the right and Vic followed as best he could, watching ahead as the vehicle pulled away and then turned right again in the distance, heading for the subdivision exit. When Vic went around a curve, he saw a white cruiser blocking the speeding car's escape. The fleeing vehicle then slowed and moved again down Cypress Street. Vic raised a questioning eyelid as he watched the grumbling car slow down and finally stop in front of Nelson Lodrigue's brick rancher. The patrolman pulled up, opened his door, and pointed his pistol toward the other vehicle.

"Driver, get out," he barked.

Slowly, a graying, soft-looking man wearing a dark shirt buttoned all the way up slid out of the Toronado, his shaking hands raised high.

"Can you please not yell?" The old man looked around at the drowsing houses.

Vic stared at him, walked close, and looked at his eyes. He holstered his weapon. "Why'd you speed away like that, Father?"

The priest was out of breath. "When you turned on those flashers it frightened me and, well, I guess I pressed the accelerator too hard and this thing took off like a rocket."

Vic looked at the car and back to the priest. "The tag is expired, and it doesn't have an inspection sticker." He went to his patrol car and reached in for his ticket book.

"Could you please turn off those flashers?"

"Have to leave 'em on. Rules, you know," Vic said in a nasty voice. "You want to show me your proof of insurance, driver's license, and pink slip?" He held out a mocking hand.

"You know I don't have any of those."

"Father, what are you doing in this wreck?"

The priest put his hands in front of him, pleading. "I can't say anything. It's related to a confession."

"Oh, is this a good deed or somethin'?"

The priest's face brightened with hope, as though the patrolman understood what this was all about. "Yes, yes."

Vic leaned in and sniffed. "You think it's a good deed to get drunk as a boiled owl and speed around town at night?" he hollered.

"Oh, please hush," Father Ledet pleaded.

Vic reached to his gun belt. "Turn around so I can cuff you."

"Have some mercy."

"Them that deserves it get mercy," Vic told him.

"God would give me mercy," the priest said, turning around and offering his hands at his back.

"Then he's a better man than I am. Spread your legs."

"This won't do anyone any good."

"It'll do me some good." Just then a porch light came on, and a shirtless Nelson Lodrigue padded down the steps to the walk in his bare feet, his moon-shaped belly hanging over the elastic of his pajamas.

"Hey. What's goin' on?"

Other porch lights began to fire up across the street and next door, people coming out to the edge of their driveways and staring.

"It's Father Ledet," Vic called out. "He's getting a ticket or two."

Nelson was standing next to the car before his eyes opened fully and his head swung from side to side at the dusty apparition. "What the hell? This here's my old car that got stole."

Vic gave the priest a hard look. "Collections been a little slow, Father?"

"Don't be absurd. I was returning Nelson's car."

"You know who stole my car?" Nelson lumbered around the dusty hood. "You better tell me right now. I didn't sleep for a year after this thing got taken. I always had a feeling it was somebody I knew."

"I can't say anything."

"It came out in a confession," Vic explained.

Nelson ran his hand over the chalky paint of the roof. "Well, charge him with auto theft and I bet he'll tell us."

Two ladies in curlers and a tall middle-aged man wearing a robe and slippers approached from across the street. "What's going on, Vic?" the man asked. "Hello, Father."

The priest nodded, hiding the handcuffs behind him. "Good evening, Mayor. This isn't what it appears to be."

"I hope not," one of the women said.

Other neighbors began walking into the circle of crackling light cast by the police car's flashers. Then the parish deputy pulled up, his own lights blazing. Vic looked on as the priest tried to explain to everyone that he was doing a good thing, that they couldn't know all the details. The patrolman felt sorry for him, he really did, felt bad as he filled out the tickets, as he pushed the old head under the roofline of the patrol car, and later, as he fingerprinted the soft hands and put the holy body into the cell, taking his belt, his shoelaces, and his rosary.

*F*ather Ledet had to journey to Baton Rouge to endure the frowns and lecturing of the bishop. His parish was taken away for two months, and he was put into an AA program in his own community where he sat many times in rusty folding chairs along with fundamentalist garage mechanics, striptease artists, and depressed wives to listen to testimonials, admonitions, confessions without end. He rode cabs to these meetings, and in the evenings no one invited him to the Ladies' Altar Society dinners or anyplace else. Mrs. Arceneaux never called to sympathize, and pretty Mrs. Barrilleaux wouldn't even look at him when he waved as she drove by the rectory in her new secondhand car.

The first day he was again allowed to put on vestments was a Sunday, and he went in to say the eleven o'clock Mass. The church was full, and the sun was bleeding gold streamers of light down through the sanctuary windows above the altar. The Gloria was sung by the birdlike voices of a visiting children's choir, and later the priest stood in the pulpit and read the Gospel, drawing scant solace from the story of Jesus turning water into wine. The congregation then sat down with a rumble of settling pews and kicked-up kneelers. Father Ledet began to talk about Christ's first miracle, an old sermon that he'd given dozens of times. The elder parishioners in the front pews seemed to regard him as a stranger, the children were uninterested, and he felt disconnected and sad as he spoke, wondering if he would ever be punished enough for what he had done. He scanned the faces in the congregation as he preached, looking for forgiveness of any sort, and fifteen minutes into the sermon, he saw in the fifth pew, against the wall, something that was better than forgiveness, more than what he deserved, a sight that gave sudden expression to his dull voice and turned bored heads up to the freshened preaching. It was Clyde Arceneaux, a plastic tube creeping down from his nose and taped to his puckered neck. He was asleep, pale, two steps from death, his head resting against the wall, but at least he had finally come inside.

Something for Nothing

Not long after he had been laid off at the truck plant, Wayne lost his new car to the bank, and his girlfriend broke up with him and moved away from Baton Rouge to Atlanta. He had to relocate from his condo to a garage apartment where the floors creaked and the water heater made a sound all night like boiling eggs knocking together in a pot. In the local paper he saw no ads that required his skills, but a new business in town, the Something for Nothing Floating Casino Corporation, ran a large announcement that the boat was hiring for "certain positions." He took a cab down to the river and was interviewed by a combed-back, portly gentleman wearing a chalk-stripe suit.

"Are you a good swimmer?" the man asked, reading from a list of questions.

Wayne told him that he had been a certified lifeguard in high school, and when the interviewer heard this, he smiled and peered over the front of his desk into Wayne's lap. "You're a thirty-four waist?"

"That's about right."

"Hey, I know waists. I used to sell suits at Loeb's before the downtown store closed. You're not the only one that's made a career change." The interviewer opened his desk drawer and pulled out an invoice. "Let me have your inseam so I can order uniforms for you if you pass the swimming test."

"What kind of work are you hiring me for?"

The interviewer clicked a pen and began to write. "You'll be in, ah, inspection. Mainly on the riverbank," he said, opening another drawer and pulling out a pair of brown swimming trunks. "There's a bath-room," he said, pointing over Wayne's shoulder.

They went up the ramp to the boat and then out on the river side of the bow.

"Where do you want me to swim?" Wayne eyed an iron ladder that descended into the murky chop.

"There's a bad eddy out there. If you think you can, jump and go straight across the current a hundred feet or so, then swim back to the ladder."

Wayne banged down into the water, fighting across the eddy and out toward the west. The river was gritty, tasting of turpentine and almonds. When he stroked back, as soon as his hand touched the ladder, the man in the chalk-stripe suit yelled down, "You're hired."

*W*ayne sat in the glass guardhouse at the edge of the parking lot sniff-ing the dye in his new gray uniform. Down the bank in the Mississippi River, the *Something for Nothing* floated in the greasy current looking like a wedding cake decorated by a lunatic. The roofline of every deck was crowded with crudely made serpentine gingerbread, a turquoise-and-lavender pattern repeated on the boxy landing building and along the top of the parking lot fence. Wayne thought the whole place was silly, and he was mourning the loss of his previous job making $37.81 an hour in a vast, clean plant where everything made sense. The mirror-like paint jobs of the leather-upholstered trucks had reflected logic as they bobbled off the assembly line on their way to farmers and carpen-ters all over America. The plant had shut down mysteriously, and when he asked a foreman why, he was told, "Let's just say it makes more sense to operate in another state."

*T*he casino manager apprenticed him to Mr. Joey, a slim, meditative man in his midforties. On Wayne's first day, he took him down to the riverside guardhouse and pointed to an aluminum skiff tethered against the bank. "Maybe later today I want you to take that little boat and run it around the casino a couple times. Get the hang of it, you know?"

Wayne studied the skiff. "Okay. But why do we need a boat?"

Mr. Joey looked down at his shiny black work shoes. "They ain't told you nothing in the main office?"

Wayne scratched an arm where the shirt's fabric made him itch. "They just asked me about nine hundred times if I could swim. What's up with that?"

Mr. Joey put his hands out in front of him, as if he were showing the length of a fish. "Here's the deal. This boat's had some bad luck, you know? Now and then we get a customer that's real mental. He's maybe depressed and loses too much."

Wayne glanced back down to the skiff, which carried two inches of rainwater in it from an early morning squall. A Luzianne bailing can floated against the seat. "I hope this ain't going where I think it's going."

"Hey, you a grown-up. What, twenty-six years old, your papers said." He took a short comb from his rear pocket and ran it straight back through his hair. "When a customer loses big, sometimes he don't want to leave the boat and face Mamma and the kids."

Wayne turned toward the Mississippi and watched a loaded tanker coming down from Exxon, pushing a mound of beige river up its bow. "Then what happens?"

"I don't know what happens to the ones that walk home. But at this boat, maybe once every two months, one of them jumps in the water."

"Oh, shit."

Mr. Joey put a hand on his shoulder. "Hey, other boats got this problem, too. Just not as bad as us."

Wayne looked at the *Something for Nothing* and its narrow shelves of open deck space. A woman stepped out on level three, not letting the door close, and glanced at Baton Rouge as if to confirm the presence of a real world beyond the dim violet fantasy of the casino. She regarded the gloss-white deck, ceiling, and bulkheads, and after a moment was scalded by the light back into the dark racket of the slot machines. "My God," Wayne said. "We're the suicide skiff."

Running his thumb down the music of his comb, Mr. Joey said, "No, we're lifeguards."

Wayne sat down on a lavender chair. Back when he'd worked at the community pool, he'd been a veteran at rescuing the nine-year-olds who had wandered out of their depth. He'd stopped children from running and even broken up fights between hormone-wracked boys driven crazy by budding subdivision girls burnished beautiful by sunshine and pool chemicals.

One day, during his second year at the pool, a fourteen-year-old girl named Valerie dove many times into the deep end, even though she had trouble swimming to the edge after she came up. She was thin and went into the water like a spear, but after her girlfriend towed her out twice, and after he had to drop in to help her when she stayed on the bottom like she'd forgotten where the sky was, he banished her to the other side of the rope at eight feet. He saw her treading water against the rope, throwing him baleful looks. Twice she hollered to him that she could swim well enough to handle the deep end, but he shook his head, *no.*

And then two busloads of third-graders arrived, and the pool became a bobbing stew of yelling bodies ringed by runners and screaming teachers, helpless in dresses. When a boy bubbled under at six feet and Wayne jumped in for the rescue, several shrieking third-grade girls fluttered to him like ducks after bread, hanging onto his neck, pulling his hair. He brought up the boy and in the hubbub didn't hear the word *mister,* or half heard it as he backed the raft of hollering kids into shallow water. He saw a boy with tomato-red hair running alongside the pool and yelled for him to stop at the same time as the boy mouthed, "Mister, mister," and later, while Wayne told a teacher that the sputtering child he'd handed to her should be made to sit on the bus, the redheaded boy came in close and pleaded, "Mister." Wayne shook the water out of his ears and looked at the freckles that covered the boy like red ants and heard, "Mister, there's a big girl in the deep end." He went under like a dolphin then, through cilia of white legs, under the eight-foot rope, his eyes open, and after forty feet he saw the one-piece aqua swimsuit the same color as the pool paint and the gray-white arms and legs coming out of the cloth, limp and drifting.

When he brought her to the surface, her mouth was open and filled with water like a pitcher. He laid the girl on the hot apron and tried to bring her back, bending over her to restart her heart, and then, mouth to mouth, sending last breaths through her lips until the ambulance crew arrived, but again she wouldn't listen and stay where she belonged.

And the worst part of it all was going to her funeral and explaining to each of her staring relatives why he hadn't been able to bring Valerie back to her family.

For three days Wayne and Mr. Joey sat in their little building, a parody of a steamboat's pilot house, with purple vinyl filigree running along the roofline and a domed top sprouting a bird-streaked gilded ball. Whenever a customer stepped out onto a riverside deck, a security camera would examine him, and an employee in the monitoring room would make a decision; sometimes the speaker clipped to the shoulder of Wayne's uniform would snarl out a code, and he and Mr. Joey would run the skiff around the casino, cruising slowly alongside, inspecting the hull, dawdling in the rolling, mud-pungent current, pointing at rust spots and algae until the customer returned to the howling machines.

Wayne began to jump every time the speaker on his shoulder made a noise. He watched the eyes of customers who walked near the guardhouse, trying to tell if any were depressed or desperate, trying to predict their future.

Mornings were the most dangerous times, Mr. Joey told him. The management wanted a strong swimmer on site before sunrise because if a poor soul was destined to become despondent after a night of losing everything, first light was usually the trigger. "Nothing kills off a bad fantasy like sunrise," Mr. Joey said.

One day Wayne was thinking about this as he walked up to the guardhouse at false dawn, the Mississippi steaming behind it like a sliding lake of phenol and diesel fuel. He washed the westward windows with glass cleaner as the sun came up across the river and charged the mists with heat, the whole July morning beginning to glow like gas in a fluorescent tube. Through the brightening panes he watched clouds rise, mile-high sooty mollusks burgeoning toward thunderhead. Mr. Joey slouched in a chair, asleep behind his dark glasses. The air conditioner in the guardhouse cycled on, and when Wayne put his hand out to the window, he could already feel heat percolating off the pane. He began to worry about the all-night gamblers who might look through one of the few windows and understand that nothing could hide from the sun.

The radio snorted, and Mr. Joey wiggled his nose.

"Four B," the radio said. Mr. Joey sat straight up. *Four* meant fourth deck, *B* meant an intoxicated customer. In the security handbook, *C* was a conflict on deck. There was a *D* in the book, but only white space after it.

Suddenly the radio stuttered an electric yell, "Four D, dammit," and Mr. Joey jackknifed out of his chair. In ten seconds they were in the skiff, Mr. Joe's spatulate fingers pulling on the starter rope, Wayne in the bow yanking the tether free.

"Heads up." Mr. Joey gunned the engine and Wayne leaned away from a lavender plank of the imitation paddle wheel zinging at his head. The skiff arced around the back of the casino, climbed a rolling swell cast by a descending tanker, and surfed down into the trough. Above them they heard a yell. A white-shirted security guard on the fifth deck pointed down to where a sour-faced man, pot-bellied and balding, was sitting on the rail, his skinny legs dangling over the water like disconnected cables. "Okay, boy," Mr. Joey said, "now's when you earn your keep."

At that moment the man lost his grip and cartwheeled into the river. Wayne tipped overboard, stroking over to a bubbling swirl where he hoped he could reach in and pull the man out of the current like a rabbit from a hat. As he beat down the waves he pictured the despairing gambler floating quietly just under the surface, beginning to have second thoughts.

The big guard on the upper deck began to gesture and shout. "Over here! Hey, over *here!*" Wayne swam upstream a few yards and his knee touched something soft, so he went under. He spread his arms, even his fingers, groping blindly, imagining his hands would soon fill with something—dirt from Minnesota, a waterlogged stick—and when he grabbed a handful of pliant cotton shirt, he was startled to be granted more than he expected. He hauled back on the cloth and kicked for the surface, where he shook the water from his hair and brought up next to him a head spitting water and gasping, a cyanic face opening its mouth, and eyes taking everything in at once and not thinking much of it. "Let me go," the face croaked.

The man began to fight, and Wayne was surprised by his own rising anger. This one wasn't going to get away. "Come on, you old bastard. You're going to the bank with me."

"Let me drown." The old fellow raised his lardy arms and flailed at the river. It was obvious he couldn't swim at all.

Wayne circled his right arm around the man's chest and began stroking toward the skiff with his left. "Be still. I *won't* turn you loose."

Mr. Joey steered the boat in close, reached over, and grabbed the jumper by his belt, hauling him in like a spent fish, staying low in the skiff to keep it from rolling over. He placed a foot on the man's biceps as he helped Wayne, who tumbled in next to them. He was trembling and his mouth was full of the scary taste of the river. "Why in holy hell did you jump?" he shouted.

The old man propped himself against a seat and wiped beads of river off his bald head, blinking up at the sky as though he expected something to fall out of it and crush him. "I been playing the ten-dollar slots," he rasped.

Wayne watched him like he was a hound that had wandered out onto an interstate. The skiff swung toward an eroded piece of riverbank next to the guardhouse. "What'd you lose?"

The man put his head down. "Bank account."

"Well, that don—"

"Checking account. CDs. Paycheck. Maxed all the credit cards." His voice rose and he picked up his head. "No machine on God's green earth could put you in a bind like the one I been feeding. It sucked me dry."

"So then you threw yourself away," Mr. Joey said.

The man cut his eyes sharply. "Why not, son of a bitch. I'm about all I got left."

"Here we go," Wayne said quickly, stepping over the bow and pulling the skiff ashore. He put a hand out to the jumper and didn't know what to say. "Watch your step," he finally told him. In the back of the skiff Mr. Joey rolled his eyes.

*T*he casino manager, Mr. Dominic, was standing next to the guardhouse dressed in a dark gray suit with the lapels perfectly rolled, the pleats in his pants like razor blades. Next to him stood a large athletic man Wayne had seen many times around the casino. Everybody called him Puck. He held a little phone to his ear and listened as if some superior intelligence were telling him everything. Puck nodded and pocketed his cell, coming to the skiff and helping the man up the bank as if he were an old relative who'd slipped down in a supermarket aisle.

"Hey, you Mr. Bradruff, right? Live up by Government Street?" Puck had a soft, friendly face, a voice like elevator music, and two long, thin scars lining his jaw.

Bradruff struggled up to the parking lot and when he started to cry, Puck held out a huge arm and gathered him in. "Hey, it's all right, you know? Everybody has a bad day at the tables once in a while." He jiggled the man in his arms. Wayne was afraid he might rest his cheek on the top of Bradruff's slick head.

A black Cadillac idled up to the guardhouse. Its door opened and Puck walked Bradruff over to it where they were miniaturized in the vehicle's tinted windows. When Puck stepped back from the smaller man his suit was dark with river, Bradruff's image printed on him as though something other than water had passed between them. Puck motioned toward the soft leather folds of the backseat, and the old man ducked in, Puck crawling after him. He spoke a word into his tiny phone, the door closed, and the Cadillac swam up the levee like a glossy reptile.

Mr. Dominic, everyone's boss, was rocking back and forth in his mirrory shoes, staring after the car.

Wayne cleared his throat. "Shouldn't that guy be in an ambulance or something?"

Mr. Dominic turned to him, and Wayne saw himself a tiny uniformed figure on the lenses of the dark glasses, his blond head the size of a match tip. "Somebody comes around, you know, like a newspaper man," he said, "you send them to me, right?"

Wayne was young, but he was not stupid. "Right," he said.

His boss gave him a stick of spearmint gum and placed a hand on

Wayne's sodden shoulder. "Not to worry. We gonna get the gennelman the help he needs."

Mr. Joey came up behind the manager and gave his partner a look. Wayne peeled away the gum wrapper slowly, popped the stick into his mouth, and chewed vigorously, trying to keep from asking questions. He watched Mr. Dominic turn and walk back to the imitation-wood office and concession area, toward his cloud-soft carpet and fragrant secretaries.

Wayne went into the guardhouse and took a dry uniform from his locker. In the tiny bathroom he closed his eyes and saw Bradruff's streaming face coming up next to his in the river, wet and squalling.

An hour later Mr. Joey came back from the main office and stood in front of the window unit, his palms spread open to the vents. "I was checking on our man."

"You find out anything about why he jumped? Was he kind of nuts or something?"

"He wiped out around two in the morning. The shift manager, Nelson, that turd, came over and told him that maybe he should lay off and play another day. But Nelson don't mean it. They taught him to say that in casino school because it drives the bad gamblers insane. Once the house suggests they should stay away from the machines, they're crazy to get back."

Wayne stopped buttoning his shirt. "How did he keep playing after he busted out?"

"Puck says he walked up the hill to the all-night pawn and sold his watch, rings, and car." He made fists and rolled them in the cold air. "When he lost that, Nelson started giving him credit, and then he really went in the hole. I mean down, down, down. About sunup he just couldn't stand to leave the boat and face his family, or whoever he was gonna have to explain the losses to."

Wayne shoved the corner of a towel into his ear. "These are, like, weak people to begin with, right?"

Mr. Joey shrugged. "I guess they're accidents looking for a place to happen." He looked over toward the purple and turquoise trim work on the *Something for Nothing.* "This must be the place."

Wayne pictured Bradruff again, how the color had returned to his face, the little broken vessels in his cheeks reddening like filaments. "He didn't look stupid. Why couldn't he understand what was happening in there?"

Mr. Joey sat down on a wobbly turquoise stool. "Does a horsefly know what's happening when it flies into a bug zapper?"

Wayne tried to imagine what goes on in a bug's brain when it sees the magic blue light, that mystical glow. He thought of the flawed trembling in a moth's wings that guides it in to death, and then he turned to watch cars pulling into the parking lot and driving under the casino's huge sign that whirled its nimbus of bad-colored magnetic neon.

A month slid by like the chocolate river, and two jumpers decided to stay among the living when they saw the silvery skiff and watchful eyes below them. The morning Wayne hauled in a three-hundred-pound woman who'd gambled away her trailer, he began to feel powerful, like a real lifesaver, a skiff angel who would never again let anyone come up limp and breathless in his arms. He began to enjoy coming to work.

One August afternoon he looked up as Puck patted the glass guardhouse door with his vast palm.

"What's going on?" Wayne asked.

"Hey, come inside and put on a white shirt and a badge. We're short a man on the floor." Puck had a habit of putting his right fist into his left hand and holding it in front of him. Wayne realized that his arms were too big to fold without splitting his suit. Puck looked as if he were built out of martinis and rib eyes, his neck so big that his tie hung eight inches above his belt.

"I didn't train for security."

Puck waved him out into the sun. "It's just one shift. You don't carry no gun or nothing. Just walk the slots and make sure the old ladies don't go crazy."

Wayne boarded the boat, found the guards' area, and drew his shirt, badge, and hat. Passing through a different door, he stepped out onto the swirling orange, fuchsia, and teal carpet. The vast room was a dinging, chime-wracked labyrinth of a thousand hooting slot machines, each one with a customer attached like a tick.

The air itself was a fabric woven of bells, coins hammering into trays, the grind and flop of levers, the electric whanging of small payoffs. Wayne surveyed the room and understood that all of the motion and sound was orchestrated to rattle the customers toward a fear that some future allocation of bells would not be theirs, that a big tolling thing was going to happen, perhaps without them—the big jackpot was coming soon, and they'd be caught unprepared, a coin in the pocket instead of whirling through the innards of a benevolent machine. Interwoven with the sound was a fog of continually rebreathed cigarette smoke.

Wayne drifted past a blackjack table as a well-dressed, elegant woman won a pile of hundred-dollar chips, then shoved the whole win out for the next bet, as if wagering two thousand dollars was meaningless. Wayne wondered if the blonde, who was pushing fifty and probably still wondering when her ship was going to come in, would win five thousand, what would that do for her? If she would parlay her money into twenty-five grand, what would that buy but a poky American sedan or a down payment on a nondescript subdivision dwelling? He imagined that most people in the casino were living from paycheck to paycheck, so they gambled against the house, the computerized house that hired geniuses to program the machines and to figure the odds down to the last fate-lubricated turn of the roulette wheel. He looked around through the smoke and the racket, feeling like a conspirator in everyone's losses.

And then he saw him. Bald Mr. Bradruff was back, stuck on a vinyl stool, rolling quarters into a slot machine, a plastic bucket in the crook of his left arm. Wayne glanced toward the door that led to the outside deck, then looked up at the ceiling camera in his quadrant and held out one finger. Stepping back around a bank of bonging poker machines, he waited twenty seconds until Gagliano, head of security for the floor, got the word through his earpiece and steered his round belly in Wayne's direction.

"What you got?" Gagliano wore a jeweled badge and gold fringe on his cap. He was old and waddled when he walked, his hands facing backward. Wayne had heard he'd once been a master machinist.

"The gentleman on number four, next row, is the guy who jumped."

Gagliano's eyes were drooping from the smoke, and Wayne figured he was near the end of his shift.

"Which guy who jumped? This month, January, last year, what?"

Wayne began to feel queasy, and his stomach read a motion in the boat, as though it were turning from its moorings. He wanted to ask how many jumpers there were in all. "It's a Mr. Bradruff."

Gagliano walked around to the next aisle, spoke into his radio, waited a while for an answer, and pretended to ignore Bradruff, who was steadily feeding his machine as if it were a beloved pet. Gagliano adjusted a wheel on his radio and held it close to a furry ear, then came back. "He's all right."

"All right my ass. He tried to kill himself."

"Puck says he's okay now." He glanced over his shoulder at Bradruff. "He's happy enough spending his quarters." The guard shrugged. He had people to observe, money to count. "If you're worried about him, just keep an eye on the door to the outside deck," he said, chucking Wayne on the shoulder. Gagliano spoke a word into his radio and walked away into the craps tables.

On his next round, Wayne wandered close to Bradruff, noted the cheap knit shirt he wore, then passed on into the pebble of hard sounds paving the air, hoping he wouldn't be called on to slam into the water from up on this deck. After his next turn around the floor, he drifted past Bradruff's machine again, and this time the man's eyes flicked up at him, sick and dark, and at the last instant before turning away, they ignited with a fearful spark of recognition. Wayne touched him on a forearm lightly, and Bradruff leaned into the aisle, his hand stupidly caught in the bucket of coins.

"How's luck treating you?" Wayne asked.

Bradruff looked toward the door. "You the one pulled me out."

"That's me. You all right now?"

He turned back to the machine. "You can mind your own business if you want to. I'm just risking a few dollars here." His eyes bounced between the machine and Wayne's badge. "You don't have to worry about me."

Wayne remembered again the wet heft of Bradruff in his arms, how the color had come back into his face. He took a step closer. "You here by yourself?"

"My son dropped me off on his motorbike. He'll be picking me up before too long."

Wayne gave him a look. "You don't have a car anymore?"

"I didn't have no car when I came into this world."

"Well, if you need something, I'll be right up in here, walking around."

Bradruff put a hand up on a lever, his fingertips blackened by the coins. "I'm all right with the management. They're a bunch of nice guys."

"Yeah?"

"They got my house back. I mean, all the other stuff's gone, but I still got a roof. My wife and my son's still living with me." He dropped his hand into the bucket, fished a quarter, placed it into the slot, and pulled the lever, all without looking at the machine. "Everything's fine." Thirty quarters banged into the tray, and Bradruff stared at them, deadpan. "See, things're looking up."

The next night, Wayne lay awake listening to his water heater knock and rumble. Toward dawn he began to imagine that if he ever had children, this is how it would be, worrying all the time about what they were doing. He went to work and spent the shift watching television and listening to the plastic speaker clipped to his shoulder like a fretting pet bird with a threatening beak. When he got off, he looked in the Baton Rouge directory, found Roy Bradruff's address, and took a bus to a peeling frame house on a sandy lot south of Catfish Town. A yellow Monte Carlo with a large red sticker on the back windshield listed in a rain-topped rut. Wayne walked in off the street and knocked, and Bradruff came out onto the splintery porch in his knobby bare feet, wearing a washed-out paisley shirt with cream-colored paramecia swimming through a burgundy background. "Hey," he said.

Wayne saw that the shirt was not washed out but coated with sawdust. "I just wanted to check up on you."

Bradruff seemed sleepy or half-drunk. He motioned him feebly inside. "You want to sit awhile? I just got off work at the cabinet shop."

"No. I feel kind of foolish worrying you like this."

Bradruff made a noise down in his chest, a cracking of phlegm. "You sure don't owe me nothing."

"You do any good at the slots?"

Bradruff looked around at his porch ruefully. "What you think."

"You gonna keep coming to the boat?" Wayne looked over to a bloated yellow dog limping up the steps.

"Only chance I got."

"Well. It's a real long shot."

"Better than no shot."

Wayne showed his teeth, trying to be pleasant, and rocked back on his heels. "I've heard the odds on the big one. Seven million to one is no shot."

Bradruff pulled his watch face around from the other side of his wrist and read the dial. "Somebody's got to win it."

Any further comment would have sounded like an argument, so Wayne nodded and turned for the steps. "I just got off myself, so I'll head on to the house."

"All right," Bradruff said, sounding relieved. "Don't set up worrying about me, now. I was pretty drunk that time I fell in the river."

Wayne bumped up against the dog, which walked backward and coughed. "Take it easy."

"Thanks for coming," Bradruff told him, under his breath.

Wayne watched him go inside. At least he was still alive, working and making money, still around for his family. Surely something had changed in him a bit—he'd seen the light, Wayne hoped, and come to the surface of things.

Ten days later, on the night shift, Wayne and Mr. Joey were playing gin to keep awake when the little speakers on their shoulders began scratching out a frantic string of syllables punctuated by "4D" sung several times staccato, and together they stumbled down the dark bank.

The outboard dug into the river, the bow rising into the moonless sky. Immediately past the paddle wheel the skiff rode over a submerged drift log and the motor kicked up with a bang and stalled. Looking upriver alongside the boat, Wayne saw what he knew he would see. When he was a child he'd waited at a rural railroad station with his mother to catch a cross-country train they both knew would be an hour late. He had stared at the empty distance between the rails patiently, knowing the void would fill, for the train was inevitable; it was on tracks and had to come to town, and now Roy Bradruff was coming on, climbing over the casino rail, right on his schedule. He was hitching his rear end off a half inch at a time, moving one buttock, then the other, squinting in the hundreds of deck lights firing up the side of the boat.

Wayne tried to figure the math of the rescue, what he'd have to do if Bradruff made it to the water. The guards on deck were hanging back, their arms extended, waiting for a chance, but Bradruff was red faced, unfocused, and drunk, yelling in a back-road voice that all their son-of-a-bitching machines were broke, that he'd poured his house back into the slots and was down to the clothes on his back. He ripped open his shirt, the buttons flying like shrapnel, and flung it off into the night, then tumbled, bald head over heels.

Mr. Joey had gotten the engine back into the water and started it; the skiff surged upriver alongside the scummy hull, sliding under the falling man who came plunging down on both of them in a percussion of bones. Mr. Joey fell overboard, and one of Bradruff's tumbling legs struck Wayne in the chest and they both fell backward into the water. As soon as he was under, Wayne kicked away from the light, afraid of the propeller, and when the water darkened to the color of syrup, he came up for air. The river drained out of his ears, and he heard the yells on deck and glimpsed Mr. Joey stroking toward the casino. His lifeguard instincts came alive and he wanted Roy Bradruff like air itself. Spitting out a mouthful of river, he yelled up at the boat, hoping that someone could point toward where he was supposed to swim in the chop, but everyone was busy pulling Mr. Joey out. Behind him he heard a man's cry, a watery scream that raised the hairs on his neck, and he struck out downriver into the black suck of current, past the end of the boat where the river faded from tan enamel to a dark, oil-laced mystery on which reflections of shore lights sparked like drowning fireflies. He swam fifty yards along the darkening channel, seeing nothing, then stopped to tread water, to listen. Wayne hoped that Bradruff was not below him somewhere, trying to breathe water and swim away to a new place where there would be no blame for whatever he'd done on the boat. He heard a swirl, like the struggle of a caught fish, and dug out toward it, clutching the water as though each stroke might touch a hand or an arm drifting away with a soul's final motion. He swam until he imagined Bradruff's body as a gray ember with only one spark at its center, but still something that could be blown back into fire. He swam until his arms went numb and a dark roller ironed him under. A charge of river stabbed up his nose, and, sputtering and lost in a new velvety blackness, he pictured his own young limbs gray as ash and cooling toward death.

The search over, his questing strength gone, he struggled toward the bank. All he could see was a dark wall ahead, and after many strokes he overhanded into the algae-padded side of a moored barge. Sapped and slipping south along its side, he found a cable dangling between two barges and hung on with one hand, letting his body go limp, giving it over to the current like a flag to the breeze. He gathered black breaths, wondering if Bradruff had come up or was journeying backward to his origin, a gamble lost, returned to the dealer.

In fifteen minutes, a Coast Guard boat's spotlight silver-plated the eddies around him, and he heard, from far off, Mr. Joey's worried voice calling out to him.

The next afternoon he came back to work and was summoned to the cool green office of Mr. Dominic. Puck politely ushered him in, and the manager was smiling. He walked around his desk and motioned with both hands for Wayne to sit in a forest-green leather armchair. The skin on Mr. Dominic's face was smooth like the hide of the chair. "You thinking of quitting us, I hear."

"Yes sir." Wayne felt himself sinking.

"We moving some people around, you know. Thought you might want to get out of that little glass greenhouse and work the boat." He sat back on the front edge of his immaculate desk.

Wayne opened a hand, looked into the palm, then made a fist. "I was thinking of going back to factory work. Maybe find another truck plant and move."

Mr. Dominic looked at him. "The Shreveport plant is the closest one, and it's closing down. You got to stay with us." He made a gun of his hand and pointed it at Wayne. "Check the want ads. We're about the only game in town anymore, unless you want to get scalded down at Exxon or elected to the legislature."

Wayne twisted the soles of his shoes into the carpet. "I guess that's true. What would I do on the boat?"

"A little security. Just a utility belt with cuffs and mace. Mr. Gagliano could train you in a couple days, teach you the radio codes, how to steer the drunks, how to watch a machine that's being emptied. Usual stuff. Plus you'd get an extra two dollars an hour." Mr. Dominic folded his hands on a thigh, waiting for an answer like a man holding all the right cards.

Wayne scanned the room for a window. He had the urge to look outside, but the room was like a plush secret. "Okay," he said.

"Good. Good." They both got to their feet, and Mr. Dominic put up a hand, clamping it on Wayne's neck, shaking it affectionately. "You know, they found that poor man's body this morning, down under a dock past the lower bridge."

Wayne's mind cut off like an engine starved for fuel, and he waited in the quiet office for it to start up again. "Ah," he said.

"The funeral's tomorrow afternoon. Just a wake type thing. You think you could show up? You know, represent the boat to the family?"

He thought of himself in this changed identity, the representative of something for nothing. "I don't know."

Mr. Dominic squeezed his neck, hard. "You could take the whole day off," he whispered respectfully. "With overtime."

The funeral home was a long, low building of streaked white brick situated across from a refinery. Wayne's cab pulled into the gravel parking lot, stopped, and he watched the dust ghosting down the potholed street. Inside, he signed the guest book and met Roy Bradruff's wife, who was much larger than her husband. She wore long, swinging gray braids and leaned into Wayne, holding his hand and trying to bend it double.

"We know you done what you could," she said with her beery breath.

He spilled out his rehearsed words. "All of us down at the casino are really sorry about this." He had to speak up to be heard over a Hammond organ being played in the vestibule by a stick of an old woman. The tune was blurry, the organist bereft of rhythm.

The wife's eyes were hard to read. "Well, we tried to keep him out of that place. We talked and talked about it, but we all knew something was going to happen. I guess we just didn't want to admit it." She looked off to the side.

"You understand it wasn't an accident?"

She lifted her head. "Yeah. You know, he always gambled, penny-ante stuff, but after they parked that damn boat uptown, he just lost control."

"The boat," he said, choking on the words, "it just doesn't want any hard feelings."

The woman's eyes focused on his. "Well, my husband don't have no feelings at all right now, so I guess the boat's happy." She grabbed his arm. "Let me innerduce you to Roy Junior."

In the rear of the funeral home chapel, against a wall of slightly buckled paneling, a slim sunburned man who seemed about forty years old leaned back in a folding chair, its front legs hovering off the carpet. Wayne reached out, and the redheaded son put his cigarette in the corner of his mouth and offered a hand that felt like a tree root. The mother gave a rattling cough, then said, "This here's the boy in the paper what tried to save him." She turned and walked away, over toward the organist.

The son rolled up his bloodshot eyes for a look. He was wearing dark dress pants, patent leather shoes left over from a wedding in the seventies, and a white dress shirt with silver collar tips. The top three buttons were undone, showing a gold chain with a Phillips 66 emblem on the end. "You almost got kilt," Roy Junior said.

Wayne sat next to him. He'd known dozens of men like him in the truck factory. "I tried to find him in the dark, but I couldn't. I just couldn't do it."

Roy Junior nodded. "Hey, you can back off on yourself half a turn." He looked over at his mother, who was choosing hymns. "The old man just didn't want to come on home to us. You know, he pawned my motorcycle to play them damn ten-dollar slots is what he done. The pawnshop come got it last night. I worked four years to save enough for that thing, and don't look at me like it was some hippie motorbike without no muffler. This was a Gold Wing, like a banker might ride with his wife on the weekend." Roy Junior put his Marlboro to his lips and drew deep and long, looking sideways at Wayne. "Daddy was okay all around, but he couldn't leave them son-of-a-bitchin' machines alone. My youngest brother had him a little college account started with money a uncle left him. Daddy lost that first off on video poker." He glanced up through his bushy eyebrows. "Aw, hell, I don't mean to bend your ear with all our goin'-ons."

Wayne listened to the thready organ music and tried to imagine Roy Senior's life but couldn't. He closed his eyes for a long while, as though it hurt to look at the room. When he opened them, he said, "Why do you think he jumped?"

The son thought a moment, looking across the chapel at the coffin. "I reckon he got tired of taking from all us," he said, shaking his head. "It's a long, long story. Always chasing some jackpot."

"What would he have done if he'd won the big one?"

Roy Junior bobbed his head. "Are you crazy, man? Nobody can't win that thing. There's billions-to-one odds against it."

"But what if he did?"

He took in a drag on the nub of his cigarette, and Wayne thought the smoke must have been hot enough to weld his lips shut. "He'd try to give it back, what he took," Roy Junior said. "But you can't do that. Once something is took, even if you get it back, it's still been took from you. It's not the same thing you get back." The son straightened in his folding chair and flicked ash on the carpet.

Wayne looked at Roy Junior's fingers, which had been burned and nipped by hundreds of machines. "But he would have given you some of it."

"I already had what I wanted," Roy Junior said, talking out the smoke.

Wayne looked toward the tinny casket and could see that Roy Bradruff's profile bore the same waxy complexion as a fourteen-year-old girl named Valerie. "I can't believe it."

"Believe what?" Roy Junior said.

Wayne put his hands together and rested his forearms on his knees. "That I couldn't save him."

The son took another hissing drag, the tobacco burning out against the filter, and he turned to Wayne with a mixture of derision and abiding sympathy on his face. He motioned toward the coffin with the dead cigarette and told him, "Listen to me now, fella, the only one could've saved anything is stretched out in that box."

Resistance

Alvin Boudreaux had outlived his neighbors. His asbestos-siding house was part of a tiny subdivision built in the 1950s, when everybody had children, a single-lane driveway, a rotating TV antenna, and a picnic table out back. Nowadays he sat on his little porch and watched the next wave of families occupy the neighborhood, each taking over the old houses, driving up in their pairs of bug-shaped cars, one for each spouse to drive to work. Next door, Melvin Tillot had died, and his wife had sold the house to migrate up north with her daughter. Mr. Boudreaux used to watch her white puff of hair move through the yard as she snipped roses. Now she was gone, and there was no movement on his street that had consequence for him. Today he sat and watched the sky for sailing wedges of birds, or an army of ranked mackerel clouds, or the electric bruise of a thunderstorm rising from the molten heat of the Gulf. Sometimes he thought of his wife, dead now eight years. He was in that time of life when the past began coming around again, as if to reclaim him. Lately he thought about his father, the sugarcane farmer, who used to teach him about tractors and steam engines.

Two months before, Mr. Boudreaux had watched his new neighbors move in, a young blonde woman, overweight with thin hair and raw, nervous eyes. The husband was small and mean, and every weekend he sat in a lawn chair in the backyard as though he was at the beach and drank without stopping. They had one daughter, a plain, slow-moving ten-year-old.

Mr. Boudreaux could not bear to look at these people. They let the rosebushes die of thirst and left the empty garbage cans sit at the edge of the street until the grass under them forgot what the sun looked like and died. They never sat on their porch and had no pets that he could see. But after a while, he tried talking to the wife when she dragged out the garbage bag in the morning. Her voice was thin, like a little squeak. She worked somewhere for six hours each day, she told him, running an electric coffee-grinding machine.

One mild afternoon, Mr. Boudreaux was going to visit the graveyard, and he rattled open a kitchen window to air the room out while he was gone. Next door, he saw the daughter come into the yard and show her father a sheet of paper. The father curled up his lip, took a swallow from a tall tumbler, and looked away. Mr. Boudreaux felt sorry for the girl when she placed a hand on the father's shoulder and he grabbed the sheet from her and balled it up. She put a forefinger to her glasses as if to bring the world into focus. The motion showed practice and patience. She was formless and looked overweight in her pleated skirt and baggy white blouse. Her carroty hair was gathered in a short tail above her neck, her lips were too big for her face, and her gray eyes hid behind glasses framed in pale blue plastic, the kind of glasses little girls wore thirty years before. She stepped next to her father's chair again, getting in his space, as Mr. Boudreaux's grandson would say. The father began to yell, something about a damned science project. He waved his arms, and his face grew red. Another child might have cried.

The next afternoon, Mr. Boudreaux was on his knees pulling grass by the backyard fence when he heard the school bus grind up LeBoeuf Street. He was still pulling when the father came home at four-thirty and sat in the lawn chair, next to the back steps. The girl appeared behind the screen door, like a shadow.

"It's got to be turned in Monday," she said. Even her voice was ordinary, a plain voice with little music in it.

The father put his glass against his forehead. "I don't know anything about it," he said. "Do you know how tired I am?"

Her half-formed image shifted at the screen, then dispersed like smoke. In a moment the mother came out and stepped carefully past her husband, not looking at him until she was safely on the grass. "I'd help her," she said, "but I don't know anything about that. Electricity. It's something a man'll have to do."

The husband drained his drink and flung the ice cubes at the fence. Mr. Boudreaux felt a drop hit the back of his spotted hand. "Why can't she do something like a girl would do? Something *you* could help her with."

Mr. Boudreaux peered through the honeysuckle. The man was wearing jeans and a white button-down shirt with some sort of company emblem embroidered on the breast, a gay and meandering logo that suggested a bowling alley or gas station.

The mother looked down and patted the grass in a semicircle with her left foot. "You're her parent too," she said. It was a weak thing to say, Mr. Boudreaux thought.

The father stood up, and the flimsy chair tipped over on its side. He turned around and looked at it for a moment, then kicked it across the yard.

After dark, Mr. Boudreaux went out on his front porch with a glass of iced tea and listened, wondering whether the girl's parents ever argued. He had never heard them, but then he remembered that since the coming of air-conditioning, he'd heard little from inside anyone's house. When he first moved to the neighborhood, up and down LeBoeuf Street he could hear the tinny cheer of radios, the yelps of children chasing through the houses, a rare hollering match about money or relatives. But now there was only the aspirate hum of the heat pumps and the intermittent ahhh of an automobile's tires on the subdivision's ebony streets. He looked over at his fifteen-year-old Buick parked in the single drive. It embarrassed him to drive such a large old car through the neighborhood where everyone stood out and washed the dust from their Japanese-lantern compacts. Maybe it was time to trade it off for something that would fit in. Next door, the father came out and walked stiffly to his candy-apple car and drove away, dragging his tires at every shift of the gears, irk, irk.

The next morning Mr. Boudreaux walked down his drive for the paper and saw the girl, Carmen, sitting on her front steps waiting for the bus to appear out of the fog. Her eyes were red. He picked up the paper and started back toward the porch, telling himself, *Don't look.* But at his front steps he felt a little electrical tug in his neck muscles, a blank moment of indecision.

He turned his head. "Good morning, little miss," he called out, raising his paper.

"Morning, Mr. Boudreaux." Her low voice was small in the fog.

"How you doing in school?" He unfolded the paper and pretended to read the headlines.

"Okay."

He bounced once on the balls of his feet. He could walk into the house and not look back. "It's springtime," he said. "My kids used to have to make their science projects this time of year."

She looked over at him, her eyebrows up in surprise. "You have kids?"

Mr. Boudreaux realized how impossibly old he must seem. "Sure. A long time ago. They're nurses and engineers and one's a policeman way up in Virginia. They all had their science projects. What about you?"

She looked down at a heavy brown shoe. "I want to do one," she said, "but no one can help me."

He banged the paper against his leg several times before he said anything more. He closed his eyes. "Is your momma home? Let me talk to her a minute."

*T*hat's how it got started. After school, she rang his doorbell, and he led her into the kitchen, where he fixed her a Coke float. Carmen smelled dusty and hot and finished her drink in less than a minute. She placed the glass in the sink and then sat down at Mr. Boudreaux's porcelain table, spreading open a spiral-bound tablet. She gave him a blank look of evaluation, an expression she might use on a strange dog.

Mr. Boudreaux sat down across from her. "Well, missy, what kind of project you interested in? Your momma said you needed a little nudge in the right direction."

Carmen pushed her brown hair out of her eyes. "What did you do when you had a job?"

He blinked. "I started as a millwright at LeBlanc Sugar Mill, and when I retired I was a foreman over all the maintenance people."

She frowned. "Does that mean you don't know anything about electricity?"

Leaning back, he rubbed a spot over his eye. "I worked on a lot of motors in my time."

Carmen moved to the chair on his right and showed him her notebook. In it she'd drawn dozens of Os with legs, all running into a narrow cylinder and jumping one by one out of the other end of it. "These are electrons," she said. Some of the figures were running through a bigger cylinder and even more of them seemed to be coming out the other side. "The tube shapes are resistors," she instructed. "Some let electrons through fast, some slow." Her short fingers led his attention along the rows of exiting electrons, which had little smiles drawn on them as though they were now in a wonderful place. She told him how resistors control current and how without them no one could have ever made a television or computer.

Mr. Boudreaux nodded. "So what you going to call this project?"

"Resistance." She said the word as though it had another meaning.

"And we gotta figure out how to demonstrate it, right?" He closed his eyes and thought back to those late-night projects of his children. His son Sid, the state patrolman, had done friction. Friction, the old man thought. That was right up Sid's alley. "We have to state a problem and show how it's solved with resistors. Then we demonstrate how they work."

Carmen bobbed her head. "You *have* done this before."

The next afternoon they spent on the rug in the den drawing and brainstorming. When Mr. Boudreaux let the girl out at suppertime, he saw her father standing on the front walk, glowering. The next morning was Saturday, and he and Carmen got into his venerable Buick to go down to the electronics store at the mall. Walking the aisles, the girl hardly looked at her list, but instead spent her time browsing the tall pegboard sections hung with diodes and toggle switches, condensers and capacitors, where she toyed with little transistors through the thin plastic bags. Mr. Boudreaux tended to business, buying a pack of foot-square circuit boards, little red push switches, 18-gauge wire. Carmen had brought him a dog-eared book called *Electricity for Children,* and from it he'd memorized the banding codes for resistors. With this knowledge he selected an assortment of plastic cylinders that looked like tiny jelly beans decorated with red, black, and silver bands, an inch of bright wire coming out of each end.

Their purchases stowed in a loopy plastic bag, they walked through the mall to the candy counter, where Mr. Boudreaux bought a quarter pound of lime slices. Carmen took a green wedge from him, saying nothing, and they walked on through the baby strollers, teenagers, and senior citizens limping along in running shoes. The children who were Carmen's age looked stylish and energetic to him as they played video games or preened at their reflections in shop windows. Carmen was mechanical, earnest, and as communicative as a very old pet dog.

When they got back to Mr. Boudreaux's house, Carmen's father was standing unsteadily in the slim line of grass that ridged the middle of the driveway. The old man got out of the Buick and greeted him.

The other man had been drinking again. He pointed a chewed fingernail at Mr. Boudreaux. "You should've asked me before you took that girl off somewhere."

"I asked your wife. You weren't awake yet."

"Well, let me tell you, I was worried. I called up the police and checked you out." Carmen came around the car and stood between them, staring down the street as if she could see all the way to Texas.

Mr. Boudreaux passed his tongue along his bottom lip. "The police. You called the police about me? Why'd you do that?"

"You can't tell, nowadays. Old guys such as yourself and kids, you know?" The father stuck his pale hands into a pair of tight work pants.

Mr Boudreaux looked at the ground. He was embarrassed because he didn't know what to think, other than that nobody used to imagine things like that. Not in a million years. "You think I'm gonna rob your kid or something?" he said at last. "Look." He held out the plastic bag. "I helped her pay for her stuff."

Carmen's father pointed a finger at him again. "She can pay for her own stuff. You keep your money in your pocket," he said. "I don't know why you think you got to do this." He gave the girl a wounded glance and then turned toward his steps.

Mr. Boudreaux looked at Carmen. She pushed her glasses up her nose and looked back at him. "Did you have a little girl back when you were a father?" she asked.

He looked at his house and then back at the child. "Yes, I did. Her name's Charlene. And I have another named Monica."

For the first time that day, her expression changed and showed surprise. "What would anybody need with two girls?"

That afternoon he watched her write her report, helped her decide where to put headings and how to divide the information up. After supper, she came back over, and they planned the display. Carmen drew out a design on lined paper with an oversized pencil. "I want those little button switches that work like doorbells here," she said. "On the first circuit I want a straight wire to a flashlight bulb in one of those sockets we bought. On the second line I want a 22-ohm resistor to the same size bulb. That'll make the bulb glow dimmer." She stuck out her tongue and bit it as she drew carbon ribbons of circuits. "The third button will turn on a line with two 22-ohm resistors soldered together in series, and the bulb will glow dimmer." She went on to draw in the fourth circuit and said it would be an ordinary pencil wired to show how current can pass through carbon, "which is what resistors are made of," she told him. A fifth circuit would have a rotary switch controlling a bulb. Carmen drew in the electrical symbol for a variable resistor at this point and put down her pencil.

"Now what?" Mr. Boudreaux asked, rubbing his eyes with his long forefingers. Since he'd reached his late seventies, he'd been going to bed around eight-thirty. At the moment, his knees were aching like great boils.

"Now we have to solder this together on the perforated circuit board."

"Ow. I don't know about that."

She didn't look up. "Don't you have a soldering iron?"

"I haven't seen it in years." They got up and Carmen helped him down the back steps into the moonlit yard. Built onto the rear of the garage was a workshop. Mr. Boudreaux opened the door and its glass panel rattled. At one time he spent long hours here fixing the house's appliances or rebuilding bicycles and gas-powered airplanes. Now he came in once or twice a year to look for a screwdriver or to store a box. Carmen found the light switch.

"A workbench," she sang, going over to a vise and turning its handle around.

Mr. Boudreaux looked for the soldering gun while she dusted the maple counter with a rag and spread out the components. "Here it is," he said. But when he plugged the instrument in and pulled the trigger, a burst of sparks shot from the vents and a smell of melting Bakelite filled the shop. Holding it by its cord, he threw it into the yard.

The girl looked after the soldering iron sorrowfully. "Do you have another one?"

"No, honey. And it's too late to go buy a new one. We'll have to finish tomorrow." He watched her look at the counter and purse her lips. "What you thinking?"

"Sundays aren't good days," she told him.

He shook his head at the comment. "You'll be over here."

She stared at her blocky leather shoes. "Mom and I have got to be there, and we've got to stay quiet." She looked up at him and her face showed that she was smarter than he ever was. "We've always got to be in the corner of his eye," she whispered.

"What's that?" He bent a furry ear toward her.

"He wants us around, but kind of on the side. Never the main thing he looks at."

The old man looked up to a rusty sixteen-penny nail jutting from a rafter and took down his Turner gasoline blowtorch. "Hey. If this thing'll still work, we can try to get our soldering done the old-fashioned way."

She clapped her hands together once. "What is it?" She put a forefinger on the brass tank.

"Well, you open it up here," he told her, unscrewing a plug in the bottom and shaking out a few spoonfuls of stale, sweet-smelling gas. "Then you put some fresh lawn mower gasoline in, turn it over, and use this little thumb pump on the side."

"To make pressure?"

"Yeah. Then you light the end of this horizontal tube and adjust the flame with these old knobs." He dug around in a deep drawer under the counter, coming up with an arrow-shaped tool with a wooden handle on one end and an iron rod running out of that into a pointed bar of copper. "You got to set this heavy point in the flame, and when it gets hot enough, you touch it to the solder, which melts onto the wires. That's what holds the wires together."

The girl grabbed the wooden handle and waved the tool like a weapon, stabbing the air.

In a few minutes the blowtorch was sputtering and surging, humming out a feathery yellow flame. It had been over thirty years since Mr. Boudreaux had used such a torch for soldering, and it took several tries before the first wires were trapped in melted silver. He and the girl strung wire and turned screws into a circuit board, and for a minute he was a younger man looking down on the head of one of his own daughters. He felt expert as he guided Carmen's short fingers and held the circuit board for her to thread the red wire through to the switch terminals. He felt like he was back at work, almost as though he was getting things done at the mill.

The girl avoided his eyes but did give him a glance before asking, "Why're you helping me with this?"

He guided her fingers as she threaded a wire under the board. "It just needed doing."

"Did you really help your children with their projects?"

"I don't remember. Maybe their momma did."

She was quiet as she turned in a stubby screw. "Did *you* ever have to do a science project?"

He looked toward the dark workshop window and closed one eye. "I don't think science had been invented yet." He checked her face, but she wasn't smiling. Then he remembered something. "When I was in fifth grade I had to read a novel called *Great Expectations*. The teacher said we had to build something that was in the book, like an old house or Miss Havisham's wedding cake or some such foolishness. I forgot all about it until the night before, and knew I was going to really catch it the next day if I showed up without it."

Carmen took the hot copper away from the torch and soldered a joint herself. "What did you do?"

He rubbed his chin. "I think I cried, I was so scared. My mother would whack me with a belt if I ever failed a course, and I wasn't doing so good in English. Anyway, my daddy saw my long face and made me tell him what was wrong. He asked me what was in the book." Mr. Boudreaux laughed. "I thought that was strange, because he couldn't read hardly two words in a row. But I told him about Pip, and Pip's father, and the prison ship. That caught his ear, and he asked me about that ship, so I told him. Then he went outside. That night I went to bed and couldn't sleep hardly a wink. I remember that because I've always been a good sleeper. I go out like a light about nine, ten o'clock, you know?" The girl nodded, then placed a bulb in a socket. "When I got up for school, Daddy had left for work at the mill, and on the kitchen table was a foot-long sailing boat, painted black, three masts, all the rigging strung with black sewing thread, deck hatches, gunports, and a bowsprit. It was all done with a pocket knife, and it was warm to the touch because Momma said he had put it in the oven to dry the paint so it would be ready for school."

The girl seemed not to hear him. "I want the battery tied in with wire," she said.

"The old man was like that," Mr. Boudreaux told her. "He never asked me if I liked the boat, and I never said anything to him about it, even when I brought home a good grade for the project."

When they were finished, all the lightbulbs lit up in the way that she predicted. He built a hinged wooden frame for the two posters that held her report and drawings. They set everything up on the workbench and stepped back. Mr. Boudreaux pretended to be a judge and clamped his fingers thoughtfully around his chin. "That's a prizewinner," he said in a mock-serious voice. Then he looked down at Carmen. Her lips were in a straight line, her eyes dark and round.

The next day was Sunday, and Mr. Boudreaux went to eleven o'clock Mass, visiting afterward with the men his age who were still able to come out. They sat on the rim of St. Anthony's fountain under the shade of a palm tree and told well-worn jokes in Cajun French, followed by an accounting of who was sick, who was dead. Mr. Landry, who'd worked under Mr. Boudreaux at the sugar mill, asked him what he was doing with his granddaughter at the mall.

"That was a neighbor child," Mr. Boudreaux told him. "My grandchildren live away."

"What was she doing? Asking you about the dinosaurs?" He laughed and bumped the shoulder of the man next to him.

"She's doing a school thing, and I'm helping her with it."

Mr. Landry's face settled into a question. "She lives on the north side of you?"

"Yes."

Mr. Landry shook his head. "My son works with her daddy. She needs all the help she can get."

"He's a piece of work, all right."

The men broke up and moved away from one another, waving. Mr. Boudreaux drove the long way home, passing by the school, along the park, behind the ball field. He felt that by helping with the science project he had completed something important and that both he and the girl had learned something. His old Buick hesitated in an intersection, and he looked at its faded upholstery, its dusty buttons and levers, thinking that he should buy a new car. He could cash in his life insurance policy and finally use a little of his savings.

When he got home, even though he felt light-headed, he began to clean out the glove compartment, search under the seats, empty the trunk of boots and old tools. He rested in the sun on his front steps, then decided to change into shorts, get the galvanized pail, and wash the car. He was standing in a pool of water from the hose and looking down at his white legs when he heard Carmen's parents arguing, their shouts pouring out the open front door, the mother's keening yell washed away by the drunken father's roaring. The girl ran out as though she were escaping a fire and stood on the withering lawn, looking back into the house. Mr. Boudreaux saw a wink of something white, and then the science project posters flew out onto the front walk, followed by the circuit board display and the little platform they had made for it. The father lurched down the steps, his unbuttoned white shirt pulled from his pants, his eyes narrowed and sick. He kicked the poster frame apart, and Carmen ran to avoid a flying hinge. She turned in time to see the circuit board crackle under a black shoe.

"Hey," Mr. Boudreaux yelled. "Stop that."

The father looked around for the voice and spotted him. "You go to hell."

Mr. Boudreaux's back straightened. "Just because you can't handle your liquor don't give you the right to treat your little girl like that."

The father staggered toward him. "You old bastard, you tried to make me look bad."

Mr. Boudreaux's heart misfired once. The walk was so slippery he couldn't even run away from the father, who was coming closer in a wobbly, stalking motion. He looked down at the man's doubled fists. "You stay in your yard," he told him. "If you give me any trouble, I'll call the cops." The father gave him a shove and Mr. Boudreaux went down hard in a grassy puddle. "Ow, you drunk worm. I'm seventy-eight years old."

"Leave us alone," the father yelled. He raised a shoe, and for a moment the old man thought he was going to kick him.

Then the mother was at his side, pulling at his arms. "Come back in the yard, Chet. Please," she begged. She was not a small woman, and she had both hands on his arm.

Mr. Boudreaux squeezed the lever on the hose nozzle and sprayed the father in the stomach and he stumbled backward against the mother, cursing. He sprayed him in the forehead. "You rummy. You a big man with old guys and little kids."

"Screw you, you old bastard." The father shook water from his hair and tried to pull loose from his wife.

"Aw, you real scary," Mr. Boudreaux shouted, trying to stand up. When he finally was able to see over the roof of his Buick, the mother was pulling her husband up the steps, and Carmen was standing under a wilting magnolia tree, her gaze frozen on the fragments of her science project scattered along the walk.

.   .   .

Mr. Boudreaux's lower back was sore. By eight o'clock he couldn't move without considerable pain. He looked angrily through his living room window at the house next door. He went out on his porch and saw the light in Carmen's bedroom window. Then he went in and watched television, adjusting the rabbit ears on his set and rolling the dial from station to station, not really paying attention to the images on his scuffed Zenith. He turned the machine off and stared at it for a long time and tapped it with his fingers. Then he got a screwdriver, removed the back panel, and peered inside. Mr. Boudreaux pulled off all the knobs on the front, slid the works out of the case, and carried it over to his dining room table, placing it under the bright drop fixture. When he turned the works over, he smiled into a nest of resistors. He read the band values, and with a pair of pointed wire snips, removed several that bore two red bands and one black. Behind the selector were light sockets, and he cut these out, noting with a grimace that the bulbs in them drew too much power.

In the living room was his wife's cabinet-model Magnavox hi-fi. He slowly ran a finger along its walnut top, then pulled the knobs off and opened it up with a screwdriver, removing several feet of red and black wire, and three light sockets containing little bulbs of the correct voltage. The volume knob was a variable resistor, he now understood, and he removed that as well. He went out to his workshop and took the little steel-tongued toggle switches off his old saber saw, his chain saw, and his Moto-Tool. He needed one more and found that in the attic on a rusty set of barber's clippers that had been his brother's. Also in the attic he found his first daughter's Royal manual typewriter. Mr. Boudreaux could type. He'd learned in the army, so he brought that down too. He emptied the new batteries out of a penlight he kept on his bedside table. They had bought extra sheets of poster board in case Carmen made a mistake while drawing the big resistors, but she'd been careful. He dug the handwritten first draft of her report out of his trash can and penciled in the revisions he could remember. Then, on paper that was only slightly yellowed, he typed her report neatly, with proper headings.

Next he drew the images on the posters, big color-coded resistors traversed by round electrons with faces drawn on. His lettering was like a child's, and this worried him, but he kept on, finishing up with instructions for operating the display. He drew in the last letter at two o'clock, then went out into the workshop to saw up a spruce two-by-four to make the poster frame again. He had no hinges, so he had to go to the cedar chest in his bedroom and remove the ones on the wooden box that held his family insurance policies. He mounted the posters with thumbtacks from an old cork board hanging in the kitchen. The tack heads were rusty, so he painted them over with gummy white correction fluid he'd found in the box with the typewriter.

At four o'clock, he had to stop to take three aspirin for his back, and from the kitchen he looked across through the blue moonlight to the dark house next door, thinking maybe of all the dark houses in town where children endured the lack of light, fidgeting toward dawn.

In the garage he found that there was no more gasoline for the old torch, which had whispered itself empty on the first project. On the front lawn, he cut a short length out of his new garden hose and siphoned fuel from his Buick, getting a charge of gas in his mouth that burned his gums under his dentures. Later, as the soldering tool heated in the raspy voice of the torch, he felt he could spit a tongue of flame.

He ran the wires as she had run them, set the switches, mounted the light sockets, soldered the resistors in little silvery tornadoes of smoke. He found the bulbs left over from the first project and turned them into the sockets, wired in the battery, checked everything, then stepped back. Though the workshop window showed a trace of dawn and Mr. Boudreaux's legs felt as if someone had shot them full of arrows, he allowed himself a faint smile.

He made a pot of coffee and sat out in the dew on the front porch, hoping the girl's father would leave before the school bus arrived. At seven-fifteen, he hadn't appeared, so Mr. Boudreaux loaded the project into the backseat of his car, started the engine, and sat there, waiting. Carmen came out and stood next to the garbage cans, and when the bus came, its seats stippled with white poster boards, for everyone's project was due the same day, she watched its door swing open, pushed her glasses up her nose, and climbed on. He followed the bus out of the neighborhood and down the long, oak-shaded avenue as the vehicle picked up kids in twos and threes, science projects at each stop. The farther he drove, the more fearful he became, thinking that maybe the girl wouldn't understand, or maybe she would think he was doing this just to get back at her father, which in part, he admitted, he was. Several times he thought he'd better pass the bus, turn around, and head home. But then what would he do with the project? He wouldn't throw it away, and it would haunt him forever if he kept it.

The bus pulled into the school lot, and he followed it in and parked. By the time he got to the covered walkway, children were pouring off, carrying jars of colored fluids, homemade generators, Styrofoam models of molecules. He had the bifold project in his arms, and when she came down the bus steps empty-handed, he spread it open for her. She stepped close, lifted a page of the tacked-on report, and checked the second and third pages as well.

"Where's the display," she asked, not looking at him.

"It's in the car there," he said, sidling off to retrieve it. When he got back, he saw she'd hitched her book bag onto her shoulder and had the posters folded up under her arm.

"Give it here," she said, holding out her free hand, her face showing nothing.

He handed it to her. "You want me to help bring it in?"

She shook her head. "No. How do the switches work?"

He clicked one for her. "Up is on, down is off."

She nodded, then squinted up at him. "I'll be late."

"Go on, then." He watched her waddle off among her classmates, bearing her load, then he turned for his car. She could have called after him, smiled, and said thank you, but she didn't.

*B*ecause he was out so early, he decided to go shopping. He considered his options: the Buick lot, the appliance dealer's, the hardware. After half an hour of driving slowly around town, he went into a department store and bought two small masonry pots filled with plastic flowers. They looked like the jonquils that used to come up in the spring alongside his mother's cypress fence. He drove to the old city graveyard, and after walking among the brick vaults and carefully made marble angels, he placed a colorful pot on the sun-washed slab of his father's grave. His back pained him as he laid down the flowers, and when he straightened up, the bone-white tombs hurt his eyes, but still he turned completely around to look at this place where no one would say the things that could have been said, and that was all right with him.

The Adventures of Sue Pistola

Sue suspected she was in trouble the day she stumbled into a Harley dealership and ordered a Little Thickburger. The salesman behind the counter was tall, and a cascade of dark hair fell to the middle of his back. He studied her eyes for a moment. "You drinkin'?" he asked, in the way locals posed that question, which really meant *Why the hell are you acting this way?*

She was a big girl herself, thirty years old, not thick, just tall and toned like a woman who'd grown up roping cattle. She stared at tattoos of flames rising up the salesman's neck, beginning to understand that she wasn't going to get her burger. "I don't drink," she told him, putting a hand on the counter for support.

He flicked his eyes up to the dealership's wall-sized windows. "Did you drive here?" His voice was smooth for a biker. "Because if I see you get into a car, I'm calling the police."

She closed one blue eye, studying the orange fire coming out of his shirt. "Aren't you hot?"

"You didn't answer my question." He drummed his fingers on the counter. She saw that four knuckles on the right hand were tattooed with the letters P O T A and four on the left T O × 2.

She tried to straighten her back, and her blonde hair swung to the side. "I went to the dentist and got a root canal. He gave me gas and then some pills. I don't drink." She threw out an arm and let it slap down on her thigh, thinking this movement was cute. Some actress had done that in a movie. Then she took a step sideways as if stepping into a skiff and again grabbed at the counter.

"You have a cell?" he asked.

She tried to roll her eyes but that made her dizzy. "Of course."

"Call a cab."

She focused on his face, trying to imagine what kind of person he was. Evaluation was hard for her. In all of her schooling she was taught to accept others no matter what their appearance. She was a modern girl, totally purged of the ability to discriminate. The in thing was to ignore all the signals, putting dark glasses on the brain, as one civics teacher told her in high school. He was her first husband, a skinny, pale guy with a tattoo of a cantaloupe on what there was of his right biceps. When she asked him what the cantaloupe meant, he told her it was a satire of Catholic marriage rules. "You know," he told her, "you can't elope." Eventually he was fired from his teaching job, and he left her for an eleventh grader. When she divorced him, she wrote on one of the legal forms, "I didn't know who he was."

"Okay, already." She slapped a phone against her ear, lowered her head, and walked out the side door of the dealership. Sue floated across the parking lot and around the back of the building, feeling the Louisiana heat light up her skull, not with illumination but with a sick, feverish wanderlust, and her ears began to pop. She forgot what she was supposed to do, got into her little bubblegum-colored car, and drove out toward the highway, slamming a passenger-side tire up over a curb. She felt like a fifteen-year-old learning to drive. She knew what she wanted the car to do, but her reflexes had turned adolescent on her. Pulling into a McDonald's, she got a cup of coffee from a trembling tattooed child behind the counter, and her vision began to regulate somewhat. In a booth she watched Fox, and her aching molar began to rage like the waif blonde anchor-girl hollering out against the Democrats. Finally, no longer able to stand the pain, she reached into her sequined purse for another of Dr. Lew's pills. The coffee was cold when the trembling child woke her up.

"You can't sleep here." She backed up after she said this.

"I wasn't sleeping."

"If you want to stay here, you have to at least buy a pie."

"What?" The room spun a quarter turn and the girl began to blur. "Okay. Bring me a couple."

"Yes ma'am," the child said, who suddenly seemed just skinny, maybe twenty years old, with runny eyes. "How many do you want?"

"A couple."

The child's voice vibrated with panic. "How many is that?"

Sue found her keys and walked out the west entrance to look for her car. When she found it on the other side of the building, she tried to start it with a house key. Backing out and moving toward the highway, she had to guess at right or left, and then the yellow lines, dotted lines, double lines, lane arrows, and traffic lights began to compete for her attention. A mile down the four-lane she sensed some type of aerial fire behind her. She could feel it like a stove element left on in a dark kitchen. When she checked the rearview she saw it was a policeman, but she couldn't imagine he was after her and kept driving. Then came the siren, loud and chirping, and she drove off the road onto the shoulder and a little bit beyond into a bank of thistles and almost into a canal.

She saw that the policeman was old-school. He had a crown of gray hair surrounding a field of shiny skin, and his gut docked against her window while she tried to remember how to lower it. In a brief moment of what she hoped was clarity, she knew she had to be friendly, logical, and not say anything, anything at all, that would indicate she was impaired. She would think up the exact right thing to say. She found the button and opened up to him with a smile.

He stooped and stuck his head through the window, a big silvery head covered with old red skin and nests of broken capillaries. He looked at her eyes and smelled her like a hound.

"You drinkin'?" he asked.

Her mind went blank.

At the station she was put in the drunk tank with a three-hundred-pound red-haired woman wearing tattooed makeup so poorly done that her eye sockets flamed with copper fire. She'd been trying to talk to Sue for half an hour. "My uncle was a cop in North Carolina," she prattled. "In that state they come after drunk drivers with three spikes and a hammer. One time my uncle testified against a eight-time repeat offender who'd chugged a pint of Early Times and drove off into the side of a school bus, killing two children. The local jury didn't even leave the box, found him guilty, and then voted for the death penalty before breaking for lunch. The next month an appeal judge reduced the penalty to 251 years, but somebody kilt him the second day he was in the penitentiary."

Sue sat on a metal bench and put her head in her hands, her mind full of smoke. "I don't drink," she whined.

The big woman sat back against the cinder-block wall, regarded Sue for signals, and huffed. "And I eat hummin'bird tongues for breakfast," she said.

Sue doubled over on the bench. "My tooth hurts so much."

"Why'nt you go to the dentist?"

"I did. I went to an endodontist and got a root canal."

"Let me see." The redhead stood up, the fat on her arms billowing.

"What?"

"I had a sister-in-law that used to work for a dentist. She told me all about it. Sometimes I'd go to the office with her and just watch. That dentist was a jackleg and couldn't handle a electric screwdriver, much less a drill goin' into a human head. Just let me see."

Sue opened her mouth and the woman slid a forefinger inside her left cheek, a surprisingly professional movement.

"I mighta guessed," she said. "Did he tell you the number of the tooth that needed the canal?"

"It was number five."

"Yep. Well, he drilled number five all right, but there's a gum abscess the size of a sweet pea next to number four."

"Jeez, and they took my pain pills."

"The problem with some pain pills is they make you stupid. Just remember that." The redhead rocked herself up and was let out by a guard.

The little jailer was paternal. "Now Marcie, the chief says we can let you out again. But you got to stop shooting those squirrels in the city limits with your twenty-two."

The big woman made a face. "Jeff, you know how much those first-class birdseed cakes cost? The little tree rats tear one apart in fifteen minutes."

He leaned into her. "You'd best switch to a pellet rifle. They don't make no noise."

Sparks flying in her vision, Sue lifted her head and yelled, "My brother-in-law binds an ear of corn to a spring-loaded skeet flinger."

The jailer cocked his head. "What's that do?"

"He puts a solenoid on the trigger and sits on the porch with a remote control. When the squirrel jumps on the corn, the flinger throws the little bastard over the house."

The redhead stared at her as she backed into the hall, and the jailer slammed the drunk tank door.

Sue Pistola, at times like this, times not particularly rare for her, wished she really had a brother-in-law to pal around with. She didn't even have a sister and had never seen her father, a person she felt closer to than her screamer of a mom. She'd wondered about the man from the day she realized he wasn't in her house. Throughout her childhood, his absence was a constant presence. She'd once heard he was somewhere in east Texas, so when the Louisiana job opened up near the border, she imagined she could go look for him when she wasn't at the fire-truck factory where she worked as an electrician.

It'd been two years since she had run away from her mother, who lived deep in western Canada. Her first day in the town of Grand Crapaud, Sue had picked up a Condé Nast magazine at the realtor's office that made Louisiana sound as exotic as the Amazon. After a few weeks she got used to the stinking alligators in the drainage ditch behind her apartment building and learned to cold-cock the nutrias that came up into her tiny backyard at night to gnaw at the few flowers she'd planted. The armadillos she found to be exotic but not when they tumbled her garbage can into the street. The big swamp she drove through to get to the fire-truck factory was otherworldly, all right, like a nightmare filled with snakes and mildewed turtles tangled in plastic six-pack holders.

She heard a noise and looked up to see her arresting officer tapping a clipboard on the bars. "We're checking out your doctor right now," he said. "Did he give you a prescription you got filled, or did he give you the pills himself?" The cop was so broad that his lungs were having trouble keeping up with the rest of him. She imagined he was a busy man, maybe the only traffic enforcer in this little town.

"He just gave me a bottle of them."

The officer nodded his huge head. "Yep. His nurse kind of let slip he rolls his own." The cop looked at the floor and grabbed the bars. "How's your head. You know where you are?"

"I'm clearing up, but my tooth's killing me."

"You want to call anybody?"

"What, like a lawyer or bail bondsman?"

"We'll tell you in a little while. I was thinkin' a friend."

She remembered Gladys, who lived forty miles away, and Fred, the headlight and siren man, but he didn't own a car. "I'm kind of unconnected down here."

"Gotcha." He walked back through the hall and the building shrunk around him, the door not possibly big enough for him to fit through.

She lay back on a bunk and drifted off. At some point the jailer ushered in an old woman who looked as if she had lived in a drain pipe for ten years. Her hair was gray and filthy, she had two missing front teeth, and her backbone was a crescent. Her whole being was a toothache, and Sue was so sorry for the woman's obvious poverty and low station in life that the throbbing in her jaw seemed to fade. "How you doing, lady?" Sue asked.

The old woman picked up her head. "Oh, all right, considering I just crashed my husband's new Mercedes into the Fifth Street canal."

Around six o'clock the jailer turned up and reported that someone had agreed to vouch for her, and they were releasing her to him. Down the hall, she saw the good-looking clerk from the Harley dealership and thought she was still drugged.

"Can I take you somewhere?" he said. "They're about to cut you loose."

She sat up and squinted at him from her bunk. "Why are *you* here?"

"I turned you in. I feel responsible. Just a bit, anyway."

The big policeman came down the hall. "When your head clears later this week, we'll need to talk to you about your endodontist."

She could remember his badge—Sydney Babineaux. "You'll give me my painkillers back?"

"Nope. We havin' them checked out."

"I don't want to cause him any trouble."

"If there's trouble, he'll have brought it on himself. Meanwhile, this fella can drive you home in his truck." The officer grabbed a section of steel grate, then paused and looked at her a long time, as if he'd known her a dozen years before and was trying to place when and where. Then he turned the key to the drunk tank.

On the way to her apartment she made the Harley clerk stop at the liquor store.

"Well, well, I thought you said you didn't drink," he said.

She shrugged. "My memory just came back."

"You don't have any more pills in you, do you?"

"They took 'em away, I said." She stepped out on the sticky asphalt melting before the Mirage Liquor Store, went in, and came out carrying a bottle of vodka by the neck. It felt like a dead chicken in her hand, and she thought of her mother, the part-time farmer, who'd taught her to kill a yard bird and pluck it like a banjo. "What's your name?" she asked.

"Percy."

Her mouth fell open. "How old are you?"

"Twenty-eight. Why?"

"What parent in the last seventy years named their kid Percy?"

He pulled away from the curb slowly. "Could be worse."

"What could be worse than Percy?"

"Leslie. Hazel."

She thought about this and looked at his big shoulders and biceps. "What do the other bikers say about it?"

"What makes you think I'm a biker?"

At her apartment, she turned to him at the door. "I'm not going to have sex with you."

He didn't miss a beat. "Good. My wife would be really pissed if you did."

They went into her stuffy living room, and she fixed herself a drink, giving him the glass of water he asked for. Then they sat on the sofa.

"I'm sorry it's so hot in here," she said. "The AC needs work."

He drained his glass in one pull, put it on a rickety side table, and turned to her. "You shouldn't drink and drive around," he said.

She banged the backs of her hands on her thighs. "I know, I know. I took the pills the dentist gave me and they didn't do the job, so I floated them on a drink or two." She looked at him. "It was a mistake, okay?" He was sweating and she couldn't stop the urge to put a finger on his neck's flame tattoo. It smudged.

"Yikes." She jerked her hand back.

He looked down at her finger. "It's just one of those transfer tattoos I wear on Tuesdays and Thursdays. The customers dig it."

She glanced at his knuckles and saw the POTATO × 2 was gone. "You only work two days a week?"

"My father owns the business. I'm his partner. Got to look the part. But I know about bikes. All about them. I just don't ride one."

"Why not?"

"I don't know. Maybe because when I was a kid and whining for one, my mother said okay, but that I had to carry a spatula everywhere I rode. I asked her why, and she said so someone could use it to scrape me off the pavement."

Sue got a chill and took a swallow of her vodka and seven. "I'm okay now. Um, I'll probably just go to sleep and get up and call Dr. Lew."

"Glad to hear that." He stood, and he was even taller than she thought. "Just stay off the juice when you're on the road. I don't want you crashing through our display window."

She found it hard to take her eyes off him. "What do you do the days you don't work?"

"I volunteer with Habitat for Humanity. Sundays I'm a deacon at Mass."

She threw up her hands, let them fall. "Man, I sure got you wrong." She took another swig and pointed at his hair. "What do your church buddies think about your Fabio do?"

He threw back his head and shook out his shiny locks. "The biker chicks like it." He smiled down at her. "How about you?" he asked, reaching up and giving the top of his hair a jerk. He pulled off a shimmering wig, held it in front of his chest, and then bowed to show an even buzz cut.

· · ·

The next morning she woke up to flaming jaw pain and a white-hot anger toward Dr. Lew. His nurse said she could have an appointment in an hour. Sue couldn't eat breakfast and wondered if he would try to charge her for a second root canal. She also wondered what was in the pills he'd given her, if maybe they were some kind of date-rape drug. She made herself a vodka and tonic, washed down two pain pills she'd found wrapped in tinfoil in her jewelry box, and before going out the door she put her little .25 automatic in her baggy jeans.

Dr. Lew's office was modest and dingy, only one chair next to a window. The curtains were held open by chains made from old linked pull tabs.

He came in wearing a vintage dentist's smock, buttoned up the right side of the breast with fourteen faux ivory buttons. He was around seventy years old, with a thin splatter of silver hair. "Hi, sweetie. Francine tells me you're having trouble."

Sue gave him a pout. "My tooth hurts like hell because you worked on the wrong one."

Dr. Lew polished his little mirror on his smock. "Well, now, that's impossible, sweetie. But I checked your X-rays, and I did miss a small abscess on the neighbor tooth, so we might have to do that one as well." He unrolled his long fingers. "Let's see."

"And you gave me some capsules you made up yourself that about drove me nuts."

Dr. Lew straightened up and held his hands close to his chest like an erect rat. "Those painkillers give you some sweet dreams, don't they?"

"They messed me up." She tugged at her bib. "Are you gonna charge me twice?"

He gave the air two quick sniffs, just like her childhood pet rat, Mr. Squeakum, used to do. "Well, a new procedure will mean a new bill."

Sue started to say she wouldn't pay it, then remembered she could just ask to be billed in the mail and then ignore the charge. As if reading her thoughts, Dr. Lew proceeded to give her a hard stick in her palate and a couple more farther back. When he pulled the needle out, she cursed him. He decided to give her some gas and, minutes later, a pill, and then he went to work.

. . .

She felt herself come out of the fog slowly and angrily. Though her lips were heavy as lead, she managed to cry out that he was the Osama bin Laden of endodontists. Like most veteran doctors, he was impervious to insult, but he seemed stung by the comment. He put his hand on her shoulder and pressed down. "You shouldn't talk to me like that, young lady."

Sue tasted blood in her mouth and dreaded the time when the lidocaine would fade. Her consciousness began to slip again, and she wondered what else Dr. Lew could have done when she was totally out. She squirmed, then imagined that her bra was unhooked, so she reached into the pocket of her jeans and pulled out her little pistol. "Get your hands off me, you old lech." The gun wavered between them, went off, and so did Dr. Lew's light.

When she fully regained consciousness, she was staring up the rails of a railroad with her head down between them. She blinked, and the towering bars of the drunk tank came into focus. She was lying on her back in a bunk, her head toward the hall. She heard some movement in the enclosure but was too foggy headed to look and also afraid of what unfortunate arrestee she would meet. She thought of her mother up in Canada, Ramona Pistola, originally from Alice, Texas, who was probably now training for the senior female calf-roping event in Calgary. She'd wanted Sue to be a barrel-racing champion, and though she was good at it and liked the horses, she felt there was life outside of Canada, the farther away, the better. She didn't ever get along with her mother, not for one second, and one reason she lay awake so much at night imagining a father was that he couldn't possibly be a worse parent. Even absent, he was better for her psyche than Ramona Pistola, a blockheaded woman with hairy ears. Sue liked the job at the fire-truck plant and hoped to God the company wouldn't fire her. She'd just been promoted to installing wiring harnesses, a skill she'd picked up at Grand Crapaud Online Technical

University, which offered a one-semester pre-associate's certificate for only $5,000.

Finally, she looked up and saw a young woman standing in the middle of the enclosure, turning slowly around. She wore an ivory dress that seemed to be made of a giant crocheted doily and, over that, a bronze Viking woman brassiere. The woman's green hair was straight and heavy, as though recently spray-painted, and there was a black star tattooed around her left eye.

Sue couldn't help asking, "What are you in for?"

The woman looked down at her, pulled out the tongue of a large metal tape measure, and let it snap back into its case. "I'm measuring for new flooring, and I just finished." She pushed on the cell door, which opened with a squeak, and then she locked it with a bright key. Sue watched her fade away down the hall and kept watching until the big balding cop bulled his way up to the drunk tank.

Sydney Babineaux gave her a look of grim evaluation, and she sat up straight.

"Well, we meet again," she told him, trying not to be groggy, putting a hand up to brush her hair and missing her head completely.

"We checked out Dr. Lew, and he's clean," the cop said. "His pills are conventional stuff and mostly placebo."

Sue frowned at him. "He gives injections like a frame carpenter. He was holding me down in the chair, and I think he got into my brassiere."

The old policeman looked down the hall. "Our matron told me you're not wearing a brassiere, so forget about that."

Sue folded her arms. "Was that her just in here?"

"No. That was Mrs. Pudlewsky. She owns the flooring business down the street. Why'd you try to shoot your dentist?"

She remembered the sound of the shot, huge in the little office. "I didn't. When I pulled the damn thing out of my jeans, it just went off."

He nodded. "Okay. I'm not surprised, that little popgun's a piece of junk. It has no safety."

"I've got a concealed-carry permit for it."

"We found that. You have to buy him a new surgical light, you know. He kind of thought it was an accident, so he's not pressing charges. I talked him out of it."

She put her head in her hands. "How much is this going to cost?"

"I think he said four-fifty for the light and then there's the little matter of the citation against you for discharging a gun in the city limits."

Sue groaned like a bear. "At least my tooth feels better."

"He's not the best dentist in the world, Ms. Pistola, but he's a fine pianist."

She looked up slowly. The statement brought back the dizziness. "What?"

Sydney bobbed his moon of a head. "Internationally famous. Plays the trickiest Chopin stuff, I hear. One reason he didn't press charges is he had to fly to Leipzig for a week of concerts."

Sue blinked slowly and placed a hand against a bar in front of the policeman's face. "I thought he was just some incompetent old perv."

The policeman made eye contact with her, his big gray irises trying to figure her out. "I've got one question for you and I want you to tell the truth, okay?"

"The truth," she mugged, crossing her heart.

"Did you drink alcohol on top of some pills before you went in to see him?"

Sue was of the generation that saw lying as a navigational aid for the river of life. "Of course not," she said, looking him right in the eye. "How stupid do you think I am?"

"I don't know anything about you." He looked at his glossy boot. "The older I get, the less I know about young people. You know, I have a daughter about your age, kind of looks like you, who just up and left town one day. Last thing we all expected. She calls about once a year but won't tell us where she lives. We never argued except for a couple usual things. My wife and me, we just don't know what to think."

Sue tilted her head. "How cruel of her."

He looked up and nodded. "I called the guy at the Harley place and got you released into his custody again," he said softly. "I'm going out on a limb for you. I guess because I'd like to think someone else would do the same for my daughter, wherever the hell she is. But the Harley guy's busy at the dealer's biker rally. His wife said she'd sign you out and drive you home."

"His wife?" Her mouth dropped open a bit.

"Look, I'm doing you a favor here. You could be in big trouble. Just promise me you'll lay off the sauce."

She put a hand through the bars and put it on his shoulder. "Do they call you Syd?"

"Sydney."

"Well, Mr. Sydney, I'll lay off the sauce."

The Harley guy's wife, Gloria, was gorgeous, bigger than life, long-legged, blindingly blonde with near lavender eyes. She picked Sue up with a minivan, two toddlers strapped in back, May and June.

Sue looked back at the girls as if they were exotics in a cage, or maybe leprechauns. She was an only child and didn't know a lot about children. "Hi, girls," she said to them, giving a little wave as an afterthought.

May, who seemed to be maybe four, said, "Are you glad you're out of the jailhouse?"

Sue glanced at Gloria, who was busy with traffic. "I sure am," she said.

June, who looked to be near seven, began singing:

> She's in the jailhouse now
> She's in the jailhouse now,
> I'll tell you once again,
> Stay 'way from that whiskey
> And leave off of that gin,
> She's in the jailhouse now.

Then she began to yodel, but her mother flashed a stern glance at her in the rearview. "Sissy, that's mean. You have to excuse her, Sue, she just loves country music. And I don't know where she got those lyrics."

"Grandpa sings it like that," June said.

May, a miniature of her mother, slowly shook her head. "Sissy mean."

At her apartment, Sue expected to be dropped off, but instead Gloria parked the big Chrysler and unbuckled the children, her bright fingernails flashing.

"I'm all right now," Sue told her, showing her palms.

"Oh, I know. I just want to come in for a minute," she said, herding the girls in through the door.

Sue found cartoons on her small TV and fixed glasses of iced tea for Gloria and herself. She moved a wad of clothes off the sofa and sat down near the glossy woman. "So, Gloria. What are you, a stay-at-home mom?"

"Nope."

Sue guessed she was a fashion consultant. Maybe a catalog model. She looked at her expensive white jeans. "Sure, you must be a dress designer, right?"

Gloria took a big gulp of tea and stifled a burp. "I work for the regional health department. I'm the sewer and septic tank inspector."

The statement made the room revolve half a turn. "Oh, is that right?"

"What about you?"

"You know, I just work down at the fire-truck plant. Stringing wire."

Gloria's perfect face became serious. "And why do you drink?"

"Whoa. Aren't we getting a little personal here? Do I look like a drunk or something?" Sue started to get up, then sat back down.

Gloria watched her closely. "You're pretty nervous. Edgy, like you're ready to jump out of your skin."

Sue looked at the television, where Disney's Princess Sofia was ice-skating around her lavender palace. She remembered winter in Canada with her mother. Washing horses in the snow. "Yeah, I need a drink."

"You need a program."

"Please. I don't know what I need."

"Yes you do, but you won't do it."

Gloria got to her feet, picked up the remote, and turned off the TV.

The girls let out a short whine in unison, then came to their mother, and hung on her long, long legs and yawned. May asked, "We leaving the lady?"

"In a minute."

"Okay," June said. "This place smells like a shoe."

Gloria put a finger gently against her daughter's lips and turned to Sue. "My husband told me you looked like a person very worthy of either advice or good luck. That's why I'm here. If you want to talk to me about anything, call him at the dealership. I can get you help."

"So he looked at me and figured me out?"

"Yes. Some people have it in them to do that. I'm not so good at it."

Sue walked to the door and grabbed the knob as if for balance. "Maybe I can get along with a little luck."

Gloria turned her perfect face to her as she walked outside and said, "We make our own luck, sweetie."

Sue Pistola tried to make it through the rest of the afternoon without a drink. She poured what was left of her vodka down the drain, holding her breath. Then she went for a stroll, up the steaming sidewalk to a coffee shop where she ate buttered French bread and drank a cup of dark roast. Farther down the street she drifted past the blowout lounge, and a man in Schlumberger coveralls pushed through the door in a wash of icy air, cigarette smoke, and something else, a little dagger of gin sailing out the door and under her nostrils. She was attacked by a manic longing for a drink, for her imaginary father to show up and tell her to control herself, for a cutting Canadian wind, a longing that nearly knocked her over with the power of a fire truck speeding to its inevitable disaster. She plodded on in the heat, feeling tentacles of air-conditioned air pulling her back to the bar. Escaping to the little downtown, she thought she was safe, but then she walked past an old hardware store where a clerk was coating the iron façade with oil-based paint, and the midday heat was cooking the thinner out of the enamel, the odor driving her wild-eyed back to her apartment, where she sat in a chair and tried to read a book of wiring schematics. Then she tried a book of jokes a friend at work had given her, a friend who'd told her she needed cheering up. But the humor was thin and pathetic, especially the one about the dumb blonde in an airplane who was told they were flying over a crater made by a meteor crashing down a million years ago. "Damn, that thing almost hit the highway," the blonde said. Sue began shaking a little and thought about calling the Harley dealership, but instead she decided to call her mother's house phone, an old beige thing that would not show her number.

Someone picked up the receiver and said, "What you know good?"

"Mom?" Sue ventured.

"Suzie, where the hell are you, gal?"

She drew her legs up against her breasts. "I still don't want to tell you."

"Aw, come on home. You'll like it. My boyfriend left and took all his smoke with him."

"Angus is gone? He left you?"

"Naw. You ain't been home in a while. Angus was two years ago. This was Clint."

Sue looked down at the ratty berber carpet in her apartment. She'd liked to pretend that one of her mother's partners, most of them nice fellows, was her real father. Angus was pretty jolly when he was sober. "Will you ever tell me who my dad is?"

The line went quiet for a minute. "Don't start on that." The easygoing cowgirl talk her mother had picked up like borrowed clothes in bars from Mexico to Kamloops suddenly disappeared. "Just don't bug me about it again, you hear me?"

"I searched the computer for Pistolas in Texas and found a few, but they didn't know of a Herbert. Wasn't that his name?"

Her mother's voice came at her like breaking glass. "Damn it, I said don't talk about him. As far as you're concerned, he doesn't exist. I hope he's dead."

"Mom."

"Where the hell are you, worthless? If you'd come up I could get you ready for next month's barrel race. If you placed I sure as hell could use the money."

Sue sponged her eyes with the heel of her left hand and turned off her cell. Then she went to the closet, and in the bottom was a quart of Old Overholt rye, a taste she didn't care for. Back in the little kitchen she poured four fingers in a water glass, two fingers of cola, and added one ice cube. She tested the root canals with her tongue, and they were fine. Walking over to her swayback sofa she tried to imagine what her father looked like, if he was tall and fair like she was, something she'd wondered about all her life. Somewhere there was this older man who was a part of her that had fallen away, making her incomplete.

If she could ever find him it would be like getting back a leg or both eyes. She would look and look at him and hope that he was someone she could figure out at a glance. Sue shook her head and took a long swallow. So far, no one in her world was who she thought they were.

About dusk she was what her mother would call knee-walking drunk, and imagined, like many in that state, that she needed to get out and drive around. She revved her dusty little car and tried to see if she could make the tires squeal out to the street, but all the compact Chevy could manage was a single eek. Soon she was galloping through traffic on old highway 90, sliding through town, clipping curbs and laughing at the horn blasts of the amazed motorists in her wake. Then she bolted into a supermarket parking lot, riding the Chevy like her old horse Jake, rolling around to the back of the store where the clerks piled the cardboard boxes before they collapsed them, and she reined the car into a big one and spurred into a circle, swinging back around the building toward the highway, sideswiping a shopping cart on the way to the exit. Sue raced again through town, the box still trapped under the floorboard and roaring like escaping steam, and somewhere around the old railroad station, here came flashing lights and a siren up to her back bumper, a really excited siren squawking at her like a six-ton bird. She slowed but didn't pull over, thinking, What will I say now? It has to be the perfect thing. It has to be the best thing a woman ever said to a policeman in the history of the automobile. She kept slowing, trying to concentrate, knowing she had to stay free so she could drive through east Texas looking for Pistolas, for leads to a father she needed like a parallel rider plucking her off a bucking horse, but she couldn't unless she came up with the words that would save her now. Finally, she drifted to a stop in a small parking lot in front of a psychiatric clinic. HELP FOR THE HELPLESS, its sign read, and she wondered how to get into the place. There was a tap at her window and she saw Sydney and the big starry symbol on his chest that gave him the right to do whatever he wanted with her whole life. She lowered the window and he stuck in his face, hangdog with disappointment, staring, trying to figure her out, and she stared back, hoping he was what he seemed to be.

"You drinkin'?" he asked.

Sue reached up and pinched a big slab of his left ear between her thumb and forefinger and said, "You buyin'?"

Died and Gone to Vegas

Raynelle Bullfinch told the young oiler that the only sense of mystery in her life was provided by a deck of cards. As she set up the card table in the engine room of the *Leo B. Canterbury,* a government steam dredge anchored in a pass at the mouth of the Mississippi River, she lectured him. "Nick, you're just a college boy laying out a bit until you get money to go back to school, but for me, this is it." She adjusted her overalls straps and looked around at the steam chests and piping, sniffed at the smell of heatproof red enamel. She was the cook on the big boat, which was idle for a couple of days because of high winter winds. "My big adventure is cards. One day I'll save enough to play with the skill boys in Vegas. Now set up those folding chairs," she told him. "Seven in all."

"I don't know how to play bourrée, ma'am." Nick Montalbano ran a hand through long hair shiny with dressing. "I only had one semester of college."

"Bullshit. A pet rat can play bourrée. Sit down." She pointed to a metal chair and the oiler, a thin boy wearing an untucked plaid flannel shirt and a baseball cap, obeyed. "Pay attention here. I deal out five cards to everybody, and I turn up the last card. Whatever suit it is, that's trumps. Then you discard all your non-trumps and draw replacements. Remember, trumps beat all other suits, high trumps beat low trumps. Whatever card is led, you follow suit." She ducked her head under the bill of his cap, looking for his eyes. "This ain't too hard for you is it? Ain't college stuff more complicated than this?"

"Sure, sure. I understand, but what if you can't follow suit?"

"If non-trumps is led, put a trump on it. If you ain't got no more trumps, just throw your lowest card. Trust me, you'll catch on quick."

"How do you win?" The oiler turned his cap around.

"Every hand has five tricks to take. If you take three tricks, you win the pot, unless only two decide to play that hand after the draw. Then it takes four tricks. If you got any questions, ask Sydney there."

Sydney, the chief engineer, a little fireplug of a man who would wear a white T-shirt in a blizzard, sat down heavily with a whistle. "Oh boy, fresh meat." He squeezed the oiler's neck.

The steel door next to the starboard triple-expansion engine banged open, letting in a wash of frigid air around the day fireman, pilot, deckhand, and welder who came into the big room cursing and clapping the cold out of their clothes. Through the door the angry whitecaps of Southwest Pass foamed up against a leaden sky.

"Close that damned pneumonia hole," Raynelle cried, sailing cards precisely before the seven chairs. "Sit down, worms. Usual little game, dollar ante, five-dollar bourrée if you don't take a trick." After the rattle of halves and dollars came discards, more dealing, and then a flurry of cards ending with a diminishing snowstorm of curses as no one took three tricks and the pot rolled over to the next hand. Three players took no tricks and put up the five-dollar bourrée.

The engineer unrolled a pack of Camels from his T-shirt sleeve and cursed loudest. "I heard of a bourrée game on a offshore rig where the pot didn't clear for eighty-three passes. By the time somebody won that bitch it had seventeen hundred dollars in it. The next day the genius what took it got a wrench upside the head in a Morgan City bar and woke up with his pockets inside out and the name Conchita tattooed around his left nipple."

Pig, the day fireman, put up his ante and collected the next hand. "That ain't nothin'." He touched three discards to the top of his bald head and threw them down. "A ol' boy down at the dock told me the other day that he heard about a fellow got hit in the head over in Orange, Texas, and didn't know who he was when he looked at his driver's license. Had amnesia. That sorry-ass seaman's hospital sent him home to his scuzzbag wife, and he didn't know her from Adam's house cat."

"That mighta been a blessing," Raynelle said, turning the last card of the deal to see what trumps was. "Spades." She rolled left on her ample bottom.

"No, it wasn't no blessing," the day fireman said, unzipping his heavy green field jacket. "That gal told him she was his sister, gave him a remote control and a color TV, and he was happy as a fly on a pie. She started bringing her boyfriends in at night, and that fool waved them into the house. Fixed 'em drinks. Figured any old dude good enough for Sis was good enough for him. The neighbors got to lookin' at her like they was smelling something dead, so she and her old man moved to a better trailer park where nobody knew he'd lost his memory. She started into cocaine and hookin' for fun on the side. Her husband's settlement money he got from the company what dropped a 36-inch Stillson on his hard hat began to shrink up a bit, but that old boy just sat there dizzy on some cheap pills she told him was a prescription. He'd channel-surf all day, greet the Johns like one of those old dried-up coots at Walmart, and was the happiest son of a bitch in Orange, Texas." The day fireman spread his arms wide. "Was he glad to see Sis come home every day. He was proud she had more friends than a postman with a bag full of welfare checks. And then his memory came back."

"Ho, ho, the merde hit the blower," the engineer said, slamming a queen down and raking in a trick.

"Nope. That poor bastard remembered every giggle in the rear bedroom and started feeling lower than a snake's nuts. He tried to get his old woman straight, but the dyed-over tramp just laughed in his face and moved out on him. He got so sorry he went to a shrink, but that just cost him more bucks. Finally, you know what that old dude wound up doin'? He looked for someone would hit him in the head again. You know, so he could get back the way he was. He offered a hundred dollars a pop, and in them Orange bars most people will whack on you for free, so you can imagine what kind of service he bought hisself. After nearly getting killed four or five times, he give up and spent the rest of his settlement money on a hospital stay for a concussion. After that he held up a Pac-a-Bag for enough money to get hisself hypmotized back to like he was after he got hit the first time. Wound up in the pen doin' twenty hard ones."

It took three hands of cards to finish the story, and then the deckhand in the game, a thick blond man in a black cotton sweater, threw back his head and laughed, *ha ha,* as if he was only pretending. "If that wadn' so funny it'd be sad. It reminds me of this dumb-ass peckerwood kid lived next to me in Kentucky, built like a string bean. He was a few thimbles shy of a quart, but he sort of knew he wont no nuclear power plant repairman and more or less got along with everybody. Then he started hanging with these badass kids, you know, the kind that carry spray paint, wear their hats backward, and light their farts. Well, they convinced the poor bastard he was some kind of Jesse James and got him into stealing cell phones and electric drills. He started strutting around the neighborhood like he was bad shit, and soon the local deputies had him in the backseat for running off with a lawn mower. Dummy stole it in December."

"What's wrong with that?" the day fireman asked, pitching in a dollar.

"Who's gonna buy a used mower in winter, you moron. Anyway, the judge had pity on him, gave him a piss-ant fine, and sent him to bed with a sugar-tit. Said he was a good boy who ought to be satisfied bein' simple and honest. But String Bean hung out on the street corner crowing. He was proud now. A real gangster, happy as Al Capone, his head pumped full of swamp gas by these losers he's hanging around with. Finally one night he breaks into the house of some gun collector. Showing how smart he is, he chooses only one gun to take from the rack, an engraved Purdey double-barrel, mint condition with gold and ivory inlays all over, a twenty-thousand-dollar gun. String Bean took it home and with a two-dollar hacksaw cut the stock off and then most of the barrel.

"He went out and held up a taco joint and got sixteen dollars and thirty-seven cents. Was arrested when he walked out the door. This time a hard-nut judge sent him up on a multiple bill, and he got 297 years in Bisley."

"All right," Raynelle sang. "Better than death."

"He did ten years before the weepy-ass parole board noticed the sentence and pulled him in for review. Asked him did he get rehabilitated and would he go straight if he'd get out, and he spit on their mahogany table. He told them he wont no dummy and would be the richest bank robber in Kentucky if he got half a chance." The deckhand laughed again, *ha ha.* "That give everybody a icicle up the ass and the meetin' came to a vote right quick. Even the American Civil Liberties Bambi-huggin' lawyers on the parole board wanted to weld the door shut on him. It was somethin'."

The pilot, a tall man dressed in a pea jacket and a sock cap, raised a new hand to his sharp blue eyes and winced, keeping one trump and asking for four cards. "Gentlemen, that reminds me of a girl in Kentucky I knew at one time."

"Why, did she get sent up two hundred ninety-seven years?" the deckhand asked.

"No, she was from Kentucky like that crazy fellow you just lied to us about. By the way, that king won't walk," he said, laying down an ace of diamonds. "This woman was a nurse at the VA hospital in Louisville and fell in love with one of her patients, a good-looking, mild-mannered fellow with a cyst in his brain that popped and gave him amnesia."

"Now there's something you don't hear every day," the engineer said, trumping the ace with a bang.

"He didn't know what planet he came from," the pilot said stiffly. "A few months later they got married and he went to work in a local iron plant. After a year he began wandering away from work at lunchtime. So they fired him. He spent a couple of weeks walking up and down his street and all over Louisville looking into people's yards and checking passing busses for the faces in the windows. It was like he was looking for someone, but he couldn't remember who. One day he didn't come home at all. For eighteen months this pretty little nurse was beside herself with worry. Then her nephew was at a rock concert downtown and spotted a shaggy guy who looked familiar in the mosh pit, just standing there like he was watching a string quartet. Between songs her nephew asked him if he had amnesia, which is a rather odd question, considering, and the man almost started crying because he figured he'd been recognized."

"That's a sweet story," the day fireman said, rubbing his eyes with his bear-sized hands. "Sydney, could you loan me your handkerchief? I'm all choked up."

"Choke on this," the pilot said, trumping the fireman's jack. "Anyway, the little nurse gets attached to the guy again and is glad to have him back. She refreshes his memory about their marriage and all that and starts over with him. Things are better than ever, as far as she's concerned. Well, about a year of marital bliss goes by, and one evening there's a knock at the door. She gets up off the sofa where the amnesia guy is, opens it, and it's her husband, whose memory came back."

"Wait a minute," the deckhand said. "I thought that was her husband on the sofa."

"I never said it was her husband. She just *thought* it was her husband. It turns out that the guy on the sofa she's been living with for a year is the identical twin to the guy on the doorstep. Got an identical popped cyst, too."

"Aw, bullshit," the day fireman bellowed.

The engineer leaned back and put his hand on a valve handle. "I better pump this place out."

"Hey," the pilot yelled above the bickering. "I knew this girl. Her family lived across the street from my aunt. Anyway, after all the explanations were made, the guy who surfaced at the rock concert agreed it would be best if he moved on, and the wandering twin started back where he left off with his wife. Got his job back at the iron plant. But the wife wasn't happy anymore."

"Why the hell not?" the engineer asked, dealing the next hand. "She had two for the price of one."

"Yeah, well even though those guys were identical in every way, something was different. We'll never know what it was, but she couldn't get over the second twin. Got so she'd wander around herself, driving all over town looking for him."

"What the hell?" The deckhand threw down his cards. "She had her husband back, didn't she?"

"Oh, it was bad," the pilot continued. "She was driving down the street one day and saw the rock-concert twin, got out of her car, ran into a park yelling and sobbing and threw her arms around him, crying, 'I found you at last, I found you at last.' Only it wasn't him."

"Jeez," the engineer said. "Triplets."

"No." The pilot shook his head. "It was worse than that. It was her husband, who was out on delivery for the iron plant, taking a break in the park after shucking his coveralls. Mild-mannered amnesiac or not, he was pretty put out at the way she was carrying on. But he didn't show it. He pretended to be his twin and asked her why she liked him better than her husband. And she told him. Now don't ask me what it was. The difference was in her mind, way I heard it. But that guy disappeared again the next morning and that was five years ago. They say you can go down in east Louisville and see her driving around today in a ratty green Torino looking for one of those twins, this scared look in her eyes like she'll find one and'll never be sure which one she got hold of."

Raynelle pulled a pecan out of her overalls bib and cracked it between her thumb and forefinger. "That story's sadder'n a armless old man in a room full of skeeters. You sorry sons of bitches tell the depressingest lies I ever heard."

The deckhand lit up an unfiltered cigarette. "Well, sweet thing, why don't you cheer us up with one of your own."

Raynelle looked up at a brass steam gauge bolted to an I beam. "I did know a fellow worked in an iron foundry, come to think of it. His whole family worked the same place, which is a pain in the ass if you've ever done that, what with your uncle giving you wet willies and your cousin bumming money. This fellow drove a gray Dodge Dart, the kind with the old slant-six engine that'll carry you to hell and back, slow. His relatives made fun of him for it, said he was cheap and wore plastic shoes and ate Spam, that kind of thing." She turned the last card to show trumps, banging up a king. "Sydney, you better not bourrée again. You in this pot for forty dollars."

The engineer swept up his hand, pressing it against his T-shirt. "I can count."

"Anyway, this boy thought he'd show his family a thing or two and went out and proposed to the pretty girl who keyed in the invoices in the office. He bought her a diamond ring on time that would choke an elephant. It was a *nice* ring." Raynelle looked at the six men around the table as if none of them would ever buy such a ring. "He was gonna give it to her on her birthday right before they got married in three weeks, and meantime he showed it around at the iron foundry figuring it'd make 'em shut up, which basically it did."

"They was probably speechless at how dumb he was," the deckhand said out of the side of his mouth.

"But don't you know that before he got to give it to her that girl hit her head on the edge of her daddy's swimming pool and drowned. The whole foundry went into mourning, as did those kids' families and the little town in general. She had a big funeral and she was laid out in her wedding dress in a white casket surrounded by every carnation in four counties. Everybody was crying and the funeral parlor had this lovely music playing. I guess the boy got caught up in the feeling because he walked over to the coffin right before they was gonna screw down the lid and he put that engagement ring on that girl's finger."

"Naw," the engineer said breathlessly, laying a card without looking at it.

"Yes he did. And he felt proud that he done it. At least for a month or two. Then he began to have eyes for a dental hygienist, and that little romance took off hot as a bottle rocket. He courted her for six months and decided to pop the question. But he started thinking about the monthly payments he was making on that ring and how they'd go on for four and a half more years, keeping him from affording a decent ring for this living girl."

"Oh no," the pilot said as the hand split again and the pot rolled over yet another time.

"That's right. He got some tools and after midnight went down to the Heavenly Oaks Mausoleum and unscrewed the marble door on her drawer, slid out the coffin, and opened it up. I don't know how he could stand to rummage around in whatever was left in the box, but damned if he didn't get that ring and put the grave back together slick as a whistle. So the next day he give it to the hygienist and everything's okay. A bit later they get married and're doin' the lovebird bit in a trailer down by the foundry." Raynelle cracked another stout pecan against the edge of the table, crushing it with such ease that the welder and the oiler looked at each other. "But there's a big blue blow fly in the ointment. She's showing off that ring by the minute, and somebody recognized the thing and told her. Well, she had a thirty-megaton double-PMS hissy fit and told him straight up that she won't wear no dead woman's ring and throws it in his face. Said the thing gave her the willies. He told her it's that or a King Edward cigar band because he won't get out from under the payments until he's using a walker. It went back and forth like that for a month with the neighbors up and down the road, including my aunt Tammy, calling the police to come make them shut up. Finally, the hygienist told him she'd wear the damn ring."

"Well, that's a happy ending," the deckhand said.

Raynelle popped half a pecan into her red mouth. "Shut up, Jack, I ain't finished. This hygienist began to wear cowboy blouses and jean miniskirts just like the dead fiancée did. The old boy kind of liked it at first, but when she dyed her hair the same color as the first girl, it gave him the shakes. She said she was dreaming of that dead girl at least twice a week and saw her now and then in her dresser mirror when she woke up. Then she began to talk like the foundry girl did, with a snappy Arkansas twang. And the dead girl was a country music freak, liked the classic stuff too. Damned if the guy wasn't waked up in the middle of the night by his wife singing all eleven verses of 'El Paso,' the old Marty Robbins tune, in her sleep.

"This stuff went on for months until he figured it was the ring causing all the trouble, so he got his wife drunk one night, and while she was asleep slipped that sucker off and headed to the graveyard to put it back on that bone where he took it. Soon as he popped the lid, the cops was on him asking what the living hell he was doing. He told them he was putting a twenty-thousand-dollar diamond ring back in a coffin, and they said, 'Sure you are, buddy.' Man, he got charged with six or eight nasty things perverts do to dead bodies, then the dead girl's family filed six or eight civil suits and, believe me, there was mental anguish, pain, and suffering enough to aggravate the whole county. A local judge who was the dead girl's uncle sent him up for six years, and the hygienist divorced his ass good. Strange thing was that she kept her new hair color and way of dressing, started going to George Jones concerts, and last I heard had quit her job at the dentist and was running the computers down at the iron foundry."

"Raynelle, chere, I wish you wouldn't of said that one." Simoneaux, the welder, never spoke much until late in the game. He was a thin Cajun, seldom without a Camel in the corner of his mouth and a high-crown, polka-dotted welder's cap turned backward on his head. He shrugged off a violent chill. "That story gives me *les frissons* up and down my back." A long stick of beef jerky jutted from the pocket of his flannel shirt. He pulled it out, plucked a lint ball from the bottom, and bit off a small knob of meat. "But that diamond shit reminds me of a old boy I knew down in Grand Crapaud who was working on Pancho Oil #6 offshore from Point au Fer. The driller was putting down the pipe hard one day and my friend the mud engineer was taking a dump on the engine-room toilet. All at once they hit them a gas pocket at five t'ousand feet and drill pipe come back up that hole like drinking straws, knocking out the top of the rig, flyin' up in the sky, and breakin' apart at the joints. Well, my frien', he had a magazine spread out across his lap when a six-inch drill pipe hit the roof like a spear and went through and through the main diesel engine. About half a second later another one passed between his knees, through the Playmate of the Month and the steel deck both, yeah. He could hear the iron comin' down all over the rig, but he couldn't run because his pants was around his ankles on the other side the drill column between his legs. He figured he was goin' to glory with a unwiped ass, but a cook run in the engine room and cut him loose with a jackknife, and then they both took off over the side and hit the water. My friend rolled in the breakers holdin' on to a drum of gasoline, floppin' around until a badass fish gave him a bite on his giblets, but that was the only injury he had."

"Ouch, man," the deckhand said, crossing his legs.

"What?" Raynelle looked up while posting her five-dollar bourrée.

The welder threw in yet another ante, riffling the dollar bills in the pot as though figuring how much they weighed. "Well, he was hurt enough to get the company to pay him a lump sum after he got a four-by-four lawyer to sue their two-by-four insurance company. That's for true. My frien' he always said he wanted a fancy car. The first thing he did was to drive to Lafayette and buy a sixty-five-t'ousand dollar Mercedes, yeah. He put new mud-grip tires on that and drove it down to the Church Key Lounge in Morgan City where all his mud-pumpin' buddies hung out, an' it didn't take long to piss about half a dozen of them hardhats off, no." The welder shook his narrow head. "He was braggin' bad, yeah."

The engineer opened his cards on his belly and rolled his eyes. "A new Mercedes in Morgan City? Sheee-it."

"*Mais,* you can say that again. About two, tree o'clock in the mornin' my frien', he come out and what he saw woulda made a muskrat cry. Somebody took a number two ball-peen hammer and dented everything on that car that would take a dent. That t'ing looked like it got caught in a tornado full of cue balls. Next day he brought it by the insurance people and they told him the policy didn't cover vandalism. Told him he would have to pay to get it fixed or drive it like that.

"But my frien' he'd blew all his money on the car to begin with. When he drove it, everybody looked at him like he was some kind of freak. You know, he wanted people to look at him, that's why he bought the car, but now they was lookin' at him the wrong way, like 'You mus' be some prime jerk to have somebody screw with you car like that.' So after a week of having people run off the road turnin' their necks to look at that new Mercedes, he got drunk, went to the store, and bought about twenty cans of Bondo, tape, and fifty cans of light tan spray paint."

"Don't say it," the deckhand cried.

"No, no," the engineer said to his cards.

"What?" Raynelle asked.

"Yeah, the poor bastard didn't know how to make a snake out of Play-Doh, but he was gonna try and restore a fine European se-dan. He filed and sanded on that poor car for a week, then hit it with that dollar-a-can paint. When he finished up, that Mercedes looked like it was battered for fryin'. He drove it around Grand Crapaud and people just pointed and doubled over. He kept it outside his trailer at night, and people would drive up and park, just to look at it. Phone calls started comin', the hang-up kind that said things like 'You look like your car,' click, or 'What kind of icing did you use?' click. My frien' finally took out his insurance policy and saw what it did cover. Which was theft.

"So he started leaving the keys in it parked down by the abandoned lumberyard, but nobody in Grand Crapaud would steal it. He drove to Lafayette, rented a motel room, yeah, and parked it with the keys in the ignition outside that bad housing project." The welder threw in another hand and watched the cards fly. "Next night he left the windows down with the keys in it." He pulled off his polka-dotted cap and ran his fingers through his dark hair. "Third night he left the motor running and the lights on wit' the car blockin' the driveway of a redneck crack house. Next morning he found it twenty feet away, idled out of diesel with a dead battery. It was that ugly."

"What happened next?" The pilot trumped an ace like he was killing a bug.

"My frien' he called me up, you know. Said he wished he had a used standard-shift Ford pickup and the money in the bank. His girlfriend left him, his momma made him take a cab to come see her, and all he could stand to do was drink and stay in his trailer. I didn't know what to tell him. He said he was gonna read his policy some more."

"Split pot again," the deckhand shouted. "I can't get out this game. I feel like my nuts is hung up in a fan belt."

"Shut your trap and deal," Raynelle said, slinging a loose wad of cards in the deckhand's direction. "What happened to the Mercedes guy?"

The welder pulled up the crown of his cap. "Well, his policy said it covered all kinds of accidents, you know, so he parked it in back next to a big longleaf pine and cut that sucker down. Only it was a windy day and soon as he got through that tree with the saw, a gust come up and pushed it the other way from where he wanted it to fall."

"What'd it hit?"

"It mashed his trailer like a cockroach, yeah. The propane stove blew up, and by the time the Grand Crapaud fire truck come around, all the firemen could do was break out coat hangers and mushmellas. His wife what left ain't paid the insurance on the double-wide, no, so now he got to get him a camp stove and a picnic table so he can shack up in the Mercedes."

"No shit? He lived in the car?"

The welder nodded glumly. "Po' bastard wouldn't do nothin' but drink up his disability check and lie in the backseat. One night last fall we had that cold snap, you remember? It got so cold around Grand Crapaud you could hear the sugarcane stalks popping out in the fields like firecrackers. They found my frien' froze to death sittin' up behind the steering wheel. T-nook, the paramedic, said his eyes was open, starin' over the hood like he was goin' for a drive." The welder pushed his downturned hand out slowly like a big sedan driving into the horizon, all eyes following it for a long moment.

"New deck," the engineer cried, throwing in his last trump and watching it get swallowed by a jack. "Nick, you little paisan, give me that blue deck." The oiler, a quiet olive-skinned boy from the west bank of New Orleans, pushed the new box over. "New deck, new luck," the engineer told him. "You know, I used to date this ol' fat gal lived in a double-wide north of Biloxi. God, that woman liked to eat. When I called it off she asked me why, and I told her I was afraid she was going to get thirteen inches around the ankles. That must've got her attention because she went on some kind of fat-killer diet and exercise program that about wore out the floor beams in that trailer. But she got real slim, I heard. She had a pretty face, I'll admit that. She started hitting the bars and soon had her a cow farmer ask her to marry him, which she did."

"Is a cow farmer like a rancher?" Raynelle asked, her tongue in her cheek like a jawbreaker.

"It's what I said it was. Who the hell ever heard of a ranch in Biloxi. Anyway, this old gal developed a fancy for steaks, since her man got meat reasonable, being a cow farmer and all. She started putting away the T-bones and swelling like a sow on steroids. After a year, she blowed up to her fightin' weight and then some. I heard she'd about eat up half his cows before he told her he wanted a divorce. She told him she'd sue to get half the farm, and he said go for it. It'd be worth it if someone would just roll her off his half. She hooked up with this greasy little lawyer from Waveland and sure enough he got her half the husband's place. After the court dealings, to celebrate the lawyer took this old gal out to supper and one thing led to another and they wound up at her apartment for a little slap and tickle. I'll be damned if they didn't fall out of bed together with her on top and he broke three ribs and ruined a knee on a night table. After a year of treatments he sued her good and got her half of the farm."

The deckhand threw his head back. "*Ha ha!* That's a double screwing if ever there was one."

"Hey, it don't stop there. The little lawyer called up the farmer and said since we gonna be neighbors, why don't you tell me a good spot to build a house? They got together and hit it off real good like old drinkin' buddies. After a couple months, the lawyer went into business with the farmer and together they doubled the cattle production, 'specially since they'd got rid of the critters' biggest predator."

Raynelle's eyebrows came together like a small thunderhead. "Well?"

"Well what?" The engineer scratched an armpit.

"What happened to that poor girl?"

All the men looked around uneasily. Raynelle had permanently disabled a boilermaker on the *St. Genevieve* with a cornbread skillet.

"Uh, she got back on her diet, I heard. Down to a hundred and twenty again."

The day fireman put up three fingers, asking for his draw. "That's the scary thing about women," he volunteered. "Marrying 'em is just like cutting the steel bands on a bale of cotton. First thing you know, you got a roomful of woman."

Raynelle glowered. "Careful I don't pour salt on you and watch you melt."

The engineer coughed loudly to derail the conversation and said, "Okay, Nick, you the only one ain't told us a lie yet. Let's have some good bullshit."

The young oiler ducked his head. "Don't know none."

"Haw," Raynelle said. "A man without bullshit. Check his drawers, Simoneaux, see he ain't Nancy instead of Nicky."

Reddening, the oiler frowned at his hand. "Well, the cows remind me of something I heard while I was playing the slot machines over in Port Allen the other day," he said, a long strand of black hair falling in his eyes. "There was this Mexican guy named Gonzales who worked with cows in Matamoras."

"Another cow farmer," the deckhand groaned.

"Shut up," Raynelle said. "Was that his first name or second?"

"Well, both," the boy said.

"What?" She pitched a card at him.

"Aw, Miss Raynelle, you know how those Mexicans are with their names. This guy's name was Gonzales Gonzales, with a bunch of names in between."

Raynelle cocked her ear whenever she heard the oiler speak. She had a hard time with his New Orleans accent, which she thought sounded Bronx-like.

"He was a pretty smart fella and got into Texas legal, worked a few years, and became a naturalized citizen, him and his wife both."

"What was his wife's name?" the pilot asked. "Maria Maria?"

"Come on, now, do you want to hear this or don'tcha?" The oiler pushed the hair out of his eyes. "The cattle industry shrunk up where he was at, and he looked around for another place to try and settle. He started to go to Gonzales, Texas, but there ain't no work there, so he gets out a map and spots Gonzales, Louisiana."

"That the rough place with all the jitterbug joints?"

"Yep. Lots of coonasses and roughnecks, but they ain't no Mexicans. Must have been settled by a family of Gonzaleses from Spain a million years ago who probably speak French and eat gumbo nowadays. So Gonzales Gonzales gets him a job working for two local lawyer brothers who run a horse farm on the side. He gets an apartment on Gonzales Street down by the train station." The oiler looked at a new hand, fanning the cards out slowly. "You know how badass the Airline Highway cops are through there? Well, this Gonzales was dark and his car was a beat-up smoker, so they pulled him over one day on his way to Baton Rouge. The cop stands outside his window and says, 'Lemme see your license,' to which Gonzales says he forgot it at home on the dresser. The cop pulls out a ticket book and says, 'What's your last name?' to which he says, 'Gonzales.' The cop says, 'What's your first name?' and he tells him. That officer leans in the window and sniffs his breath. 'Okay, Gonzales Gonzales,' he says, real nasty, 'Where you live?' 'Gonzales,' he says. 'Okay, boy. Get out the car,' the cop says. He throws him against the door, hard. 'And who do you work for?' Gonzales looks him in the eye and says, 'Gonzales and Gonzales.' The cop turns him around and slams his head against the roof and says, 'Yeah, and you probably live on Gonzales Street, huh, you cocky son of a bitch.' 'At 1226, apartment E,' Gonzales says."

The deckhand put his cards over his eyes. "The poor bastard."

"Yeah," the oiler sighed, "he got beat up and jailed that time until the Gonzales brothers went up and sprung him. About once a month some cop would pull him over and give him hell. When he applied for a little loan at the bank they threw his ass in the street. When he tried to get a credit card, the company called the feds, and they investigated him for fraud. Nobody would cash his checks, and the first year he filed state and federal taxes three government cars stayed in his driveway for a week. Nobody believed who he was."

"That musta drove him nuts," the welder said, drawing four cards.

"I don't think so, man. *He* knew who he was. Gonzales Gonzales knew he was in America and you could control what you was, unlike in Mexico. So when the traffic cops beat him up, he sold his car and got a bike. When the banks wouldn't give him no checks, he used cash. When the tax people refused to admit he existed, he stopped paying taxes. Man, he worked hard and saved every penny. One day it was real hot and he was walking into Gonzales because his bike had a flat. He stopped in the Rat's Nest Lounge to get a root beer, and this drunk asshole from west Texas was in there making life hard for the barmaid. He come over to Gonzales and asked him would he have a drink. He said sure, and the bartender set up a whiskey and a root beer. The cowboy was full of Early Times and pills, and you coulda lit a blowtorch off his eyeballs. He put his arm around Gonzales and asked him what his name was, you know. When he heard it, he got all serious, like he was bein' made fun of or something. He asked a couple more questions and got downright pissed off big-time. He pulled out an engraved Colt revolver from under a cheesy denim jacket and stuck it in Gonzales's mouth. 'You jerkin' me around, man,' that cowboy told him. 'You tellin' me you're Gonzales Gonzales from Gonzales and you live on Gonzales Street and work for Gonzales and Gonzales?' That Mexican looked at the gun, and I don't know what was going through his head, but he nodded, and the cowboy pulled back the hammer."

"Damn," the welder said.

"I don't want to hear this." Raynelle clapped the cards to her ears.

"Hey," the oiler said. "Like I told you, he knew who he was. He pointed to the old phone book by the register, and after a minute, the bartender had enough balls to open it up and hold it out to the cowboy. Sure enough, old Ma Bell had come through for the American Way, and Gonzales was listed, with the street and all. The cowboy took the gun out his mouth and started crying like the crazy snail he was. He told Gonzales he was sorry and gave him the Colt. Said his girlfriend left him and his dog died, or maybe it was the other way around. Gonzales went down the street and called the cops. In two months he got a ten-thousand-dollar reward for turning the guy in, since it turns out he'd killed his girlfriend and his dog too, over in Laredo. He got another two grand for the Colt and moved to Baton Rouge, where he started a postage stamp of a used car lot. Did well too. Got a dealership now."

The day fireman snapped his fingers. "G. Gonzales Buick?"

"That's it, man," the oiler said.

"The smilin' rich dude in the commercials?"

"Like I said," the oiler told the table, "he knew who he was."

"Mary and Joseph, everybody's in this hand," the pilot yelled. "Spades is trumps."

"*Laissez les bons temps roullet*," the welder sang, laying an eight of spades on a pile of diamonds and raking in the trick.

"That's your skinny ass," Raynelle hollered, playing a ten of spades last, taking the second trick.

"Do I smell the ten-millionth rollover pot?" the engineer said. "There must be over nine hundred fifty dollars in that pile." He threw down an eight and covered the third trick.

"Comin' gitcha." Raynelle raised her hand high, plucked a card, and slammed a jack to win the fourth trick. That was two. She led the king of spades and watched the cards follow.

The pilot put his hands together and prayed. "Please, somebody, have the ace." He played his card and sat up to watch as each man threw his last card in, no one able to beat the king, and then Raynelle jumped like a hooked marlin, nearly upsetting the table, screaming and waving her ample arms through the steamy engine room air. "I never won so much money in my life," she cried, falling onto the pile of bills and coins and raking it beneath her.

"Whatcha gonna do with all that money?" the welder asked, turning his hat around in disbelief.

She began stuffing the bib pockets of her overalls with coins. "I'm gonna buy me a silver lamé dress and one of those cheap tickets to Las

Vegas where I can do some high-class gamblin'. No more of this piss-ant stuff with old men and worms."

Five of the men got up to relieve their bladders or get cigarettes or grab something to drink. The pilot stood up and leaned against a column of insulated pipe.

"Hell, we all want to go to Las Vegas. Don't you want to take one of us along to the holy land?"

"Man, I'm gonna gamble with gentlemen. Ranchers, not cow farmers." She folded a wad of bills into a hip pocket.

Nick, the young oiler, laced his fingers behind his head, leaned back, and closed his eyes. He wondered what Raynelle would do in such a glitzy place as Las Vegas. He imagined her wearing a Sears gown in a casino full of tourists dressed in shorts and sneakers. She'd drink too much and eat too much, and the gown would look like it was crammed with rising dough. After she lost all her money, she would start a fight with a blackjack dealer and get thrown out on the street. Then she would cash in her plane ticket, go back to the slot machines, and lose every penny, winding up on a neon-infested boulevard, her tiny silver purse hanging from her shoulder on a long spaghetti strap, one heel broken off a silver shoe. He saw her at last walking across the desert through the waves of heat, mountains in front and the angry snarl of cross-country traffic behind her until she sobered up and began to hitch, getting picked up by a carload of Jehovah's Witnesses driving to a convention in Baton Rouge in an un-air-conditioned compact stuck in second gear. Every thirty miles the car would overheat, and they would all get out, stand among the cactus, and pray. Raynelle would curse them, and they would pray even harder for the big sunburned woman sweating through the metallic dress. The desert would spread before her as far as the end of the world, a hot and rocky place empty of mirages and dreams. She might not live to get out of it.

The Safe

When the safe came in, Alva's head was down sideways on his desk. He heard the junkyard's box-bed truck grind through the main gate, so he got up and stepped out of the office door, giving a hand signal for the driver to accelerate so he could make it onto the scale through the slurry of mud, battery acid, cinders, burned insulation, asbestos, and grease. The tires pinwheeled in the olive-colored slop, and the truck waddled into place, dripping and sizzling. Alva noted the weight, and the crane operator swung an electromagnet over the truck bed to pick up clumps of cast-iron fragments, dropping them in a pile next to the yard's wracked fence. Alva checked an invoice and saw that this was another load from the demolished sewing-machine factory, tons of rusted-together treadles, fancy flywheels, ornate stands. The magnet crane finished its work in twenty minutes, and Alva, who owned the junkyard, would have returned to his nap, but he noticed that the truck was still squatting low. He watched the crane operator disconnect the magnet and attach a hook to the end of the cable. Little Dickie, the welder, got up into the truck's box to attach the cable to something. At his signal, the cable jerked taut, and the whole truck rose on its springs. An antique office safe, at least eight feet high and six feet wide, swung up into the sooty air.

The rambling brick sewing-machine factory had been out of business for sixty years, its huge inventory of parts and partially assembled machines rusting in heaps even after most of the buildings were taken over in the late forties by a tire-manufacturing plant. The new management jammed all the left-behind equipment into the owl-haunted foundry building and went about their business until their tire process became obsolete in the 1970s. A millworks took over the hulking factory but soon failed and was replaced by a warehousing firm, which gradually vacated the crumbling plant as roofs fell in and smokestacks tumbled across the storage lot, startling only pigeons and rats. Finally, a chicken processor bought the site, and the owners decided to tear the factory down as quickly as possible and sell all the scrap metal to Alva. Hills of sewing-machine components, and the machinery that made them, had been coming in for two weeks. The truckload containing the safe was the last shipment.

Discarded safes showed up at the junkyard a few times a year, but this one was older and larger than most, a symbol of a substantial business. He admired the safe's thick arched legs that showed off rusty iron lilies, and he noted the precisely cast rope design rising along the borders of the double doors. He was a man who enjoyed the artful details of things, even of objects he shipped daily to the smelter. The crane operator pulled a lever in his cab and the safe came down, slowly falling back and flattening a Chambers range. Alva walked over as Little Dickie climbed out of the truck's box. The crane engine died, and they stood there listening to the stressed porcelain popping off the range's shell.

Alva climbed up on the safe and tried the dial, which was pitted and green, and it rotated with a gritty resistance. The safe looked as though it had been dug up, and it was slimed with a rusty wet clay. Alva hollered to the driver, "This thing hasn't been opened. Who told you to bring it on?"

The driver had only his right eye, so he turned his head severely in the truck window. "The head construction foreman hisself."

Alva stepped back to the ground and bobbed his boot toes in the mud a few times. "Hell, this thing might be full of diamonds."

The driver shook his head. "It was facedown in a pile with the rest of the junk. Foreman said you bought every piece of iron out there including this thing."

"Well, I better call him."

"It was left behind in a sewing-machine factory," the driver hollered. "What could be in it?"

Alva bit into his cheek. "That foreman didn't want to know?"

"He had thirty cement trucks lined up and ready to pour around where the safe was. Soon's I loaded up, he run me off."

"All right, then. Go on to the transmission shop." The truck slithered away toward Perdue Street, and Alva turned to the burner. "Open it up."

Little Dickie grabbed a cutting torch off a nearby tank dolly then stopped to give the safe a look. "I don't think so."

"What's wrong?"

"Remember Larry Bourgeois?"

"Oh." Larry had worked for the yard when Alva's father ran it. An old riveted safe came in one day, and when Larry started to cut it apart with a torch, it blew up. Larry and the door came down two blocks away. The safe had belonged to a construction firm and held a box of dynamite. "Ain't you curious?" Alva said.

Little Dickie pressed the lever on his torch and let out a derisive spit of oxygen. "I'm curious about what's on TV tonight. I'm curious about what Sandra's gonna make for my supper."

Alva walked to his office, a cinder-block cube, and pulled open its leprous steel door. The room's interior walls were lined with possibly functioning automobile starters, tractor transmissions, boiler valves, chain saws, bumper jacks, and one twin-floppy computer. Though he made good money, Alva was not particularly proud of his business. He had started out working part-time for his father, intending to move on after high school and live in New Orleans—maybe take drafting or even art lessons, since he loved to draw things—but somehow his hours had gotten longer, and then his father passed away, leaving him with a business that nobody but Alva knew how to run. He looked out his dusty window at the taken-apart world of his scrapyard, a place where the creative process was reversed and the burnt-umber insides of everything were spilled across his property.

His eyes fell on the safe. He thought about how his yard workers had no curiosity, no imagination, how too many people glanced at the surface of things and ignored what was inside. For the rest of the afternoon he tallied the scale sheets and figured his little payroll, but between tasks he daydreamed about the contents of the safe, wondered how many times in its life it had been opened and shut. He closed his eyes and pictured himself inside, a witness to the light-flashed face of the employee who opened the doors each day to retrieve patent drawings, payroll, gold leaf for the fancy embellishments on the machines' black-lacquered bodies.

That night at supper he sat with his wife, Donna, and their two daughters, Renée and Carrie. He told them about the safe, and Renée, a somber child of eight with a narrow head and watery eyes, stopped eating for a moment and said, "Maybe a ghost is inside."

Alva frowned, but was delighted by the way she was thinking. "Couldn't a ghost get out by just passing through the metal?"

Renée stabbed at her potato salad. "At school Sister Finnbarr says our souls can't get out of our bodies."

Her sister gave her a sharp look. "Oh, be quiet." Carrie was eleven, already pretty, and smarter than all of them. Alva dreaded her growing up and leaving them behind like bits of her broken shell. "A ghost isn't a soul."

Alva avoided her eyes. "How do you know?"

Carrie made a little huffing noise against the roof of her mouth. "A soul is either inside you or it's in heaven or hell. It sure isn't hiding in some rusty safe sitting in a Louisiana junkyard."

"Then what's a ghost?" Alva asked.

Renée put up her hands, palms forward alongside her pale face, and began to sway from side to side while speaking in a wavering voice. "It's this smoky thing that drifts around and talks."

"You're crazy," her sister told her. "A ghost is something made up, like in comics or movies." The girls began to bicker in rising complaints until their mother stopped them.

Donna put a hand on her husband's arm. "When you gonna open that thing up? It might have some money in it."

Alva noticed for the first time since he could remember that her brown eyes were bright, glistening under her sandy bangs. "There's probably nothing in it but drawings of sewing machines and stuff like that."

"Or the last payroll."

"Don't count on it." Over the years he'd noticed that his wife's interest in him depended on how much money he brought home. Three years before, when the margin on copper was high, she was his best friend. Last year she'd cooled off a bit. "But there might be something interesting."

She took a swallow of iced tea and banged the glass down. "What's more interesting than money?"

He glanced at her, wondering if she had finally defined herself. "I don't know. Maybe I'll find out." He looked into the darkening back-yard, where his yellow dog, Claude, sat placidly with a forepaw planted on the back of a large toad. He was an older dog, vaguely like a golden retriever, but really just a yellow dog, which is what happens when every breed on earth is mixed up in the course of a hundred years. The animal had been a gift from Alva's brother, who worked for a federal agency. Claude had been trained to find bodies but was never a stellar performer, so he'd been retrained to find drugs at airports, a task at which he excelled only too well. If he found marijuana, he tried to eat it all in one gulp.

The next morning, a yard crew was busy crushing all the old washing machines and dryers that had come in from the burned-out coin laun-dry at the edge of town. Snyder Problem, a big ex-preacher whose job it was to stand at an anvil and break bronze and copper out of the ferrous scrap, was cracking open rheostats with a maul when Alva walked by. Snyder was an old man, but his arms were still round and firm. The sleeves had been cut off his blue work shirt at the shoulders, and his biceps jumped each time the hammer fell against the anvil. It was a hot day, and sweat rolled off his bald head in beads. Alva couldn't imag-ine Snyder in a shiny suit addressing his congregation back in the days before his church burned down. "Seal welds," Snyder announced in his big preacher voice.

Alva stopped and looked over his shoulder. "What?"

"Me and Little Dickie was lookin' over that safe, and ever' door seam and joint on it's welded with thin seal welds. Looks like Heliarc work, too, so that dates it."

"How's that?" Alva walked over and saw that the mud had dried on the doors and someone had swept it off with a broom.

"Heliarc wasn't used till the early forties." Snyder picked up a brass bibcock and broke the iron handle off with a sparking blow of his hammer. "Somebody welded it up about when the sewing folks went out of business. That big ol' thing's tight as a sardine can."

"What for, do you think?"

Snyder shook his head slowly and looked Alva in the eye. "It's a mystery, and I don't know if you want to solve it or not." He spat a dart in the safe's direction. "Some men would just get a backhoe and bury the thing."

"It's a safe, not a coffin."

Snyder picked a brass doorknob off the ground and shook the iron shaft out of it. "I *hope* it's a safe," he said.

Alva took a step back. "You're letting your imagination run away."

"I thought that's what an imagination was for. It didn't run away, it'd just be like seeing."

His boss looked at him a long moment. "I didn't know you thought like that."

Snyder waved his hammer at the safe. "You got to use your imagination. You can make stuff with it, like ideas nobody never had before."

In the cluttered office, Little Dickie draped an arm around the water-cooler jug, holding a triangular paper cup in his free hand. Alva pointed at him. "Seal welds, huh? You decided to burn off the hinges yet?"

Little Dickie shook his head, his long bronze-colored hair shining like a schoolgirl's. For a welder, he took uncommonly good care of it, always putting it in a ponytail when he was using a cutting torch. "Taking the hinges off won't help open that type. Big iron rods come out the door and pass into the frame. It's lying on its back, so it'd be easy to drill it and sniff at the hole to see if dynamite's in this one. It has a pretty plain smell."

Alva opened a rusty file cabinet's bottom drawer and pulled out a ⅝-inch tungsten drill bit. "Here. Put a hole in it, then."

By standing on the doors and taking turns with an enormous drill that smoked and spat sparks as it ran, Snyder and Little Dickie managed to drill two holes in the safe, one in each door. A quarter-inch-thick iron skin covered a deep layer of cement backed by another plate of steel. Dickie's sinuses were smarting and running from all the dust raised by the drill, and he couldn't smell a thing, so Snyder got down on all fours and put his big red nose close to one of the holes. Alva walked up behind him and watched.

Little Dickie coughed as he wound up the big drill's cracked cord. He'd been a foreman at the wire plant, Alva recalled, but had been let go because he couldn't do enough math. Though he'd signed on to work in the scrapyard temporarily, he'd been on the payroll for three years. Alva looked through the windows of a '79 Volare that Dickie had been cutting up and thought about how his junkyard employees generally had fallen down the work ladder for one reason or another. The crane operator had been a trained mechanic, and even the old one-eyed truck driver had once made good money, back when he owned his own shrimp boat. Alva had always been what he was, going neither up nor down in fortune. He thought about how he was forty-five and envious of his workers because they at least had done something else in their lifetimes. He looked over at the wrecked and rusted chain-link fence forming the west corner of the yard, where a bramble mountain concealed a heap of uncrushed car bodies and refrigerator doors. The notion that he might straighten the place up a bit crossed his mind and kept on going.

Snyder Problem stood up and blew his nose into a red shop cloth. "Just smells like a hundred-year-old safe to me. Dynamite has a sweet smell, maybe with some rubbing alcohol mixed in." He gave Little Dickie a look.

"I don't know," Little Dickie said. "I guess I could grind off those little seal welds to start with, if you want me to."

Alva looked at his wristwatch. "Lunchtime. We'll get on it when I come back at one."

His house was just down the street, and for a change Donna had a hot lunch waiting for him. She walked over from the stove and stood by the table. "How about that old safe? You get it open yet? We rich?"

He swallowed and looked past her out into the yard, where Claude's blond body mounded above a bed of asparagus fern. "If nothing's in it, will you start serving me a cold sandwich again?"

Donna didn't blink. "I might. It's the old hunter-gatherer thing. You bring home an ox, we eat ox. You bring home a little squirrel, that means slim pickings around here."

The analogy pleased him for some reason. "This is good stew."

"Thanks." She sat down across from him and began to eat. "You suspect I don't think much of you?"

"No," he lied, taking another bite. "But you know, I'm the junkman."

"You're Alva." She pointed at him with her fork. "And *you're* the one who decided you're the junkman."

He thought about what she might mean. "You're saying I could be something else?"

She began wiping her plate with a pinch of white bread. "Only you can decide what you want to be."

"The junk business is all right, I guess, though sometimes I feel like I'm going about it wrong."

Looking out the window, she said, "I wouldn't worry about it too much. Be like Claude and take a nap."

When he finished eating, Alva stood up. "Where's his leash?"

"Hanging on the coat hook by the door. Why?"

"I'm going to take him down to the yard."

"What on earth for?" Donna put down her fork, alarmed. "You'll drop something on him."

"Naw. I just need his nose for a minute."

Snyder and Little Dickie were already back at work when Alva walked through the big yard gate pulled along by Claude, who was panting, his long pink tongue dripping beads on the dirt.

"Hey, boy," Snyder said, holding out a blackened hand. Claude put his nose in Snyder's palm, wondering at the paint, silicon, putty, zinc, cupric oxide, lime scale, and graphite he smelled there.

"I figured I'd let him get a sniff of the safe," Alva said. "See if he gives a reaction."

Little Dickie looked doubtfully at the dog. Claude sat and returned his steady gaze. "That the dog trained for dead bodies and dope?"

"Sort of."

Little Dickie extended his arm in a sweeping motion. "Well, be my guest."

Alva pulled the dog over to the safe and grabbed his collar, bringing his nose close to the door. At first Claude seemed uninterested, but then he put one nostril to a drilled hole and sniffed in short intakes as if pumping his head full of air. He snuffed loudly, blew his nose free of scent, then smelled again, putting his forepaws on either side of the hole. Drawing back, he cocked his head sideways, rolled his ears forward, then raised his snout to the gray sky, howling a long, sorrowful note that flew over the fence and haunted the whole neighborhood.

Little Dickie took a step backward into a puddle of dark fluid leaking from a refrigerator compressor. "Damn. That yell could peel paint off a porch." Claude howled again and began scratching at the safe's door, drawing scent from one hole and then the other. Alva had never seen the dog express anything close to excitement, and for the past few years had considered him to be little more than a slow-moving lawn ornament. He was the kind of dog that didn't do tricks, didn't ask to be scratched or to be let in or out. He was a drifter dog, a brassy apparition noticed only when he was on the sofa or blocking the walkway to the mailbox. But now he was pulling the leash like a caught fish, dancing on the rusty safe like someone convinced a relative was locked inside. He made so much noise and got so upset that Alva towed him over to the office and shut him in.

Snyder Problem rested a hip against his anvil. "Know what I think?"

"No, I don't."

"If you call the chief of police and tell him what that dog did, he might could find someone to unlock the safe. Save you the price of a locksmith."

"What about the seal welds? A safecracker can't get past those."

"They're thin," Little Dickie said, reaching up to put a rubber band in his hair. "I can take them off with an angle grinder before the law gets here."

Alva looked back toward the office and could hear Claude's muffled barking. He didn't like the idea of bringing police into the yard. He lived in secret envy of their clean uniforms, nickel-plated decorations, and shiny boots, the possibility that one of them might be promoted to something other than what they already were. Claude was now howling like a wolf.

"Tell the operator to get the crane and stand the thing up, then."

The policeman who answered the phone wasn't interested at first, but when Alva explained how the dog had been trained, the receiver went dead for a minute, and then the chief of police came on the line. "What brand of safe is it?"

"It says *Sloss* on the knob. Why?"

"I'll tell that to Houston, the locksmith."

"I thought he was dead. You think he can open it?"

"Is it a real old safe?"

"Yes."

"That's exactly his game."

In an hour the chief's cruiser pulled up, a freshly waxed black Crown Victoria with an elaborate gold-leaf badge on the door. Alva saw that even the tires were shiny, and he whistled. The chief was a short, balding man, and with him was Jack Houston, who slowly rose out of the passenger side and seemed so pained by a general arthritis that he stayed bent over, almost in a sitting position, as he walked around the hood.

"Hey, junkman," he said.

"Mr. Houston." Alva took his soft hand and then the chief's big paw.

"You say your yellow dog alerted on a smell coming from a safe?" the chief asked.

"It's unusual for him to get upset."

The chief hitched up his gun belt. "I'll listen to a dog's opinion before that of most people I know."

Jack Houston looked around and seemed surprised at the big safe sitting upright under the crane. "That thing ain't gonna topple over on me, is it?"

"It's stable where it is. The legs have sunk into the ground."

"If it fell on me, that'd be a sad end," he said, moving along in his creaky bowlegged stride. He pulled out a stethoscope from his baggy khakis. "You say it's a Sloss?"

"Yessir."

"Is it marked on the door or the dial?"

They had walked up to the safe by then, and Houston was looking right at the dial. "Well?"

"It's on the knob there," Alva said, noticing the locksmith's milky eyes.

The old man touched the dial. "I need a spray can of brake-parts cleaner."

"I got some spray lubricant."

"Is it got the little plastic squirter?"

"Yessir."

"That'll have to do." Houston twisted the combination dial back and forth, trying to work the grit from under it. When Alva returned with the spray, he used all of it blasting behind the dial, pitched the can, and plugged the stethoscope into his hairy ears. He worked the dial for five minutes or so, then his head came up sharply. "Damn it, turn off the crane engine." He looked over at the office. "That air condition, too." He bent again to his work and ten minutes later he pulled off his earpieces and stuffed the stethoscope into his pants pocket.

"Give up already?" the chief asked, his tongue fat in his cheek.

Houston chuckled. "Stethoscope's mostly for show. It don't tell much." He cracked his knuckles, clapped his hands, and hung his arms at his sides. "Got to let the blood build up in my fingertips."

Alva looked around at the other men, who were waiting patiently for something to happen, a treasure or a body to fall out onto the crushed battery casings and muck. For the moment at least, Alva envied the crippled and near blind Jack Houston. "How'd you learn to crack safes?"

"Pressure," the old man said.

"What kind of pressure?"

"The pressure of eating a sandwich every day. Of paying the light bill." He looked down, closed his eyes, and allowed only the very tips of his fingers to touch the dial. "One time a little four-year-old girl got into the Mosler safe down at the dime store, and damned if she didn't pull the door shut on herself. If you don't think *that* wasn't a scene, with me on my knees in the storeroom in August heat and her mother crying down my back while I'm trying to feel my way through those tamper-proof Mosler tumblers. It took so long we all knew she was dead, a pretty little girl with black hair and violet eyes. The daddy comes in and starts punching me in the neck to hurry me up like I'm a balked mule, the Catholic priest is praying in Latin behind the safe, and here comes my young wife to stand to the side and eyeball me while I worked. The store manager offered me two hundred extra dollars to hurry me up, like a boxcar full of money would have done any good." He pulled his hand away and brushed his fingertips with a pale thumb.

Little Dickie settled slowly into a squat next to him. "Well, what happened?"

"What happened? What you think happened? I got the door open and jerked her body out like a fish and gave her to Doc Prine. She was blue in the face and limp, but after a pretty scary while he brought her around. And when she opened her eyes, in that instant I went from the stupidest ox in town to some kind of saint. You never heard such noise in your life."

"That was the Delarco girl?" Snyder Problem asked.

"It was. She grew up and is a school principal over in Pine Oil. Had four children and one of 'em's named Houston." He put his right hand on the dial and began to move it slowly.

"How long's this gonna take?" Alva asked.

Houston closed his eyes. "Shut up and we'll see. This big, nasty-looking baby was made in the 1800s. It's simple as a box of Cracker Jacks. I'd as soon put my money in a cigar box behind the piano."

The men walked over to the entrance gate and stood in a little circle in the shade of a hackberry growing through a rotted tractor tire. "You know," the police chief began, casting a long look around the yard, "I had a complaint or two about the rats living in this place."

Alva put a foot on an engine block. "You want me to talk to the rats about it?"

"No. But you could teach them to work a weed whacker."

Snyder guffawed. "Chief, you could loan us a couple prisoners to pull up the brush."

The men went back and forth like this, weaving a meaningless talk just to pass the time. They knew what they were doing, clouding their minds' eyes to the fact of what might be in the safe—some sign of murder, a crumbling body falling to gray ash as the air reached it, or of thievery, a stingy payroll never given out to the perhaps starving laborers at the factory, or the stale air of nothingness, a seventy-year-old breath of fiscal shame. They talked and tried not to think for an hour, moving with the ball of shade thrown down by the hackberry tree. At last, Jack Houston's voice came around a hill of tire rims: "I've got it."

They all walked slowly, as if toward a grisly diagnosis. Houston beckoned them with his thin arms, then turned to the door and spun the wheel that drew out the deadbolts from the frame. "Someone will have to pull the right door open for me. If there's another thin door inside, I'll have to deal with that one a few minutes."

Snyder stepped up and muscled open the squalling door, an antique and sweet air gliding past his face and on into the universe. He worked a lever and swung wide the other door. They saw no inner barrier, just a system of low metal shelves that stopped halfway up and then what appeared to be a large pile of sacks wedged into the remaining space. Snyder seemed disappointed. He cocked his head and stepped back. "I guess the dog was smelling those hemp sacks."

Little Dickie looked back at the office. "He got a snootful and thought he was in for a real good buzz. Thought it was hashish."

Alva walked up and felt around in the sacks, which were whispery as dry hay. He turned to the men. "Something's inside the pile." He and Snyder pulled the sacks away, revealing a maple crate with dovetailed corners. The men slid it off its shelf and carried it into the office, where they placed it on the gray metal desk. The lid was nailed on, and Alva pried it up with a small crowbar. Inside the box he saw a layer of thick burgundy velvet cloth, which he unfolded as the men gathered around.

"Hey," the chief said, "it's made out of thick glass, whatever it is."

Snyder picked up the desk lamp and held it high. "It's a big glass dome with a handle on top. Kind of shaped like a suitcase. What's that in it?"

"Let's see." Alva pulled up on the handle, which was textured and also glass, and he raised something—what, he couldn't tell—out of the enveloping cloth. It was too close to see for a moment, heavy, two feet long and a foot wide. Snyder moved the crate to the floor with a wheeze, and Alva set the object on the desk where the crate had been. He stepped back.

The locksmith adjusted his glasses and leaned in. "Oh my gosh," he said. "Will you look at this!"

The men bent down at the waist, hands on knees like schoolboys, and studied the oblong cut-glass dome etched broadside with the emblem of the Wiewasser Sewing Machine Company, a large shield with a waterfall in the middle surrounded by alternating stars and lightning bolts and fine, careful cross-hatching. Covering the surface beyond the emblem's borders was a cloud of small hand-cut leaves. Female figures in Grecian dress walked up a mountain path through these leaves toward a tunnel of overhanging limbs. On the other side of the dome the etched waters of a rock-studded stream ran before a long temple whose fluted pillars framed the figures of goddesses, their hands held aloft to a white-gold sun. With a forefinger Alva traced the handle, a glass dolphin. On the two long sides, near the bottom, four damascened latch hooks swung on golden rivets in the glass. Inside the dome, the men began to comprehend an elegant sewing machine, antique, with a hand crank on the wheel. Alva slid the latches through their bright arcs, lifted off the dome, and placed it under his desk.

Little Dickie whistled. "Man, they coulda sewed a suit for the pope on this thing."

The base of the machine was shaped like a fiddleback, made of intricately cast and clear-lacquered brass. The edges stepped down in a triple ogee to four detailed turtle feet, each cast toenail bearing an amber jewel the size of a small kernel of corn. The feet planted themselves on a dark subbase of burled rosewood, showing a carved border of miniature ocean surf. "I know they didn't make them like this to sell," Alva said.

"Not hardly." The locksmith's face brightened in the machine's glow. "In the old days, there were international machinery expositions in the world's largest cities. Factories would make up special exhibit versions of their products and go all out trying to best the other makers, no matter what it was they manufactured, even putting together fancy locomotives and giant mill engines, and steam gauges that looked like religious items off an altar. This thing's got to be way over a hundred years old."

"They used to crank them by hand?" Alva touched the flywheel's bone-white handle. "This an early plastic?"

The locksmith's eyes swam and focused. "Ivory. Do you see a pattern?"

Alva looked closer. "Little shallow fish scales. Helped you grab it, I guess."

Snyder straightened up and laughed. "It's a tree."

"Damned if it ain't," Little Dickie said. The machine's bright gildings placed star points in his eyes. "The whole body of the thing's like a bent-over tree."

Alva was gradually disheartened by the cleverness of the design. The main body of the machine was gold plated, indeed rising like a tree trunk and then leaning into an arch that ended in the machine's head, a flattened mass of bunched metal leaves. The presser foot and needle protruded from the bottom. The bark pattern Alva knew well—water oak, like the big one in his yard—but this metal tree showed sinewy ridges of gold. Out of the machine's leaf pattern stared the embedded garnet eyes of birds, squirrels, and toads hiding in the foliage. The casting and fine engraving showed the handiwork of what must have been the factory's most talented worker. Near the flywheel was the maker badge, a repeat of the design on the glass cover, but here the stars were inlaid with small diamond-cut rubies, and the lightning bolts were coated with alternating layers of gold and silver. The flywheel itself was gold plated and scalloped along the rim, and on its face ran a serpentine row of hyacinth inlaid with ivory dyed apple green.

Alva felt belittled by the apparatus, as though his abilities were suddenly small and unrealized. He suspected the feeling would pass after a while, but really, who could make this? He hardly understood how to look at it. Every surface was a surprise of coherent innovation. The men pointed and stared for fifteen minutes before the police chief motioned toward a small wishing well protruding from the lower frame of the machine, exclaiming, "The little crank and shaft for the well bucket is the bobbin winder!"

It was a good while before anyone thought about value, which even to the scrap men seemed beside the point. Little Dickie pushed back his hair and straightened up. "What's this thing worth?"

Snyder closed one eye. "Even if somebody just busted it up into scrap and jewelry, it'd bring a good bit."

Alva put two fingers on the flywheel handle and turned it around through a cycle. The machine made no sound, and the motion was as smooth as water pouring from a teapot. "Mr. Houston, who could appraise something like this?"

"Oh, everybody knows everything nowadays because of that Internet. Just get your wife to take a picture and e-mail it around to some antique dealers. You'll get a ballpark figure, anyway."

At the end of the day, after everyone had left, Alva sat in his desk chair and toured the sewing machine, touching the inlaid slide plates, the platinum tension adjustment, and, on the fiddleback base, the mosaic peacock inlaid with bars of amethyst. He even examined the machine's innards where the shuttle in the bottom was engraved with boat planks and false oarlocks. The machine's glow was warming, clarifying, and when Alva looked away, he saw that his dingy office had changed. He could see it for what it was.

Nearly every day, some of the men would come in during break and look through the glass at the machine where it rested on a wide filing cabinet. His wife took photos and sent them to appraisers. She spent a great deal of time with the photography; in fact, she spent a whole afternoon shooting frame after frame, finally just sitting in front of the machine with her mouth open a little, as though exhausted by looking.

He walked up behind her and asked what she thought they ought to do with it.

"Well, I can't sew any curtains with this thing, can I?" She closed up her camera case. "But I'd hate to see it go."

Alva discovered that a small number of exhibition machines were in private collections, and those with semiprecious stones were worth upward of $10,000. One dealer responded with a letter, not just an e-mail, admitting that this was the finest he'd ever seen, and could bring up to $19,000 at auction. Alva's wife said that it was his choice whether or not to sell, but his daughters wanted to bring it home and put it on the mantelpiece. What Alva decided to do, after the final appraisal came in, was to have a beefed-up security system installed in his office so he could keep the sewing machine there. If the appraisals were right, he couldn't even buy an average sedan with the proceeds. And what would $19,000 buy him that wouldn't turn to junk in ten years and wind up piled on the oily ground outside his office window?

He moved the dusty spare parts lining the room's walls to a storage shed and then painted the inside of the office antique white. He bought a new desk, chairs, and filing cabinets, as well as a rubber plant and brass lamps. Sometimes his daughters brought their friends to the yard to study the machine, and these were the first visits Renée and Carrie had ever made to their father's place of business. His wife, who'd always liked to sew, bought an expensive Italian machine and began a small alterations business; in her spare time she embroidered elaborate name-tags embedded in crests on his work shirts and even on Claude's soggy collar. One day she followed him back to work from his lunch break and recorded his invoices for the week. Sitting in his padded chair, she looked over at the machine. "If you want, one of these days I could get some new velvet and make a dustcover for it with a little lifting strap on top. Run some embroidery around the bottom with gold thread."

He stepped next to the desk, followed her line of sight, and rubbed his chin. "Yeah. That'll work."

She reached out, put a forefinger through one of his belt loops, and gave it a tug. "I won't charge you hardly nothin'."

Over the next several weeks he paid a crew to pull up all the brush and saplings from the hills of twisted metal that had lain unexplored since his father's death, and he had the exposed junk crushed and shipped out in a railroad gondola. He graveled the yard and put up silvery new fencing.

Snyder would wipe his feet and come in during hot weather and linger at the water cooler next to the sewing machine, looking down on it where it rested in a cone of light cast by a brass floor lamp. When he was at his anvil, he seemed somber and bored, hammering away as if he was angry at steam gauges and toilet valves. Two months after they'd cracked the safe, Snyder began meeting with his old congregation from the low neighborhood behind the sawmill, and during August he leased the empty Woodmen of the World hall and reopened his church there. Alva was surprised when Snyder told him he was leaving, but not as surprised as when a month later Little Dickie departed for an exotic welding school in Dallas.

"What brought this on?" Alva asked the day Little Dickie turned in his notice.

He shrugged. "I don't know. I figure I can do better if I learn some real welding. You know, Heliarc, and some good pipe-joining technique."

"I guess I can give you a raise, if it'll change your mind."

"It's not all money," Little Dickie said, snapping his gate key down on the shiny desk.

"What, then? I still can't get used to Snyder not being here."

Little Dickie looked around at the room and its fixtures. "I just figure I can do better than burning stuff apart. Time to put some stuff together for a change."

In the next month Alva hired two new workers, mildly handicapped men provided by a federal program. His truck driver and crane operator stayed on, but they hardly ever came into the office. One or two times he saw them look briefly at the sewing machine, but he could tell they didn't understand what it was and that they thought it was some shiny plastic thing he'd bought on vacation in Gatlinburg, Tennessee.

About once a week, right before leaving the office in the evening, he'd lift Donna's sea-blue dustcover, which flowed and rippled like an expensive gown. He'd remove the cut-glass cover and turn the machine through a few cycles with its ivory handle. On one of these occasions, five months after he'd opened the safe, he bent down to examine the machine yet again and discovered that even the needle was engraved. The next day, he brought a magnifying glass from home and squinted at the script running along the lightning-silver shaft. It read, ART STITCHES ALL.

He sat back in his chair, feeling as though his skull had become transparent, letting in a warm illumination he didn't comprehend any more than an animal standing in a winter's false dawn understands the physics of the sun. He turned and looked out the office window at a hill of steel beams cut into rust-red chunks, and he wondered for the first time about the mill where the pieces would be reborn into bars and plates and rolls. Closing his eyes he saw a long, running image of steel panels night-riding across the Great Plains toward a factory where they would be stamped into automobile frames, surgical instruments, brackets for church bells, braces for thick glass shelves holding diamonds and pearls, and he felt that he was now part of this flowing upward toward all the things that people make. He reached down to replace the dome, and the glass dolphin swam in his palm.

Welding with Children

*T*uesday was about typical. My four daughters, not a one of them married, you understand, brought over their kids, one each, and explained to my wife how much fun she was going to have looking after them again. But Tuesday was her day to go to the casino, so guess who got to tend the four babies? My oldest daughter also brought over a bed rail that the end broke off of. She wanted me to weld it. Now what the hell you can do in a bed that'll break a iron rail is beyond me, but she can't afford another one on her burger-flipping salary, she said, so I got to fix it with four little kids hanging on my coveralls. Her kid is seven months, nicknamed Nu-Nu, a big-head baby with a bubbling tongue always hanging out his mouth. My second oldest, a flight attendant on some propeller airline out of Alexandria, has a little six-year-old girl named Moonbean, and that ain't no nickname. My third youngest, who's still dating, dropped off Tammynette, also six, and last to come was Freddie, my favorite because he looks like those old photographs of me when I was seven, a round head with copper bristle for hair, cut about as short as Velcro. He's got that kind of papery skin like me, too, except splashed with a handful of freckles.

When everybody was on deck, I put the three oldest in front the TV and rocked Nu-Nu off and dropped him in the porta-crib. Then I dragged the bed rail and the three awake kids out through the trees, back to my tin workshop. I tried to get something done, but Tammynette got the big grinder turned on and jammed a file against the stone just to laugh at the sparks. I got the thing unplugged and then started to work, but when I was setting the bed rail in the vise and clamping on the ground wire from the welding machine, I leaned against the iron and Moonbean picked the electric rod holder off the cracker box and struck a blue arc on the zipper of my coveralls, low. I jumped back like I was hit with religion and tore those coveralls off and shook the sparks out of my drawers. Moonbean opened her goat eyes wide and sang, "Whoo. Grendaddy can bust a move." I decided I better hold off trying to weld with little kids around.

I herded them into the yard to play, but even though I got three acres there ain't much for them to do at my place, so I sat down and watched Freddie climb on a Oldsmobile engine I got hanging from a willow oak on a long chain. Tammynette and Moonbean pushed him like he was on a swing, and I yelled at them to stop, but they wouldn't listen. It was a sad sight, I guess. I shouldn't have that old greasy engine hanging from that Kmart chain in my side yard. I know better. Even in this central Louisiana town of Gumwood, which is just like any other red-dirt place in the South, trash in the yard is trash in the yard. I make decent money as a now-and-then welder.

I think sometimes about how I even went to college once, a whole semester to LSU. Worked overtime at a sawmill for a year to afford the tuition and showed up in my work boots to get taught English 101 by a guy from Pakistan who couldn't understand one word we said, much less us him. He didn't teach me a damn thing and sat there on the desk with his legs crossed, telling us to write nonstop in what he called our portfolios, which he never read. For all I know, he sent our tablets back to Pakistan for his relatives to use as stove wood.

The algebra teacher talked to us with his eyes rolled up like his lecture was printed out on the ceiling. Most of the time he didn't even know we were in the room, and for a month I thought the poor bastard was stone blind. I never once solved for X.

The chemistry professor was a fat drunk who heated Campbell's soup on one of those little burners and ate it out the can while he talked. There was about a million of us in that classroom, and I couldn't get the hang of what he wanted us to do with the numbers and names. I sat way in the back next to some fraternity boys who called me Uncle Jed. Time or two, when I could see the blackboard off on the horizon, I almost got the hang of something, and I was glad of that.

I kind of liked the history professor and learned to write down a lot of what he said, but he dropped dead one hot afternoon in the middle of the pyramids and was replaced by a little porch lizard that looked down his nose at me where I sat in the front row. He bit on me pretty good because I guess I didn't look like nobody else in that class, with my short red hair and blue jeans that were really blue. I flunked out that semester, but I got my money's worth learning about people that don't have hearts no bigger than bird shot.

Tammynette and Moonbean gave the engine a long shove, got distracted by a yellow butterfly playing in a clump of pigweed, and that nine-hundred-pound V8 kind of ironed them out on the backswing. So I picked the squalling girls up and got everybody inside where I cleaned them good with GOJO.

"I want a ICEE," Tammynette yelled while I was getting the motor oil from between her fingers. "I ain't had a ICEE all day."

"You don't need one every day, little miss," I told her.

"Don't you got some money?" She pulled a hand away and flipped her hair with it like a model on TV.

"Those things cost most of a dollar. When I was a kid I used to get a nickel for candy, and that only twice a week."

"ICEE," she yelled in my face, Moonbean taking up the cry and calling out from the kitchen in her dull little voice. She wasn't dull in the head; she just talked low, like a bad cowboy actor. Nu-Nu sat up in the port-a-crib and gargled something, so I gathered everyone up, put them in the Caprice, and drove them down to the Gumwood Pak-a-Sak. The baby was in my lap when I pulled up, Freddie tuning in some rock music that sounded like hail on a tin roof. Two guys I know, way older than me, watched us roll to the curb. When I turned the engine off, I could barely hear one of them say, "Here comes Bruton and his bastard-mobile." I grabbed the steering wheel hard and looked down on the top of Nu-Nu's head, feeling like somebody just told me my house burned down. I'm naturally tanned, so those boys couldn't see the shame rising in my face, and I got out pretending I didn't hear anything, Nu-Nu in the crook of my arm like a loaf of bread. I wanted to punch the older guy and break his upper plate, but I could see the article in the local paper and imagine the memories the kids would have of their grandfather whaling away at two snuff-dripping geezers. I looked them in the eye and smiled, surprising even myself. Bastardmobile. Man.

"Hey, Bruton," the younger one said, a Mr. Fordlyson, maybe sixty-five. "All them kids yours? You start over?"

"Grandkids," I said, holding Nu-Nu over his shoes so maybe he'd drool on them.

The older one wore a straw fedora and was nicked up in twenty places with skin cancer operations. He snorted. "Maybe you can do better with this batch," he told me. I remembered then that he was also a Mr. Fordlyson, the other guy's uncle. He used to run the hardwood sawmill north of town, was a deacon in the Baptist Church, and owned about one percent of the pissant bank down next to the gin. He thought he was king of Gumwood, but then every old man in town who had five dollars in his pocket and an opinion on the tip of his tongue thought the same.

I pushed past him and went into the Pak-a-Sak. The kids saw the candy rack and cried out for Mars bars and Zeros. Even Nu-Nu put out a slobbery hand toward the Gummy Worms, but I ignored their whining and drew them each a small Coke ICEE. Tammynette and Moonbean grabbed theirs and headed for the door. Freddie took his real careful when I held it out. Nu-Nu might be kind of wobble-headed and plain as a melon, but he sure knew what a ICEE was and how to go after a straw. And what a smile when that Coke syrup hit those bald gums of his.

Right then Freddie looked up at me with his green eyes in that speckled face and said, "What's a bastardmobile?"

I guess my mouth dropped open. "I don't know what you're talking about."

"I thought we was in a Chevrolet," he said.

"We are."

"Well, that man said we was in a—"

"Never mind what he said. You must have misheard him." I nudged him toward the door and we went out. The older Mr. Fordlyson was watching us like we were a parade, and I was trying to look straight ahead. In my mind the newspaper showed the headlines, LOCAL MAN ARRESTED WITH GRANDCHILDREN FOR ASSAULT.

I got into the car with the kids and looked back out at the Fordlysons where they sat on a bumper rail, sweating through their white shirts and staring at us all. Their kids owned sawmills, ran fast-food franchises, were on the school board. They were all married. I guess the young Fordlysons were smart, though looking at that pair you'd never know where they got their brains. I started my car and backed out onto the highway, trying not to think, but to me that word was spelled out in chrome script on my fenders: *bastardmobile.*

On the way home Tammynette stole a suck on Freddie's straw, and he jerked it away and called her something I'd only heard the younger workers at the plywood mill say. The expression hit me in the back of the head like a brick, and I pulled off the road onto the gravel shoulder. "What'd you say, boy?"

"Nothing." But he reddened. I saw he cared what I thought.

"Kids your age don't use language like that."

Tammynette flipped her hair and raised her chin. "How old you got to be?"

I gave her a look. "Don't you care what he said to you?"

"It's what they say on the comedy program," Freddie said. "Everybody says that."

"What comedy program?"

"It comes on after the nighttime news."

"What you doing up late at night?"

He just stared at me, and I saw that he had no idea what *late* was. Glendine, his mamma, probably lets him fall asleep in front of the set every night. I pictured him crumpled up on that smelly shag rug his mamma keeps in front of the TV to catch the spills and crumbs.

When I got home I took them all on our covered side porch. The girls began to struggle with jacks, their little ball bouncing crooked on the slanted floor, Freddie played tunes on his ICEE straw, and Nu-Nu fell asleep in my lap. I stared at my car and wondered if its name had spread throughout the community, if everywhere I drove people would call out "Here comes the bastardmobile." Gumwood's one of those towns where everybody looks at everything that moves. I do it myself. If my neighbor Miss Hanchy pulls out of her lane I wonder, Now where's the old bat off to? It's two-thirty, so her soap opera must be over. I figure her route to the store and then somebody different will drive by and catch my attention, and I'll think after them. This is not all bad. It makes you watch how you behave, and besides, what's the alternative? Nobody giving a flip about whether you live or die? I've heard those stories from the big cities about how people will sit in an apartment window six stories up, watch somebody take ten minutes to kill you with a stick, and not even reach for the phone.

I started thinking about my four daughters. None of them has any religion to speak of. I thought they'd pick it up from their mamma, like I did from mine, but LaNelle always worked so much she just had time to cook, clean, transport, and fuss. The girls grew up watching cable and videos every night, and that's where they got their view of the world, and that's why four dirty blondes with weak chins from Rapides Parish thought they lived in a Hollywood soap opera. They also figured the married pulpwood truck drivers and garage mechanics they dated was movie stars. I guess a lot of what's wrong with my girls is my fault, but I don't know what I could've done different.

Moonbean raked in a gaggle of jacks, and a splinter from the porch floor ran up under her nail. "Shit dog," she said, wagging her hand like it was on fire and coming to me on her knees.

"Don't say that."

"My finger hurts. Fix it, Paw-Paw."

"I will if you stop talking like white trash."

Tammynette picked up on fivesies. "Mamma's boyfriend Melvin says *shit dog.*"

"Would you do everything your mamma's boyfriend does?"

"Melvin can drive," Tammynette said. "I'd sure like to drive."

I got out my penknife and worked the splinter from under Moonbean's nail while she jabbered to Tammynette about how her mamma's Toyota cost more than Melvin's teeny Dodge truck. I swear I don't know how these kids got so complicated. When I was their age all I wanted to do was make mud pies or play in the creek. I didn't want nothing but a twice-a-week nickel to bring to the store. These kids ain't eight years old and already know enough to run a casino. When I finished, I looked down at Moonbean's brown eyes, at Nu-Nu's pulsing head. "Does your mammas ever talk to y'all about, you know, God?"

"My mamma says God when she's cussing Melvin," Tammynette said.

"That's not what I mean. Do they read Bible stories to y'all at bedtime?"

Freddie's face brightened. "She rented us *Conan the Barbarian*. That movie kicked ass."

"That's not a Bible movie," I told him.

"It ain't? It's got swords and snakes in it."

"What's that got to do with anything?"

Tammynette came close and grabbed Nu-Nu's hand and played the fingers like they were piano keys. "Ain't the Bible full of swords and snakes?"

Nu-Nu woke up and peed on himself, so I had to go for a plastic diaper. On the way back from the bathroom I saw our little bookrack out the corner of my eye. I found my old Bible stories hardback and brought it out on the porch. It was time somebody taught them something about something.

They gathered round, sitting on the floor, and I got down among them. I started into Genesis and how God made the earth, and how He made us and gave us a soul that would live forever. Moonbean reached into the book and put her hand on God's beard. "If He shaved, He'd look just like that old man down at the Pak-a-Sak," she said.

My mouth dropped a bit. "You mean Mr. Fordlyson? That man don't look like God."

Tammynette yawned. "You just said God made us to look like Him."

"Never mind," I told them, going on into Adam and Eve and the Garden. Soon as I turned the page they saw the snake and began to squeal.

"Look at the size of that sucker," Freddie said.

Tammynette wiggled closer. "I knew they was a snake in this book."

"He's a bad one," I told them. "He lied to Adam and Eve and said to not do what God told them to."

Moonbean looked up at me slow. "This snake can talk?"

"Yes."

"How about that. Just like on cartoons. I thought they was making that up."

"Well a real snake can't talk, nowadays," I explained.

"Ain't this garden snake a real snake?" Freddie asked.

"It's the devil in disguise," I told them.

Tammynette flipped her hair. "Aw, that's just a old song. I heard it on the reddio."

"That Elvis Presley tune's got nothing to do with the devil making himself into a snake in the Garden of Eden."

"Who's Elvis Presley?" Moonbean sat back in the dust by the weatherboard wall and stared out at my overgrown lawn.

"He's some old singer died a million years ago," Tammynette told her.

"Was he in the Bible too?"

I beat the book on the floor. "No, he ain't. Now pay attention. This is important." I read the section about Adam and Eve disobeying God, turned the page, and all hell broke loose. An angel was holding a long sword over Adam and Eve's down-turned heads as he ran them out of the Garden. Even Nu-Nu got excited and pointed a finger at the angel.

"What's that guy doing?" Tammynette asked.

"Chasing them out of Paradise. Adam and Eve did a bad thing, and when you do bad, you get punished for it." I looked down at their faces and it seemed that they were all thinking about something at the same time. It was scary, the little sparks I saw flying in their eyes. Whatever you tell them at this age stays forever. You got to be careful.

Freddie looked up at me and asked, "Did they ever get to go back?"

"Nope. Eve started worrying about everything and Adam had to work every day like a beaver just to get by."

"Was that angel really gonna stick Adam with that sword?" Moonbean asked.

"Forget about that darn sword, will you?"

"Well, that's just mean" is what she said.

"No it ain't," I said. "They got what was coming to them." Then I went into Noah and the flood, and in the middle of things Freddie piped up.

"You mean all the bad people got drownded at once? All right."

I looked down at him hard and saw that the Bible was turning into one big adventure film for him. Freddie had already watched so many movies that any religion he would hear about would nest in his brain on top of *Tanga the Cave Woman* and *Bikini Death Squad*. I got everybody a cold drink and jelly sandwiches, and after that I turned on a window unit, handed out Popsicles, and we sat inside on the couch because the heat had waked up the yellow flies outside. I tore into how Abraham almost stabbed Isaac, and the kids' eyes got big when they saw the knife. I hoped they got a sense of obedience to God out of it, but when I asked Freddie what the point of the story was, he just shrugged and looked glum.

Tammynette, however, had an opinion. "He's just like O. J. Simpson!"

Freddie shook his head. "Naw. God told Abraham to do it just as a test."

"Maybe God told O.J. to do what he did," Tammynette sang.

"Naw. O.J. did it on his own," Freddie told her. "He didn't like his wife no more."

"Well, maybe Abraham didn't like his son no more neither, so he was gonna kill him dead and God stopped him." Tammynette's voice was starting to rise like her mother's did when she got to drinking.

"Daddies don't kill their sons when they don't like them," Freddie told her. "They just pack up and leave." He broke apart the two halves of his Popsicle and bit one, then the other.

Real quick I started in on Sodom and Gomorrah and the burning of the towns full of wicked people. Moonbean got interested in Lot's wife. "I saw this movie once where Martians shot a gun at you and turned you into a statue. You reckon it was Martians burnt down those towns?"

"The Bible ain't a movie," I told her.

"I think I seen it down at Blockbuster," Tammynette said.

I didn't stop to argue and pushed on through Moses and the Ten Commandments, spending a lot of time on number six, since that one give their mammas so much trouble. Then Nu-Nu began to rub his nose with the backs of his hands and started to tune up, so I knew it was time to put the book down and wash faces and get snacks and play crawl-around. I was determined not to turn on TV again, but Freddie hit the button when I was in the kitchen. When Nu-Nu and me came into the living room, they were in a half circle around a talk show. On the set were several overweight, tattooed, frowning, slouching individuals who, the announcer told us, had tricked their parents into signing over ownership of their houses and then evicted them. The kids watched like they were looking at cartoons, gobbling it all up. At a commercial I asked Moonbean, who's got the softest heart, what she thought of kids that threw their parents in the street. She put a finger in an ear and said through a long yawn that if they did mean things, then the kids could do what they want to them. I shook my head, went in the kitchen, found the Christmas vodka, and poured myself a long drink. I stared out in the yard to where my last pickup truck lay dead and rusting in a pile of wisteria at the edge of the lot. I formed a little fantasy about gathering all these kids into my Caprice and heading out northwest to start over, away from their mammas, TVs, mildew, their casino-mad grandmother, and Louisiana in general. I could get a job, raise them right, send them to college so they could own sawmills and run car dealerships. A drop of sweat rolled off the glass and hit my right shoe, and I looked down at it. The leather lace-ups I was wearing were paint spattered and twenty years old. They told me I hadn't held a steady job in a long time, that whatever bad was gonna happen was partly my fault. I wondered then if my wife ever had the same fantasy: leaving her scruffy, sunburned, failed-welder husband home and moving away with these kids, maybe taking some kind of courses and getting a job in Utah, raising them right, sending them off to college. Maybe even each of their mammas had the same idea, pulling their kids out of their parents' gassy-smelling old house and heading away from the heat and humidity. I took another long swallow and wondered why one of us didn't do it. I looked out to my Caprice sitting in the shade of a pecan tree, shadows of leaves moving on it making it shimmy like a dark green flame, and I realized we couldn't drive away from ourselves. We couldn't escape in the bastardmobile.

In the pantry, I opened the house's circuit panel and rotated out a fuse until I heard a cry from the living room. I went in and pulled down a storybook, something about a dog chasing a train. My wife bought it twenty years ago for one of our daughters but never read it to her. I sat in front of the dark television.

"What's wrong with the TV, Paw-Paw?" Moonbean rasped.

"It died," I said, opening the book. They wiggled and complained, but after a few pages they were hooked. It was a good book, one I'd read myself one afternoon during a thunderstorm. But while I'm reading, this blue feeling's got me. I'm thinking, What's the use? I'm just one old man with a little brown book of Bible stories and a doggie hero book. How can that compete with daily MTV, kids' programs that make big people look like fools, the Playboy Channel, the shiny magazines their mammas and their boyfriends leave around the house—magazines like *Me,* and *Self*—and *Love Guides,* and rental movies where people kill each other with no more thought than it would take to swat a fly, nothing at all like what Abraham suffered before he raised that knife? But I read on for a half hour, and when that dog stopped the locomotive before it pulled the passenger train over the collapsed bridge, even Tammynette clapped her sticky hands.

The next day I didn't have much on the welding schedule, so after one or two little jobs, including the bed rail that my daughter began to rag me about, I went out to pick up a window grate the town marshall wanted me to fix. The clouds burned off right after lunch, and Gumwood was wiggling with heat. Across from the cypress railroad station was our little red-brick city hall with a green copper dome on it, and on the grass in front of that was a pecan tree and a wooden bench next to its trunk. Old men sometimes gathered under the cool branches and told each other how to fix tractors that hadn't been made in fifty years, or how to make grits out of a strain of corn that didn't exist anymore. That big pecan was a landmark, and locals called it the Tree of Knowledge. When I walked by going to the marshall's office, I saw the older Mr. Fordlyson seated in the middle of the long bench, blinking at the street like a chicken. He called out to me.

"Bruton," he said. "Too hot to weld?" It didn't sound like a friendly comment, though he waved for me to come over.

"Something like that." I was tempted to walk on by, but he motioned for me to sit next to him, which I did. I looked across the street for a long time. Finally, I said, "The other day at the store, you said my car was a bastardmobile."

Fordlyson blinked twice but didn't change his expression. Most local men would be embarrassed at being called down for a lack of politeness, but he sat there with his face as hard as a plowshare. "Is that not what it is?" he said at last.

I should have been mad, and I was, but I kept on. "It was a mean thing to let me hear." I looked down and wagged my head. "I need help with those kids, not your meanness."

He looked at me with his little nickel-colored eyes glinting under that straw fedora with the black silk hat band. "What kind of help you need?"

I picked up a pecan that was still in its green pod. "I'd like to fix it so those grandkids can do right. I'm thinking of talking to their mammas and—"

"Too late for their mammas." He put up a hand and let it fall like an ax. "They'll have to decide to straighten out on their own or not at all. Nothing you can tell those girls now will change them a whit." He said this in a tone that hinted I was dumb as a post for not seeing this. He looked off to the left for half a second, then back. "You got to deal directly with those kids."

"I'm trying." I cracked the nut open on the edge of the bench.

"Tryin' won't do shit. You got to bring them to Sunday school every week. You go to church?"

"Yeah."

"Don't eat that green pecan—it'll make you sick. Which church you go to?"

"Bonner Straight Gospel."

He flew back like he'd just fired a twelve-gauge at the dog sleeping under the station platform across the street. "Bruton, your wild-man preacher's one step away from takin' up serpents. I heard he lets the kids come to the main service and yells at them about frying in hell like chicken parts. You got to keep them away from that man. Why don't you come to First Baptist?"

I looked at the ground. "I don't know."

The old man bobbed his head just once. "I know damned well why not. You won't tithe."

That cut deep. "Hey, I don't have a lot of extra money. I know the Baptists got good Sunday school programs but—"

Fordlyson waved a finger in the air like a little sword. "Well, join the Methodists. The Presbyterians." He pointed up the street. "Join those Catholics. Some of them don't put more than a dollar a week in the plate, but there's so many of them, and the church runs so many services a weekend, that those priests can run the place on volume like Walmart."

I knew several good mechanics who were Methodists. "How's the Methodists' children's programs?"

The old man spoke out of the side of his mouth. "Better'n you got now."

"I'll think about it," I told him.

"Yeah, bullshit. You'll go home and weld together a log truck, and tomorrow you'll go fishing, and you'll never do nothing for them kids, and they'll all wind up serving time in Angola or on their backs in New Orleans."

It got me hot the way he thought he had all the answers, and I turned on him quick. "Okay, wise man. I came to the Tree of Knowledge. Tell me what to do."

He pulled down one finger on his right hand with the forefinger of the left. "Go join the Methodists." Another finger went down and he told me, "Every Sunday bring them children to church." A third finger, and he said, "And keep 'em with you as much as you can."

I shook my head. "I already raised my kids."

Fordlyson looked at me hard and didn't have to say what he was thinking. He glanced down at the ground between his smooth-toe lace-ups. "And clean up your yard."

"What's that got to do with anything?"

"It's got everything to do with everything."

"Why?"

"If you don't know, I can't tell you." Here he stood up, and I saw his daughter at the curb in her Lincoln. One leg wouldn't straighten all the way out, and I could see the pain in his face. When I grabbed his arm, he smiled a mean little smile and leaned in to me for a second and said, "Bruton, everything worth doing hurts like hell." He toddled off and left me with his sour breath on my face and a thought forming in my head like a rain cloud.

After a session with the Methodist preacher I went home and stared at the yard, then stared at the telephone until I got up the strength to call Famous Amos Salvage. The next morning a wrecker and a gondola came down my road, and before noon, Amos loaded up four derelict cars, six engines, four washing machines, ten broken lawn mowers, and two and a quarter tons of scrap iron. I begged and borrowed Miss Hanchy's Super A and bush-hogged the three acres I own and then some. I cut the grass and picked up around the workshop. With the money I got from the scrap, I bought some aluminum paint for the shop and some first-class stuff for the outside of the house. The next morning I was up at seven replacing screens on the little porch, and on the big porch on the side I put down a heavy coat of glossy green deck enamel. At lunch, my wife stuck her head through the porch door. "The kids are coming over again. How you gonna keep 'em off all that wet paint?"

My knees were killing me, and I couldn't figure how to keep Nu-Nu from crawling out here. "I got no idea."

She looked around at the wet glare. "What's got into you, changing our religion and all?"

"Time for a change, I guess." I loaded up my brush.

She thought about this a moment, then pointed. "Careful you don't paint yourself in a corner."

"I'm doing the best I can."

"It's about time," she said under her breath, walking away.

I backed off the porch and down the steps, then stood in the pine straw next to the house painting the ends of the porch boards. I heard a car come down the road and watched my youngest daughter drive up and get out with Nu-Nu over her shoulder. When she came close, I noticed her dyed hair, which was the color and texture of fiberglass insulation, and the dark mascara and the olive skin under her eyes. She smelled of stale cigarette smoke, like she hadn't had a bath in three days. Her tan blouse was tight and tied in a knot above her navel, which was a lardy hole.

She passed Nu-Nu to me like he was a ham. "Can he stay the night?" she asked, dropping a diaper bag at my feet. "I want to go hear some music."

"Why not?"

She looked around slowly. "Looks like a bomb hit this place and blew everything away." The door to her dusty compact creaked open, and a freckled hand came out. "I forgot to mention I picked up Freddie on the way in. Hope you don't mind." She didn't look at him as she mumbled this, hands on her cocked hips. Freddie, who'd been sleeping, I guess, sat on the edge of the car seat and rubbed his eyes like a drunk.

"He'll be all right here," I said.

She took in a deep, slow breath, so deathly bored that I felt sorry for her. "Well, guess I better be heading on down the road." She turned, then whipped around on me. "Hey, guess what?"

"What?"

"Nu-Nu finally said his first word yesterday." She was biting the inside of her cheek, I could tell.

I looked at the baby, who was going after my shirt buttons. "What'd he say?"

"Da-da." And her eyes started to get red, so she broke and ran for her car.

"Wait," I called, but it was too late. In a flash she was gone in a cloud of gravel dust, racing toward the most cigarette smoke, music, and beer she could find in one place.

I took Freddie and the baby around to the back steps by the little screen porch and sat down. We tickled and goo-gooed at Nu-Nu until finally he let out a "Da-da"—real loud, like a call.

Freddie looked back toward the woods, at all the nice trees in the yard, which looked like what they really were now that the trash had been carried off. "What happened to all the stuff?"

"Gone," I said. "We gonna put a tire swing on that tall willow oak there, first off."

"All right. Can you cut a drain hole in the bottom so the rainwater won't stay in it?" He came close and put a hand on top of the baby's head.

"Yep."

"A big steel-belt tire?"

"Sounds like a plan." Nu-Nu looked at me and yelled, "Da-da," and I thought how he'll be saying that in one way or another for the rest of his life and never be able to face the fact that Da-da had skipped town, whoever Da-da was. The baby brought me in focus, somebody's blue eyes looking at me hard. He blew spit over his tongue and cried out, "Da-da," and I put him on my knee, facing away toward the cool green branches of my biggest willow oak.

"Even Nu-Nu can ride the tire," Freddie said.

"He can fit the circle in the middle," I told him.

What We Don't See in the Light

Joe Adoue worked in a Baton Rouge chemical plant in the days when the pipe fitters washed their tools with hot varsol or methylene chloride or whatever product was steaming out of the test valve. Sometimes he rinsed grease from his hands with tolulene or MEK, quickly wiping them to keep his skin on. On damp afternoons, he walked through ground-hugging clouds that could boil the paint off a bicycle.

In his forties Joe began losing his wind, was no good on the silver ladders that ran up the cracking towers, and could no longer walk the length of the plant with a 48-inch pipe wrench rattling on his shoulder. Management put him in the supply shack, out of the sun, but each year he seemed to lose a little more of his breath. Not a worrier, he just suspected he was more sensitive to fumes than other men; though when some of his friends moved on to cleaner companies, and a couple died in old Baton Rouge General of cancer, he started wearing his respirator out among the pipes and valves. At fifty Joe threw away his last cigarette, but things kept getting worse. Occasionally men from upper management, who worked beyond the fence, would visit him in his supply building and ask how he was doing. They were worried about something, he could tell. The test valves were locked, break rooms were pasted with notices forbidding the use of "product" for cleaning. Everyone was ordered to work with gloves or respirators out in the clouds and drips.

Joe's wife, Lorena, was a stern little woman who dragged him along to church until his faith was damaged. She carped at him for not having any energy, for cussing, for taking off his shoes and socks and parking his cyanic feet on the coffee table he'd given her for Christmas. She hated his dirty jokes, though they really were harmless antiques. Sometimes he told her one just to get her goat and start her pouting, because that silence was better than her occasional carping about the state of everybody's character. One day they were driving to her old aunt's house, the one who still kept her blinding-white hair in flat buns wound against the sides of her head. His wife examined her seat belt and mentioned she'd had a dream about being injured in a wreck he'd caused. Joe remembered that she hadn't always been so stiff-necked, and imagined she was just going through a stage. When they were young parents they'd go out and drink a couple of beers and jitterbug. But that day she wouldn't stop finding fault, so when he drove past a buxom girl jogging up the sidewalk wearing short shorts he said, "Man, that gal's so sexy she makes my arteries hard." His wife didn't say a word to him for the rest of the afternoon.

At work, his breathing got a bit worse. He sat in the supply building doling out globe valves and steam packing to the pipe fitters and welders until the day the company gave him an early retirement. He turned in his keys, hearing protectors, respirators, steel toes, and hard hat and went home to his wife. He was fifty-five and looked it, mostly gray, his skin sun crinkled, his hands plagued by minor benign tremors, and his arms showing strange little white warts. But his back was still straight.

At night Joe coughed a lot, and sometimes he'd feel his wife's small hands on his back, which meant he should go sleep on the sofa. He didn't think that was fair, but he'd drag a blanket through the dark house and prop himself on three pillows so he could breathe.

After he retired, things got worse. Twice he passed out right on the tile at the Piggly Wiggly. His pulmonary doctor told him on several visits that he ought to consider moving from Baton Rouge to a place where the air wasn't a gumbo of acetone, methyl mercaptan, bug killer, hundred percent humidity, pollen thick as a dust storm, and aromatic plants steaming sweetly at night like vegetable whores named jasmine, honeysuckle, sweet olive, and magnolia. But his daughters, who loved the funny, easygoing man he was, still demanded that he stay and fix all the broken things in their households, because their husbands knew only how to press buttons and couldn't manage an adjustable wrench to save their lives. One morning Joe sat huffing at his kitchen table, taking in the stink from the Exxon plant. He considered that his daughters were married and settled, that his wife wouldn't leave the neighborhood if it caught fire. He couldn't imagine living in a place alone, though. He would miss Lorena's cooking and occasional hugs. But breathing was pretty important, too.

At Easter Sunday dinner he blacked out and tumbled from his chair. His daughters were hysterical, and the grandchildren wept and howled, running out into the yard shrieking, "Grandpa's dead! Grandpa's dead!" While dialing the ambulance, his wife complained that he'd ruined the big meal, but he could tell she was crying for him and frightened for them both. Joe lay on the floor like a beached fish, thinking that he was a drag on the whole family.

The next Saturday he got together with his daughters and told them that if they wanted him to stay alive, he had to find a place out west. But where? None of the families were wealthy, and even together they couldn't just buy him a house. He heard his wife banging around in the kitchen, so he kissed the girls good-bye and padded toward the noise. Joe gasped to his wife that he loved her, and moving away would make things a hell of a lot easier for them all.

She slammed down the lid on a pot of green beans. "If you loved me," she snapped, "you wouldn't curse and fall asleep in church." Then her eyes softened, and she put a balled fist to her mouth. "But I don't want you to die just smothering."

He gave her a hug from the side, which was sort of like hugging a manikin. He wondered what had happened to her softness. He guessed it had been worked out of her by living in a big family in a big house where everybody visits. He touched her hair and said, "All my life I been buying company stock in dribs and drabs through Cousin Albert. He told me when I laid off work that it's gone up a lot over the years."

"I know," she said, "and you thought you were gonna buy a new car and boat with that. A nice boat the family can use."

He turned her loose because she was beginning to arch her back like a cat ready to scratch. "Our boat days are over. I'll get with Albert on his computer and see what I can buy or rent where it don't never rain."

He walked back to his recliner, feeling that she was sorry that he might leave, but not as sorry as he'd expected. He'd been around the house so many years he guessed she didn't see him anymore. He was just something to fuss at, like the television. It wasn't her fault. Happens to everybody. He didn't exactly watch her like she was a parade, either.

So that's how he wound up somewhere near the Chihuahuan Desert on one acre of leased land generally southwest of Water Tank, New Mexico, a remnant village where steam locomotives once stopped to fill their tenders. The first time he saw his place, he stopped his truck on an endless two-lane blacktop and stared past his mailbox down a mile-long graveled easement. In the middle of maybe five thousand acres, maybe a million, an azure single-wide trailer faced west, as out of place as a jewel on a corpse. Nowhere in that high, flat valley surrounded by red mountains was there another habitation. As he rattled down the driveway, he felt like an astronaut driving on the moon. His truck was a 1958 Apache classic he'd restored himself, even installing air-conditioning. The door to the trailer was unlocked, so he went in and turned on the AC, which seemed to work fine. Once a wayside shelter for government agents, it had been declared surplus. He went out and stood in the shade of the metal box, waiting for its insides to cool down a bit. He could see forty miles in each direction over empty desert, sandy hummocks, leathery plants, every one bearing thorns, and bordering it all to the north were bare mountains raising coppery ridges sharp as hatchets. He hardly knew where he was on the map, but in such empty land it didn't matter. The air was dry as hot crystal, and clean, though it faintly stung his nose. In all that space he could see not a single other building. The mountains on all sides seemed to be nothing but naked rock, the range to the west white topped and unimaginably tall, the one to the east as rusty as old nails. Behind him, to the south, lay putty-colored foothills and then Mexico. In Louisiana he could never see more than a city block, or maybe three hundred yards if he was driving around outside town. Here he could shoot a cannon and the projectile would just run out of speed and skid to a stop, maybe bowling down a cactus ten miles away.

He sat on the aluminum steps and coughed for a while. He had new prescriptions from his Louisiana doctors and had contacted a pulmonary specialist in Grind, a copper mining town fifty miles away. It was September and not too hot, maybe ninety. It didn't feel like ninety because he wasn't sweating. Running his fingers along his bare arms, he heard his skin whisper that he ought to drink some water. The dry air was still as death. On one of the mountains someone had laid out a cross with white rocks that, judging from the distance, must have been two hundred feet tall. It should have been comforting, but the man who laid out the cross could have died over a hundred years ago. Or it might have been put there by Martians. Joe wondered if he could live here. He'd just have to take life as it came, he guessed, one day after another, like labored breaths.

After a month, he began to feel a little better. The doctor in Grind, an old bald man who smoked, told him he mainly suffered from bronchitis with the beginnings of emphysema. He didn't seem to be allergic to anything, but they'd be able to tell in the spring.

"Are you walking?" the doc asked.

"Some."

"Well, walk some more. You can do it."

So every day except Sunday he walked that mile to his mailbox. There was no fence there or anywhere else that he could see, even with binoculars. Once or twice he saw some black cows on the horizon and imagined there should be a fence somewhere, but the country was too big for them to escape to wherever cows would want to go.

He wrote letters to his wife because his land line had not been installed yet and no cell phone on earth could get a signal here. She wrote back a long letter that began in clipped sentences, but toward the end her tone softened a bit, and the last sentence was "We been eating well, but the kids miss that chicken stew you make. Lorena."

He began to walk toward Mexico, a mile out and a mile back. The going was rougher, with little mounds of cholla and prickly pear rising among a welter of other armed vegetation. Now and then a big rattle snake crossed his path, and he began to step carefully. After seeing ten or twelve during one walk, he got used to them, but not to the jeweled gila monsters that rested in the mouths of their burrows and watched him like fate as he passed by.

Although he had mostly lost faith in God, he wanted something to do on Sundays, so he attended a small, sun-blasted church in Fuse. The Mass was in Navaho, and during the handshake of peace, no one looked at him. He was the only person in church who did not take communion.

In October, the winds picked up. His trailer was well anchored, but it still jiggled when a big roller of air slammed against it from across the open land. He wore a cap and light jacket on his walks and noted an increase of birds, both on the ground and high overhead, including the biggest geese he'd ever seen going somewhere he couldn't imagine.

He got a phone line and could receive television over it. Even though he could talk to his wife whenever the mood struck him, they both continued to write letters, as they had when they were dating and he was in the army. In writing they could say what they meant and not just what sounded good. Joe looked forward to the long walk to the mailbox. His breathing got a little easier, and he began to sit outside once it was totally dark and study an amazing sky dusted with diamonds. The sky was half the world at night, and he understood how unimportant he was, the things he did, the thoughts he had. Especially what he thought. Maybe he was wrong about everything. He imagined the sun rose in his daughters' eyes, but all their lives they were after him for money, which he gave them for cars, silly dresses. Not much practicality in their nearly pretty heads. His wife, he realized, had held the family together like an ugly glue job.

With his binoculars he could see wolves at a great distance, and now and then he could see Mexicans coming up from the border and laboring under backpacks three or four miles away, moving like ants to the north. Sometimes he wished one would wander close enough so he could call out to him, "*Buenos días.* Do you want some water?"

Every two weeks or so he would wake up to the sound of a cow nibbling at the conduit leading up to his electrical panel outside. He would shoo it off with a pebble and a few running steps. Also he would drive to Water Tank to shop at an adobe store that seemed abandoned until he stepped inside to study the sagging shelves of canned goods protected behind long counters. In the back were old peeling coolers holding milk and meat. The clerk had the complexion of schoolhouse brick and only nodded when Joe paid his bill. He tried to make small talk with him, and on one trip, exasperated and desperate for the sound of anyone's voice, Joe said, "Why don't you talk to me? Is it a tribal thing or something?"

The man's eyes were two onyx stones. "You are a tourist."

"Like hell I am," Joe told him. "I own property here. I'll die out here."

The eyes didn't move. "Then you'll be a dead tourist," the man said.

By November his walks were up to a mile and a half, and he managed to climb a hillock and could see holes in a red mountainside where native Americans had lived a thousand years before. In December the cold hurt his lungs, but a man at church told him it didn't snow there much and the winters were not hard. Joe missed Louisiana's food and missed his family, but he loved his breathing. He also loved writing letters, caressing the pages with a smooth-rolling ballpoint he'd bought at the adobe store. Touching the soft paper was like sliding his fingers over the clean hair of his grandchildren.

In February, his truck's battery gave out and he was stranded for a long time, running low on provisions. One morning he woke up and looked out the window to see an old man, the adobe store owner, standing fifty feet away, still as a stone.

Joe pushed his door open. "Hey. Come on in before you freeze."

The man looked around, puzzled. "Not cold."

But he came in anyway, and Joe fixed him a cup of coffee. "I'm glad for some company. You know my name, it's on my credit card."

"My name's Joe also."

"Well, that's confusing. Do you have a tribal-type name?"

He glanced down at the linoleum. "Snow in Face. I was born outdoors."

"No kidding? What brings you way out here?"

"You didn't come in for groceries."

Joe's eyes opened wide. "You were worried about me?"

Snow in Face shook his head. "I need your money."

Joe looked out at the man's pickup. "Let me get my jacket." And the two of them rode to the store and later came back, sliding through the wind and spits of snow in the old man's rusty Dodge with a large grocery order.

That evening before sundown, Joe fixed himself another pot of Community Coffee his daughters had mailed to him and watched through the little window by his dinette table as black cows and large deer pulled democratically at the tough grass coming up around his trailer. He thought of Snow in Face and the logic of his coming out to rescue him. In such a harsh land, such thinking prevailed. Things were done according to hard reason. Listening to local news on his radio, he noted that locals seldom died of unnatural causes, but that drug dealers stepped on rattlesnakes, hikers fell to their deaths when exploring cliff-dweller sites, off-roaders broke their necks by running their glossy machines over dunes into dry creek beds. Visitors who were there for no practical reason were the most vulnerable, more likely to die of thirst or a desert dope party. He developed a respect for the fact of his presence in New Mexico, where he could breathe.

When he opened the door, the deer took off, and the cows raised their heads to watch him. He sat on the steps, zipped his jacket, and looked up at the stars, which seemed to be a vast interpretation of a gila monster's hide. He considered how such a sky could be formed, and why he was privileged to witness it. Was it just an accident, all of these things that bring a person delight, like a slice of cold watermelon on a hot Louisiana day when his lungs were on fire and the cold crush of juice runneling down the inside of his chest gave at least a moment of blissful relief, a moment pinned to his memory until death? He wondered if his trailer could be seen from outer space, from the moon or Mars or Saturn or from even beyond that, a distant tin rectangle glinting in the corner of God's eye. The next day was Sunday and he decided to go to confession before Mass.

January and February were not harsh where his trailer was. He watched a great deal of television, read some used books Snow in Face had sold him, walked on an old thirdhand machine he bought at a church yard sale, and followed sports on television. And he wrote letters, many letters, until his ballpoint ran out of ink. After a call from a daughter he would sit down and finish the communication in two or three pages of small cursive with a pencil, the letters growing thicker as he wrote.

He dreaded spring and the desert flowers coming alive with pollen, and the first week he was coughing up mucus and had to see his doctor in Grind, who tested him at the little hospital in town and cocked his head at the results, gave him some antihistamines, and sent him home. In a few days he was better, but feeling as if he were walking the edge of a sheer cliff. Joe wasn't sure how long he would live, and he never asked the doctor. He tried to look at each day as his lifetime.

The letters from his wife gradually changed in tone. The latest even confessed that she was sorry she had hassled him so much about every little matter, that she knew she'd grown cold even though she believed she was not a cold person. She wrote that she always thought he could have done better at some things and that was why she got angry with him, but since he'd been gone she realized he was at least good enough at everything.

One day in June he traveled to the adobe store and traded a few sentences with Snow in Face. He'd decided to cook up something special and tasty, a meal that started with a roux and continued with sautéed onions, diced celery, and garlic, and Snow in Face sold him some chicken meat he said came from pullets in his own yard that would be so tender over fluffy white rice. Joe invited him to come to supper, and the old man told him he couldn't promise anything because he had to wait for the gasoline delivery for the pumps out front.

He made it back to his trailer earlier than he'd thought, so he decided to clean the battery terminals on his truck. He picked up the broad hood and cleaned the posts with a little wire brush, doped the positive one with grease, and was going to tighten it onto the battery when the phone rang. It was Snow in Face, who said the gas man had arrived and he might come over after all.

About five o'clock he put the skillet on the gas range and turned on the stove hood, which for some reason wouldn't work. While trying to repair it, he heated the oil too much, so he threw in the chopped vegetables and chicken and dumped in the broth to lower the temperature, but the little kitchen nook was suddenly charged with flavor and steam and smoke, smothering him, and he started to cough, at once feeling a deep stiffening in his chest. In only a few seconds, he couldn't catch his breath and had to sit on the floor. The smoke from the stove thickened throughout the trailer, and he was forced to turn off the burner and flee, stumbling out into the yard where five cows were gathered around the front of his truck with their heads in the open engine compartment, eating the wires off his motor. One raised his nose, a plug wire dangling from his mouth like a piece of black spaghetti. Joe sat in the sand, coughing up phlegm and sneezing over and over. With the truck, he could have made a try to reach Grind, but now, with little air coming in and almost none going out, he figured he had run out of chances. Sitting up against the steps, he stared at the cows, then at the empty road in the distance. He thought some revelation might be at hand, but all he felt was sleepy and dizzy, so he watched the cows nudge against his favorite old truck, and hoped it was all right to die. It was, after all, what he'd come out here to do.

The day of the big chicken stew, Snow in Face had an argument with the man who was driving the gasoline truck, and he was late getting on the road. Then around sunset his cousin the drunk flagged him down three miles away from the store and asked for a ride as far as his wife's house, which was down a steep drive paved with loose rocks the size of skulls. After dropping him off, he debated whether to go on to the white man's trailer. What difference would it make if he didn't show up? The tourist couldn't get angry and shop somewhere else. There *wasn't* any-place else. Snow in Face stopped his truck at the main road and for a while considered both directions. He looked up in the sky and saw the first star lodged in his windshield, right above his fingers. Then he put on his blinker, his hands turning the wheel without his making the decision.

Snow in Face found him lying face up in the yard and called the Navaho police, who sent a helicopter to bring Joe Adoue to the hospital in Grind. He watched the machine ascend in a thundering whop of blades and kept vigil until it was a dot of pepper against a purple after-glow in the west. Then he went into the trailer, finished cooking, and ate half of the chicken stew, nodding his approval as he chewed.

A week later, Joe was packing his few things to leave the hospital, when his bald old doctor came in carrying a clipboard, raised an eye-brow, and told him that his mild emphysema had not advanced much at all.

"That so?" Joe said.

"Yeah, I guess you're lucky, all right. What laid you low out there at your place was your bronchitis. A bad attack. I don't see how you ever stayed alive in Louisiana with that stuff." He held up a page on his clipboard and said, "Two things you need is an electric stove and a new range hood. Plus your medicine, of course."

Joe studied the pockets in the doctor's smock. "I don't see any smokes. You quit?"

The doctor gave him a long look. "They got too damn expensive."

The next day he was sitting at his table catching up on his mail, when the phone rang and his wife said she was coming to see him. She told him she was worried about him because somebody else named Joe had called to say a family member ought to visit him. "That you'd been real sick. He'd said something about protecting his investment."

Joe kept his trailer clean, but not wife clean. Three days after he returned from the hospital, he slipped on a mask and raked the sand around his trailer, washed the dishes, changed the linens in his bedroom, and put on fresh sheets in the tiny bedroom at the other end of the trailer. He scrubbed, dusted, and wiped down every surface until he collapsed, winded, on a small sofa in front of the television. Lorena was fifty-six years old, younger than he was, and she had better eyesight. He pictured her spotting a raisin under the table and frowning, so he got up and swept again.

The next afternoon at three o'clock, he saw a car turn in from the main road. He knew she would take a plane into the regional and rent the cheapest vehicle she could. As it got closer, however, throwing up a wave of dust to the cloudy west, he saw it was a nice midsize sedan, and he wondered if it carried his wife after all. But the person who got out next to the trailer's steps was indeed Lorena, wearing a light sundress with a nice pattern of abstract, indistinct dots. He was used to her in pants and sweatshirts and figured these were her traveling clothes.

He went out to meet her and she gave him a quick wet kiss that startled him. "Joe," she said, pushing him back a foot, "you don't look bad at all. Look at those pink ears."

"Well, the humidity's about right today." He thought he felt his chest wall relax a bit, though it might have been his heart. "The doc says I'm hanging on."

She looked over at the mountains to the north. "So this is the land of enchantment? Looks like Mars." She glanced at him. "But in a good way."

Inside she went to the little bathroom and then did a general inspection. "I see you cleaned up for me," she told him. He made coffee and they sat looking out the window. An Angus walked around the corner of the trailer and gazed longingly at the hood of Joe's pickup.

"I'm glad you came for a visit," he said. "I didn't realize how much I missed people until you showed up." He watched her as he would a rare animal he'd come across on one of his walks.

She rested an arm on the table. "I'd have come sooner, but the girls need a lot of help with their kids, and you know me. Always afraid to spend down savings, what there is of it."

He started to touch her hand, then held back. "I just want you to know that I miss you. Life in Baton Rouge." He lifted his chin toward the east. "I'm not happier out here or anything. But man, it's nice to feel okay most days."

"I could tell from your letters. You write a hell of a letter, by the way."

He shrugged. "I guess I can say more when I think as slow as handwriting."

She laughed and covered her mouth with her hand. Suddenly, she stood up. "Hey, you know what I have in the trunk on ice? Some andouille sausage and big shrimp. I'm going to cook you a pot of gumbo."

He tried a joke. "Man, I should move away more often."

She got serious at that and sat back down. "Joe, when you left, I began to see you."

"What? I don't understand."

"I know. I mean a hundred things. Like when in hot weather you wore a white T-shirt, and I'd tell you not to dress like a bum in the house, and you'd make that clown face instead of calling me down for saying something like that. After you left, I remembered you built that house for me, paid for it and nailed a lot of it together. A couple months after you left town, I found a few of your Ts in your drawer and thought they were yellowed, so I took them out and bleached them."

He snorted. "That's like you. Washing clean laundry."

"When I was folding them, I thought how there was no one in them.

I actually felt through the cloth for you. And there was nobody there."
She began to cry softly and they put their heads together and closed
their eyes for a long moment.

Later, supper was like a visit to the old land of moss and fumes, and
Joe ate two bowls of gumbo. Lorena changed her shoes and he took her
out for a walk down to the mailbox, cautioning her not to touch any of
the prickly plants. She wasn't impressed by a big rattler on the highway, or a brace of tarantulas skittering across the blacktop, but she was
taken with the openness of this world, the distance, the red vistas, and
the big white cross on the mountain. Coming back they talked a year's
worth, watched television, and at ten he decided it was time to turn in.
When he showed her the little bedroom, she asked, "Is your own bed
big enough for two?"

He was confused for a moment. "Sure, sure. It's a double. I just
thought . . ."

"Nah, it'll be okay. We're still married, if you remember."

He brushed his teeth and took a handful of pills in the kitchen while
Lorena was in the bathroom. He climbed into bed and looked forward
to not being the only one in the trailer, the little woman making him
feel safer, as silly as that seemed. His eyes were closed when she came
in and turned off the light. He heard her slip off her dress or her robe,
he wasn't sure exactly what she had on, and then lift the covers and
roll up against him. He smelled soap and felt her arms slip around his
chest, squeezing him as though he were a tree. He touched her and
understood with a shock that she wasn't wearing anything at all. "Oh,
my God," he said, laughing, "this is like our honeymoon. And you're
going to kill me."

"No I'm not," she whispered. "Just take a breath."

Acknowledgments

Thanks to Winborne, my wife, for reading and suggesting improvements for these stories. I owe a great deal of thanks to my agency, Sterling-Lord Literistic and my long-term advocate there, Peter Matson. Short stories are a hard sell nowadays, and he and Jim Rutman have done well for me, and for that I thank them. To Gary Fisketjon, who has to be the hardest working editor in New York, I again take off my hat.

A Note About the Author

Tim Gautreaux is the author of three novels and two earlier short story collections. His work has appeared in *The New Yorker, The Best American Short Stories, The Atlantic, Harper's,* and *GQ.* After teaching for thirty years at Southeastern Louisiana University, he now lives, with his wife, in Chattanooga, Tennessee.

A Note About the Type

This book was set in Apolline, a typeface created in 1993 by Jean François Porchez (born 1964), the director of the French Typofonderie type foundry.

Derived from drawings of Porchez's calligraphy, Apolline was designed to suggest the rhythm of handwriting.

Typeset by Scribe, Philadelphia, Pennsylvania

Printed and bound by Berryville Graphics, Berryville, Virginia

Designed by Betty Lew